In the lounge, time had frozen. Everything was the same as it had been that afternoon when she had gone into labour; the afternoon which had preceded Laurel's birth at twenty past eight the following morning. Twenty past eight, Ruth thought suddenly, remembering Grandma Price calling it the Hour of the Angel. The Hour of the Angel, she repeated to herself as she closed the front door and walked down the path for the last time.

The train took hours to reach London. When it finally arrived, Ruth got off unsteadily, a man glancing at her as she passed. There was an all-pervading smell of smoke and damp, the first September warmth having given way to mist and bare twigs of Autumn. Ruth stood before the barrier, handed in her ticket, and walked to the Ladies toilet.

It was only after she had washed her face that she looked into the mirror and saw an understanding which had not been there for many months. She stared. Her eyes looked back at her with an expression of complete and terrifying disbelief. In that one moment, Ruth knew that Derek was dead and that she had given away her own child. Panicking, her head spinning, she gripped the basin . . . and then she was sick, painfully and violently, the tears running down her cheeks like ribbons.

ALEXANDRA CONNOR

The
HOUR
of the
ANGEL

ARROW

Reprinted in Arrow Books, 2004

3 5 7 9 0 8 6 4 2

First published in the United Kingdom in 1989
by William Heinemann Ltd

Arrow Books
The Random House Group Limited
20 Vauxhall Bridge Road, London, SW1V 2SA

Random House Australia (Pty) Limited
20 Alfred Street, Milsons Point, Sydney,
New South Wales 2061, Australia

Random House New Zealand Limited
18 Poland Road, Glenfield
Auckland 10, New Zealand

Random House (Pty) Limited
Endulini, 5a Jubilee Road, Parktown 2193, South Africa

The Random House Group Limited Reg. No. 954009

www.randomhouse.co.uk

A CIP catalogue record for this book
is available from the British Library

Papers used by Random House are natural, recyclable products made
from wood grown in sustainable forests. The manufacturing processes
conform to the environmental regulations of the country of origin

ISBN 0 7493 0494 4

Printed and bound in Great Britain by
Bookmarque Ltd, Croydon, Surrey

To the town where I was born
and the people that I loved there

Prologue

Her own childhood smelt of camphor and damp clothes hanging on a rack over the fire. Five o'clock mornings got her father up for work, making his own breakfast and dressing for his job in the park, where he worked for the Corporation. At six in the evening he came home, cutting through the ginnel beside the fruit shop and whistling if it was summer, or coughing in the winter when the nights drew in.

She never liked this place; this place where she was born. It held no magic for her then and holds none now. It became clear to her from an early age that she wanted more for herself and for the children she would have.

Soot on the washing; smudges of ash from fires; and rain-spotted cobbles coloured her childhood, and made her determined that her own children would never have to endure the smell of cheap soap and Izal, or be caught in early marriages and grinding jobs. Her life would be different – would be special; as would her children.

They were, after all, Ruth's children.

PART ONE

Beginnings

One

OLDHAM

It was raining. Tippling off the roof and drumming against the windows when the wind caught it. The sky had darkened, the clouds low over the school, forcing lights on, even at three in the afternoon. Ruth glanced out of the window, her chin cupped in the palm of her right hand. It seemed to be always raining, she thought dully, imagining how her mother would be watching the downpour from the shop. It required very little effort to picture the look on her face – rain was bad business, it kept people in their homes, away from the shops, especially the small milliner's on the corner of Union Street. She'll be tidying out the drawers again, Ruth thought, rearranging the same tired out stock, or re-dressing the window where the yellow blind came down at night.

'Ruth Gordon! You're day-dreaming again.'

Ruth's attention snapped back to the present. 'Sorry, Miss Kemp.'

'It's no good saying sorry,' the teacher insisted, her anger rising as her face reddened; 'No good at all. You have to learn to control yourself.'

Ruth nodded, dumbly miserable.

'Do you understand what I'm saying?'

'Yes, Miss Kemp.'

'Are you sure? It's important, you know.'

Ruth looked up, her gaze steady, fully aware of how it infuriated the woman to be stared at. Her expression said that she understood exactly what the teacher was saying – and thought it rubbish. 'I understand, Miss Kemp.'

The teacher flushed deeply and walked away, turning her attention back to the rest of the class.

Miss Kemp was the first person Ruth disliked; disliking her attitude as much as her appearance, her milk-whey face and cream-coloured hair which was never really tidy. Ruth also realised that she wasn't that much older than herself, which made it doubly difficult to take her seriously. For Miss Kemp's part, she understood only that Ruth Gordon was stubborn and resentful.

Ruth was thirteen when she entered Miss Kemp's class and fourteen when she left it, having learned no more than a couple of good textbooks could have told her more quickly and with less aggravation. Her mother knew she was unsettled at school, but, being overworked and overtired, was never deeply curious.

'You have a good day, Ruth?'

'Fine.'

'Everything going well?' she continued, unpacking a shopping bag and bending down to put something in the cupboard under the sink. A copy of the *Oldham Chronicle* was lying on the kitchen table, its front page spotted with rain.

'Yes, everything's fine.'

She straightened up and looked over to her daughter. 'Are you sure?'

'Of course, I'd tell you otherwise, wouldn't I?' Ruth answered, glancing back to the paper. She knew the reply was enough to reassure her mother; enough to absolve her of worry.

Poverty had been Ruth's closest companion from birth, and as a child she had cried as she was carried to her grandmother's along dark streets on early mornings when her mother had to go to work. Her father, Jack Gordon, worked long, hard hours for the Corporation, but there was never enough money and his wages had to be supplemented by his wife's. Knowing that so much depended on her, Lilian worked hard running the shop, sometimes taking on jobs elsewhere to keep their heads above water. In later years, Ruth understood her situation, but then it was hard to explain to a child why it was carted about from one home to another; why it was carried in a blanket to a cold house on the other side of town. If Ruth had dared, she would have asked to stay with Grandma Price in the tiny house

4

on Mapleshaw Road, safe by the coal fire with her talamanca cat. But she never questioned Lilian, and night after night she would be wakened and taken home. With very little effort Ruth could still feel the chill of night air on her face and the sense of the damp blanket against her skin. When they got back the fire had always gone out, and as she fell asleep the kettle whistled into her dreams.

Lilian believed she had done the best for her daughter, who never said otherwise, but when Jack Gordon came home from work in the evenings, it was to him that Ruth turned.

'Come on, flower, let your Dad take you out.'

'Don't let her get cold,' Lilian shouted to him, glad to be rid of them so she could get down to some work at the shop.

He winked at Ruth. 'Would I let my little girl catch cold?'

'Well, mind you don't,' was her familiar parting shot.

In perfect unison, they set off for a walk. There were numerous places they could have gone – Oldham Edge, the high ground where they could look out to the Pennines and over to Shaw, counting the mills which loomed out of the hollows, stretching away from the tight little towns around their feet. Or they could have gone to Tommy Fields and the open air market. Ruth liked it there, she didn't even mind the rain on Tommy Fields, not if it was only a light drizzle and she could shelter under the tarpaulins; and in the winter, when the days were really short before Christmas, they lit naphtha flares, hanging them on the stalls, where they hissed in the darkness.

There were many places they could have gone, but they always went to the park where Jack Gordon worked in the gardens. There he walked round holding his daughter's hand, a tall man in a raincoat and a trilby, pulled rakishly down over his forehead ever since the time someone told him he looked like Ray Milland. As they walked, he pointed to each of the trees, telling Ruth their names, and how big they would grow: 'This one should make twenty feet.'

'Twenty feet!' she repeated, her voice rising with excitement.

He warmed to his subject. 'Maybe bigger – maybe *thirty*.'

'Thirty,' she said softly. That was huge, wasn't it? Thirty feet ... surely that was close to God?

Jack Gordon looked down at his daughter and winked. He was proud of the skinny child next to him; proud of her poise, 'class' Grandma Price called it. He knew that Ruth was too shy, knew that Lilian gave her little affection, but at least she had taught her manners, and that would stand her in good stead. He found it impossible not to love Ruth, but her slight reserve made him careful with her, and, although she was only a child, he realised then that he was a little in awe of his own daughter.

Ruth knew only that she adored her father and his sense of fun, laughing when he put his trilby on the back of the larder door and it fell off and tripped Lilian up. She loved his humour and took sides with him, ganging up on her mother constantly. Many times he would tie a wooden spoon into the bow of Lilian's apron or undo the strings so that it fell to the floor as she moved.

'Jack, stop that, I'm working even if you're not.'

'It was a joke – '

'Some joke! I could have fallen over that.'

His temper flared quickly. 'Oh, stop going on – you're all right, aren't you?'

So father and daughter became willing companions, and because Ruth was an only child she needed her father's company as much as he needed hers. Jack Gordon never wanted to get on and left the ambitions to his wife, who, had she been as successful as she was hard-working, should have ended up running the London Stock Exchange. Instead the breaks never came her way, and although she did reasonably well in her millinery business, the big time eluded Lilian and made her bitter. It also made her irritable.

'You should want more for your family, Jack. You should try and get a better position, with more prestige – instead of being content to work for the Corporation.'

It was an old argument. Wincing, Ruth kept her head down over her comic and pretended to read.

'I'm happy where I am.'

'But we could do better for ourselves,' Lilian persisted, knowing that he was set against the idea; against any idea which altered the pattern of his life.

'We can pay our bills, and we owe nothing. What more could anybody want?'

'A damn sight more,' Lilian replied, and turned away from him, wounded.

Ruth listened and judged her mother, seeing her as unreasonable, demanding, inflexible. She wondered why she couldn't leave her father alone and be happy with him, and, as though by proxy, Ruth suffered for her father and the atmosphere became strained as mother and daughter learned to resent one another.

Believing herself thwarted at home, Lilian was also finding life difficult in the shop. The days of the cotton barons were already numbered, the war having been the high point for production. Orders began to fall off and the areas which had been so blatantly prosperous, declined. The real money had gone. People bought hats, but not as often, and Lilian never managed to raise enough money to buy a shop in one of the 'posh' areas, like Lytham St Annes. She longed for the social graces, and could have held her own anywhere – which made it harder to bear. What tied her was the marriage to Jack Gordon.

Having been an only child, Lilian was brought up by her mother, Grandma Price, a woman widowed early, but with enough spirit and determination to see that her daughter lacked none of the essentials in life. Materially they were poor, but Grandma Price had dreams for her only child . . . dreams which extended beyond Oldham. She brought Lilian up to be courteous and proud, a deadly combination in most circumstances, but in a mill town like Oldham it was devastating.

Lilian reached twenty and began to look for a suitable mate. None were found. She had no background, apart from the one Grandma Price had instilled into her psyche – and that was not proper currency in the real world. Lilian was looked upon as an attractive young woman with too big an opinion of herself, and as the years passed and she did not marry, she became desperate. With the little money Grandma Price and Lilian had saved, they bought the hat shop on the corner of

Union Street. A small shop with a square window, on whose door was painted in gold letters the legend – Lilian's Millinery. Sneer they might, but Lilian had style, a commodity in very short supply in Oldham. People could joke behind her back, but they came to buy her hats, or peer, transfixed, into the window. On the days leading up to the Whit Walks, Lilian would dress the shop with a plethora of feathers, net and straw, showing hats which she knew the women passing would not buy, but hats which were enticing enough to draw them into the shop, and once they were in, well ...

So when the handsome, unambitious Jack Gordon came courting, Lilian was too close to thirty to shoo him away. Ten years earlier would have seen her looking down her nose, but now she was pleased to have him walk her home, and willingly accepted his offer of a boat ride on the Park Lake. His friends teased him unmercifully, but Jack Gordon saw something under the hard polish, and fell in love with Lilian.

'Did you really love her?' Ruth asked him during one of their walks. It was blowing hard, the lake water slapping up against the concrete steps.

'Of course I did, flower.' He stopped and lit a cigarette.

'Why, Dad?'

'Oh, she was so ... different. Unusual like.'

Ruth thought about her mother, seeing the hard lines from her nose to her mouth. Yes, she could be attractive when she smiled, but there was no softness there. '*How* was she different?'

'She had class. You know ...' He inhaled deeply. 'People thought she was a snob, but it wasn't that. She just wanted more from life.'

She still did, but the 'something more' never materialised, and after she married Jack Gordon she was more tied, not less. Women did not divorce in those days, unless they could face the scandal, and even if Lilian had chosen to leave her husband, what possible reason could she give? He was hard-working, clean-living and he didn't drink. In most people's eyes, she was amongst the lucky ones.

So she kept on the millinery business and he stayed working in the park, and she learned how to make the best of her situation and she learned how to cope.

'It won't fit, Mrs Gordon,' the woman said, passing the hat back over the counter to Lilian, her voice carrying into the poky back room of the shop where Ruth was doing her homework. 'It's too small.'

Ruth could imagine her mother looking at it carefully: 'Would you hold on just a moment? I do believe that I have another in the back.'

Behind the curtain Lilian glided and, giving Ruth a quick look, yanked the hat on her knee and pulled sharply. She then adjusted the brim again and walked out into the shop, smiling. 'This must be your lucky day. I'd nearly forgotten that there was another one in the stock room.'

Time and time again Ruth sat silently watching her mother perform various routines, smiling, always polite, before diving into the back room and ripping off trimmings and sticking in a feather here or a flower there before re-emerging with an apparently new article. As a child it bemused her, but the first time Ruth laughed her mother was merciless. 'Be quiet! This means money to us. Now just be a good girl and read your comics.'

The rebuke silenced her and widened the gulf between them.

But if her mother lacked affection her ingenuity meant that, although they were bitterly poor, they survived. Striking hard bargains and cultivating the right people, Lilian ensured that Ruth was fed well and dressed adequately. Living so carefully, however, any sudden alteration in her reckonings could throw them into confusion.

'That blasted woman!' she shouted, exasperated, throwing down her case on the kitchen table where Ruth was sitting. 'She's cancelled the order for her hat. Says she's "short of cash at the moment".' Lilian sat down heavily by the fire. 'It couldn't have come at a worse time ... God, whatever can I do?'

Ruth turned round in her seat. She could see the back of her mother's head and, looking up, the clothes-horse hung with its variety of drying clothes.

'Do you want a cup of tea?' she asked quietly.

Lilian glanced up. Her face looked very white under the light, her slim legs extended, the court shoes kicked off. She *did* have class, Ruth could see what her father meant. But it was out of place, and somehow shockingly sad.

'Yes ... thank you, Ruth, that would be nice.'

She nodded, walking past her mother's chair, and as she did so Lilian took hold of her hand. The gesture was unexpected, and left Ruth confused as she smiled and moved away.

Lilian's maternal instinct faded almost as soon as it had given birth. Her quick brain decided on a plan of action and, without even finishing the cup of tea, she grabbed her bag, called for Ruth, and set off for the better part of town and one particular customer who lived near the park. It was a foggy night, the street lamps making smudges in the thick air. Lilian walked quickly, her heels knocking the cold pavement, Ruth following behind like an echo. The house had a large garden and a big car parked outside. Ruth glanced at it curiously – there were never cars on Carrington Street.

'Mrs Carter, how are you?' Lilian began pleasantly as the door opened.

'I'm well, Mrs Gordon, won't you come in?'

They went through into the hallway. Several pieces of silver reclined on a small table, and a vase of flowers stood to attention by the window. Lilian only ever had flowers in the house if someone was sick.

'I was just passing and I wondered if you would be interested in seeing some new designs. I received them only this morning, and the fabric is extremely reasonable.'

The woman looked pressurised, but curious. 'You said they were new? Does that mean no one else has them in the town?'

Lilian nodded confidently. 'No one.'

'In that case, I'll call in at the shop tomorrow after I've been to the hairdresser's.' The woman moved towards the door and they followed her. 'Until then, Mrs Gordon.'

Lilian kept smiling until they rounded the corner of the road, and then her patience snapped. 'Going to the hairdresser's! What she spends there would keep us going for a couple of days.'

The fog swung round both of them; it seeped into Ruth's coat and made her hair damp.

'Do you have some new hats?' she asked without thinking.

'Of course not!' Lilian replied sharply.

They walked home the rest of the way in silence.

For most of the night she worked, making two net hats from the remnants at the shop, and when she finished she put them in tissue paper for Mrs Carter's approval the following day.

Mrs Carter bought the cheaper of the two.

Ruth never really knew what her mother expected of her, but as a child she was undemanding and stayed out of the way as much as possible, learning early on how to dance that particular jig of childhood: with her father, she sought love, with her mother, she sought approval.

Jack Gordon also sought approval from his wife, letting Lilian make all the decisions and handing over his wages so that she could take care of the finances. As long as he had enough for cigarettes and the occasional beer, he was blissfully content. He even looked happy, and as they aged their personalities became obvious from their faces, and the grinding bitterness inside Lilian came to the surface. Tall, inclined to thinness, and constantly busy, she was still stylish, although as she aged her body took on a brittle appearance and her mannerisms bordered on affectations. The easy conviviality which had earned her customers, at times became ingratiating and made Ruth wince when she heard her, not realising then that disappointment makes liars out of people. The more weary Lilian became, the more Ruth wanted to love her, but closeness was impossible.

It was not a problem with her father. He allowed Ruth to do what she liked, and was constantly tolerant. Although his hair was thin she would tie it into little pigtails and fix her coloured ribbons on them. Once she did so when he was asleep and forgot about it. Apparently he woke up, put on his hat and went for an evening paper. None of this would have mattered if he hadn't met one of Lilian's customers on the way back and raised his hat to her.

'You didn't, Jack! Not with those things on your head.'

He could hardly talk for laughing. 'She looked so bloody amazed, and walked past so quickly I wondered what the hell was the matter with her.'

Ruth was laughing with her father as Lilian continued. 'She's a good customer of mine! This could mean money for us.' She swung round and pointed at her daughter. 'This is your fault!'

Ruth's smile faded. 'But – '

'Leave her alone, she's only a child!' her father snapped, rising to Ruth's defence as he always did.

'Don't tell me how to speak to my child.'

'Our child!' he shouted.

'It's her fault – ' Lilian continued.

'Stop it, you'll upset her,' he said, turning to Ruth. 'Come here, flower, I'm not cross.'

Lilian's face crumpled and she began to cry. 'You always take her part.'

Lifting his daughter, he turned to face Lilian. 'She's only little! You shouldn't shout at her.'

'I just meant – '

He smiled at his wife quickly and then turned his attention back to the child in his arms. 'No harm done, eh, little one?'

Ruth knew then how she divided them.

When Ruth was fourteen Lilian managed to make a modest profit at the shop, and in a rush of long-suppressed ambition bought a small, second-hand car which was the talk of the neighbourhood for months. The driving lessons were expensive and Lilian, not wanting to waste money, passed first time, and took the whole family, including Grandma Price, to Southport for the day. The roads were quieter then, because few people had cars. In silence, Lilian drove along, her mother in her church clothes, and Ruth's father in the back, sitting with the window wound down so that he could smoke without choking anyone to death.

'You drive well, Mother,' Ruth said, after a few miles had passed.

Grandma Price rummaged in her bag for some mints and offered them round. 'You certainly do, Lilian, that's a fact,' she agreed, folding a sweet paper and putting it into her pocket. Her pride was palpable. 'I always knew you'd do well.'

Ruth leaned forward from the back seat. 'Do you know the way, Mother?'

'Of course. Be quiet now, and talk to your father.'

They lunched at a small restaurant on Lord Street, Grandma Price sitting erect, her expression autocratic, whilst Lilian fretted endlessly about where she had parked the car. Turning to her mother, Ruth was momentarily shaken by the rush of pride which welled up in her. Lilian was wearing a small blue hat, her fine ash-blonde hair curling underneath. Beside her, she had tucked her leather gloves under her bag, and was carefully adjusting the collar of her blouse. At that moment Ruth finally understood her mother. Saw her craving for position, for enough money to be able to eat regularly in restaurants in elegant towns, and own a flourishing business. She saw it . . . and knew it was impossible.

They spent the rest of the day walking in the Gardens and then Lilian drove them to the beach, parking on the coast road and watching her daughter as she ran out to the sea. When she was out of breath, Ruth stopped and waved. She could only just make out the formidable shape of Grandma Price sitting in the car, but she could see her father clearly and watched as he looped his arm around her mother's shoulder. She thought then that they could still be happy. That away from the smog and the soot smudges of Oldham they would be content. Southport was suddenly Utopia, and standing with her eyes shaded against the sun, watching that special closeness of her parents, Ruth wished childishly that they could stay there transfixed, for ever.

But they left soon afterwards and crawled back to Oldham under the bridges and curl of the buildings, dropping off Grandma Price at her house on Mapleshaw Road. The car was parked carefully and Ruth and her father brushed all the seats before tying a tarpaulin cover over it. They were inordinately proud of the machine, but, as though it was too good to last, when Ruth got home one day from school the car had gone.

'Mother, where's the car?'

'I sold it ... I got a fair price.'

'But that was your car! You paid for it. It was yours.'

She looked amused. '*Mine!* "Mine", she says! Well, what is mine, is your father's, dear girl, and that goes for his debts.'

'But you didn't have to sell the car – '

'Yes I did!' she shouted, close to tears. 'What was the good of it anyway? I was only trying to get on, but I obviously got above my station.'

'Mother – ' Ruth said, putting out her hand.

Immediately Lilian stepped back. 'I don't want sympathy! Sympathy won't pay the bills. Your father's always lent a sympathetic ear ... and look where it's got us.'

Ruth was baffled. 'But you'd made such a big profit at the shop. You said – '

'Your father took care of that,' Lilian said, and began to sob. 'He lent the money to some distant relative of his ... *my* profit! He said that he needed it more than we did ... He said that he'd pay him back – '

'Maybe he will – '

She swung round: 'That was three weeks ago! The money's gone.'

Ruth had never seen her mother out of control before. 'But maybe – '

Ignoring her daughter, Lilian turned and walked out of the room. When she came back she was dressed in her outdoor clothes.

'Where are you going?' Ruth asked.

'To the shop. Somebody's got to make some money here. Tell your father that if he wants his supper he can get it himself.'

There was never any mention of cars after that. Indeed Lilian seemed so altered by the experience that all her desire to advance herself faded. She kept the shop going, but only enough for it to tick over, and spent more time with Grandma Price, who was then Ruth's only surviving grandparent. Lilian aged because she was beaten; Jack Gordon remained the same.

But without realising it, Lilian had taught her daughter something which would influence her throughout her life. From then on, the image of her mother in that blue hat, driving her own car, stayed with Ruth, and taught her a lesson she would never forget. What Ruth earned, she would keep. No one, but no one, would take what was hers.

Two

The age of fourteen was important because Ruth discovered friendship, marking out one girl for particular attention because she was most of the things Ruth was not. Nina O'Donnell's family was apparently indifferent to her comings and goings, and through her Ruth enjoyed a vicarious freedom which would have been impossible with any of the other girls.

The O'Donnells had come to Oldham from Bolton, Nina's mother buying a newspaper shop on Rock Street beside a tripe shop and a derelict church. On the corner was a place where before the war they kept live chickens in cages. Passers-by went in, picked the one they wanted, and half an hour later it was dead, plucked, and ready for cooking. Her father, Terry O'Donnell, worked as a panel-beater, chatting up every woman from Shaw to Little Lever, and getting acquainted with every pub on the way.

Nina O'Donnell arrived at school badly dressed, badly spoken, and wilful. 'You're so bloody polite all the time, Ruth,' she grumbled, fixing her hair in front of the chipped mirror in the cloakroom.

'You shouldn't swear, you know what they said – '

'Oh, dry up,' she snapped good-naturedly. 'You worry too much.'

Stung, Ruth changed the subject. 'How many brothers and sisters *have* you got? I keep hearing different stories.'

Nina looked over her shoulder and smiled. 'That's because I keep telling everyone something different.'

'That's immoral,' Ruth said self-righteously, staring at her feet.

'That's show business,' Nina responded, walking out.

Nina's attitude was one of bravado, and after a while she couldn't have dropped the act even if she'd wanted to because

16

the girls at school needed her fantasies as much as she needed the audience. Only middlingly attractive, she was, however, blazingly red-headed, always quick with a snappy come-back no matter what anyone said, and brim-full of that kind of down-at-heel charm which is very potent. When she was quiet, which wasn't often, her face was that of an older woman, the expression of someone who'd already seen it all and was on her second or third time round. But when she smiled, people automatically smiled back because she made them feel special. That was her gift.

The two girls became quick friends and swapped stories of family life, although Nina soon admitted that she only had two brothers and that the rest were phantoms.

'It doesn't matter,' Ruth said, inordinately relieved that her home life wasn't that remarkable.

It was not the reaction Nina wanted, so she added quickly, 'Well, they're very unusual brothers.'

Ruth swivelled round to face her. 'How?'

'They work on the docks,' she said uncertainly.

'Which docks?'

Irritation stiffened Nina's face as she snatched up her satchel and began to stuff her school books into it. 'What's the difference? Why all the questions?'

'Your brothers aren't on the docks, you know they're not,' Ruth said quietly, seeing Nina's colour rise, 'but it doesn't matter . . . honestly.'

Pity was the last thing Nina wanted. 'Well, my father's a drunk,' she added smartly and left.

She was an incorrigible liar. Determined that her life should be full of drama, Nina invented scenarios, cleverly making sure that most of her stories were credible enough to be believed. Ruth watched her progress, horror-struck. 'They'll catch you out, you know,' she said, as they walked down the street together. 'They're bound to.'

'Not if I keep one step ahead of them.'

'But why? It's going to get very tiring. Besides, everyone's going to get to know your mum – and they'll tell her.'

Nina shrugged indifferently. 'She wouldn't give a damn

anyway. She only cares about my brothers. She can't stand the sight of me or my dad.'

Curiosity made Ruth press for details. 'Don't they get on?'

Nina laughed loudly, 'With him as drunk as a fiddler's bitch half the time?' She winked. 'I'm not getting married. I'm going to get on. And I *don't* mean owning my own shop.'

The words bounced round Ruth's head. She felt firstly anger on behalf of her mother and Nina's – and secondly, guilt. Even then Ruth hated the hat shop and everything it represented ... but if she could think it, she couldn't admit it; that was too much like treachery.

So instead she said, 'What's wrong with running a shop? It's a living.'

'So's pest control, but I wouldn't do that either.'

'You're always the first to criticise, aren't you?' Ruth said, annoyed because Nina had the courage to speak her mind. 'Well, I hope your life works out for you the way you think. But you needn't be so smug.'

Stunned by such an outburst from the usually diffident Ruth, Nina looked at her for a long moment. 'Fancy getting some chips on the way home?' she said finally.

It was obvious that Lilian would come to hear of the friendship, and it was equally obvious that she would not approve. She tackled Ruth on the subject only a few weeks after Nina had started at school. 'That friend of yours – Nina,' she began evenly, her hands folded together over her account books, her ankles crossed neatly. 'I've been hearing some stories about her parents, her father in particular, and I think it would be advisable if you didn't mix with her too much.'

Ruth looked down at her shoes. The kitchen was cold, the fire nearly out. 'She's good fun.'

Her mother regarded her coolly. 'No doubt she is. Look, Ruth, I don't want to make life difficult for you but you'll be influenced by her if you remain friends. You know the old saying ...' Ruth knew it. ' "Birds of a feather flock together",' she smiled, already certain her daughter understood. 'I know that life can be unfair, but that's the way it is.'

It was over and done with in Lilian's mind; there was no question of Ruth remaining friendly with a girl who was beneath her daughter in social class and whose father had thrown up in more bars than her husband had visited. To Lilian it was an unpleasant but necessary duty; to Ruth it was the first decision she ever made which opposed her mother.

'Very well, Mother,' she lied.

'Good girl,' Lilian responded, already turning back to her account books.

But the friendship was too vital for Ruth to abandon. Her upbringing had made her into an obedient child, quick to feel guilt, but her character was too much like her mother's to make her completely pliable. Having never had any reason to be defiant before, Ruth was amazed by the hot rush of anger she had experienced, and decided there and then that the friendship would last.

Nina noticed the change in her manner the following day. 'What's the matter with you?'

They were sitting at the back of the class, almost hidden behind the two boys in front of them.

'I'm all right.'

Nina looked round and then leant further over her desk. 'It's your bloody mother, isn't it?'

'Stop talking!' the Maths teacher shouted as he peered round for the offenders. Adopting innocent poses they scribbled away frantically. When the bell went Nina grabbed Ruth's arm. 'Well? What has your mother been saying?'

Ruth shook her off. 'Nothing.'

'Like hell,' she replied, dropping into step beside her. 'I bet she was calling us – I just bet she was.'

'She wasn't.'

Nina stopped walking and confronted Ruth. 'Would you *swear* that – if God was suddenly to appear here and now – would you *swear* that your mother hasn't been calling my family ill to burn?'

Visions of hell reared up in front of Ruth's eyes. 'My mother never said anything unkind about you, or your mother,' she said diplomatically.

Nina's eyes narrowed. 'But she did mention my father?'

Ruth shifted around uncomfortably. 'Well...'

'I knew it!' Nina shouted triumphantly. 'We've only been in this bloody town for a few weeks and everyone's talking about my father.'

It appeared to Ruth that Nina was enjoying something of the reflected glory. 'Not everyone,' she said quietly.

'They soon will be.'

'Well, that won't be surprising, will it? After all, your father hardly keeps himself to himself.'

Ruth expected Nina to come back with a quick rejoinder as she always did. But instead, she looked surprised and then hurt, her face becoming pale, and her blue eyes filling. Mortified, Ruth touched her shoulder. 'I'm sorry, I didn't mean – '

Nina brushed her eyes with the back of her hand. 'It's OK, I know.'

'Nina?' Ruth persisted uncomfortably.

'It's OK, really.'

A feeling of relief washed over Ruth. 'Then we'll still go to the cinema tonight?'

'I can't – I said I'd go with Richard.'

'Richard?' she repeated dumbly, watching as Nina recovered her balance, adopting a victorious look in her eyes as she paid her back in full measure for her cruelty.

'Yes, Richard. It's a shame you don't have a boyfriend, we could have made a foursome. Still, you wouldn't want to be a gooseberry, would you?'

The words slapped Ruth in silence. She was used to Lilian's swings of mood, but this was Nina – her friend – the person for whom she had lied to her mother. Family or friendship, she decided unwillingly, was very unreliable.

But by the end of the week they were back on the old slanging-match ground. Nina took a lively interest in boys, and pursued them with a ferocity usually reserved for wild boar hunting. Ruth watched, mesmerised by her astonishing ability to bounce back from a rebuff which would have rendered her incapable for a year. 'You should find a boyfriend,' Nina said for the thousandth time, glancing over to her friend and seeing a tall shy girl with a fine face. Refined, some would have called her.

'I can't – my mother would kill me, you know she would.'

Nina was brushing her hair, making it prickle with electricity. 'You could meet them at my home.'

Ruth thought of the flat over the shop in Rock Street; of Nina's mother and the terrible shabbiness of the place. They had linoleum on the floor, bought for ten bob the roll off the market. It cracked when you walked on it.

'Well?' Nina persisted.

Ruth dragged her attention back to the present. 'No, it's not worth it.'

'It would be fun.'

'Let it drop, Nina, please.'

In order to protect herself, Ruth used her mother as an excuse not to go out with boys, whilst in reality she was terrified of them. She wondered fleetingly if she was abnormal, but was too ashamed to confide in Nina, and too embarrassed to ask her mother. To Ruth even the idea of kissing a boy made her face colour up and her palms sweaty. So she continued in her small, enclosed world, and, entering puberty, sky-rocketed from an average five feet four to a dwarfing five feet ten, developing a stoop that Quasimodo would have envied.

Nina, comfortably six inches smaller, was constructive. 'It's elegant to be tall.'

'I can't see my head in the bedroom mirror any more,' Ruth muttered, staring into the dressing-table mirror in Nina's room.

'Being tall suits you. You look regal and – '

'Tall.'

Determined to be helpful, Nina shifted her tactics, sitting on the edge of the bed and looking at Ruth with her head on one side, 'You have good bones.'

'Except that they're all too long.'

'Models have to be tall.'

Ruth sighed deeply. 'I couldn't be a model, even if I wanted to.'

'You could earn a fortune cleaning out people's gutters then –

think of the money you'd save on ladders.'

As Nina laughed uproariously at her own joke, Ruth turned back to the mirror. Carefully she tipped the glass until her face came into view; until she recognised the chin line, the long mouth and the eyes which looked back at her. Her height made it easy for her to look slim, almost thin like her mother, and the same keenness of feature was obvious in her face, making it rather severe for her years. Only the eyes remained constant, the eyes of her childhood. Unremarkable in colour and deep-set, they gave Ruth a peculiarly wise look, which was more a look of the woman she was to become, rather than the girl she was. In the mirror she could see her mother standing where she should have been.

'You hypnotising yourself, or something?'

'Huh?'

'You're standing there like a great goon. What's the matter?' Nina asked, watching her friend with fascination.

'Do I look like my mother?'

'Yes – and no.'

Ruth let the mirror fall back into place. 'Thanks, that was a great help.'

'Well, your figure's like hers, and your face, but you aren't.'

'Is that good or bad?'

Nina shrugged. 'I dunno. I'm not like either of my parents ... maybe I was adopted,' she said dreamily, already changing the subject.

'They'd have told you.'

She smiled mysteriously and leant back against the bedhead. 'Not necessarily. Maybe my mother had an affair with an Arabian prince in the desert when she was young, and I was the result.' Ruth thought of Nina's mother – she would have been lucky to have had an affair with his horse. 'Maybe the reason she can't stand me is because I remind her too much of him ... possibly they wanted to marry and his parents kept them apart ... maybe they still meet now and then – '

'In Oldham?' Ruth asked, practically.

Nina looked pained. 'He could come in disguise.'

'You're right – maybe he's the Paki at the fruit shop.'

22

'Well, it does no harm to fantasise,' Nina added thoughtfully. 'If you dream enough, it might come true.'

'About the Paki at the fruit shop?' Ruth asked, ducking as she threw a pillow at her.

At sixteen, Nina dropped off from school, losing interest in work and reserving all her energy for boys. Due to her own reluctance and the almost hysterical control of her mother, Ruth did not go out with anyone, even the determined ones, and after a while they went their separate ways with the more obliging girls from the school across the park.

Despite Lilian's intervention, the friendship survived and Ruth visited Nina's home frequently, finding another kind of world in Rock Street. Nina had two brothers: Gavin drove lorries and the other, Trevor, qualified as one of the archetypical wide boys of Oldham. Flashy like his father, Trevor worked on the market and as a bookie's runner. He had the same kind of looks as Terry O'Donnell, and the same lack of scruples.

'Oh God, she's not coming here again, is she?' he asked Nina one night when Ruth was due.

Nina was quick to the defence. 'So what's the matter with her now?'

Trevor pushed his plate away from him and leant back in his chair, his hands behind his head. 'The same that's always been the matter with her – she's a bloody snob.'

'She just seems that way.'

'Her mother seems the same,' he said, echoing the town's sentiments.

'She's nice when you get to know her. You should have a talk with her.'

Trevor got to his feet. 'Talk to her!' he shouted, laughing. 'What the hell would I "talk to her" about? The opera?'

Nina put her tongue out at him and he left, banging the door behind him. She could hear the shop bell ringing as he walked out on to the street. It was six-fifteen when Ruth arrived, exchanging a few words with Mrs O'Donnell on the back stairs before coming in to see Nina. She walked with her

23

head down, unaware that her friend was watching her.

'Are you all right?'

Ruth looked up, startled. 'I didn't see you.'

'No, well, you wouldn't, would you? Not with your nose jammed up against the stair tread.'

'It's Mother,' Ruth volunteered, using the verbal shorthand they understood instinctively.

'Oh God,' Nina said, opening the door and stepping back for Ruth to walk in. 'Serious or critical?'

The story soon came out – Ruth had always wanted to take her exams and go on to train as a nurse. When she first mentioned it to her mother Lilian had been absent-mindedly pleased, but as the time came closer her view had begun to alter, and that afternoon matters had come to a head.

'The shop's not doing so well, and if you went in for nursing you'd be training and not earning anything for years.' She smiled the smile she used on her customers, the professional expression Ruth loathed. 'Perhaps you could help me out at the shop so I wouldn't have to pay for an assistant and I could have more time to do the bookkeeping. We would save money that way.'

The suggestion had made Ruth's stomach churn. Since child-hood she had loathed the hat shop; loathed the poky back room with the scratched table on which she had done her homework for years. She had flinched at the sound of the doorbell, and hated the faint odour of felt and the dark velvet curtain in between the shop and the back room. For years, Lilian's Mil-linery had been a place endured; a place visited after school; the place remembered vividly from her earliest years when she used to play behind the counter, out of sight.

With a rare feeling of panic, Ruth's throat tightened and her hands clenched in her blazer pockets. She wanted to scream at her mother; tell her how much she hated the shop; how much she hated the smell and the yellow blind which came down at night, and the tired hat boxes on shelves in the back.

Instead, she said quietly, 'Mother, I wanted to train – '

Lilian cut her off. 'I never thought you'd grow up to be difficult, really I never did. I need help and this is what

24

happens...' She stopped, swathed in self-pity and indignation, her hands snapping together the lid of the cash-box on the kitchen table.

'Mother –'

. 'No, I don't want to discuss it! Perhaps you ought to think back, young lady, and see if you don't owe me something.'

When her father came home Ruth waited until Lilian left to visit Grandma Price and then tackled him. Ever loving, he listened carefully. 'But, love, your mother only means it to be for a short time.'

She knew then they had discussed it. She knew then they had already decided what she would do. Ruth was to have no part in the matter – it was only her life, that's all. Shaking with rage, Ruth leant forwards in her seat and put her hand on her father's arm. 'Dad, you've been wonderful all my life. No one could have had a better father.' He looked down, touched. 'But I need you now to stand up to Mother and get her to see it my way. I don't want to work in a shop ... especially that shop.'

'Your mother loves you, you know,' he added, as though she had questioned it.

'I know that, but in her own way. We're so different, and we wouldn't get on ... it wouldn't work.'

'You could give it a go –'

'No, Dad!' she said sharply.

The fire was only just in, the coal making erratic shifts as it settled. Outside, the light was pooling from dusk to darkness. The kitchen was the same as usual: small, tidy, nothing out of place, the clothes-rack full of washing, the cooker and sink all old-fashioned, well cleaned, but past their prime. Well past.

'Please, just give it a try, Ruth, just until things ease off a bit, then you can go to the hospital.'

She looked at him, incredulous. 'Dad, can't you see how much this means to me? Can't you?' She gripped his arm. 'Please don't ask me to do this, I'm relying on you.' He looked at her and opened his mouth to speak. 'No, Dad, don't say it! Please, think before you say it.' Ruth pleaded.

A long moment lay between them, and then he coughed and said, 'It won't be for long, Ruth. Do this for me, hey? Just for me?'

'What are you going to do?' Nina asked her.

'What would you do?'

'Bugger off and go nursing anyway.'

Ruth nodded slowly.

'Your father's ruled by your mother, you know that,' Nina continued, hating the look on Ruth's face and knowing how much Trevor would have enjoyed this. "Getting her come-uppance" he would have called it. 'Your dad would do anything for a quiet life.'

Ruth got to her feet and walked over to the window. The street lamp was lit and made her face look jaded. 'I'll be at her beck and call all day and all night. I'll have to listen to her and watch her struggling to keep the damn business afloat.' Ruth stopped, catching hold of the grimy net curtain. Underneath them came the sounds from the shop. 'Why should I?' she said hopelessly.

'You don't have to.'

'Really?' Ruth said, spinning round on her friend. 'What's my choice?'

'She's counting on your doing the right thing. She's hoping to make you feel so bad you *have* to do it.'

Ruth shook her head in exasperation. 'I wanted to get away from the shop, I wanted to better myself – is that so wrong?'

Trevor walked in before Nina could answer. He looked at his sister and then at Ruth standing by the window. 'Oh, sorry, I didn't realise Lady Muck was here,' he said unpleasantly.

Taking a deep breath Ruth walked out.

Ruth went to work in the hat shop, apparently accepting the situation completely, although inside, the frustration burned her. She altered. Having discovered that her much loved father was fallible, Ruth retreated further into herself. Always polite and courteous with the customers, she found times when her repressed anger broke out with astonishing violence – but these times were rare and always in private. Her pride dictated that, to the rest of the world, she was in control of herself and her life. The only person with whom she let down her guard was Nina.

'You should never have let yourself get stuck in that bloody shop,' she said, when they met for coffee. 'I'm not tied like that.'

'Oh no, you're the original free spirit – serving on the toiletries at Boots.'

Nina bristled. 'You've lost all your sense of humour since you left school, Ruth ... you're not a bit like you were.'

'Neither would you be – penned in like this.'

'So get out.'

Ruth looked at her bitterly. 'And how do you suggest I do that? Poison Mother?'

'She only seems so bad because you're with her all the time. If you got away things would seem brighter.'

Ruth raised her eyes to heaven. 'That's the flaming point – I can't get away.'

Nina looked at her coolly. 'Well, in that case, you're stuck.'

And to her that was it; she had no further advice she could offer. Or at least, none that Ruth would act upon. It seemed to Nina that her friend was pinioned into her circumstances like a moth in a butterfly cabinet, and if she wasn't careful she would powder away as they did, or mummify, becoming the oldest and probably the tallest spinster in captivity. Looking at Ruth, Nina could see the shadows under her eyes which said she wasn't sleeping properly, and the faintest trace of a line running from her nose to her mouth. The mark of her mother was on her.

The shop continued in its usual fashion, however, becoming a little more faded and just about breaking even. Lilian's style remained, but her patience was frequently strained serving people she thought beneath her, and the veneer cracked now and again with a ferocity which was almost audible. Instead of confiding in her daughter, she nagged her, and at the end of the day Ruth would make for Nina's home, running away from a situation which threatened to close in on her.

Lilian did give Ruth a small wage, but she always felt guilty about taking it, knowing how hard up for money they were. Alternatively, Ruth was reminded that she could have any hat in the shop for nothing; Lilian blind to the fact that her daughter needed the extra height like she needed a pair of roller skates. As an obvious solution, Ruth relied more and more on Nina to provide light relief, seeing her as a contact with the outside world and yet realising at the same time that she could not continually burden her with problems.

And so, in a valiant attempt to widen her interests, Ruth joined the library ... where she met Derek Collins. His main attraction was that he looked down on her, being six feet three inches tall and somewhat hefty, though by no means fat. Carrying some books out one lunch-time he held the door open for Ruth and smiled; and the next week when he was there again, they began to talk. He looked at least fifteen years older than she was and – glamour of glamour – he was a teacher. He was also safe.

'Perhaps you would like to come out with me?' he asked politely.

Ruth smiled. 'Lovely. When?'

'Tomorrow?'

They made the arrangements easily, and when he came to the house to collect her, Lilian seemed to approve and Ruth's father shook his hand warmly. 'We've heard a lot about you,' he said.

'Good,' Derek replied.

'You go to the same library as Ruth?'

'Yes.'

'That's nice.'

Ruth winced.

'Well, have a good time and be back by eleven,' Lilian said brusquely, concluding the conversation and bustling them out into the evening air.

It would have been wonderful if Ruth could have convinced herself that Derek was her ideal man. But he was neither sensual nor witty and each moment with him was not heaven – but it

28

wasn't hell either. Ruth enjoyed his company; his conversation was easy and he was earning a reasonable salary as a junior teacher in Physics. Every time she looked at him she was mentally waving goodbye to the hat shop, and each time he kissed her her mind wandered and she saw herself in her own house. Home free. And oddly enough, he grew on her, not just because of the escape he would offer her, but because of his kindness.

'I think you're beautiful.'

'Thank you,' she replied clumsily, totally lacking in Nina's intimate small talk.

'Really – I feel proud to be with you.'

But it was really Derek's mother who decided Ruth should marry her son. Mrs Collins was a widow living in Greenacres, in a small house smelling of furniture polish which she shared with Derek. Each surface was burnished to a supernatural shine, the wood polished, the windows glistening and the brass fender brilliant. The contrast between the O'Donnells' flat and Mrs Collins's house was marked, to say the least.

The energy Mrs Collins put into her housework apparently left her with little interest for anything else, other than her Pekinese, Toby. She adored Toby, and carried on long talks with him, including him in conversations. Small and rather stout, Florence Collins had a dowager's hump and pale blue eyes which seemed incapable of resting on any object or person for longer than a moment. Seeing Ruth, she came to a quick decision – the girl had class and would suit her son. That momentous conclusion having been drawn, she turned her full attention back to the dog.

Ruth was a little harder to persuade. Looking at Derek, she saw eyes which were honest and a mouth which was never drawn into a bitter line. She never knew if it was merely his size or his easy personality, but Ruth felt at peace with him and oddly protected. Constantly pleasant, as some people are who have little temperament, Derek wooed her, and by the end of the month Ruth had convinced herself that she loved him.

'Derek, I care for you very much.'

29

'And I love you.'

'Yes. Well ... I love you, too.'

'We could be happy,' he said. 'We could buy a small place down on the Coppice, and I could carry on at the school.'

'And what would I do?'

He smiled benignly. 'Look after me.'

'Full time? I'd get bored,' Ruth said stubbornly, realising that her desire to nurse had not disappeared, but merely faded into the background. 'I've always wanted a career.'

Derek seemed genuinely puzzled. 'When you're married?'

'Well, why not?'

His answer was to hug Ruth and ruffle her hair just as her father would have done. The old tug of anxiety nudged her, but she convinced herself that she could bring him round to her way of thinking. All that was needed was a little persuasion and it would work out. It just needed time ...

The hat shop had a good summer that year, largely due to the fact that the weather stayed warm and there had been a rush on straw hats with wide brims. Invigorated by her profits, Lilian became almost light-hearted. 'Take the afternoon off, Ruth, and you go out with Derek. It'll do you good.'

She accepted gleefully. 'Are you sure you can manage?'

'I think I know how to run a hat shop by now,' she said briskly.

Every day Ruth anticipated her mother's interference in her relationship with Derek, but it never came. In a state of total indecision, she vacillated. Sometimes Derek seemed easy and loving, sometimes he seemed too old and too stodgy. It was as she waited for a bus outside the town hall on Yorkshire Street that she spotted Nina.

Waving, she came over, her red coat flapping recklessly. 'I was just wondering why you hadn't been round lately. How's your love life?'

Several of the assembled queue turned to look at Ruth.

'Flourishing. How's yours?'

'It has its ups and downs,' Nina replied, grinning broadly.

Despite herself, Ruth smiled back. 'I've missed you.'

'What? With lover boy around?'

'You've heard then?'

She pushed her hands into the pockets of her coat. 'Uh huh. Not bad. Teacher, well-paid job, good prospects. Pension fund?'

'I suppose so.'

'Well, from what I hear, he'll be needing it soon.'

Ruth winced. 'He's only fourteen years older than I am.'

'That means when you're thirty-nine, he'll be fifty-three.'

The fact had not escaped Ruth.

'Not that it matters,' Nina continued smoothly. 'It beats the hell out of working for your mother.'

The words found their mark. 'I'm not doing it for that!'

Nina looked heavenwards. 'Would I suggest such a thing? But, *if* the thought ever does cross your mind, it would be a way out. You could go nursing then, if you still wanted to.'

'Why are you so keen to get me married off?'

'Less competition, besides, I could come and see you when you've got your own home. Think of that. Your own front door key, no one to tell you when to come in, or bossing you around. If you take my advice you'll snatch his hand off and get him up to St Mark's before he knows what's hit him.'

For a moment Ruth thought she was laughing at her, but Nina was serious and seemed tired. 'Are you OK?'

'Me?' she asked, pointing to her chest. 'I'm in the rudest of rude.'

'Yes, I know that – but are you all right?'

Laughing loudly, Nina waited until the bus came. When it arrived, Ruth turned round at the window and waved, but Nina was already walking up the street. She moved like an older woman.

That Sunday, when Ruth went round for tea at the house in Greenacres, she waited until Mrs Collins was in the kitchen before she said, 'Derek, I want to ask you something.'

'What is it?'

'Do you really think we could be happy?' she said, not realising that if you have to ask the question, the answer is no.

Derek looked at her carefully. 'We could be blissfully happy,' he said. 'Let's have a try – what do you say?'

Ruth hesitated. Duty and obedience, the long walk of her childhood, flooded into her mind at that moment, as did a picture of the hat shop, the clothes-horse, and the carpet, thin with wear. Without answering in words, she nodded. Triumphantly, Derek leant forward and kissed her, but for some reason Ruth's attention wandered and she thought about the first boy who had kissed her when she still wore braces. She kept wondering if he had noticed, although it must have been like kissing a gin trap.

All the time Derek was holding her, she kept trying to remember that boy's name.

Three

Lilian could hardly have been more delighted when the engagement was announced. To her it was not like losing a daughter and a shop assistant; more like gaining a Physics teacher who could realise her own dreams vicariously. In Derek Collins she saw the certainty of a house on the Coppice, and later, possibly, Queen's Road. She hardly dared let her imagination run on, but, as she said to Jack, even Lytham St Annes wasn't out of reach for a young, ambitious teacher.

'Oh, leave them alone, Lilian, they'll sort themselves out.'

Lilian trimmed the pastry in front of her. The kitchen table was covered with cooking ingredients, flour powdering the board and the rolling-pin she was holding. 'I'm not nagging them, Jack, I'm just saying that they could really get on.'

Her husband didn't even bother to look up from his paper. 'I'm glad just so long as Ruth's happy.'

Lilian ground the rolling-pin into the flattened pastry. 'Well, so am I. But ambition never hurt anyone.'

'Pride comes before a fall,' Jack said evenly.

Without answering, Lilian placed the pastry in a dish and cut two air holes in the top of the pie. She glanced over to where her husband was sitting, totally obscured behind his paper, a thin plume of cigarette smoke curling over the top. Leaning down, she put the pie in the oven, closing the door gently because it always stuck now. Too old, she thought bitterly, too old and too worn out. Like me. She yawned and then straightened her apron, untying the cord to the clothes-rack and lowering it down from the ceiling.

Uncharacteristically silent, Lilian began to fold the dry clothes, laying them on the chair next to her. They were mostly well worn, some mended or altered to give them a new lease of life. Derek Collins wouldn't let his wife wear shabby clothes,

33

she thought. No, from now on Ruth would have good things, a new coat each winter and money in her bag. The thought was soothing to Lilian. After years of scratching to make a living, her whole life would make sense with her daughter's wedding. The neighbours were already complimenting her on her son-in-law-to-be; envious, every one of them. Lilian thought back – it had taken a long time, but she was now going to be a person to be reckoned with. Not just Lilian Gordon from Carrington Street, but Lilian Gordon with a daughter married to a teacher and living in Lytham . . .

She stopped, smiled to herself, and continued to fold the dry clothes. The conversation she had had with Ruth the previous night came back to her. They had been making plans for the wedding and Lilian had said, 'You've made a wise choice with Derek.'

Ruth had stopped writing her wedding list and glanced over to her mother. 'Yes, I know. He's a kind man.'

'And he'll get on,' Lilian added quickly. 'I wanted to get on. I never wanted to sound or look as though I was born in Oldham. It's not conceit,' she said, defensively. 'It's just that I've always felt out of place here, that's all.'

Ruth was unprepared for such confidences. 'You've always been smart . . .' she said lamely.

'Oh yes, I've always looked after myself, but my husband still works for the Corporation and I still run a down-at-heel hat shop.' She sounded bitter and Ruth winced. 'Still, that's my life, not yours. You could go a long way with a man like Derek – he might even get to be a headmaster one day.'

But for all the excitement in her mother's voice, the prospect of marriage to a headmaster didn't thrill Ruth, and a faint nagging sensation began in the base of her head.

'You don't seem to realise how lucky you are,' Lilian continued, 'to have a house when you're first married – and a car.' Ruth nodded obligingly as her mother continued. 'I've never said this to you before, but you've been a good girl and I've never had reason to be ashamed of you.' She was shifting around the outskirts instead of coming to the point. 'Thank you, dear.'

If her father had said it, Ruth would have jumped up and hugged him, but instead she merely looked at her mother with a banal smile on her face, and after another minute, went upstairs.

The bedroom was the same one Ruth had had since childhood. The wallpaper was slightly faded, and although the nets were scrupulously clean, they sucked up most of the daylight and made the walls close in. It was a room she had grown up in, the one next to the stair-well where her mother had hung a Rembrandt print many years before. Always trying to be something more than she was, Lilian added little touches to her home like the picture or the dried flower arrangement in the sitting-room window; but they were sad instead of impressive, and made Ruth ache when she thought of them. She swore that when she was settled in her own home she would invite her mother round and make an effort to get to know her. But though the intention was good, it was based more on guilt than concern, and although she wanted to be close to her mother, she also wanted to make peace with her own conscience.

Of course, Ruth's father was delighted by the coming wedding, rushing his daughter towards the altar and to that idolised state, recognisable by the almost spiritual label 'Mrs'.

'No more nonsense about that nursing then?' he asked Ruth after breakfast.

'Well ...'

He smiled broadly. 'You'll have no time for a career with a husband to look after.'

Ruth bristled. 'Mother found time.'

He wasn't at all discomfited. 'Well, we needed the money.'

'Maybe I need the stimulus.'

'What?'

She sighed audibly and laid down her fork. 'Derek will be bringing in a good wage and so that means I could go and train to be a nurse, without having to bring in my own money.'

He blinked. 'You weren't that unhappy at the shop, were you?'

He had never realised what it had meant to her, after all; he hadn't been unkind, merely unperceptive. Somehow, she

35

thought that was worse. 'Dad, I wasn't unhappy really. It's just that I couldn't do what I wanted when you and Mother were so pushed for cash. But married to Derek, I could.'

An expression of tolerant patience spread over his face and he touched Ruth's hand. 'We'll see. We'll see.'

The wedding was set for 24 September, and in the months which ran up to the ceremony Lilian decided that the future in-laws should get more acquainted. Deeply resenting the fact that Florence Collins had a house in Greenacres, she was enormously comforted by the fact that Derek's mother spoke with a Lancashire accent.

'It's so lovely to think that your daughter is marrying my Derek,' Florence said, pouring out some tea. Lilian and Jack were sitting on the settee next to her, Derek and Ruth having gone out for a walk. 'She's such a nice girl.'

Lilian sipped her tea and accepted a sandwich. She noticed the china tea service and thought of her own – evidently Mrs Collins was not forced to shop at the pot market.

'Derek's a good man,' his mother continued, feeding Toby a piece of crust and stroking the top of his head. The dog regarded them all dispassionately. Unhealthy, Lilian thought, '. . . and a kind one. I know all mothers say good things about their own. We all think our ducks are swans.'

Lilian smiled, some swans were more duck-like than others, she thought ungenerously. 'Ruth will make him a very good wife, Mrs Collins, I can assure you,' she said, admiring her own accentless voice as it bounced around the walls of the front room. 'I've never had a moment's trouble with her.' She turned to her husband. 'There's never been a moment's trouble with her, has there?'

'Not a moment,' he responded, on cue.

All three of them smiled at each other and slipped into an uneasy silence, relieved only by the steady snoring of Toby on his mistress's lap.

Ruth and Derek were by that time high on Oldham Edge. A sharp wind was blowing and pulled at their hair.

'I can hardly wait until we're married,' Derek said, clasping

Ruth's hand and smiling at her. 'Now we've got the house and everything.' He paused mysteriously. 'You know, the headmaster said yesterday that because I was getting married, he was thinking of me in a different light. He then went on to compliment me on my work with the Lower Fourth.'

Ruth smiled, but she felt no excitement. 'Good.'

'Yes, isn't it? It means that he'll take me more seriously.'

She pulled her jacket round her against the wind. 'Derek, I've been thinking – could we talk about my going to train as a nurse?'

A light went off in his eyes. 'What?'

'You remember, I've mentioned it before.'

He looked slightly aggravated. 'Yes, I know. You're not serious, are you?'

'Of course I am. I wouldn't mention it otherwise.'

'I thought you'd be happy looking after me.'

Ruth turned and looked at him. 'You're not a baby.'

'That's not the point.'

'Isn't it? Then what *is* the point? What are you expecting, Derek? You may have been looked after by your mother all these years but I won't be at your beck and call!'

His face went from white to red as quickly as a traffic light changing. 'You're supposed to *want* to look after me.'

'As a wife!' Ruth shouted. 'Not as a damn nursemaid.'

'You're being unreasonable,' he said, turning away from her and looking out towards the mill chimneys. 'Maybe we should go home now and I'll see you tomorrow.'

'I'll say the same then,' Ruth said, sounding much braver than she felt at seeing her escape route slowly disappearing.

'Think carefully, Ruth. I need a wife who loves me and wants to take care of me.'

'I could do all that at the same time as I was training to be a nurse.'

He hesitated, trying to understand, and when he bent over to kiss her, his mouth was gentle. 'Good night, I'll see you tomorrow.'

Nina was colouring her hair, the dye dripping off her head on

37

to a towel round her shoulders as she called down the stairs: 'Come on up, but close the door behind you. Mother's out.'

Ruth took the stairs two at a time and walked in. Nina's father was sitting reading the evening paper, a glass of beer next to him. He screwed his head round to greet her. 'Hello, m'dear, how's yourself?'

'Fine, Mr O'Donnell,' Ruth responded evenly. 'I came to see Nina.'

He got to his feet unsteadily, his dark hair falling over his forehead, his eyes unfocused. 'You're always welcome here, so you are. That's what we all say – it's your second home.'

In the doorway, Nina raised her eyes heavenwards, 'Come through, Ruth.'

Politely Ruth smiled and moved away. Terry O'Donnell raised his glass to her before collapsing back into his chair.

'Pig,' Nina said simply as she closed the door.

'I had to come and see you.'

'Good, I wanted someone to rinse this bloody stuff off my head, it's burning my ears.'

Patiently, Ruth began to rinse the soap off Nina's hair.

'Ouch!'

'What?'

'My ear! Watch my bloody ear! God, Ruth, you should cut those nails.'

In reply Ruth poured a jug of cold water over Nina's head. She jumped up, cursing, and wrapped a towel round her head. 'That was freezing! What colour d'you think it'll turn out?'

'Maroon,' Ruth responded, exasperated.

Whilst Nina towelled her hair she looked round. There was something boiling on the stove and a pile of dishes on the draining board. On the window-ledge, there was a pot of dead flowers and the smell of damp came up from the back wall.

Nina gave Ruth a sidelong look. 'What is it?'

She shrugged.

'Oh, do go on, the suspense is awful!'

'I'm wondering about Derek and ... marriage,' she began hesitantly, unable to explain how she felt.

'People only get married to have sex and babies – '

38

'Nina!' Ruth said aghast, terrified that Nina might ask her how much experience she had had. 'That's an awful thing to say. Don't you want children?'

'Kids mean trouble. The wrong people always have them – have you noticed that?' Nina replied, drying her ears. 'Your mother isn't that loving, is she? And my parents don't give a damn what happens to me.'

'I do,' Ruth said quietly.

'I know you do, but that's not enough, is it? You want your parents to care, and mine never did.' She rubbed her hair with the towel. 'That's why I'm not having kids – I don't want them to suffer what I did. Besides, I don't want to do anything I can't do well.'

'So what are you going to do? Stay at Boots?'

'Why not?'

'You used to say you were going places – '

'I *used* to say that I was going on the stage.' She winked. 'I always was a terrible liar. Besides, you used to want to be a nurse.'

Ruth winced. 'I still do.'

'Derek's in favour of his wife having a career, is he?'

'Well – '

'I see. Whether he likes it or not, you're going to do it,' Nina said, frowning. 'That's not fair. You're marrying him for the wrong reasons, just to get away from that bloody shop – '

'You've changed your tune!' Ruth retorted, outraged.

'Maybe,' Nina said, shrugging. 'Maybe I have ... anyway, it's none of my business. You'll do what you want in the end.'

The temperature in the room having dropped several degrees, Ruth said coldly, 'Are you still coming to my wedding?'

'Has your mother asked me?'

'No.'

'In that case,' Nina said wickedly, 'nothing would stop me.'

'Come on, you're going to be late for the shop, Ruth,' Lilian shouted up the stairs the next morning. Minutes later, Ruth materialised in the kitchen, leaning over the fire and poking the coals.

'Are you all right?'

'I'm fine, Mother. Derek and I had an argument yesterday, that's all.'

Lilian stopped short. 'You haven't broken off the engagement?' she said sharply.

'No, nothing like that. It was nothing important. Nothing at all.'

'Thank God. I thought for a minute . . .'

'Don't worry, Mother,' Ruth repeated carefully. 'It was nothing important, nothing of any importance whatsoever.'

The Saturday they married it rained, the water tippling down the windows and along the streets, making pools by the pavements and gurgling down the throats of the gutters. The night before, Ruth had been down to the new house on the Coppice, relishing the feel of the key in her hand and unlocking the door with so much pride it almost choked her. Inside were the wedding presents, some of them unwrapped and in pride of place, like the cut-glass vase in the window and the vacuum cleaner in the cupboard under the stairs. The house was small and slightly cramped, but it smelt of new paint and there wasn't a clothes-horse in sight as Ruth looked round. She touched everything, her euphoria more for the bricks and mortar than for the man she was marrying.

In fact, she remained there for hours, and when she left the image of her new home stayed with her through the night and into the following morning as Lilian helped her into her wedding dress. After many arguments, Ruth had managed to keep the wedding small, inviting about forty guests, mostly distant relatives on Lilian's side and acquaintances of Mrs Collins, whilst Derek invited a few close friends, and the headmaster of his school, with his flaccid wife.

The service was short, and when Ruth went to sign the Register with Derek she tripped on her dress and lurched forwards towards the vicar, who smiled as he caught her. A ludicrous desire to laugh welled up in Ruth and only the fixed

40

expression on Derek's face stopped her. Leaning forwards he kissed her cheek. 'You look beautiful,' he said kindly. 'The beautiful Mrs Collins.'

'Thank you, Derek.'

'I'll make you happy,' he added for good measure, and after the rain stopped they posed for nearly half an hour for the photographer.

Lilian wore blue and hung on to Ruth's father for support, her face vividly attractive, the expression one of achievement. Next to Derek stood his mother, her short little figure dressed in an expensive suit from Marianne Grey's. Ruth could see her mother calculating the price and working out how many hats she would have to sell to pay for Florence Collins's lizard-skin bag. On cue, everyone smiled and then made their way to the buffet eagerly. There was no sign of Nina.

Suddenly ill at ease, Ruth wandered round until she found her mother, and clasped Lilian's hand with a form of bewildered affection. 'Mother . . . thanks.'

Her eyes filled. 'Be happy, dear.'

'I will, Mother, I will. It's just . . .'

Jack Gordon interrupted both of them. 'You look lovely, flower, really lovely.'

'Thanks, Dad.'

Lilian's eyes were fixed on her daughter. 'What did you want to say?'

'Go on, girl, your husband's waiting,' her father said, butting in again.

'Dad, I wanted to talk to Mother . . . just a minute.'

But he was adamant, and slightly tipsy. 'Women! You'll see her again, you know,' he said, pushing Ruth gently towards Derek. 'Good luck, flower.'

Ruth walked over to her husband and then turned to look at her mother. For an instant their eyes met, and for the first time they understood each other completely.

They had decided not to go away on a honeymoon, preferring to use the money on their new house, and after the reception went home to spend their first night together. Unfortunately,

41

the wedding night was a humiliation on both their parts. Ruth was embarrassed and surprised; Derek was apologetic and then angry. They both slept fitfully and in the morning Ruth was up and had made breakfast by the time her husband was stirring. When he came downstairs he looked different, his stubble and untidy hair making him unfamiliar. 'Morning,' he said joylessly.

Ruth missed Nina, missed the good laugh they could have had to lighten the atmosphere. 'Morning. How would you like your eggs?'

'I'm not bothered.'

'Boiled? Or poached?'

'However they come,' he muttered.

'Raw then,' Ruth said peevishly.

He looked up. 'Sorry, Ruthie, it's just that after last night ...'

'What the hell,' she said, shrugging her shoulders. 'It's probably like tennis and improves with practice.'

He seemed embarrassed that she had brought the subject up directly. 'Yes, of course.'

Mortified, Ruth did not dare to touch him or even attempt to cajole him into a better humour. 'What time will you be home?'

'The usual time,' he answered, opening the newspaper.

Ruth stood silently, a plate in one hand and a fixed smile on her face. Her wedding band looked painfully new. 'About five then?'

'About five,' he agreed and after eating his breakfast went off to dress.

Ruth kissed him at the step and waved, but when he disappeared round the corner she slammed the door shut and raged in the kitchen. What the hell was it all about, she asked herself. Was this the supposed Valhalla that all women strove to achieve? Was this the mystery of sex? No wonder they tried to keep it quiet, she thought bitterly, no one would bother if they knew the truth. With a dull feeling of misery, Ruth Hoovered the floor and dried the breakfast things, understanding for the first time her mother's disenchantment, and why the shop had provided her with a welcome escape from the drudgery of it all. Ruth had been married for nearly a day – and it seemed like a decade.

By the following weekend she was convinced that the marriage was a failure. Derek became even more uncommunicative and his previous tenderness vanished. Feeling guilty in a way she couldn't understand, Ruth was resentful, unhappy, and too embarrassed to ask her mother for advice. It seemed light years away from school or the shop, and Ruth even began to long for the sight of the hats on their wooden poles and the smell of the felt. She actually took to shopping twice a day, calling in to see her mother, without actually telling her anything.

'Are you happy?' Lilian asked her, packing up a straw hat to put away for the winter. After September, no one bought straw.

'Yes.'

'Is Derek happy?'

'Blissfully,' Ruth lied, helping her stack some boxes – helpful as she never was before.

'Come round for your tea on Sunday then,' her mother said, and seemed slightly surprised at how willingly Ruth accepted her offer.

So they staggered through the first weeks, and it was only when Ruth finally lost her temper and challenged him, that Derek confided in her. It appeared that he loved her too much; that he was unable to see Ruth as a wife, instead of a girlfriend. He found that even though he longed to be with her, he couldn't relax. Suddenly aware of a compassion she had long suppressed, Ruth listened and held him. It was the beginning of her life as a woman, the first time she allowed herself to give unconditionally, and by the end of the evening they made love.

From that night onwards Ruth loved her husband totally, and he loved her. Their sex life was happy, but beyond that there was a contentment and a security which was previously unknown to Ruth. When they were together there was such closeness that she missed him when he wasn't there, and at night just the sound of his breathing made her smile in her sleep. The dream of a career evaporated in a welter of Cornish pasties, meat pies and fruit cakes; and the disquiet Ruth had felt before the wedding disappeared entirely when Derek came up the small path to the front door. Ruth was ludicrously happy; mindlessly, childishly content, and when she met Nina for lunch the difference between them yawned across the table-cloth almost audibly.

'You never came to the wedding,' Ruth began quietly. 'I looked for you.'

Nina glanced up at her friend; she saw a woman glowing with contentment, even a little filled out, her skin smooth as a child's.

'So?'

' "So?" I missed you – that's so,' Ruth responded. 'What's the matter with you?'

'We single girls can't hang around all day having coffees in town, we have to work.' Nina's mouth was set, and her skin looked tight and pallid.

'Hey, this is me you're talking to – we're not enemies.'

'Not yet, anyway.'

Ruth stirred her coffee without replying. 'What's the matter?'

'Nothing.'

'Really? That's why you're being so charming, is it? Life just a bowl of cherries?'

Nina looked up bitterly. 'For you, obviously.'

'Nina – what is it?' Ruth pressed her, ignoring the barb. 'Can I help?'

'No.'

'Are you sure?'

'Oh, I'm sure.'

Ruth laid down her coffee cup. 'Listen, Nina, I'm sorry if you've got problems, but I won't be made to feel guilty for my happiness – '

'Especially when it was so unexpected,' Nina countered, adding quickly, 'Listen, I'm sorry. It's just that I'm in a jam. I need money. I lost some ... and I can't pay it back.'

'You *lost* it?'

'Yes, I bloody lost it!' she hissed, looking round. 'Why don't you get a megaphone then everyone in Oldham can hear?'

Ruth lowered her voice. 'How much?'

'Fifty quid.'

'Fifty!' Then it was a lot of money.

'Yes, fifty. I haven't got it, Ruth, I can only raise twenty-two, and that's it.'

Visions of her mother's car appeared before Ruth's eyes. She could still hear Lilian telling her that her father had lent their money to a distant relative; so distant, he was never heard from again ... But this wasn't a fortune; this was twenty-eight pounds, and Nina was in trouble. Ruth smiled half-heartedly. 'I'll ask Derek.'

Nina's face brightened instantly. 'I hate to ask ... you know that. But it would help me out. I promise I won't do it again.'

'How did you lose it?'

'On a horse.'

'A horse!'

'It was supposed to be a safe bet.' She smiled and raised her eyebrows. 'Ran like a bloody frog.'

Derek gave Ruth the money without a murmur, even though she told him what it was for, and even though he had never liked Nina. The following day Ruth rang her at work and Nina collected it on her way home, standing on the doorstep in the pouring rain. 'For God's sake, come in. It's throwing it down!'

She was shivering, her thin legs rattling in her boots. 'I can't. I'll be in touch,' she said, running down the path and turning to wave. 'Take care, Ruth ... and thanks.'

She was in touch more quickly than either of them thought – sending ten pounds in a letter, the following week.

Dear Ruth,

This is all I've got to pay you back – so far. I'll get the whole amount just as soon as I can. As you must have gathered from the postmark, I've left Oldham *and* Boots – I don't know which was the biggest wrench! Wales looked interesting in the travel agency, but now I'm here it just looks like Oldham without

45

the buildings. Off to pastures new, no doubt – I'll be
in touch with the rest of the cash.

Cheers,
Nina.

Aware of her own security, Ruth worried about Nina. Because
she was profoundly happy, she altered, even changing physically. Whereas before she had been quick in her movements,
Ruth was now more relaxed, her voice calm, as though she
now had time for the world which had previously intimidated
her. Confidence touched everything she did: the way she
shopped, the easy way she made friends with the neighbours,
even the manner in which she visited home was altered. The
bird was out of the cage and could afford to sing. But with her
new freedom Ruth cared more deeply about the people she
loved and became unreasonably worried about Nina. Never
one to let sentiment rule her, Nina had always seemed in
control, but under the bravado she was rootless and isolated,
and her fragility made Ruth uneasy. Because Nina lived by her
own rules, she had severed any links to respectability; cut herself
off from the men who made good husbands; and alienated
herself from women who kept homes and aspired to bridge
classes and a silver tea set. Secure and safe from the world,
Ruth reread the letter and wondered about her.

The following year Derek was asked to go to a conference in
London, an honour which the headmaster had explained in
great detail and which Derek relayed to Ruth. She listened, by
this time genuinely interested in her husband's career, always
aware, in the back of her mind, that she could have chosen
wrongly and never gone through with the marriage.

'This could be the beginning for us. Maxwell wouldn't be
sending me unless he thought I had potential.'

'Of course you have. You must be the best teacher at that
school.'

He swivelled round and smiled at her. 'Mrs Collins, I do
believe you're biased.'

'Only with the right people,' she responded, laughing.

She packed his case the day after, ironing his shirts twice and buying him a new tie for the occasion. Her mother asked Ruth to sleep at their house, but she wanted to stay on her own and besides, Ruth had a phone and her parents didn't. Even Derek's mother offered to come and stay with her – bringing Toby as company for them both. Ruth declined graciously.

Derek left early in the morning, kissing Ruth repeatedly and waving from the pavement.

'Go on, knock 'em dead,' she called out into the cold morning air. The tabby from Mrs Davies's next door sat on the gate-post and watched them.

'I love you,' he called, his tall figure lurching over to one side with the weight of the suitcase she had packed.

'I love you.'

'See you soon,' he yelled. 'I love – '

Ruth ran out to the gate. 'Yes, I know, but if you don't hurry you'll miss your train and think of the impression you'll make then.'

He kissed her on the forehead and ran off waving, without looking back.

Having never been separated from Derek before, Ruth wandered aimlessly round the house all day, and then spent the evening hovering over the phone. The instant it rang she snatched it up.

'God, I thought something had happened to you.'

'It's OK, Ruthie, I'm here and I'm safe. The hotel's bloody awful though.'

'Do you have to stay there for the three days?'

'If everyone else is, I've no choice,' he said dully. 'I miss you.'

'I know. I've been hanging around all day waiting for you to ring.' She clung to the mouthpiece. 'Have you eaten?'

He laughed loudly. 'Yes. Besides, there's nothing else to do here.'

'Thank God for that!'

'I want to bring you down to London, Ruthie, and show

you the sights. They've got everything here, it's like another world.'

'We'll have a few days there in the summer.'

He sounded far off. 'I have to go ... I love you, and I'll see you soon.'

The following morning Ruth woke feeling slightly light-headed. Strange. Not ill, just altered. Going up to town, she called in her mother's shop, and sat on one of her upright seats as she waited. There was a large woman buying a small, pink hat with a feather. Ruth kept imagining what it would look like on her and caught Lilian's eye. Immediately, she frowned.

'Lovely, Mrs Ison, really lovely. You can carry a small hat. Not everyone can.'

Mrs Ison looked in the mirror. 'I'm not sure ...'

'Ruth, dear,' Mother said, turning to her daughter, 'what do you think? Doesn't this hat suit Mrs Ison perfectly?'

Ruth's mouth refused to work for a moment. 'Oh yes ... ideal, I would have said.'

Mrs Ison looked pleased. 'You are sure? I mean, I know I can trust your judgement, Mrs Gordon, but it's so unlike anything I've worn before.'

'It's unique,' Mother continued.

She could say that again, Ruth thought to herself.

'I'll have it,' Mrs Ison decided, opening her bag and getting the money out. 'It's always a pleasure to come in here and choose a hat. You have such good taste.'

It was Lilian's turn to look pleased. When the customer left, Ruth glanced at her mother, grinning. 'How *could* you sell that hat to that poor woman? She'll be a laughing-stock.'

'Nonsense. If people stare, she'll think it's because they're admiring her.' Lilian put the money in the cash-box and snapped the lid closed. 'I know her type.'

'I just thought I'd pop in,' Ruth said vaguely.

'That was nice, dear.'

'How's Dad?'

'The same as ever.'

Her mother was being evasive, Ruth knew that, and it worried her. 'Are you feeling all right?'

48

'Oh, I'm feeling all right. How are you?'

Ruth frowned slightly. 'Bit odd really.'

'Yes, I'm not surprised ...' Ruth wondered what she meant and looked at her. 'Your being pregnant, that is.'

'What?'

'You're pregnant, Ruth, I'd stake my life on it.'

The words wrapped round Ruth and rocked her. A child. The culmination of her loving; the final proof of her happiness. She was having a child ... no more misery and uncertainty, there was going to be another person she could love and protect, someone who would need her. Someone of her own. Not her parents, not her husband, but a child born of her body, of herself. That moment made sense of Ruth's life.

'Didn't you know?' Lilian asked.

'Well ...' Ruth's voice trailed off. Certainly she had missed a period, but that was something which often happened. 'I can't be,' she smiled, a high summer smile. 'It's wonderful,' she said, grabbing hold of her mother without thinking. 'It's marvellous.'

Lilian stiffened in her arms and Ruth let go of her quickly. A slight blush of colour rose in her mother's face. 'I'm happy for you, Ruth. Very happy indeed.'

Her voice was strained and with astonishment Ruth realised she was close to tears.

'I'll need your help, Mother. You know about these things, I don't.'

'Oh, there's nothing to it,' Lilian replied, regaining her composure and picking up some material. 'But you'd better go to the doctor.'

Ruth went to see Dr Nuttall that afternoon, sitting in the waiting room with a stupid expression of ecstasy on her face. The thought that inside her she was carrying a child was so powerful that it made her fingers numb and her mind churn over endless possibilities. This was to be the first of Ruth's children. The first child which was hers; hers to carry, to give birth to, and treasure.

Ruth had known Dr Nuttall since she was a child. He looked pleased for her when she told him, and examined her, taking

49

a specimen for tests. 'The results will be here tomorrow. What do you want, a boy or a girl?'

Ruth shrugged. 'It doesn't matter – as long as it's healthy I don't mind. I suppose Derek will want a boy though.'

Dr Nuttall put down his notes. 'Is he pleased?'

'He doesn't know yet. He's at a conference in London, and doesn't get home until tomorrow.' Ruth grinned. 'Just in time to find out.'

'Well, I can't see that there will be any problems, Ruth. You're fit and healthy and if this is a false alarm, there's nothing to stop you from starting a family just as soon as you like.'

She looked at him, puzzled. 'Oh, this isn't a false alarm, doctor. I know I'm having a baby.'

He smiled and got to his feet. 'And I presume that I will continue to look after this little offspring into the next generation?'

'You can count on that.'

Ruth went home through town, stopping to buy some baby clothes and a tiny hair brush, before turning her steps towards Mapleshaw Road. Grandma Price had been unable to come to her wedding, having been admitted into hospital with a heart attack only a week beforehand. The family had expected her to die, in fact Ruth had wanted to postpone the wedding, but soon afterwards Grandma Price came home fully recovered and apparently unchanged, except that her previously grey hair was now completely white.

She answered on the third knock. 'Ruth, love, I was just thinking about you. Come on in.'

Ruth followed her grandmother, Bobby, the talamanca cat, nuzzling against her legs when she sat down. 'How are you feeling?'

Grandma Price's blue eyes twinkled. 'Very well – and you?'

'Fine,' Ruth said, wanting to enjoy the moment and postponing it for as long as possible. She glanced at the small table next to her. A photograph of Lilian looked back; Lilian at sixteen, refined, polished, ready to be disappointed with life.

'Nothing to tell me?' Grandma Price asked, putting a cushion behind her back and leaning against it. 'Nothing exciting to tell me?'

Ruth looked at her grandmother. 'You know?'

She nodded, smiling broadly. 'Your mother came over this morning.' She stared hard at Ruth. 'You've done so well for yourself, and she's so proud of you. Don't be vexed with her for telling me, she was so excited.'

Ruth shook her head, too deeply content to resent anything. For a while she stayed talking to her grandmother and on the following morning rang for the test results. They were positive. Whistling all the way to the hat shop, Ruth found her mother composed, her eyes bright with excitement. From under the counter she pulled out a small box and opened it. Inside there was a silver egg-cup and spoon, set in a satin surround.

'Oh, Mother. It's beautiful.'

'It's for the baby,' Lilian said quietly, running her hand over the side of the cup. 'I wanted it to have the best, right from the start. When it's born, we can have his or her name engraved on the side ... if you like,' she added quickly.

'It's perfect, and we will have it engraved. Thank you, Mother, I know how expensive it was.'

Lilian smiled stiffly. 'Oh, there's a bit more money now than there was before. Nothing much, but I've saved and worked hard. There's something in the bank.' She closed the lid on the box and pushed it over the counter towards Ruth. 'I hope this baby is everything you want.'

Ruth couldn't take it, and pushed it back. 'No, Mother, I don't want to take it. You give it to the baby yourself ... when the time comes.'

Nodding, Lilian put the box away, and when she spoke again it was about some hats she was making.

Waiting for Derek to come home, Ruth impatiently paced up and down the small front lounge and peered through the curtains for any sign of him. When he didn't return, she walked around the house restlessly, walking from the lounge to the kitchen and then up to the bedrooms. The house was small, but on the right side of town, the neighbours consisting of the

51

Davies next door, Mr Davies being a chemist; and the Sutcliffes on the other side, Mr Sutcliffe being a clerk at the town hall. It was a good start for any girl born in Oldham, to be living on the Coppice and married to a professional man.

She waited impatiently, even going next door to talk to Joan Sutcliffe when the suspense became too much for her. In fact, she was sitting in their front room when she saw Derek pass the window. 'Derek!' she shouted, running up the path.

'Well, I thought at least you might be waiting for me at the gate,' he said, grabbing hold of her and burying his face in her blonde hair. 'God, I've missed you.'

She held on to him as they walked into the house together. 'Home looks good,' he said, looping his arm round her shoulder as he glanced round. 'You've dusted.'

Ruth laughed and punched him lightly in the stomach. Her news bubbled up inside her.

'I've got something to tell you,' he said, collapsing into a chair and pulling Ruth down beside him.

'So have I.'

He pretended to frown. 'Well, mine first.'

'OK, have it your own way.' After all, she thought, hers was going to last another seven and a half months.

'Maxwell's offered me that promotion.'

'Does that mean more money?' Ruth asked, shaking with excitement. First the baby and now this. Life was so good to them.

'Yes, quite a lot more.'

'That's good ... because we're going to need it. I'm pregnant.'

He looked at her for a few seconds in silence and a dreadful feeling of panic tugged at her – perhaps he didn't want a child. Perhaps the child would ruin their happiness, not add to it ... she waited for his response, dry-mouthed, and then he leant forwards and kissed her gently, as though he hardly knew her. The kiss of a man falling in love for the second time.

'Does that mean you're pleased?' Ruth asked, when he drew away from her.

'Pleased? Pleased, she asks! What do you think?' He touched

her cheek, and looked at her, saw in her everything he wanted, a wife any man would be proud of. A woman who would give his children the poise and confidence to go anywhere. 'We're on our way, Ruthie,' he said softly. 'This is the beginning of our good times.'

And she believed him.

They sat side by side until it was nearly dark and Derek got up to draw the curtains. His suitcase was still in the hall where he had dropped it, and until one in the morning they sat there holding each other, the fire burning in the grate in front of them.

Four

Ruth didn't have time to get bored, or to miss working before the excitement of the marriage was over and the baby was on its way. If she ever looked back and remembered how she had wanted a career, she put the thought away firmly and settled down to the profession of motherhood. Almost immediately the neighbours adopted a different attitude. Instead of a dizzy newly-wed, Ruth was now to be a mother and that meant responsibility and respect.

'I imagine your husband's pleased,' Joan Sutcliffe said, as they drank coffee one morning. 'My Tom was thrilled when I had the twins.'

Ruth smiled and leant back into her chair. The lounge was tidy, a weak sun patterning the curtains.

'Tom said that it was a good thing to have a family young. You grow up with your children that way.'

Ruth glanced at her companion. Joan looked comfortable, a little too plump, her hair a little too permed, but settled. I wonder if I will look like that when I'm older, Ruth thought. Perhaps I'll be dull too; but then dullness was quite suitable for the wife of a teacher, and a young mother.

'How many do you want?'

Ruth stopped day-dreaming. 'I haven't thought about it. I'm too preoccupied with this one for the moment.' She touched her stomach, her hand lingering for an instant.

'Well, one at a time,' Joan said, pausing. 'Is that your door?'

Ruth had just glanced round when her father walked in, exchanging greetings with Joan, and helping himself to some coffee. 'I've just been to the shop, and your mother said that she's got you some Harrington squares for the baby.' He sat down and pulled the paper out of his pocket.

'Well, I'll be on my way,' Joan said, getting to her feet. 'It's all right, Ruth, don't bother to see me out.' She nodded towards Jack. 'Goodbye for now, Mr Gordon.'

'Bye,' he said, grateful to have his daughter to himself. 'Well, Ruth, as I was saying . . .'

It had been the same ever since he'd heard about the baby. Each day saw him on the doorstep with something for the layette, or a message which had to be delivered personally. If he had been pleased with Ruth's marriage, he was ecstatic with her pregnancy and as time passed the closeness between father and daughter grew.

Being tall, Ruth carried the baby well, her pregnancy not obvious until the sixth month when she blossomed as the trees in the park did and bought herself maternity dresses in bright colours – much to Lilian's dismay, as she believed a woman should try and hide her condition as long as possible, not flaunt it. Grandma Price was of the same opinion.

'But I like bright colours,' Ruth said, pulling on a turquoise smock and looking at both of them for approval. Two pairs of blue eyes met hers.

'But, Ruth, it makes you look . . . so conspicuous.'

'I'm pregnant, Mother, not deformed.'

Lilian gave Grandma Price a pained look. 'I'm not criticising you, Ruth,' she began, making it perfectly obvious that she was about to, 'but I hope you intend to go to the school meeting in something a little more suitable.'

Peevishly Ruth went over to the wardrobe and pulled out a red and white polka dot dress. 'I was thinking of this, actually.'

Both women gave it a hard look. 'Oh, I don't think so, dear,' Grandma Price said kindly. 'Dignity is important, you know.'

Because Nina had disappeared without trace in Wales, Ruth was unable to contact her and tell her the news, even though she doubted that her friend would have been all that interested in the approaching birth. Then by strange coincidence, a letter arrived postmarked Birmingham.

Dear Ruth,

What a hell-hole this is! We thought Oldham was
bad – this is appalling. I left Wales a month or so
ago, having had enough sheep and enough bloody
choirs to last me six lifetimes. 'Land of Song', they
call it – 'Land of Daff Taffs', I'd call it. So, I packed
up my cases, stuck a pin in the map and . . .
BIRMINGHAM. The only good thing I can say for
it is that I'm never likely to find anywhere worse.
Enclosed find another five quid to knock off my IOU –
I bet you never thought I'd pay you back, or if you
did, your husband didn't. How is he? Is marriage the
bliss you thought, or more to the point, is he? I've
got to go, I'm meeting some bloke in a pub around
six . . . I miss you. The address above is where I'm
staying at the moment. If you want to write, well,
you know.

Cheers,
Nina.

Ruth read the card and laughed, sitting down to compose a
letter in reply. But try as she might, the words seemed smug,
complacent, as though she was saying – 'look at you in such a
mess, and look at me, I've got it made'. In her heart of hearts,
Ruth realised that there was no longer any common ground
on which to communicate with Nina, and on the third attempt
she gave up, looking for a telephone number on the letter
instead. There wasn't one. With a feeling of real guilt, Ruth
found it increasingly difficult to remember Nina. She could
hear her friend's voice and see that brittle little figure walking
down the street . . . but she was so far away, both physically
and mentally, that they seemed to have nothing in common
any longer.

Summer came and sweltered the little house, filling the minute
garden with flowers. They made the second bedroom a nursery
and bought a cot from Drummonds, hanging lace curtains at
the window which looked out over the front. Derek settled into

his new post and thrived, whilst Ruth spent languid afternoons talking to her mother at the shop, or listening to the neighbours who dropped in. Sally Davies took a particular shine to Ruth, calling by to see her most days with tips about child-rearing. 'I had three myself. No problem,' she confided as she drank her tea. Her voice was low-pitched and full of concern. 'You're a healthy girl, you'll have no trouble.'

Ruth smiled easily. 'I'm not worried.'

'Good. Good. No point worrying, I always say,' Sally leant back and adjusted the neck of her blouse, the heat making her movements languid. 'My husband was always a kind man, you know, like yours. Some women have a rough time.' She sipped the tea thoughtfully. 'Not much more a woman could want out of life, really, other than a good man and a nice home.'

'I agree,' Ruth said, laying her hand on her stomach.

'Things changed though, after the war. People seem so different now. Wanting this, that and the other, and greedy for money.' She sniffed disapprovingly. 'Can't be doing with it myself – there's only so much anyone needs out of life.'

There was a fly droning as she talked, and the nets blew softly against the kitchen window.

'When's the baby due?' she asked suddenly.

'Early September. They've given me the tenth.'

The information was duly digested. 'I'll tell you what – I could find out the sex of the child, if you like. There's an old gypsy – '

Ruth cut in quickly. 'I don't want to know.'

Sally looked at her, puzzled. 'I was only thinking – ' she began, but again Ruth interrupted her.

'No, thanks, really. I'd rather not know.' Unaccountably upset, Ruth could hear her voice rising.

'Suit yourself, dear, I was only thinking you might be interested.'

It was obvious that she was offended and to placate her Ruth stretched out her hand and touched her on the arm. 'Sorry if I snapped at you, Sally, but I'd like the sex of the baby to be a surprise.'

Accepting the apology, Sally continued to talk, but Ruth's

own equilibrium was shattered and something inside her was setting off warning bells, so much so that she went to see Dr Nuttall again.

He was sympathetic, but firm. 'There's no problem. Nothing at all. I would tell you if there was. Now you go home and settle down.'

Ruth shook her head. 'I thought ...' She looked at him, smiling half-heartedly. 'Something strange happened, that's all. As you say, it's probably nothing.'

He was right, nothing unpleasant happened and the summer burned on. The park was crowded with people when Derek took Ruth for a walk one Sunday in August, the boats filled with lovers, whilst numerous small toy ships were being pushed out over the lake by enthusiastic fathers, much to the consternation of their children.

'Look at that,' Derek said, pointing to a child who was crying loudly. 'He was playing happily until his father came along to help him.' He shaded his eyes with his hand. 'If we have a son I'll bring him here with his boats.'

'What about the train set you promised him?'

He turned to Ruth. She looked well, her skin slightly tanned, her blonde hair lightened with the sun and swinging against the smooth curve of her shoulder.

'Oh, he can have that, naturally.'

'And if it's a girl?' she asked, leaning against him as they walked.

'She can have a turn now and again,' he said, squeezing her arm.

She was obviously pregnant then, the baby making its presence felt and causing Ruth to walk with her back arched so that it ached almost perpetually. They were just stopping for a breather when Ruth's father spotted them across the lake and came over, his coat across his arm, his hat tipped back.

'You look wonderful, Ruthie, you really do,' he said, dropping into step beside them as they set off again. 'Not long now till the baby comes.'

'Six weeks,' Ruth chimed in proudly. 'Where's Mother?'

He paused and lit his pipe before answering, his hand cupped around the match although there was only a slight breeze. 'At the shop, where else?'

'She should be out in the fresh air,' Ruth continued. 'It would do her more good.'

'Not really, she'd only be fretting to get back,' he replied, inhaling deeply. 'Don't worry, that shop won't see her much when the baby comes.'

Ruth walked between the two men she loved, the sun bouncing off their shoulders and the ground warm under their feet. As they walked, they talked about the conference Derek was attending the next day in Manchester, when he was standing in for Maxwell, who depended on him more and more. They finally parted at the park gates, Jack kissing his daughter's cheek. 'Your mother will ring you later.'

'Good thing you had that phone put in,' Derek said, rubbing the back of his neck with a handkerchief.

'Makes sure we can keep tabs on our girl,' Jack said, turning back to Derek. 'You take care of yourself, you hear. Come back home soon, you're needed.'

'I'll be there,' Derek said firmly.

'Well, mind you are,' Jack countered, parting from them at the park gates, and whistling his way up Park Road.

When the alarm went off in the morning Ruth jumped and then got up clumsily, forgetting for a moment that she was pregnant. Beside her, Derek stirred. She kissed him on the mouth lightly.

'That was a lovely wakening,' he said, rubbing his eyes and yawning.

'Come on, you've got to be off. Maxwell's prodigy can't be lying in bed like this.'

He caught hold of Ruth and kissed her throat. 'I love you, Mrs Collins,' he murmured.

She looked down at the top of his head and stroked his hair. 'I love you too, you don't know how much.'

'I hate having to go away,' he said childishly.

'I know, but it's only one night. You'll be home before you know it.'

He rolled on his side and looked at her, his head resting on one hand. 'You make me happy,' he said suddenly, then, getting to his feet, went into the bathroom.

Breakfast was protracted and difficult. For some reason, Derek kept making excuses to pack and repack his things, so that in the end the suitcase looked messy and would hardly close. Ruth was unreasonably annoyed. 'Look what you've done! I spent an hour packing it, and much longer ironing those things for you.'

He turned round, impatiently. 'I don't feel prepared for this trip somehow. Maybe I've forgotten something.'

'Everything's in,' she said, leaning forward and slamming the case shut. 'Go on, the sooner you go, the sooner you come back.'

He stopped and glanced at Ruth, then the case, and then nodded. 'Cheerio then.'

'Cheerio.'

They kissed on the doorstep, Ruth's bulk making the action clumsy.

'God, you are a size, Mrs Collins,' he said, laughing and touching her stomach with the palm of his left hand. 'But I love you.'

Before Ruth had a chance to say anything he ran off down the path, waving without looking round.

Sally came visiting after lunch, leaving a pie and a dog-eared baby book which looked as though it had gone through the tortures of labour itself. They chatted listlessly for a while, but she left soon after, waving as she closed the gate behind her. Lying down later in the cool lounge for an afternoon sleep, Ruth found herself unable to doze off. The air was full of noises: flies, bees and children all melting together in a heady concoction which made her head buzz. The temperature was sticky and the cushion under her head felt hard and oddly unfamiliar. Fitfully, Ruth slept.

At first she had no idea what had wakened her, then she heard the doorbell, and a quick succession of knocks. Hurriedly, she struggled to her feet and caught sight of the clock. It was seven-fifteen . . . she had been sleeping for three hours.

The front door handle was stiff and slipped through Ruth's fingers twice before she managed to wrench the door open. There was a police officer standing there, the same one who had chased Nina once for climbing up on to the bakehouse roof.

'Mrs Collins . . . Ruth.'

She knew as soon as he used her first name.

'What? What is it?' she asked loudly, although the voice came out tinny and high-pitched. Her back ached, the baby dragging her down bodily.

'It's Derek.'

She looked at him dully. 'What?'

'He's – he's dead, luv.'

She stared blankly at the man in front of her and then tried to close the door on him. The policeman stepped forward and caught hold of her arm. 'Come on, luv, come on.'

Angrily she tried to shake him off. He shouldn't be bothering her like this. Where was Derek?

'Come and sit down. Come on, Ruth.'

She turned on him furiously. 'He's not dead! He's my husband. You're wrong.'

With considerable gentleness, the policeman led Ruth to a seat in the lounge. She caught hold of his hand suddenly and said, 'Tell me it's a mistake . . . please.'

His throat dry, he looked at the woman in front of him, remembering Ruth as a skinny, shy kid who never seemed to have much to say for herself. She had the same bewildered look in her eyes now. 'There's been a train crash. Derek's dead. I'm sorry.'

'Dead?'

'I'm so sorry.'

She didn't appear to understand him. 'No, I'm afraid you're wrong. You see, I'm having a baby and my husband is coming home tonight.' She stopped, her voice tiny, frightened. 'He's only in Manchester.'

'Your mother's coming,' the man said, still holding her hand.

She could feel the baby moving inside her and, looking over

61

to the chair opposite, she could see Derek sitting there, smiling, his head resting in one hand. 'My husband's coming home,' she said softly to the empty chair. 'You see, he promised me.'

Far away, she could hear the policeman's voice telling someone to fetch her father home from work.

Time ended. Ruth didn't remember when she arrived, but her mother suddenly materialised, stroking her daughter's hair as she stood by the side of the settee in her severe navy suit, the one she wore in the shop. Her face seemed resigned, almost as though she was prepared. In a muffled whisper, a voice said that her father was on his way, and another asked if she needed a doctor. Disjointed conversations filtered through to Ruth. Voices in the kitchen, muffled.

'Thank you for calling, Mrs Davies,' Lilian said, 'but there's nothing you can do.'

Sally's voice sounded further away, obviously she was being kept on the doorstep. 'Ruth won't have the baby early, will she?'

'I doubt it. My daughter is a strong, sensible girl, and she and the baby will be perfectly all right.'

'If there's anything – '

'Nothing ... thank you.'

'Well, if you're sure.'

'Quite sure,' Lilian said, closing the door. The lock clicked as it closed.

In the lounge, Ruth pressed her hands against her stomach and held her breath.

'What are you doing?'

Snapping open her eyes, she saw her mother watching her. 'Will it come early?'

Without answering, Lilian handed her the cup of tea she'd brought in. 'You don't want to listen to that stupid woman – '

'Sally isn't stupid.'

Lilian sighed audibly. 'Whatever you say, dear.'

'Don't say that, don't say that!' Ruth shouted. 'Don't humour me.'

The shock of her outburst silenced Lilian. She looked at her daughter, saw the dull expression in her eyes and her rapid breathing and held her tongue. At the same time, Ruth watched her mother and wanted to lunge at her, wanted to make her leave; wanted Derek there instead, in the house they had made together. She knew then that she had lost everything; knew that Derek would never have thought of insurance; knew that she would have to return home to live with her parents in order to look after the child – after all, she couldn't get a job with a baby to look after. And in the end she would have to go back to the shop ... back to where it all started.

Without saying another word, Ruth struggled upstairs and locked herself in the bathroom. Alone, she huddled against the door and cried, her arms wrapped round herself, her head down. Grief mingled with disbelief – how could she have been so happy? How could she have found Derek and be carrying his child ... just to lose him.

'I love you,' she shouted aloud, hearing the sounds of her mother's feet on the stairs. 'Oh God, I love you, Derek.'

Lilian knocked on the door. 'Let me in, Ruth. Please.'

'He's not dead!' she shouted back. 'It's another man.'

'Ruth, listen to me – '

'No, I won't listen to you! I've always listened to you, but you're wrong. It was another man, and that's final. I want to see the body and sort this out.'

A few minutes passed, and then Ruth heard another voice on the other side of the door and knew her father was there. Softly, he called to her. 'Ruthie, it's me.'

'Tell them, Dad!' Ruth shouted, the tears running down her face. 'Tell them they're wrong. Please...'

'Ruthie, let me in.'

She shook her head. 'He's not dead, Dad! Derek's not dead. It's a mistake.'

There were tears in his eyes as he listened to her and with his fists clenched, he rested his forehead against the bathroom door, saying sadly, 'Ruth, I've seen him, it's Derek.'

And that was the moment she knew. Her father never lied to her, and from then on she knew that there was no mistake. Derek was dead; her father had seen him.

The remaining weeks before the baby was born became a nightmare. Derek's mother or Lilian stayed with Ruth in the little house on the Coppice, and she ate what they gave her and drank what she was given and she kept on living.

'She's sick,' Lilian said to her husband after Ruth had gone up to bed. 'She doesn't even cry for Derek any longer.'

'She should have gone to the funeral,' Jack said. 'It would have been a shock, but she would have accepted his death better that way.'

'Oh, don't be so damn stupid!' Lilian snapped. 'She's too near her time to have risked that.'

'So what do you suggest?'

'Wait until the baby's born. Then she'll come round. It'll give her something to live for. You mark my words,' Lilian said firmly. 'Ruth will be another person once that child arrives.'

But much as they tried to encourage her, Ruth would hardly talk about Derek or the baby and seldom set foot in the little nursery, leaving Lilian to organise everything in readiness for the birth. Florence Collins, visibly reeling from the shock of her son's death, visited frequently, agreeing with Lilian that the child's birth would bring Ruth out of her torpor. 'Has she thought of a name for the baby?' she asked, watching as Lilian counted the nappies piled on the top of the small chest of drawers in the nursery.

'She said she wanted to wait until it was born before deciding,' Lilian said, glancing round. 'Have you seen the cot blanket?'

Florence looked round and shook her head, her voice dropping to a whisper. 'How is she?'

'In shock, Dr Nuttall said.'

'Shock,' Florence repeated, as though the word would explain everything. 'It was an awful shock for me too. Derek was my only son. First my husband and then my son ... it makes no sense.'

Lilian turned away as Florence pulled out a handkerchief and hurriedly wiped her eyes. 'Well, never mind, Mrs Collins, there's still the baby to think of.'

'I don't know how I'd have got through these last weeks

without that to look forward to. I just don't know.' She pushed the handkerchief into her bag and tried to smile. She looked older, her hair needing a perm, her clothes hanging loosely, underlining the weight she had lost since Derek's death. 'But we have to make the best of things.'

'That's right,' Lilian added brightly. 'We'll just have to make the best of things.' She ushered Florence out of the nursery and down the stairs. 'Would you like a word with Ruth?' she asked, as they approached the front door.

Florence glanced towards the lounge and then nodded, a little figure, trying to put on a brave face.

'You've a visitor,' Lilian said, opening the door and going in. 'It's Mrs Collins.'

Ruth was sitting by the window, her blonde hair pulled back into a ponytail. In a maternity smock her bulk was obvious, and as she looked up her expression was dull, the attempt of a smile forced and perilously close to tears. 'Hello, Mrs Collins.'

'Hello, dear.' Florence hovered. 'Is there anything I can get for you ... or the baby?'

'Nothing, thank you,' Ruth answered, twisting her wedding ring round her finger, her voice flat, without emotion. 'Mother's taking care of everything.'

'I don't know how we'd manage without Mrs Gordon,' Florence continued, smiling at Lilian who was watching both of them. 'She's been a tower of strength since Derek died.'

Ruth's face suddenly altered. Her eyes filled and she turned away. Touched, Florence walked over and took her hand. 'There, there now. Things will look brighter once the baby comes. You'll see. There's nothing like a baby for putting some love back into your life.'

But there was no response, and after a moment, she patted Ruth's shoulder and left.

On the doorstep she turned to Lilian. 'Can you cope?'

'Of course. Don't worry.'

'But it's so near her time now.' Florence continued. 'Will she live with you? I mean, she can't carry on alone, can she?'

'She doesn't seem to want to talk about it. Mr Gordon and

I thought we'd wait until the baby was born and then sort things out.' She dropped her voice. 'Better not to force things just at the moment.'

A light drizzle started. Florence looked up and undid her umbrella hurriedly. 'This baby will have its work cut out for it – making up for Derek. Still, Ruth's an affectionate girl – she'll find life's worth living when she has something to love and care for.'

'I know my daughter,' Lilian said evenly. 'When this child comes, it'll mean a new life for her.'

Ruth could hear them talking. She could hear them and wondered why it was that they kept pestering her, asking her questions when she wanted to be left alone. Since Derek's death ... she shivered and pulled a shawl around herself ... since then, she hadn't been alone for a moment. It made grief impossible, she thought hopelessly, when she couldn't walk round the house and touch his things, think of him, remember him. How could she cry when there were people always telling her to be brave, and to think of the baby? She didn't need to be told to think of the baby. She kept thinking of it constantly; kept wondering what she could do for the child inside her, wondering how she could feed it and clothe it on her own. A vision of the shop came in front of Ruth's eyes and she shook her head – no, not that way, there must be some other way ... but how? Derek had left no money, what money they had had been used to buy the house. She could get a job, she thought, but who would look after the baby ...? Her mother.

The thought was immediately rejected – Ruth did not want any child of hers being brought up by Lilian to endure the same lack of affection, the arguments, the poverty, and the fact that Oldham would probably be the place where it would live out its days. No – Ruth wanted more for her child. She had had no choice in her own upbringing – but the child deserved more.

Lilian materialised soon after with a cup of tea.

'Here you are ... a nice drink,' she said, sitting down. 'I've been thinking. We really should talk about the future, you know. Are you going to come home and live with us?'

'I don't know.'

She looked at her daughter, noticed the dark rings under her eyes and the flat monotone of her voice. Depression can be a terrible thing, Dr Nuttall had said. 'Listen, I think you should sell up this house – '

'This is my house!' Ruth shouted. Her house, her furniture, her bed. The bed she and Derek had slept in, the bed she still lay in, wrapping herself in the dressing-gown which still smelt of him. They couldn't take the house from her! 'This is my house,' she repeated. 'It's mine – '

She stopped short, clutched at her stomach, and leant forwards, moaning. Knowing instinctively what was happening Lilian jumped to her feet and immediately rang for an ambulance. Alone in the lounge Ruth rocked herself gently, glancing over to the photograph of Derek and saying, 'It's all right, darling, it's all right. I'll do what's right for our baby, you can depend on it.'

The hospital was old-fashioned, a labyrinth of corridors interrupted by an occasional ramp for wheelchairs and stretchers. Tall Gothic windows stretched up to the high ceilings, and uniform green paint covered the walls. Time, and a multitude of sick people, had left their mark on the place, and as Ruth's parents waited with Florence Collins, a steady procession of nurses and patients passed along the corridor where they sat.

'My husband died here,' Florence said, taking off her hat and laying it on the seat next to her. 'He was sick for a long time ... bad chest.'

Ruth's father glanced at the woman sitting opposite them in the corridor. Only three feet divided the families. 'Was he gassed in the war?'

'No, cancer.' The word bounced off the green walls. 'He suffered something terrible.'

Totally immersed in her own thoughts, Lilian walked over to the window. 'It's been a long time now. I wonder how Ruth is.'

67

'I left Toby with the next door neighbour,' Florence said to Jack Gordon. 'He frets, you know, but what could I do? You can't bring a dog to a hospital. Not that he's like a dog, more a companion – '

Lilian cut her off in mid flow. 'She's been in labour for more than six hours.'

'That's not long for a first child,' Florence said confidently. 'No time at all.'

'She looked so pale.'

'She was in pain,' Jack said to his wife, walking over and joining her by the window. 'She'll be fine. And when the baby comes – '

'We'll all look after it,' Lilian said, her eyes bright. 'We can take it out and buy it toys. Ruth won't have a thing to worry about . . .' Her voice faltered, 'She's been so strange lately.'

Jack touched her hand. 'She's grieving.'

'No, not that; it's not that. There's something else. I've seen people grieve before, and this was something different, Jack. She's down, really down.'

'But she'll rally when the baby's born, you'll see.'

'I hope you're right, Jack, I hope to God you're right.'

'I'm afraid she won't see the baby,' Dr Nuttall repeated to Lilian.

'Won't see it! She must see it,' Jack said, turning to his wife. 'What the hell is going on?'

Lilian looked back to the doctor. 'Why? I mean, why won't she see the child?'

'She wants it to be adopted.'

There was a cry behind them as Florence Collins sat down clumsily, her face ashen. 'But that's Derek's child. She can't give his child away – '

'Is she ill?' Lilian asked frantically. Ruth had to be ill, she thought, that had to be the only explanation, Ruth wasn't in her right senses.

'She's deeply depressed and believes that she can't give the child the right start in life,' Dr Nuttall paused and glanced

68

over to Jack Gordon, sitting with his head in his hands. 'She's determined.'

'She can't,' Florence said softly. 'Not now, not with my Derek dead ... it's not natural.'

'I'm going in to see her,' Lilian said, walking quickly down to the ward. There were four beds in the room, two of them empty, and the third occupied by a large middle-aged woman still pregnant. Ruth was asleep, or so Lilian thought, but as she approached the bed, her daughter opened her eyes and looked at her impassively.

'Now, what's all this about?' she asked firmly. Ruth's eyes were dull, even Lilian could see that. Nothing flickered; no life, no spirit. The eyes of the dead in her daughter's face. Panicking, she caught hold of Ruth's hand. 'Listen to me, dear. You can't give your own child away.'

'I can.'

Lilian heard the words and dropped her daughter's hand. 'You stupid girl, snap out of it! You can't give up. You have to pull yourself out of this.'

Ruth's face expressed nothing. No emotion. Blankness. Withdrawal. 'Stop it, now, do you hear?' Lilian continued frantically. 'You should count your blessings. You have a home with us, and a mother and father who'll support you and the baby. It may not be what you want, but it's better than nothing.'

'I wanted more for my child,' Ruth said dully. 'I wanted her to have everything.'

'Be practical, Ruth! We all have ambitions, but you have to see life for what it is.'

'I can't look after her.'

Lilian breathed in sharply. 'You'd change your mind if you saw her. Look at her, Ruth, and then tell me you don't want her. She's beautiful.'

The words had no impact, and a moment later, Lilian left.

Ruth continued to think. She had made her decision and knew that she was right. The pain would pass, it had to, but her child had a right to the best in life, and that she could not provide. Other people would take her child, love her and bring her out into the world stronger and safer than Ruth ever could.

'I promised you, Derek. I said I'd do my best,' she said, slipping off into a fretful sleep.

Three days passed. Lilian talked to Ruth several times, but the answer was always the same. After much discussion, Florence Collins made a visit, initially outraged and then shocked into silence by Ruth's appearance. Totally devoid of emotion, Ruth carried on; hardly sleeping and impervious to the endless remonstrations.

Jack Gordon's world began to shake under his feet. Distressed by his daughter's condition and by circumstances well beyond his control, he turned to his wife. 'I've been thinking. We'll have to bring the child up ourselves.'

Lilian stopped walking. They were in the entrance hall of the hospital, the reception desk on their right and the large front doors in front of them. 'No,' she said simply.

He looked at his wife in total disbelief. 'What! I said we'd have to – '

'I heard what you said and I said no.' Lilian turned to him; her eyes were cold. 'It is Ruth's child, not ours ... she's chosen to reject what we're offering.'

'This is no time for injured feelings!' Jack answered, slapping his hat against his thigh in frustration. 'What does it matter what you or I feel when there's a child at stake?'

Lilian was not about to be convinced. Her heart banging, she faced her husband knowing what it would cost her. 'I want nothing to do with this child.'

Florence Collins came to the same painful decision, although the judgement was based more on her poor physical condition than any feeling of grievance. 'You mean Ruth's really going to give the baby away?' she asked Lilian. 'No Derek ... no baby,' she said sadly. 'Nothing.'

The two women sat hopelessly in Florence's front room amongst the polished furniture and the shiny bric-à-brac. Neither wanted to talk, neither wanted to accept that the one thing they had looked forward to, the one thing which would fill their lives, had gone.

'Is there no one else?' Florence asked, too timid to suggest that Lilian should take on the responsibility.

'Only my mother,' Lilian said sharply, 'and she's hardly an age to cope with a child. She was more than a bit upset about all of this, I can tell you.'

Florence nodded. All gone, she thought, first her husband, then Derek, and now the baby. It made no sense. 'So the little one's going . . .' she said, almost to herself. 'When?'

'They're coming to the hospital tomorrow.'

Florence let out a small cry and then bent over Toby to hide her face. The dog continued to sleep. 'What are they like?'

The reply balled up in Lilian's throat. 'I don't know. Apparently they can't have children of their own and they have a nice house in Yorkshire somewhere . . .' she trailed off. This can't be my grandchild we're talking about, she thought. What are we doing?

'You don't suppose – ' Florence began.

Lilian rose to her feet quickly. 'No, I don't suppose my daughter will change her mind.'

Sick and bewildered as she was, Ruth remembered one conversation perfectly. The day the baby was to be adopted a nurse came in and asked her if she had a name for the child. Ruth had shaken her head, but inside she had decided that the baby was called Laurel, after the tree in the park, the one her father had showed her.

'If you've no ideas then we'll call her Mary,' the woman had said.

(No, Ruth thought, Mary's too simple for her. She will always be Laurel to me.)

When the nurse walked out Ruth was still turning the name over and over in her mind, like a pebble in the palm of her hand.

On the morning Ruth left for London she dressed quickly and discharged herself from hospital, calling in at the estate agent's

71

on the way home and asking them to sell the house and contents as quickly as possible. The negotiations were to be handled by Derek's bank manager, with whom she would keep in touch. When she had concluded all her arrangements, Ruth went home on the bus, passing her parents' house and turning away as it approached St Mark's Church.

No one was about as Ruth entered her house, packing a few clothes and looking round each room before walking into the nursery. Nothing of the baby remained. Everything, every nappy, every toy, every piece of soap had been moved, even the little mobile which had hung over the cot. Ruth glanced around, her eyes blinded with tears, and then walked out.

In the lounge, time had frozen. Everything was the same as it had been that afternoon when she had gone into labour; the afternoon which had preceded Laurel's birth at twenty past eight the following morning. Twenty past eight, Ruth thought suddenly, remembering Grandma Price calling it the Hour of the Angel. The Hour of the Angel, she repeated to herself as she closed the front door and walked down the path for the last time.

The train took hours to reach London. When it finally arrived, Ruth got off unsteadily, a man glancing at her as she passed. There was an all-pervading smell of smoke and damp, the first September warmth having given way to the mist and bare twigs of autumn. Ruth stood beside the barrier, handed in her ticket, and walked to the Ladies' toilet.

It was only after she had washed her face that she looked into the mirror and saw an understanding which had not been there for many months. She stared. Her eyes looked back at her with an expression of complete and terrifying disbelief. In that one moment, Ruth knew that Derek was dead and that she had given away her own child.

Panicking, her head spinning, she gripped the basin . . . and then she was sick, painfully and violently, the tears running down her cheeks like ribbons.

'I'm so sorry to hear about your trouble,' the woman said,

leaning towards Lilian over the counter. 'Your daughter always seemed such a nice girl.'

Lilian's expression betrayed nothing. 'There's trouble in every family,' she said, changing the subject. 'Would you like to have a look at that small beret in the window?'

Her disappointment palpable, the woman smiled stiffly and tried on the hat.

For weeks, people had been talking about the Gordon family. Not a day passed when someone didn't ask Lilian after her daughter, or sympathise, some barely able to conceal their delight that Lilian Gordon had been brought down a peg or two – and by her own daughter. Stiff-necked and proud, Lilian said little and carried on from day to day.

It was more difficult for her husband. He missed Ruth, and resented Lilian's attitude to the baby, feeling the loss of the child as grievously as he would have felt the loss of one of his own. And so, from a distance Lilian had herself enforced, Jack Gordon watched his wife change, how the lines from her nose to her mouth became deeper, the lips pressed tightly together, the bitterness apparent. And for what? he asked himself repeatedly. Ruth had been ill, he knew that, she had been ill and now she had gone. His world seemed empty without her.

'I always said she'd get above herself,' Trevor O'Donnell confided to his sister over the phone. 'Jumped up, that was all she was.'

'Oh, shut up, you always hated her,' Nina said, rising hotly to Ruth's defence. 'I just rang to ask where she was.'

'No one knows. Buggered off good and proper. Bloody snob.'

The pips went suddenly. Struggling with her bag, Nina found some more money and crammed it into the slot. 'Trevor! Can you hear me?'

'Of course I can hear you.'

'Ask Mum to find out where Ruth's gone, will you?'

'She doesn't know.'

'She might find out!' Nina shouted impatiently. 'She hears all the gossip in the shop.'

'I'll ask, but around here everyone's saying the same thing –

Ruth Gordon couldn't face the world. Gutless, that's what she was. Giving away her own child – who'd do that? All that posh front,' he laughed spitefully, 'and not even the common decency to keep her own kid – '

Nina's temper flared. 'You're a fine one to talk about decency!'

'Listen, I live my life my own way.'

'That's what I mean!' she said, grimacing down the phone. 'You're an unfeeling sod, Trevor. No doubt when your turn comes, Ruth'll enjoy having a good crow over you.'

'That'll be the day!'

Before she had time to respond, the line went dead.

Outside the phone-box Nina zipped up her bag and leant against the wall, thinking of Ruth. Thinking of the lanky kid with whom she was at school; the shy girl who was always trying to please everyone; the girl who had married Derek Collins and then bloomed. She thought of her and in a fit of frustration, kicked a tin can all the way up the road.

In a small village outside Skipton, a child slept in a newly decorated nursery, with cartoon characters painted on the walls around her. The house was closed and locked against the night, the only light supplied by a faint moon sneaking through a gap in the nursery curtains.

The child slept on her back, one arm extended, her breaths even. She was small, delicate, and breathed with her lips slightly parted. She could have been anyone's child in the dark; anyone's child at night; but in the day, under the sun, her hair was the same dark blonde as her mother's . . . and it made her Ruth's child.

PART TWO

Successes

Five

LONDON

The winter had done its damage; trees were stripped, roads icy
or black with dead snow, the skies heavy with biting winds.
The place in which Ruth had come to rest was a small bed and
breakfast hotel off the Bayswater Road. The type Nina would
have described as 'colourful'. Because she was obviously ill, no
one took advantage of her, and Rita, who ran the hotel, was
wise enough not to ask questions. Ruth·paid her for a week in
advance, curled up on the bed, dry-eyed, and stared at the
ceiling.

She could not go back, she knew that, and she also knew
that she could never find out who had adopted her child.
Besides, if she discovered where Laurel was, she could hardly
take her away – not now, never. Everything slotted into place,
piece by painful piece, until, sick to her stomach, Ruth turned
and buried her face in the pillow. Throughout the next few
days she wondered if she could remember and remain sane.
The thought of Derek, and how she had let him down, was
compounded by the almost hysterical guilt she felt about her
child. My own child, she kept repeating to herself, my own
child – and I gave her away.

The nights were the worst. The long nights which lengthened
out and exaggerated the hours of the dark. Huddled in the
thin blankets, Ruth dozed fitfully, returning in her dreams, to
the house on the Coppice. Then she would wake suddenly,
one hand reaching out for Derek ... Recall was always immediate, and turning on the light, she would slump against the
bedhead, awake until morning. Incredibly, it never occurred
to Ruth to blame her mother for not taking the child. Too
guilty to share any of the blame, she wondered only why her

father had not understood that she was ill. Alone and desperate, Ruth waited for daylight, not knowing where to go, or what to do.

The hotel room was cramped and badly decorated, the bedspread so cheap that it creased as soon as she lay on it. Loneliness became her enemy, so powerful that she thought of it as a person, hating it as she hated the sad sounds of people coming in at night, and the muffled rumble of a cheap radio in the next room. London pressed down on her and made her keep to her room.

Rita, however, soon became curious. 'You seen that girl in No. 8?' she asked her husband. He looked at her blankly. 'Tall and thin. Good-looking, but sickly. Oh, for God's sake!'

'I can't say I remember her when I don't,' he replied angrily.

Rita slammed the register shut, and after a moment's thought, walked up to room No. 8 and knocked. There was a muffled answer from inside, and then the door opened. Rita walked in. She kept the room tidy, she thought, but she looks really sick, and she's been crying. 'You OK?'

Ruth nodded, not trusting her voice. Rita hesitated for a moment, and then said, 'You looking for work?' Ruth glanced at her blankly. 'It was just an idea, but I could find you something, if you're interested.'

Ruth sat down on the edge of the bed. 'I need work, yes. But I've ... not been well.'

Rita nodded sympathetically. 'It's not heavy work, and it's not far away. Usherette.'

Ruth smiled woodenly. 'You mean a cinema usherette?'

Rita bristled and moved towards the door. So the girl was down on her uppers, she thought, but still full of herself. Flaming snob. Probably got herself in trouble, if the truth be known. Ill, like hell! An abortion more like. 'Well, if you think it's below you –'

Ruth shook her head. 'I never said that.'

'It's the cinema in Kensington,' Rita explained, suitably placated, 'the one in the High Street. I happen to know they're looking for a nice girl. They'll offer you a price, but hold out for more – they can afford it.'

'Thank you,' Ruth said, uncertain what to say in response to such kindness.

'No bother, dear,' Rita continued, opening the door. 'I was at the end of my rope once, like you. It's not a good feeling.'

The cinema was busy, but clean, and George Armani, the manager, was extremely welcoming as Ruth followed his short, overweight body to the office. He talked unendingly, with a heavy foreign accent, his own verbosity making up for Ruth's diffidence. After half an hour he decided that the girl in front of him had more class than his usual usherettes and offered Ruth the job. She accepted there and then and began the following day.

It wasn't hard work, Rita had been right about that, although occasionally they would get some louts in, or a drunk making trouble. 'You just come and get me,' George Armani said, 'and I'll sort them out.'

'I can manage,' Ruth insisted, knowing that she was usually immune from abuse of any kind, her shyness being interpreted as aloofness and intimidating the trouble-makers. To them, as to all the girls with whom she worked, Ruth appeared cool and very much in control. No one realised that, inside, Ruth's fear and guilt ate away at her.

Most of the audience were young couples, or kids having a night out. At that time the cinemas were a means of escape, for Ruth as much as any of the audience, and she would lean against the back wall in the uniform which was too short for her, switching off the torch on which someone had scratched their name, and lose herself in the film. In the interval she showed people to their seats, sold them ice-creams or cigarettes, and thanked the ones who gave her a tip, although that wasn't often, and slapped down the straying hands of the boys who tried it on.

She would probably have continued in that fashion for months had it not been for the intervention of George. 'Miss Gordon?' he called out, using Ruth's maiden name, to which she had reverted since coming to London. 'Can I have a word with you?'

He showed her into a small back office, complete with a reproduction desk and a photograph of his wife and two children. Flinching, Ruth looked away. 'I've been thinking lately. You seem an educated girl, more educated than the rest.' He paused. She said nothing. 'And my secretary left me this morning ... I wonder if you could fill in for the time being?'

'I don't type,' Ruth said stiffly.

'There's very little typing,' George continued, motioning for Ruth to sit down. He had thought she would have welcomed the idea, but instead she was looking at him with those cool grey eyes and making him feel uneasy. 'Could you take over the bookings for me?'

'I don't understand.'

He smiled patiently. 'I need someone to help me run the cinema, someone to learn the trade. It's an opportunity –'

'For which one of us?' Ruth asked suspiciously.

He was stunned by the question. 'Sorry?'

'What is this all about, Mr Armani?' Ruth asked, panicking inside. She had been safe in the usherette's job. Why did he want to change everything? Couldn't she rely on anything any more?

'I'm talking about a job, Miss Gordon. I'd like you to learn how to book the films; I'll teach you all you need to know.' He shrugged, obviously baffled by her lack of enthusiasm. 'I just thought you might be interested in promotion. You're obviously intelligent –'

'And desperate,' she added, ashamed of her own lack of manners.

He laced his fingers and leaned forwards. 'OK, I'll explain the position. I'm good friends with Rita at the hotel ... we go back a long time, before my wife.' He glanced over to the photograph and back to the girl in front of him. 'She told me about you, and said that you weren't the usual kind of girl who arrives alone in London without a place to stay and without a job. She said you'd been ill.' George stopped but Ruth said nothing. 'I've watched you working here, you get on with people and you give the place a bit of class. I thought you might like to try the job. It would be more money for you. A new start.'

She could hear Derek's voice saying, 'We're on the way, Ruthie, this is the beginning of the good times,' and she looked down, too choked to speak.

'Are you all right?' George asked, seeing how the colour drained from her face.

'Yes,' Ruth said finally. 'I'm sorry if you thought I was throwing your kindness in your face. I didn't mean to do that ... I'd like to have a try at this job, Mr Armani.'

He smiled and leant forward to shake hands on the deal, surprised that Ruth's hand trembled slightly in his own. She really was a strange one, he thought.

The winter was ceaselessly cold, the temperature hovering around zero. Ruth worked without pause, trying to convince herself that she could absolve some of the past and make something out of the present. Laurel, however, haunted her.

Mr Armani was a kind and patient man. If he looked like a fat gangster, he didn't act like one, and took his cue from Ruth, who never allowed herself one moment of relaxation or of light-heartedness, and worked to fill the days, before returning to the tired little hotel alone. They made a great team, and George was as good as his word, teaching Ruth what he knew and explaining how the system worked, how he hired the films they showed and who were the good companies with which to deal. Cinema was big business in the early sixties, and all the major chains competed frantically with one another to capture any new films which had been released.

After a few months, Mr Armani invited Ruth home to meet his wife, a small Armenian woman with a slight moustache. 'Come in, please, George has told me so much about you. He's pleased with your progress.'

'Your home is lovely,' Ruth said politely, looking around at the mixture of English and Oriental furniture. A joss stick burned on the sideboard.

'Some of these things I brought with us, some we bought as we went along. Please sit down.'

Ruth was astute enough to realise that she had been invited to meet George's wife for the sole purpose of being given the stamp of approval. Apparently her employer depended upon his wife's advice and had wanted her to meet Ruth so that she could form her own opinion. Mrs Armani was a gracious hostess, recognising in Ruth Gordon the same diffidence she had herself experienced when she first came to England. We may be of a different race, she thought, watching Ruth, but we're sisters under the skin. 'You have no family, Miss Gordon?'

'Please call me Ruth.'

She smiled and returned to her topic. 'No family?'

'My parents live up North.'

'Are you close to them?'

Ruth hesitated, momentarily wrong-footed. She liked George, but his wife was making her uneasy and she found herself automatically drawing back, something she did whenever she felt threatened. It was the only way she knew to protect herself, but to Mrs Armani it looked suspiciously like arrogance.

'Yes, we see a lot of each other.'

'And yet you came to London alone when you were ill?' George's wife continued, her black eyes fixed on the girl sitting beside her. 'They must have been worried about you.'

'Yes.'

Her smile froze like water in a duck pond. 'Then why . . .?'

'Mrs Armani, I came to London for my own reasons, and I've stayed for my own reasons,' Ruth explained quietly. 'I do a good job and I won't let your husband down. But my private life is my own concern.'

Mrs Armani's face stiffened. So the girl has real spirit, she thought, her expression softening as she smiled. 'I'm so sorry, I've upset you and I didn't mean to. In our culture everyone asks about the family.' She shrugged, her palms outstretched. 'Forgive me.'

Ruth returned the smile. 'Of course,' she said politely, wondering what she would say to her husband after she had gone.

But his attitude did not alter towards her at all, and he was as courteous and helpful as ever, teaching Ruth and advising her as he piled more responsibility on to her shoulders. 'You understand quickly. It's a relief to find someone who can be told how to do something once, and that's enough. I've wasted so much time with people before.'

'But I'm not qualified for this kind of work,' Ruth said, looking at the stack of papers in front of them. She had changed since she began working with George, and he had noticed how the strained look lifted when she smiled, realising, with a jolt, how very young she was. 'You're a natural,' he said. 'That's different.'

He was right, she was a natural, loving the cinema, loving the films themselves and the business. And as her knowledge grew, so did her confidence. There were a great many wide boys around then who would pay over the odds to persuade managers to choose their films, but most of the people George Armani dealt with were the reputable companies who were hard, but fair. Ruth learned about costing, about which performances brought in the most money, and which ran at a loss. And she learned how to forget herself. Watching *Who's Afraid of Virginia Woolf?* she was consumed by the characters' relationship, and in *Modesty Blaise* she found herself smiling again, but *A Man for All Seasons* she loathed, seeing someone who was prepared to sacrifice everything for his principles. In his courage she saw her own cowardice.

And George moulded her, seeing in Ruth something original, some breeding, together with an ambition which was only half explored. He liked her reserve, and was the only person who understood that her cool manner covered a great deal of heartbreak. He taught her unselfishly, passing on tips it had taken him years to learn, telling her which food sold well, and explaining how to keep people comfortable throughout the film. 'They tell me I could save money on the heating, but if people are uncomfortable they don't come back. Many of my customers are regulars.' She nodded and remembered.

Then, on a Friday evening, just before the late showing of an old Humphrey Bogart film, Ruth was carrying a stack of papers and collided with someone. 'What the hell!'

Startled, Ruth peered over the top of the pile. 'I beg your pardon –'

The eyes looked at her with pure, undisguised joy. 'Bloody hell! Ruth!'

It was Nina; standing there, bright and brittle as ever, her hands on her hips, and her hair a staggering shade of blonde.

'What happened to your hair?' Ruth asked dumbly.

'Never mind my hair – what happened to you?' Nina responded, taking the papers and scrutinising the girl in front of her. 'You look . . . different.'

'I know.'

'Thin,' Nina concluded.

'I'm so pleased to see you,' Ruth said, with a rush of real affection. 'Things have been . . .'

'Bloody?' Nina said simply.

Ruth nodded. 'How much do you know?'

'I heard about Derek's death . . . I'm so sorry.'

The words stuck in Ruth's throat. 'Anything else?'

'Lots,' Nina said, 'most of it about the baby.'

'It wasn't like they said!' Ruth said hurriedly.

'I had a feeling it might not be,' Nina replied. 'Listen, can you get off for a while?'

'Yes easily . . . I should have left now anyway, the late staff have come on.' Ruth said, turning back to her, her voice edgy. 'Can you wait for me?'

Nina nodded, seeing Ruth's attempt at a smile and then watching as her face crumpled. Automatically, she caught hold of her as Ruth cried softly on to her shoulder. After a moment she pulled away. 'Go on, get ready,' she said, pretending to brush her jacket. 'And go easy on the coat, it's not waterproof.'

They left soon afterwards, walking into an icy night. 'God, it's freezing,' Ruth said as they rushed down the street.

'Where do you live?'

'Off the Bayswater Road,' Ruth said, her eyes running with the cold. 'Bed and breakfast.'

'Ugh, that sounds ghastly. I've got a flat in Maida Vale, we'll go there.'

It turned out to be on the third floor of a building which had seen better days and failed to live up to them. A series of tattered cards by the bell listed the occupants, and a man with a bald head and a guitar pushed past them as they walked in.

'Up three flights, door on the left,' Nina said calmly.

The house became shabbier floor by floor. A vague attempt at redecoration ended on the first floor and the carpet ceased somewhere around the second landing. Nina's flat was at the top, the only light provided by a 40-watt bulb and a skylight looking upwards to a few indifferent stars. With a flourish, Nina unlocked the door and Ruth walked in.

'It's fabulous,' she said admiringly, looking round at the tiny, well-furnished room in front of her.

'Not bad, hey? It's the only way I can afford to live in London – rent somewhere cheap and make it a palace inside. Fools everyone, even the burglars.' She smiled. 'Would you like a drink?'

'What kind?'

'Gin?'

Ruth shook her head. 'No thanks. You go ahead, but I'll make myself some tea.'

'Through there then, and don't mess the place up.'

'So what happened to the baby?' Nina asked as soon as Ruth came back into the lounge.

The suddenness of the question shocked her. 'I was ill,' she said quickly then changed the subject. 'How are my parents?'

'How would I know? Come on, Ruth, I never see them, I just rely on what my mother tells me.'

Ruth's voice was suspicious. 'I thought you didn't get on with your parents.'

'I don't – that's why I'm in London and not in Oldham.'

Ruth shrugged. 'Sorry.'

'I'm not,' Nina replied phlegmatically, pouring herself another drink and looking carefully at Ruth. She could see nothing of the girl she remembered from the recent past, nothing of Mrs Derek Collins. Instead, there was a vulnerability which Nina thought Ruth had left in the playground, or the hat shop on Union Street. Everyone in Oldham was wrong – Ruth Gordon was paying the price for what she had done.

'You said you were ill?'

'Of course I was! I didn't know what I was doing. It was

like a dream – all of it. I couldn't make out what was real and what was fantasy. All I wanted was the best for the baby.' Ruth paused, trying to stop the tears. 'Then afterwards ... all there was was pain ... no past, no future.' She caught hold of Nina's hand, desperate to make her understand. 'I wanted to let her go because I had nothing to offer her. After Derek died there *was* nothing. I thought I would lose our home and have to bring the baby up without a husband and ... Oh, God, I don't know *what* I thought.' She stopped, then added quietly, 'What can I have thought to let her go?'

'Come on, Ruth,' Nina said brightly, 'there will be other children. You'll have other children.'

'But not her, not her! I gave her away. How can I ever come to terms with that?'

'Listen, she's got a good home, remember that. Derek's death was a bloody awful thing to happen, you weren't in your right mind when you had the baby adopted ... it wasn't your fault.'

'But she's gone,' Ruth said quietly. The hopelessness in her voice made Nina flinch.

'Yes, she's gone. Out there,' she said, jerking her thumb towards the window. 'She's gone to make her own way ... but she's gone to people who wanted her. You can have other children. They won't replace her, but they'll fill the void. Don't try to forget the baby, just thank God that someone loves her.'

Ruth nodded and changed the subject, pressing Nina for news, a dull sense of disappointment nagging at her. She had longed to see Nina again, longed for the one friend with whom she could relax, the one person she had always trusted. What Nina said was right – there would be other children – but those children were not yet born and seemed too distant to be real. Neither the words, nor the hope for the future, lifted the memory of Laurel.

For a while they talked on, but Ruth's attention wandered. Nina told her news of Oldham, carefully omitting the fact that Grandma Price had died. She had no desire to rock Ruth's unsteady composure, knowing enough to realise that her friend was not living, merely working through the days, the guilt of what she had done bearing down on her like the night.

Ruth missed her father constantly, writing letters to him in an attempt to explain; but each one was crumpled and thrown into the bin half finished. When she did think of Lilian a cold stab of disquiet lodged in her heart, and that, together with the certain knowledge of her mother's disapproval, nagged at her. Seeing the situation through Lilian's eyes she could hardly blame her; after all, she had rejected the support and home offered to her, turning her back on her mother with what appeared to be a callous finality. At times, if it was early in the morning before light, Ruth wondered if her mother was actually pleased to be rid of her, pleased to have finally disposed of the child who had monopolised her husband's love. But when she woke the thought seemed absurd.

But an answer to Ruth's struggle came in the form of the redoubtable Nina. Within a week of meeting her old friend, Nina had disposed of her flatmate and asked Ruth to share with her.

'Are you sure?' Ruth asked, overwhelmed by her action.

'Why? Is there something wrong with you?'

'No . . . it's just that you're doing so much to help me. I can't pay you back.'

She smiled. 'You'll help me out one day.'

In fact, Ruth was so grateful that she didn't dare to ask how Nina earned her living or paid for the flat. It seemed disrespectful to pry. But after several days of Nina departing and arriving at odd hours, her curiosity got the better of her.

'Nina, where do you work?'

'In town,' she said, walking into the kitchen to turn on the kettle.

'Where in town?' Ruth called out after her.

'Around.'

'Around where?'

Nina came to the doorway and looked at her friend. 'Why do you want to know?'

Ruth had the grace to blush. 'Sorry. I didn't mean to be nosy.'

'Listen, I work in the West End and the money I earn pays for the rent here. That's all there is to it.'

It wasn't, but Ruth didn't push it.

The flat was not spacious, but the room Nina had so conveniently provided for Ruth was ample and faced south, basking in sunshine for most of the day. There were several pieces of heavy Edwardian furniture and a window which overlooked the tired little garden opposite. It was many times better than the hotel, but sometimes the emptiness crowded in on Ruth as she lay on the bed and gazed out, wondering what everyone in the rest of the world was doing.

She had forced herself to stop thinking of Derek or of Laurel; such thoughts came only at night or when she was caught off guard – seeing the photograph of George's family on his desk, or looking at a couple on the underground. In order to function she controlled her grief. As her mother would have said, she had made her bed and had to lie in it.

By summer, George had taught Ruth everything he knew and was leaving her to cope with the cinema on her own, as he spent more time with his family business – the one she wasn't supposed to know about. His free rein provided Ruth with an opportunity to find her own feet and discover not only that she was capable of handling money but that she could handle the staff as well. Days began at eight-thirty. Sometimes Nina was still in bed, sometimes not, and only scribbled notes pushed under Ruth's door told her she was in residence:

Ruth –

Get some food in, will you? Thanks for the rent.
I'll see you later – maybe.

Nina.

No explanations were offered, and Ruth learned not to ask for any. Aware of Nina's generosity, she waited until the time came when she would confide in her. When they did meet, conversations were usually hurried. 'You must be mad getting a cab home,' Nina said disbelievingly. 'It costs a fortune.'

'I don't like the underground when it's late ... there are some funny types about.'

'Yeah, and they aren't all on the trains,' Nina said drily, lighting a cigarette.

'I can't help the way I feel. I just hate crowds.'

'You're such a baby, Ruth.'

'What's that supposed to mean?'

'Oh, nothing.'

Ruth's voice was sharp, irritated. 'Yes it was – come on, let's hear it.'

Nina turned round to face her. 'It's just that for a woman who's been married and widowed, you seem kind of naïve.'

'So?' Ruth said coldly.

'Listen, I didn't mean it as an insult, just an observation,' she said, noticing the hurt look in Ruth's eyes. 'Don't look so pained – men like your sort.'

'And what sort is that?'

'The marrying sort.'

Ruth flinched. 'And you, Nina, what sort are you?'

'The kind they don't marry,' she responded evenly.

At times, Nina would invite friends round; a variety of London low-life which generally stayed until the small hours. In vain, she tried to include Ruth, although she lacked small-talk and was hopelessly out of place amongst the musicians and artists with whom Nina mixed. Old beyond her years, Ruth began to dread the invitations, and took to going out whenever people were invited round. Besides, there was always a late-night movie on at the cinema to watch, or work in the office. The heady atmosphere of London then, with its mixture of drugs and money, largely eluded her, and she was frequently leaving for work just as Nina was getting in. Only their messages, hurriedly scrawled on scraps of paper, kept up any form of continuous communication.

Nina –

I'll be home late, so don't worry if you hear noises.
The landlord's phoning you later about the bath.

Love,
Ruth.

Ruth –

That bloody cat from next door's been in my
bedroom again, so I've closed the window. Can you
open it for me when you get in?
If John rings tell him I've left London, and if he
asks you where, say you're not sure. DO NOT TELL
HIM WHEN I'LL BE IN THE FLAT, or I'll never
get rid of the moron.

Love,
Nina.

Time after time the phone rang for Nina in the evenings, or in
the early morning, making Ruth late for work. They were
curious calls, but she took the messages faithfully, leaving them
on the small table under the lounge window. No one telephoned
Ruth, and she soon learned not to expect any callers. Besides,
as her parents didn't know where she was, who could be
expected to phone?

Ruth could have kept the line busy if she'd chosen to, as men
often asked her out, her fine, careful beauty seeming to attract
them. Lonely at times, she toyed with the idea, but inside she
was still Ruth and still tied to her husband. She loved Derek
after his death, deifying him and blaming him at the same time
for her loneliness, carrying on a form of marriage in her mind,
imagining what they would have done together, closing her
eyes and remembering their home and the baby. Frequently,
Ruth wondered about the people who had bought their house;
who used her bed and put their heads on her cushions. Sometimes, if she was very tired, her mind skipped back and she
could feel the weight of the baby and laid her hand on her
stomach automatically, only to wince and snatch it away again.

Not one moment in Ruth's life had prepared her for the pain of loss; nothing had hinted at what was to come. From Oldham she had staggered to London, her previous security falling off like a skin; and the longer she left it, the more impossible it became for her to contact her parents or return home. So she concentrated on her job and her one friendship, little as it was. Nina was her prop, even in an offhand way, and although they saw little of each other in the week, Ruth knew that she would see her on one of Nina's numerous trips to the cinema, the little, upright figure pacing in, perched on high heels, sometimes accompanied, sometimes not. She'd wave when she saw Ruth and make arrangements to meet after the show. 'See you round the corner at Black's?' she said, jerking her head towards her companion who was waiting patiently in the foyer. 'I'll dump him – he's about as much good as a chocolate fireguard.'

But one Friday evening Nina didn't come, for once breaking her rule, and it was only after the film had ended that there was a sharp knock on the office door. 'Can I come in?' she said, hovering uneasily and looking round.

Ruth was surprised to see her so late. 'Of course you can. George has gone home.'

Nina seemed preoccupied and was wearing a scarf tied around her neck, although it was summer and the night was mild.

'I looked for you earlier,' Ruth said anxiously.

'I . . . couldn't come.'

'Have you got problems?'

'Who, me?' Nina said brightly, crossing her legs. 'With all this talent?' She seemed tight, her whole manner artificial and strained. Under the light her hair was untidy and her make-up had worn off.

'What's the matter, Nina?' Ruth asked, watching her carefully.

'Nothing.'

'Then why do you keep touching your throat?'

She blinked slowly like a cat, and then peeled off the scarf. There was a large, bluish bruise running from her chin to the base of her neck on the left side.

'God . . .' Ruth said, stunned. 'Who did that to you?'

'An admirer,' Nina replied shortly.

'An admirer?' Ruth repeated, suddenly alarmed and angry. 'Stop fooling around, Nina, and tell me what happened.'

'I was at work –'

'Wrestling?'

Nina gave her a cold look. 'Very funny. Actually, I was at the club.'

Ruth had expected it to be that kind of work, but when she heard the words it seemed almost an anticlimax. 'Which club?' she asked calmly.

'A club in Soho. I work there as a hostess – and that's all, Ruth, I swear it – I get drinks, listen to the customers, dance, and encourage them to buy more drinks, and more drinks.' She looked at the girl opposite her and shrugged. 'It's a living.'

'You could do better than that –' Ruth began.

'Listen, what makes you think I want to do better? I'm not you, I don't think like you.' She breathed in deeply. 'The tips are good and it pays for my lessons.'

Ruth leant forward across the desk. 'Which lessons?'

Nina's embarrassment was palpable. 'Acting lessons, if you must know. I've made good progress since I came to London – I'll be off and running before long, you see if I'm not.' Her face flushed and she looked away. 'Oh, I know what you're thinking, Ruth . . . that it's just another bloody silly pipe dream, but you're wrong. I can act, and I can dance, and I'll get a break . . . I will.'

She seemed suddenly so tiny and childlike, that Ruth ached for her. 'So why work in a club, Nina? You could get a job in an office or a shop –'

Nina raised her eyes heavenwards. 'Firstly I would *hate* that kind of work; secondly I wouldn't make as much money; and thirdly, I wouldn't have the days off to go for auditions.'

'But you can't work anywhere where they treat you like that.'

Nina touched her throat. 'It was the trumpet player,' she said, trying not to laugh. 'It was a one-off, honestly. It's the first time it's happened . . . Really it is.'

Ruth knew that there was nothing she could say to change Nina's mind. Her friend was not about to take any advice from her, or change her way of life. Sighing, she changed the subject and told Nina about the film she had booked for the following week, amazed at how quickly she responded, all tiredness gone, her voice curiously accentless and at odds with her appearance.

A chance meeting with a film company representative led to Ruth hearing about a small cinema which had been unused for years and which now required a manager. Apparently the company wanted a man over thirty; Ruth was female and barely twenty. With a confidence which surprised her, she applied for the position, toiling over the letter and hovering uncertainly before posting it. The first stirrings of ambition had begun and as the day passed, Ruth found herself repeatedly thinking of the job.

She was just about to leave for the day when George came in. 'Someone called Trevor O'Donnell rang. He wants to talk to you about your friend Nina.'

Ruth glanced round, surprised. 'Did he leave a number?'

George passed her a slip of paper. Apparently Trevor wasn't ringing from Rock Street.

He was actually ringing from a pub somewhere in Oldham, and when Ruth phoned back, she could hardly hear what he said for the deafening background noise.

'It's m'Dad,' Trevor said bluntly.

'What's wrong with him?' Ruth asked, aware of his animosity, aware too that he had only rung her because he couldn't get hold of his sister.

'Heart attack. Nina left your number at the cinema in case of an emergency. There was no answer at the flat.'

'I'm glad I was here,' Ruth replied, raising her voice to be heard. 'How bad is your father?'

'Very bad. He's in Oldham General.'

'I'll get Nina to ring you,' Ruth said quickly.

'Yeah, do that, will you? M'mother's going spare up here. Nina should be helping out.'

'Leave it with me. I'll get her to call.'

'And quick, hey?' he said, ringing off.

Ruth had no telephone number for the club where Nina worked, and after searching uselessly through directory enquiries and the phone book, finally hailed a taxi to take her to the Harry Lime, off Frith Street. Having never been to a club before, nothing prepared Ruth for the sight which greeted her as she made her way down a flight of indifferent stairs to a basement smelling of stale cigarette ash and cheap spirits. As it was early, there were very few customers around, only a collection of girls talking in one dim corner, and what passed for a jazz band rehearsing on a small stage. Poor lighting had the effect of covering the shabby décor and stained carpet, although it was less kind on the occupants, and gave each a hunted, cadaverous look.

Her heart thumping, Ruth walked to the bar. 'Is Nina O'Donnell here?'

The band struck up behind her with an indifferent rendering of Dave Brubeck's *Take Five*.

'In the back,' the woman replied, pointing to a door.

'The back' turned out to be a store-room complete with a small cooker and a table covered with make-up and a pile of coats. Ruth looked round, turning as she heard someone behind her. 'Nina.'

'Ruth,' Nina said in reply, her embarrassment obvious. 'Have you come to see how the other half live?'

She ignored the remark. 'I came about your father. He's in Oldham General – a heart attack.'

Nina's aggression crumbled. 'Oh God! How is he?'

'Trevor rang me at the cinema. He said he was bad ... I'm sorry.'

Nina looked round blindly. 'I've got to go! Where's the bloody phone?' she said, pulling some coats off the table and grabbing the receiver.

'I didn't know you had a phone. I couldn't find a number,' Ruth said in astonishment.

'It's unlisted,' Nina replied. 'We run a very exclusive joint here.'

For nearly fifteen minutes she talked to her mother, Ruth

watching her. In the shabby surroundings Nina looked even smaller than usual, her short dress riding high over her thighs as she leant against the table, her face old under the heavy make-up and false eyelashes. As she talked her expression became serious, making her seem a generation away from her age and long-past innocence.

'He's stable,' she said to Ruth when she put the phone down. 'Do you think I should go up home?'

'See how he is in the morning. If he's no better, go then.'

Nina nodded, biting the nail of her first finger. 'I can't stay here. Let's go back to the flat.'

Out on to the street they walked together, Nina in her short skirt, her hands deep in her pockets, and Ruth, tall and elegant, her own skirt a moderate couple of inches above her knees, her head bent low as she talked to her friend.

They talked through the night; Nina because she needed to keep the spectre of her father's death at bay, and Ruth because she wanted to comfort. Then, around five in the morning, they fell into an uneasy silence, having finished the bottle of wine stood on the table in front of them, and feeling that particularly unfriendly chill of the early hours.

'He's going to die,' Nina said at last. 'I know it. I can feel it in my bones.'

'No. You just think that. He won't die.'

'My mother adores him, you know.' She chewed at her nail frantically. 'Always said she hated him, but when he ran off with Carrie Fisher she was heart-broken.' Ruth thought back. The whole town had been talking about Terry O'Donnell and Carrie Fisher at the time. 'Pig ...' Nina said thoughtfully. 'He always resented me, being born unexpected like that, and taking everyone by surprise.' Her eyes burned, bright in the white face. 'A surprise baby – some bloody surprise!'

Ruth said nothing and let her talk.

'He always preferred the boys. Always ... said I was like my mother.' She went into the kitchen and came back with another bottle of wine. 'Have you noticed how you can't get drunk when you want to? Just like life, that – you can't rely on anything.' She filled the glass quickly and took a gulp. 'Mum loved him because he was so good-looking.' Nina glanced over to Ruth. 'He was too – you should have seen him when he was young before the booze puffed him up. Tall and black-haired, like something out of a book ...' She stopped for a moment, close to tears. 'He's going to die, I know it, like a premonition... But you know what really makes me cry? If the positions were reversed he wouldn't give a damn.' She buried her head in her hands, sobbing. 'Jesus, what a bloody joke.'

The phone rang at seven. It was Trevor. Apparently Terry O'Donnell had lived through the night and had been seen by a doctor. Ruth watched Nina's face turn from relief to outrage. Slamming the phone down, she said, 'Indigestion! He had indigestion! Not a heart attack, just a stomach ache.' She drank another glass of wine, finally unsteady on her feet.

Trying not to laugh, Ruth drained her own glass and raised it in a toast. 'To your father. May he live long –'

'Indigestion!' Nina repeated, weaving her way to the kitchen.

Light-headed herself, Ruth called out to her, 'Some premonition you had! "I know he's going to die,"' she mimicked, laughing. '"I can feel it in my bones, I know he's going to die."'

Nina's face re-emerged around the kitchen door. She was deathly pale, one false eyelash missing. 'Well, so what? He will die ... some time.'

That night Ruth realised that she had hidden away from the world too long. The whole episode with Nina galvanised her into action and made her realise that other people suffered too. She knew she would always feel guilty about Laurel, but she also knew, with complete certainty, that she wanted to join the world again.

So when the letter came which rejected her for the cinema job, Ruth took a deep breath and rang the firm, asking to be put through to one of the directors. After a composed and convincing plea, the man agreed to see her. 'I can't promise anything,' Ted Morrison said over the phone.

'I understand that, but thank you for saying that you will see me,' Ruth said before ringing off.

The appointment was for the following day and after dressing herself in what she considered to be a typical working woman outfit, Ruth checked her reflection in the mirror. It was perfect. She looked at least thirty ... and just like her mother. Half an hour after her arrival, the commissionaire showed her to the lift.

'If you get out at the seventh floor, Mr Morrison will meet you there.'

He was waiting as the lift doors opened. A middle-aged man with dark red hair, wearing a bow tie. 'Miss Gordon – how good of you to come.' His hand was cool and dry in her own. 'Come on in, we'll have a chat.'

He ushered her into a large room overlooking the park, and took his seat behind the desk. 'At first sight you don't appear to have the qualifications we asked for – being female...' he smiled apologetically, '... and somewhat younger than the other applicants.'

Summoning her courage, Ruth leapt in. 'I have some good experience –'

He continued, ignoring her interruption, 'But you impressed me on the phone and I thought it would be worth while seeing you ...'

He went on to describe the duties of the manager, pulling the lobe of his left ear each time he ran out of words. The cinema, he said, had been neglected for several years. The company now wanted to update it and have it in use, thereby bringing in some revenue. They wanted to show films there, and they wanted the vast empty space on the first floor to be made available for conferences. He talked for almost half an hour and then showed Ruth round.

The cinema was separated from the main building by a small alleyway-cum-courtyard, and as Morrison opened the door, a smell of damp wafted out to greet them. The same air of neglect hung over the foyer which was filled with boxes, packing cases, and a few old posters which hung rakishly from the dull walls. It looked depressing.

'The company is prepared to let the successful candidate have sufficient resources to enable them to refurbish the premises,' Morrison continued. 'It's in a prime position and should bring in some considerable revenue.'

The area upstairs was vast and echoed as they talked. Windows lined both sides of the walls and looked out over London although the view was obstructed by several years of accumulated grime. Ruth walked round and then followed Morrison into the cinema downstairs. It was a good size, with 100 seats arranged carefully in front of the large screen, obliterated behind a pair of dusty blue curtains. When she turned round and glanced up Ruth could see the balcony above, and the look-outs from the projection room. The air was thick with dust.

'It's splendid,' she said suddenly, almost intoxicated by excitement.

Mr Morrison seemed faintly bemused. 'Well, it will need work.'

'Of course – but it has all the potential in the world. It could be a gold mine.'

He smiled warily and tugged his left ear. 'Possibly, possibly ... but I think we should return to the main building now, Miss Gordon.'

The interview had been going so well that for a moment Ruth was confused and her confidence faltered. Maybe she had jeopardised her chances by being too enthusiastic, she thought bitterly, too willing to please. Subdued, she followed him back across the courtyard, knowing even then that she was determined to have the job.

Mr Morrison was polite but inconclusive about the vacancy. He had told Ruth that she was an interesting candidate but that he had others to see. In short, he tried to fob her off. For a week Ruth waited for the decision and then rang the personnel department who told her that someone would 'be in touch'. With a mixture of anger and irritation Ruth confided in George, knowing that she at least owed him the courtesy of telling him that she had applied for another job.

He took the news calmly. 'I expected it,' was all he said. 'My wife told me that you were too good to stay here and that you would move on.' He smiled anciently. 'I always listen to my wife.'

Ruth thought of the dark eyes and the way Beta Armani had questioned her. 'I'm sorry I have to leave you, George.'

He seemed preoccupied. 'Would you be running this new place as manager?' he asked, reaching into a drawer for a pen.

Ruth nodded. 'Yes. I'd be totally in control – running the cinema and the conference facilities as well.'

He scribbled as he talked. 'You'll do well,' he said at last, pushing the pad towards Ruth. 'That's my private number at home. I seldom give it to anyone, but if you're ever in trouble, give me a ring.'

Touched by the gesture, Ruth put the piece of paper carefully into her bag. George watched her – 'bright birds fly away' his wife had said.

'Thanks, George. Thanks for everything.'

'It's nothing, we all have to make our own way,' he said, getting up and leaving without another word.

But if Ruth was convinced the job was hers, the company was much slower in coming to the same conclusion. She pestered them; they stalled her. She rang; they never returned the calls. Finally, two weeks later, they summoned her back for another interview. This time Ted Morrison was accompanied by a younger man who was slim and very solemn in his manner, holding his mouth stiffly like a child caught sucking a sweet in church. When Ruth stood up to shake hands with him they were the same height.

'Miss Gordon, this is Geoffrey Lynes. He is the gentleman to whom you would be directly responsible. If you got the job, that is.'

Mr Lynes smiled tightly.

'We've given the matter a good deal of thought, and Mr Lynes and myself would like to have just a few more words with you before we make our decision.'

Lynes glanced at Ruth. 'Your record,' he began, making long pauses in between phrases as though he was trying to remember something by rote, 'is interesting. We applied to Mr ...' he looked down at his notes, '... George Armani for a reference and he spoke highly of you.' He seemed disappointed. 'But I was wondering if you really had the temperament for this kind of demanding position ...'

On and on he droned, agonisingly long-winded, while Morrison gazed longingly out of the window towards Green Park. It took Geoffrey Lynes three-quarters of an hour to assess Ruth's suitability and when he had finished he shook hands with her with little enthusiasm. 'I'll let you know the outcome of this interview tomorrow afternoon. Will you be at the number you gave us?' Ruth nodded. 'Good,' he said simply, to signal the end of the interrogation.

When Ruth came out into the cold winter night it was nearly five o'clock and the street lamps were already lighted. People jostled past her as she walked along for a while, looking in shop windows and crossing over when the lights were with her. Her whole body tingled with excitement. I have to get this job, she kept saying to herself, I have to. I can't go back, I have to make a life here. There are opportunities here, money, success ... maybe one day, a man. She stopped walking and turned her face up to the dark sky. A star winked at her. No going back, she promised herself, I go on now ... and up.

She had just rounded the corner to Albemarle Street when she saw Nina, standing alone and looking totally lost.

Six

She had not seen Ruth, that much was apparent, and as she approached, Nina was glancing round and tapping her foot childishly on the pavement. Ruth was beside her before she turned.

'Oh hi,' Nina said flatly.

'Hi, yourself. What are you doing?'

She pulled up the collar of her coat. 'Freezing to bloody death – what are you doing?'

'I was going back to the flat, but we could get a coffee.'

Nina glanced round again, and then as though she had made up her mind, shrugged, and fell into step beside Ruth.

'I went back for a second interview this afternoon,' Ruth began. 'I think they'll offer me the job.'

'That's good.'

'It would mean a lot more money.'

Nina sounded unimpressed, her shoes clicking on the pavement.

'Yeah ... well, that's good.'

'You aren't interested at all!' Ruth snapped suddenly, her enthusiasm withering. 'You don't give a damn about what I do.'

Nina stopped walking. There was a tiredness about her face, and the look of someone who had been living on their wits for too long. She had dyed her hair back to its strident red but underneath her face was pale and small and brightened only when she smiled, the old pazzazz returning.

'Yes I do,' she said, leaning towards Ruth, grinning, her hands dug deep into her pockets. 'I care, care, care, care deeply about what you do. In fact, I want nothing more at this moment than to sit in a tatty café drinking grotty coffee and listening to your tinpot dreams.'

Without another word Ruth struck her on the head with the newspaper she was carrying and ran down the street to the café, Nina after her, yelling like a couple of kids.

'How can you eat that stuff?' Ruth asked Nina as she demolished two doughnuts greedily.

'Because I'm hungry.'

She watched her for a while before saying, 'I was thinking of getting in touch with my parents.'

Nina glanced up, still chewing. 'Really?'

'I thought I should try and explain, tell them how it was, that I couldn't think clearly after Derek died, and that I would never have given the baby away if I'd been in my right mind.'

'Are you going to see them?'

Ruth shook her head. 'No. I was going to write to my father I think he'd understand better than Mother,' she looked down at her coffee. 'I've got myself together now and I know I'm going to get this job and earn a really good wage. Things are different – they would be proud of me again, if they knew.'

'You're lying,' Nina said, wiping her mouth on a paper napkin.

'What?'

'You're lying. Oh, no one else would realise, but I know you too well, Ruth. You're thinking of the baby. You're thinking that if you can get settled you can get her back, and it's not on. She's gone, she's not yours any longer.'

Ruth could feel her face tighten. 'That was cruel.'

'Cruel, but necessary,' Nina said, leaning towards Ruth with her voice lowered. 'Stop buggering about mooning over the past. You've had a bad time, no one would deny that, but if you try and dig it all up again it will fall in on you.'

'But what about my parents?'

'They haven't tried to find you, have they? They could have got in touch with you through the bank manager or the solicitor; after all, they did all the negotiations for the house sale. If they wanted to see you they would have done something before now. Face it, Ruth, your mother's angry with you and your father does whatever she says.'

'You never liked her,' Ruth said automatically.

'Well, I was a good judge, wasn't I?'

What she said was right, and Ruth knew it. Her parents could have contacted her if they wanted to – but then she could have been in touch with them. Struck by an overwhelming feeling of homesickness, Ruth wondered if her mother remembered her in the shop, or if her father ever thought of her when he was working in the park.

'Well – are you going to write to them?' Nina said, butting into her thoughts.

Ruth looked away from her quickly. 'No. Maybe another time.'

The following day Geoffrey Lynes rang Ruth and said, in his stilted way, that they had decided to offer her the job and wondered if she would be free to begin in a month's time. Elated, Ruth accepted, and told George Armani, who took the news calmly and with no trace of rancour.

So on 14 March she began working in a cinema over which she had total control. Wading in, Ruth instructed the cleaners where to begin and had a skip brought round to take the rubbish away. Her office was to be at the back of the first floor beside the kitchen, so that she could keep an eye on what was going on. It was Ruth's intention to make the upper room available to anyone who hired the cinema, taking a gamble on the fact that the patrons would want food as well as a bar. No one gave her advice; they merely watched her.

It took three weeks to get the cinema building into order with the firm of decorators working overtime. Numerous colour charts were tried and rejected, along with endless rolls of material sent over from Peter Jones. In the end Ruth decided against any strong colours, and chose a warm oyster shade for the walls and a deep gold carpet with an embossed pattern, which would wear like iron. While the rest of London reeled under a sea of psychedelic red and orange, the cinema luxuriated in simple, understated taste. Even the lights were carefully chosen, the sign over the entrance indicating the cinema with a muted whisper rather than a football whistle.

Geoffrey Lynes watched Ruth avidly. When she turned

round, he was there; when the phone rang, he was on the line; and when she left he was leaving just as she was, raising his hand in acknowledgement as he pulled out of the car-park in his large Rover. He never once offered her a lift.

Their conversations were consistently strained, and one morning he caught Ruth up a ladder putting some curtains in place.

'Good morning.'

She looked down on him, surprised to see that his hair was thinning although she wouldn't have put him past thirty-five.

'Morning.'

'How's everything going?'

'Very well,' she said, smiling, and hoping that she was showing none of the nervousness she felt.

'You're making great improvements,' he said, walking round. 'Mr Morrison said you wanted to do some advertising in the press.'

Ruth sat down on the top step of the ladder. 'We need it. No one realises the cinema is going to be back in business and we could get some good coverage if we had an opening.'

'That sort of thing is expensive.'

'I agree. But on the other hand it brings in business, and once the customers come, they'll keep coming.'

'I'm not sure.'

'Well, I am,' Ruth said, her insecurity making her over-react. 'A big opening would get the ball rolling – everyone's sick of the crummy little places down in Wardour Street, most businessmen want comfort and something to eat and drink. We can do all that – we even have parking facilities, something unique in London.' She realised she was trying to fire his enthusiasm. 'All we need are some regular customers. That, and a few big screenings, would do the trick. We'll be raking the money in.'

He looked at her dubiously and then walked towards the kitchens and peered round the doorway. 'Good sized kitchens.'

'Mr Lynes,' Ruth continued, following him, ' – can I have the money to put on an opening and advertise it?' He did not reply, merely walked round, turning several items over in his hands like a gardener looking for greenfly.

'Can I have the money?' she asked again.

He looked at her intently. He had never seen Ruth in anything other than business suits before and the difference in her appearance fascinated him. Gone was the composed, severely tailored young woman; in her place was a slim girl in jeans and a smock, her hair protected by a headscarf. 'Yes, of course,' he said, walking out.

The night of the opening Ruth was agitated, walking around the cinema straightening curtains and checking the lights, before going off to change into a bright yellow shift-dress with a heavy gold belt. She had chosen to show a comedy, one of the satirical kind which were popular, and had invited luminaries from the press, television and literary world. Many more than she had hoped for arrived, greeting friends in the foyer and exchanging phone numbers as they made their way into the cinema.

Mesmerised, Ruth watched them, recognising the lead singer of a rock band who arrived with his latest escort, a girl wearing a short skirt and a long hangover. The more people arrived, the busier Ruth became, organising the food and rearranging the dishes on the table. There was smoked salmon, avocados, rib of beef, and a formidable array of fresh salads, next to which the desserts were lined up, ready for inspection. She looked carefully at each of them, hearing the deafening hum of conversation as the guests moved out of the cinema when the film ended and, *en masse*, entered the reception rooms.

Jostled by people, Ruth smiled and mingled, greeting everyone. Lord Durkett, who had given the opening speech, congratulated her and she responded, the empty feeling in her stomach increasing instead of decreasing. Faces peered into hers, flattered her, asked for her opinion, and when she walked off, watched her avidly. By eleven-thirty, the place was crowded with people all raising their voices to be heard, the air thick with cigarette smoke and the carpet already stained with wine.

The panic settled on Ruth suddenly, making her mouth dry

and her hands shake. Valiantly she continued a conversation with a television producer, only to find her attention drifting.

'It's a huge success,' someone said, as, stiff-backed, she walked off to her office and closed the door. In the darkness, she leaned against the wall, the sound of laughter from the next room drumming in her ears. My triumph, she thought bitterly, moving over to the window and looking out. The road was still busy with traffic, the lights dancing in the night sky as she stood there, not seeing anything, knowing only that this evening for which she had worked so hard, meant nothing. The idol of success was ephemeral, she thought, only an illusion, something which fades as you touch it. Nothing ... Her mind turned to Laurel and she leant forwards, her forehead touching the cold glass. Did anything matter, she thought, after her? After Derek ... Certainly she could fool herself and pour her life into work, but that was only a palliative, something temporary to cure a sick mind and an empty bed. She knew she was past crying, long past, and after another moment she opened the office door and walked back into the gathering with a smile on her face.

At one in the morning the last guests left. Ruth was just locking up when she heard someone pipping a car horn and turned.

'Miss Gordon, do you want a lift?'

Cautiously she walked over and found herself looking into the tipsy face of a man who had attended the opening, a wealthy, well-known journalist called Ken Floyd. 'Mr Floyd?'

'Call me Ken.'

Ruth shrugged. 'OK – Ken. Thanks for the offer but I don't think so.'

He pulled an exaggerated expression of regret. 'You're breaking my heart.'

'You'll live.'

She began to walk away but he followed her, crawling along the kerb-side in his car. 'I'm lonely,' he said.

'You're drunk, you mean.'

'Never! Hardly a drop passed my lips all night.'

Irritated, Ruth glanced round. 'No. Judging from the look of you, most of it went down your suit.'

He laughed good-naturedly, his face lit by the overhead street lamp. Heavy-featured, he could hardly be classed as handsome, but there was an upper class assurance about him which was attractive and a confidence which was deadly. 'Oh, come on, jump in.'

She paused and then opened the driver's door. 'Only if you let me drive.'

He smiled widely. 'Bully.'

'That's what they all say,' she said quietly, pulling out into the traffic.

As she drove, Ken watched her. He had been watching her since the evening began, knowing who she was and wondering why she hadn't been more pleased with her triumph. Her hands gripped the car wheel tightly as she drove, her grey eyes perfectly made up, their expression unfathomable. After a few minutes' scrutiny, the wine took effect and he fell asleep.

Ruth drove him to the address he had given her in Hampstead, arriving at a very imposing property and turning off the engine. On cue, a dark, attractive woman materialised, opening the double gates and looking at her with frank hostility. 'Yes?'

Ruth was tired and out of patience. 'I'm delivering your husband. He's drunk.'

The woman blinked, her hard face set. 'How kind, but he's not my husband, he's my brother.'

'Unfortunately that doesn't make him any the less drunk,' Ruth added coldly, helping her to get him out of the car.

The night air slapped him back into consciousness. 'What the ... where...?'

'You're home, Kenneth. Come on now.'

All three of them lurched up the steps to the front door, hurling him on to the lounge settee where he fell asleep again. The woman looked at her brother and then at Ruth. 'It's absurd.'

'What is? Getting drunk?'

'Oh no,' she said, genuinely amused. 'I meant that it was absurd being brought home by the office staff.'

Ruth flinched and without bothering to reply, walked out and hailed a cab home to Maida Vale.

The following day three separate organisations rang and made bookings, two of them asking for catering facilities as well. When Geoffrey Lynes came in, Ruth was quietly triumphant. 'Three already, and there's more to come.'

'You had a good attendance last night,' he said, sitting down opposite her desk.

'Yes, we did, didn't we? You should have come.'

'Oh, I popped in and had a look round.'

'Really? I didn't see you.'

He smiled patiently. 'You were busy at the time, talking to that newspaper man, Floyd.'

Ruth smiled wryly. 'Mr Floyd was drunk last night.'

'Mr Floyd is seldom sober.'

Her smile faded. It was the first time she had heard Lynes criticise anyone and it seemed out of character. 'That's a shame and a waste of time,' she said carefully.

'Ken Floyd is good at wasting time, besides, he doesn't have to do anything, his father runs the paper and he drinks the proceeds.' His hostility was wafting over in cold draughts.

'But I thought he was a good journalist. Someone told me that last night.'

'I suppose he is, when he's not falling down drunk. I'm sure he can be very amusing.'

Ruth wanted to change the subject fast. 'Oh well, let's hope he'll bring in some business.'

'I'm sure he will, he seemed to like you.'

There was an unsteady shift in the atmosphere and she felt threatened. 'As you say, Mr Lynes, the man was drunk, he would have liked anyone.'

'Not enough to give them a lift home,' Geoffrey Lynes added, regretting the words as soon as they left his mouth.

Keeping her voice steady, Ruth said, 'For your information, Mr Lynes, he did *not* give me a lift home. I drove him home because he was drunk, and when I got there his sister helped me get him into the house. Then I left.'

He had the good manners to look discomfited. 'Your private life is your own concern.'

'I'm so glad you see it that way,' she added quietly as he walked out.

His spying left her with a bad taste in her mouth which even persistent enquiries about the cinema couldn't wholly dislodge. Having thought of him as a cold fish, his interest seemed disturbing and very unwelcome. From that moment on Ruth avoided direct contact with him and if she saw him coming walked off in the other direction immediately.

It was the Thursday of the same week that she received a telephone call from Ken Floyd's office. 'Miss Gordon, this is Mr Floyd's secretary. We would like to make a booking for the cinema for a private showing next week on Wednesday. Would that be convenient?'

'That's fine,' Ruth said, with a feeling of mounting excitement. 'Can you give me some more details?' Carefully she listed what was required, making note of the fact that Mr Ken Floyd would arrive early to see how everything was getting on.

That Wednesday she made sure everything ran perfectly, fooling herself into thinking that it was merely her desire to do a good job rather than an attempt to impress Ken Floyd. Then, just before the showing began, Geoffrey Lynes walked in. 'So your Mr Floyd is coming with his cronies today, is he?'

Ruth stood up to him. 'There's a showing in the cinema this afternoon, if that's what you mean.'

'What else could I mean?' he countered sharply before leaving

At a quarter to two there was a knock on the office door and a hand holding a box of chocolates appeared. 'Friends?' Ken Floyd asked, walking in and putting the box down on Ruth's desk.

'What is this for?' she asked, smiling.

'An apology for my appalling behaviour the other night,' he replied easily. In the daylight he appeared stockier, his features a little exaggerated, his skin grainy.

'It was a nice thought, but not really necessary.'

'So I didn't disgrace myself thoroughly the other night?'

'Not really, you were quite a disappointment actually, you never threw up once,' she countered, surprised at her own high spirits.

He put his hands up to his forehead. 'Miss Gordon, you shock me.'

Ruth smiled and glanced away, suddenly aware that she was attracted to the man. Equally astute, he noticed her hesitation and leant forward across the desk. 'Let's go out for dinner tonight.'

'I can't, I'm working.'

'Tomorrow?'

'Yes, tomorrow,' she accepted easily. It seemed natural that she would go with him, even though she had avoided any involvement with other men. He smiled and chatted comfortably until the visitors started to arrive and Ruth went into the cinema to greet them. As though they were already familiar, Ken accompanied her, squeezing her arm lightly as he moved on.

That night, Nina tackled her. 'You look good, what's happened?'

'I thought you'd be at work,' Ruth said evasively.

'I've got a cold and I'm not going in. Men resent the hostesses coughing into the club's champagne.' She screwed up her eyes. 'So what's new?'

'I'm going out for dinner tomorrow night – '

'About time.'

'With a newspaper man.'

'Aaargh.'

'What's that supposed to mean?'

'They're only after one thing, they drink too much, and worst of all they've never got enough money.'

'This newspaper man's father owns the paper.'

'Randolph Hearst is dead,' she said smartly.

'Kenneth Floyd isn't,' Ruth responded, equally smartly.

She chewed the information over and sniffed. 'What are you wearing? The mink's in cold storage.'

Ignoring her, Ruth went for a bath.

Ken Floyd lived up to his reputation; he was amusing and

good company and he drank too much. It wasn't obvious at first, but by the time they were on to the dessert he was slurring his words slightly and leaning on the table. 'You are charming ... charming. I thought that the first moment I saw you ...'

Ruth glanced round, mortified. 'Ken –'

'Come home with me.'

'Oh, for God's sake!'

He looked at the girl in front of him, realising his error and trying hard to focus. 'Sorry, force of habit.'

Humiliated, Ruth knocked his elbow off the edge of the table. He fell forward clumsily. 'Sorry, force of habit,' she said, walking out.

It was raining, naturally, and there wasn't a cab about. Ruth walked with her head down, her heart thumping, asking herself repeatedly why she had been so naïve; why, after protecting herself for so long, she had let down her guard with a man who was too old and too worldly for her. Nina could have coped with him, Ruth thought, crossing over the road, Nina could have played him like a fish on the end of a line. But not her. Quite aside from her own discomfort, it galled Ruth to think that the likes of Geoffrey Lynes were right, and that she had been taken in just like every other impressionable female. Feeling more than a little angry with herself, Ruth walked for nearly a mile before finally hailing a taxi to take her home. Mercifully, Nina was out.

When she arrived at work the following morning, there was a letter waiting for her. Hand delivered.

> Dear Ruth,
>
> What a slob you must think I am. I'd like it if you'd let me explain, perhaps we could meet tomorrow? Give my office a ring and leave a message with my secretary.
>
> > Ken.

With great satisfaction Ruth tore up the letter and turned back to her work.

*

Secure in a job which paid a good salary, Ruth decided to find a flat of her own. Nina had proved her friendship many times over – offering Ruth a home and providing support as she had climbed, unsteadily, out of the mire, Ruth knew how much she owed Nina, but also realised that her friend's life was too alien for her to share. To Ruth, family was not important, it was vital. She had no wish to live for today; her mind looked ahead to the possibility that somewhere, somehow, she could make a home again. What Nina loathed, she prized. What Nina despised, Ruth needed. For all Nina's attempts to include her, Ruth remained forever on the outside looking in, the heady freedom and indulgence of the swinging sixties hurtling by her like a rally car.

Having made her decision, Ruth set to work, and by the end of the morning had spoken to several agencies and was about to ring another, when an advertisement in the paper caught her eye: 'Pleasant ground floor flat to rent. One bedroom, one reception room, own kitchen and bathroom. Ring ...'

She phoned the number and made an appointment to see the property after work, following the directions to a wide Kensington road bordered with trees.

'The last people were here for nearly six years,' the owner, Mrs McBain, told Ruth as she showed her round. 'They loved it, said it was just perfect.' A large picture window faced them, wide with sunshine and looking out over a small, well-kept garden. The furniture was unremarkable, but solid, the walls hung with a collection of good watercolour landscapes.

Mrs McBain followed Ruth's glance. 'My husband was an artist. Not professional, just a Sunday painter.' She paused. 'Do you like it?'

'It's lovely ... the boat's excellent.'

Mrs McBain smiled. 'Not the painting, the flat.'

Ruth looked around before replying. The kitchen was small, but manageable, the bathroom likewise. Yet it was the bedroom which decided her. Decorated with a fine wallpaper of roses, it gave the impression of warmth and light and smelt faintly of violets.

'I love it.'

'So you'll come?' Mrs McBain asked eagerly. 'I would so like to have you here.' She smoothed the bedcover as she talked. 'You're not like most of the girls who've come to look.' She glanced at Ruth, seeing a smart young woman with a classical face; a respectable girl. 'I would like to think you were living in my house.'

'So would I, I'll take it,' Ruth said quickly, paying the woman a month's rent in advance before going back to Maida Vale to tell Nina.

The news stunned her. 'Why are you leaving? Are you unhappy here?' Nina asked, her hand poised over the kettle.

'Oh, it's not that. I've loved it here, but you knew I would have to find a place of my own eventually. I've told you often enough.'

She pulled her mouth down at the corners. 'Oh, I know you *said* it, I thought it was just talk, that's all.' She scooped coffee into two mugs and poured on the boiling water.

'I've been talking about it for nearly six months,' Ruth said quietly, trying to justify herself.

'I just thought you were OK here. That's all,' Nina continued, glancing at Ruth, whose face was strained. Always trying to please, Nina thought, even now when she wants to make a decision for herself, she's worried about what I'll say. 'Don't fret about it. I know you need your own space,' Nina continued, sipping her coffee. I'll miss you, she thought. Even though you don't get on with my friends, even though you look too bloody good for this place, I'll still miss you. 'You'll be happier with your own flat.'

'I'm not unhappy here.'

'But you don't feel comfortable, do you?'

Ruth hesitated. 'You've been so kind – '

'That's not an answer. I did what you would have done for me. That's not kindness, just instinct.' Nina paused, and returned to her original point. 'You don't feel at home here, do you?'

Ruth shook her head. 'I don't know why, but I don't feel at home anywhere. It's as though I'm always watching everyone else from the sidelines. I see everyone having a great time, no inhibitions, drugs, drink, sex. No worries.' She smiled wryly. 'But I can't join in. I don't *want* to feel like everyone's mother, I just do.'

'It's just the way you are – '

'The way I am!' Ruth replied, her voice rising. 'I don't want to be like this! I want to be like everyone else.'

'Bullshit,' Nina responded, pulling Ruth to her feet and planting her firmly in front of the mirror. 'Look in the glass, Ruth, and tell me that you really want to be like the rest of us. You've got something special, and that's class, kiddo. You can't steal it, fake it, or buy it. It's something bred in you and it sets you apart. You look expensive, elegant, a cut above the rest, and much as you hate it now, there'll come a time when you're grateful.' She smiled. 'Believe me, Ruth, this isn't the place for you. You're not the type to live off your wits. Don't settle for second rate, go for the top.' She turned away. 'So when are you leaving?'

'I'll pay you this week's rent and next, to tide you over – '

Nina waved aside the suggestion. 'I don't need the money. The club's doing well, and I've got some other work coming in now. I can run this place on my own.'

The implication struck Ruth with the force of a truck. 'So why have you put up with me for so long?'

'I like the company,' Nina said simply. 'Anyway ... we'll have more fun now you've got your own place. I can visit.'

'You will, won't you? And you will look after yourself?'

She pulled a face. 'Christ, you do nag!'

'But we'll keep in touch?'

'Haven't we always?' Nina said quietly, before turning back to her magazine.

Ruth moved into the new flat the following week. Nina's home had been a refuge, a hiding place from the world, but it had been too full of old memories. Too often, Ruth had cried in that bedroom, sitting alone and waiting for Nina. Each piece of furniture reminded her of the pain; each plate, or spoon took her back to those first agonising months.

Now this was her home, these were her rooms, and the walls stood guard around her.

The cinema gathered momentum just as Ruth had promised it would. Within weeks they were booked for six months ahead and her bosses were pleased with her, showing their appreciation by granting Ruth a small rise and her own secretary. In short, she had arrived. Ken Floyd had been on the phone constantly after their disastrous dinner date, but Ruth's life was too full to welcome any complications. After a while, he stopped ringing, but she still thought of him occasionally, wondering what he was doing, and who he was with. But if Ken Floyd drifted into the background, Geoffrey Lynes was another matter. He hummed round Ruth like a fly round a jam tart, losing his usual composure and becoming mildly flirtatious. Treating him in an offhand manner had no effect, and it was only after an argument that he took offence and changed into an implacable enemy overnight. His antagonism showed itself frequently.

'Mr Lynes, I want a word with Mr Morrison, could you tell me when he's free?'

He looked at her coldly. She was wearing silver-grey that morning, the same colour as her eyes. The colour of winter, he thought suddenly, 'I'll ring you.'

Ruth waited nearly an hour for him to contact her, and then rang Morrison's secretary direct. Later, when she challenged Lynes he apologised, but there was a look of triumph in his eyes and from then on she watched him carefully.

And as Ruth found her feet and climbed steadily, England was swinging as it never had before. Fashions changed and youth was everything. Carnaby Street intoxicated foreigners, and the city rocked with scandals. At the same time Jeremy Thorpe became leader of the Liberal Party, Desmond Morris had just written *The Naked Ape* and *The Forsyte Saga* was running on television.

It was the era of Liverpool's Catholic Cathedral and the end of Che Guevara. England was shining bright and everyone in

London was enjoying the rich pickings. And for Ruth, there was the ever present promise of success. She had arrived in the right place at the right time and if the dull shadow of her past caused any anxiety, it was controlled, shut off in some kind of mental gloryhole.

Until one morning, when she was talking to the projectionist and her secretary called for her. 'There's someone to see you in your office.'

'Who is it?'

She shrugged. 'He wouldn't say. Just said he'd wait.'

Irritated by the interruption, Ruth went to her office and stopped dead in her tracks. Silhouetted against the window stood her father. Turning towards her, he smiled and held out his arms.

'Oh, Dad,' Ruth said quietly and went to him.

'There, there ... come on, it's all right. It's all right, Ruthie.'

She laid her head on his shoulder, smelling the warm scent of childhood, the faint smell of earth on his clothes from the gardens. They held each other tightly for a minute and then he pulled away and looked at her. There was very little trace of his daughter left, he thought regretfully, admiring the serene face, slimmed down to show off the perfect bone structure. 'You are bonny, you really are. You look older though. Are you eating enough?'

Ruth nodded. 'I've missed you so much, Dad ... I don't know what I was doing when I left ... I was ill.'

He caught hold of her hands. 'I know. I thought about it time and time again, and I realised that you couldn't have known what was happening, what with Derek dying so sudden like that.'

'Dad, where's the baby?' she asked suddenly.

'I don't know, flower, I really don't. Only that she was adopted and that they were a nice young couple who couldn't have any of their own.'

'I gave her away ...' Ruth said, her hands limp in his.

'You were ill, Ruthie, I understand that.'

'And Mother – does she understand?' She could feel his hands stiffen. 'She doesn't know you're here, does she?' He shook his head. 'It doesn't matter,' Ruth lied. 'How did you find me, Dad?'

'I've kept tabs on you ever since you left, through the bank manager. And Nina's mother.' He laughed. 'By God, she's a rum one! Anyway, I found out where you were and where you'd moved to. I thought of coming before, but it was too ... well, you know.'

'Yes, I know.'

The intercom buzzed on Ruth's desk and she glanced over, startled. 'Dad, I have to go now. Here are the keys to my flat, I'll be home later.' He took the keys from her hand. 'Where did you tell Mother you were going?'

'To visit my father's grave in Durham. I told her I might stay over.'

Ruth smiled grimly. 'I bet she knows the truth.'

'Maybe,' he said. 'Maybe she does, at that.'

He was reading the paper when Ruth got home, perfectly relaxed, as though they had never been apart. Ignoring the subject closest to her heart, Ruth prepared a meal for them, chatting incessantly about her job. He listened, laughed, and then both of them fell silent. Her heart banging, Ruth pushed away her plate and leant towards him. 'Dad, I'm so sorry for all the trouble I caused ... I never even saw Derek's grave.'

'He's up at Lees Field. I look in now and again, just to have a word with him, you know.'

She smiled. 'Does he ever answer back?'

'Not so bloody often that you'd notice.'

They both laughed.

'I feel so bad about the baby, Dad. They called her Mary at the hospital but I called her Laurel,' she glanced at her father, 'after the tree you showed me in the park ... What did she look like, Dad? And why didn't you take her for me?'

He glanced down at his hands. 'I only saw her once. After you said you wanted her adopted I just couldn't face it.' He paused. 'She was very little, with hair the same colour as yours. I wanted to pick her up, give her a bit of a cuddle, you know how it is. But what with one thing and another ...' He stopped suddenly. Ruth was sitting rigid and staring straight ahead, her eyes bright. 'There'll be others, Ruthie, I promise you.'

'But not her,' she said softly. 'Not her, Dad, she's gone.'

'You'll have other children – '

Abruptly, Ruth got to her feet and walked into the bedroom, coming back with blankets to make up a bed on the settee, 'I'll sleep here, Dad.'

'You'll do nothing of the kind,' he said, surprised by the sudden change in her. She always was a strange child, he thought sadly, wondering how she could be so unfeeling; not realising that long after he slept, Ruth would be awake crying, her grief always private, her sorrow her own.

The following morning Jack Gordon was up before his daughter, splashing about in the bathroom and whistling to himself.

'You will come and see me again, won't you?' Ruth asked him.

'Can't you come home and see us?'

'It's too early, Dad, you know that. Mother hasn't forgiven me yet.'

'Then I'll come down here again. I don't know what I'll tell your mother, but I'll think of something.'

'Soon? Come soon, Dad, please.'

He caught hold of her hand. 'Just as soon as I can, flower.'

He left at eleven, and that afternoon she had another set of keys cut for his use. Hardly daring to hope, Ruth saw through her father a way to reach Lilian and repair their relationship. She pictured a reconciliation, a longed-for return to her home, a retreat back to security. That was how simple it seemed then.

The cinema was soon heavily booked, customers delighted to find a select watering-hole in the middle of London away from the grime of Soho. Ruth had judged the market well, having sized up the opposition by dragging herself up numerous dingy staircases to rooms which buzzed with inactivity and smelt of coffee and old cigarettes. At first Ruth's cinema was considered a bit of a joke by the old professionals, who apparently had a few laughs over their beers and prophesied a short career –

'this show will run and run ... right out of town'. But as Ruth got a toe and then a complete foot on the ladder, they revised their opinions and cleaned up their act. Soon she was working flat out, and only the anniversary of Laurel's birth made her pause momentarily. Ruth's devotion to the job did not go unnoticed.

'We were lucky with Ruth,' Ted Morrison said to Geoffrey Lynes, the accounts department having just told him that the cinema was nearly breaking even, 'she was quite a find.'

'Quite a find,' Lynes echoed cheerlessly.

Ted Morrison looked up. So the little green eye has got to you, has it, he thought, studying the man in front of him. 'She could go a long way,' he continued. 'Besides, she's even attracting the attention of the board now.'

'She's female. Any woman would attract their attention. It's novelty value, that's all.'

Morrison raised his eyebrows. 'Don't you like her, Geoffrey?'

'She's very efficient,' he responded, dodging the question.

'But you find her hard to deal with?'

Lynes flinched, and looked at his boss. Whatever he said he would be in the wrong. Ruth Gordon was the company's darling now, he thought bitterly, realising that from then on he would have to watch his step. 'She's very easy to work with,' he said carefully, studying Ted Morrison's face and trying to read his mind.

'I'm so glad you both get on,' Morrison said, after a moment's pause. 'I know how well everyone upstairs thinks of you, Geoffrey. We all want you to make a success of the cinema – with Ruth's help.'

The words did not fall on deaf ears. Geoffrey Lynes was too politically adept to allow hurt pride to foul up his chances. He smiled at Morrison and walked to the door. 'You can rely on me to help her all I can.'

Morrison's expression was bland. 'Oh, I do hope so, Geoffrey, I really do.'

The flat was ideal for Ruth's needs and the perfect haven after a long day, although the keys she had had cut for her father were still in the top drawer of the bureau, unused. He kept in constant touch by letter, saying he would visit, but as the months passed Ruth came to realise that he was still bound more to his wife than his daughter.

Nina tippled in and out like a pigeon making stop-overs. She was getting more acting work and had even managed to secure a part in a show which was going to France for the winter. 'I told you,' she said smugly, declining Ruth's offer of a drink. 'I said I'd go places.'

'Like France, you mean.'

She ignored the remark. 'This is the first break, Ruth. If they like me I can go on from there ... anywhere. I could be an international star.'

'Be careful, that's all.'

'I can take care of myself, Ruth,' she said impatiently. 'What about you?'

'What about me?'

'Well, why aren't you going out with anyone?' She scratched her knee thoughtfully. 'What happened to that Lloyd fellow?'

'Floyd.'

'What?'

Ruth repeated the name slowly. 'Floyd. He was called Ken Floyd.'

'Yeah – him. What happened?'

'He was like the rest.'

'Well, that's what you get for going out with an actor.'

'Nina, he was a journalist.'

She shrugged. 'Same difference.'

Nina was to be away from October until March of the following year, and when she visited Ruth before leaving she was cheerful until the time came for her to go, and then she stopped on the steps and turned back. 'I'll write,' she said simply.

'Me too.'

'Write something interesting then, your letters are always so dull.'

Ruth smiled ruefully. 'Thanks, Nina. For a minute there I thought I was going to miss you.'

She leant forward and kissed Ruth on the cheek. Her skin was cold and smelt of soap. 'Cheers for now.'

Unable to reply, Ruth smiled instead, waving as Nina made her way down the road, an umbrella leaning against one shoulder and the rain tapping on her PVC mac.

Ruth's arrival had not gone unnoticed by her neighbours. Only days after she had moved in, the couple next door had sent over their son, Nicholas, to assess the situation. An engaging seven-year-old, he had soon wheedled his way into Ruth's flat and discovered a wealth of information.

'Is she married?' Inger asked him when he returned.

'Nope,' he replied, glowing with pride at being the carrier of such vital news. 'Does that matter?'

'Not really. I just wondered.' Inger nudged her son off the table and unpacked her shopping. 'What's she like?'

'Tall.'

'Anything else?'

'Nice,' he said simply, biting into an apple. 'Her flat's only small but she's got flowers everywhere. All over the place ... she owns a cinema,' he said finally.

The last words proved too much for Inger. Within minutes she was knocking on Ruth's front door, pleading a sudden bread famine. But if she was curious about Ruth, she was equally willing to divulge her own background, explaining that she was a German, married to an American, and that they had come to London from Munich a year ago. 'What brought you to London?' she asked Ruth finally.

'Better job prospects.'

Inger nodded, knowing the answer was a lie, just as she knew Ruth disliked being questioned. With commendable tact, she changed the subject. 'I love all your flowers. Even Nicholas noticed.'

Ruth followed her gaze. 'I like flowers. The Buddhists believe that if you have a sum of money, you should spend half on bread and half on flowers.' She smiled uncertainly. 'It's just a whim of mine.'

Inger smiled back, her teeth white and rather large in the

little, tanned face. 'It's a nice idea. And original, I like people who have their own idiosyncrasies.'

She had plenty herself, as Ruth soon discovered. Being totally unconcerned about anything, her tolerance was immense. She was a hippy before the real influx of that culture made its mark, and her husband, a tall, shabby American who spoke five languages and lectured at some obscure private school nearby, was as radical as she was. On their frequent outings they made a strange trio and were totally mismatched – one tall, classically dressed English girl with a couple who looked like they had fallen off a record sleeve. Inger had a love of bright colours and earned her living as a photographer, creeping around Kensington Gardens and leaping out of the undergrowth to snap whatever unfortunate species of wildlife was passing at the time. From what Ruth could gather she had a few devoted patrons in London, but otherwise the great British public remained unimpressed.

Their friendship developed quickly, Inger taking over Nina's role and encouraging Ruth to widen her social life. 'You should go out more, Ruth. You should have your own man.'

'I can't, I still feel tied to Derek.'

She looked at Ruth, frowning. 'After so long? You can't go on like this – it's unhealthy.'

'I'll meet someone . . .'

'I met Sam in Berlin,' Inger said dreamily, 'He was on a course. All the girls were following him round – but he chose me.'

Ruth had a vision of the gregarious, long-haired Sam playing the American abroad.

'We made love in a train.'

'Was it crowded?' Ruth asked, nonplussed.

'Oh no, there was no one around. It was at night.' Inger smiled. Apparently even the thought of the laconic Sam could make her smile. 'He was alway so romantic.'

'How long have you been together?'

'Nine years. Two years before Nicki we met, and we're still together.' She smiled again. 'All the girls at home envied me.'

Ruth buttered the bread in front of her and thought about Sam. Much as she liked him, she could never have been attracted to him; he was too easygoing, too much the free thinker, for her taste. She also knew instinctively that he lacked courage and that he cheated on Inger, although she had no proof and no intention of passing on her thoughts. Instead, she listened to Inger and thought of Derek ... and wondered.

It was during the run-up to Christmas that Ruth's life took another sharp corner. Shopping for a present for Nina, she felt someone pull at the sleeve of her coat and turned round quickly.

'What!'

'It's OK, I wasn't after your wallet,' he said smiling.

'Hello, Ken.'

He grinned broadly. 'You remembered the name. That's good to know.'

'I wouldn't take it as a compliment, I can still remember the name of our school dentist.'

Laughing, he walked in step with her. He smelt of expensive whisky and looked prosperous. 'Are you well?' he asked. Ruth ignored the enquiry and let him continue. 'I was sorry about what happened ... about us, I mean. I treated you badly.'

'Oh, I don't know, the meal was quite good,' Ruth responded lightly, her voice betraying nothing.

'Aren't you ever serious?' he asked, taking the parcels out of her hands and clasping her arm. 'Come on, we'll get out of here.'

Fighting through the Christmas shopping crowds they made their way out into the street, where the wind snatched at Ruth's hair.

'It's freezing.'

'We'll go for a drink,' he suggested, catching her eye and smiling. 'Non-alcoholic.'

Ruth knew then that she should have made an excuse and gone her own way, but it was cold and the thought of a cup of tea seemed inviting ... besides, it was nearly Christmas. They stopped at a plush hotel on Park Lane, Ken dropping one of Ruth's parcels as they got out of the taxi. She watched him as the wind blew it out of his hand, smiling as he ran after it and caught it, holding it aloft in triumph.

'It's a long time since we saw each other,' he said, when they entered the foyer. 'I kept ringing, but you kept ignoring me.'

'I didn't think we had much in common,' Ruth replied, suddenly aware of how much she had missed him.

'You thought I was a drunk, you mean.'

Ruth shrugged and glanced round. There were many people in the restaurant, some struggling to their seats with their parcels, others eating, their shopping resting against their legs. Under the chandelier, they were all wealthy; inherited wealth, earned wealth, but wealthy none the less, and not one of them would have paused at the window of Lilian's Millinery ... Ruth thought of her mother, knowing how much she would have enjoyed being there; knowing how much she wanted it.

'What are you thinking about?' Ken asked suddenly, breaking into her thoughts.

'My mother.'

He was immediately interested; he had always wanted to know about her background. 'Does she live in London?'

'No. Oldham.'

He was surprised and showed it. 'Oldham? Isn't that up North?' Ruth nodded. 'You don't have a Lancashire accent.'

'I don't wear a flat cap either.'

'*Touché*,' he said, saluting her, aware that the sharp wit covered a well-disguised insecurity. 'It's good to see you again, Ruth, you're more interesting than most women.'

'That makes me sound like an old fossil,' she answered lightly, pretending to be looking at something in her hand. ' "This is a pretty interesting example of a Miss Gordon, quite rare now, I believe." '

He laughed easily. She admired that, the way he was so perfectly confident.

'You're fun,' he said, composing himself. 'I'd forgotten that women can be fun. My bloody sister's such a sour piece – '

'And your girlfriends?'

'My girlfriends,' he said, pausing, 'are after money and

a good time. They seldom work, and they seldom laugh at themselves.'

'Sounds dull,' Ruth said drily.

'Oh, I get by.'

'I feel certain you do.'

They fell into an ungenerous silence. Ken finished his sandwiches and then leant back in his chair. To Ruth, he had the look of a man who would put on weight easily, his features coarsening. 'I give in,' he said finally. 'I can't sit here another minute in silence, it seems such a waste of the company. Let's go out to dinner.'

'Tonight?' Ruth asked, surprised. 'I could already have a date.'

He looked at her evenly. 'But you haven't – so I'll pick you up at seven.'

When Ruth got back to the flat, a letter from Nina was waiting for her, postmarked Paris.

Ruth,

What a frost! The flaming show has folded, due to poor notices and a manager with no flair and a beer gut like a Zeppelin. He paid us off, so at least I've got something to live on, and I've decided to stay on here for a while – see if I can pick up something interesting and preferably curable. How's things with you? Thanks for all the letters, I felt like a prisoner in a POW camp. Could you pop in and have a look at the flat for me? Just in case someone's broken in. There's half a bottle of gin in the lounge, take it if you want. Nothing else to say for now, only that I'll write again and see you soon.

Cheers,
Nina.

Ruth read it hurriedly and then went off to change, her nervousness making her clumsy. She was just putting on some earrings as the doorbell rang.

'You look fabulous,' Ken said, surprised at the change in her. Under the porch light, she looked very young, her hair loose on her shoulders and her eyes brilliant.

'Do I look all right?' she asked anxiously, misreading his hesitation.

'Wonderful,' he responded uneasily.

Despite his apprehension, the evening went well. Ken laughed at her jokes and Ruth returned the compliment, although she suspected that much of his humour was rehearsed. Well used to women, he touched her arm several times, and at one point clasped hold of her hand, although the gesture was oddly gentle and left her baffled, rather than intimidated. He told her that his father was still running the newspaper, employing him as a freelance writer. Apparently, they did not get on.

'My father lives at the Belmont.'

'The club?' Ruth asked. 'Isn't that rather strange?'

'Why? He hated the house after my mother died and handed it over to Joanie and me.'

Ruth remembered Joanie, remembered the smooth oval face and the spiteful tongue. 'Why do you live with your sister?'

Ken threw down the last of his wine. 'Because I need someone to look after me.'

Memories of Derek welled up. 'You could afford a house-keeper.'

'I could, but Joanie suits me. She's a cow, but she runs the place well and keeps an eye on the staff.'

'Isn't she married?'

'Has been. Twice. But she's a hard woman with a short temper and a lot of pride. Men don't like that, she makes them feel inferior.'

'Has she any children?'

'My sister?' he asked, amused. 'The very thought of kids makes her hair stand on end. Besides, as I said, she has me to look after.'

'Doesn't she get lonely?'

'Do you?'

Ruth bristled. 'What's that got to do with it?'

'Nothing. It's just that you're asking me if my sister gets

lonely living with me, when you're in the middle of London on your own.'

'I have a job.'

'Oh, that makes all the difference, does it?'

They fell into an uncomfortable silence.

'I'm sorry,' he said finally.

'It was my fault,' Ruth said, apologising. 'I'm over-sensitive sometimes.'

'That's what I like about you. You're vulnerable.' He sipped at his brandy thoughtfully before adding, 'But you're too young for me.'

Ruth was suddenly anxious. 'Does that matter?'

'I'm forty-one years old,' he said, shaking his head. 'Old enough to be your father.'

'But you're not – I would have thought that was the important thing.'

'Ruth,' he said, smiling, 'I was wrong to ask you out. I drink too much, fool around too much, and I hate responsibility. I'm running down, and you're on your way.'

The logic chilled her, and, as she always did when she was unsettled, she reacted with coldness. 'So why bother to take me out if I was such a dead loss? I mean, if I'm such a child you shouldn't be wasting your time.'

'I didn't mean it like that,' he said gently, surprised by the tone of her voice. 'It's just that the world looks great at your age –'

'After being widowed and losing a child?' Ruth said, getting up. 'Don't bother to see me home, I've got a pair of leading reins and a toy train waiting out front.'

Immediately Ken got to his feet. 'What did you say?'

'About the reins, or the toy train?' Ruth asked bitterly, walking out. He caught up with her on the street, taking hold of her arm and jerking her round to face him. 'What did you say about being widowed?'

'My husband was killed in a train crash,' she said, with no emotion in her voice.

'And the baby?'

Ruth looked away. Across the street a man was hailing a taxi.

'Where's the child?' he asked hoarsely. The man Ruth was watching got into the taxi and the driver turned off his yellow light. It was horribly cold.

'Ruth! Where's the child?'

'I don't know!' she said suddenly, her voice rising. 'I had her adopted, you see. Isn't that an appalling thing to do? Isn't that unnatural for a mother to give away her child?'

She started to walk off down the street, Ken running after her. 'Ruth, listen to me –'

'Why? Why should I?' she said, spinning round on him, her eyes blazing. 'What will you do? Bring her back? With all your money and power, can you bring her back, Mr Floyd?' she laughed harshly. 'Go away! You know the type of person I am – I've just told you. You don't want to know anyone who would give away their own child.' She stopped, tears running down her face, the pain and bitterness pouring out of her. 'Go away! You can't help me ... no one can help me.' He caught hold of her, holding her so tightly that the wool of his coat pressed against her skin. 'Don't say you care for me. Don't!' she pleaded. 'Don't promise me anything ... I would only disappoint you in the end.'

She was too young for him, he knew that. Just as he knew why their lives had crossed. He had enough money, position and power to ensure that Ruth would be protected from herself and the world – and he wanted her.

Seven

After such sudden confessions, trust followed. They spoke each morning on the phone and saw each other virtually every day. Thankfully, Ken's drinking appeared to have lessened, although Ruth was only too well aware that he tried to disguise it sometimes, the smell of peppermint on his breath an obvious give-away.

Unfortunately, Geoffrey Lynes did not approve of Ruth's relationship with Ken Floyd and, unable to put his feelings into words, he became even more obstructive. Messages were wrongly delivered, or not delivered at all, and each day brought further annoyances.

Finally, Ruth confided in Ken. 'He's being bloody imposs-ible, I can't understand it.'

'I can. He thought he had rights over you. After all, he was the one who had the final say on your appointment.'

'But I worked hard to get that job! I've made a success out of it. They're earning money hand over fist because of me.'

Ken smiled. 'Mind you, he fancies you as well,' he said, grinning. 'That's why he's so pissed off about me. Listen, Ruth, the man's a small-minded little bookkeeper who's been beaten to the post. It's not important.'

'If it affects my job, it's important.'

'If a career matters that much to you, I could get you a better job any day.'

Ruth slumped back in her chair. 'You've missed the point, Ken. I *earned* this job. I don't want you or anyone else to hand me anything on a plate.'

'Suit yourself, but just remember you've got options.'

Their relationship strengthened as they got to know each other, although it was weeks before Ruth met Ken's father, and when she did, he was courteous, but indifferent. Joanie was another matter. Ever interested in her brother's affairs, she was quick with her judgement. 'She's too young for you.'

'We've been through that one, Joanie.'

She sighed and moved across the lounge, her high heels leaving imprints on the thick carpet. Pausing by the window she looked out, her perfectly made-up face impassive, one elegant hand resting on the back of a chair. Quite a pose, Ken thought admiringly.

'I can see how you find her fascinating,' Joanie went on. 'She does have a certain air about her ... Is it serious?' In the sunlight her skin was flawless, the dark eyes with their arched brows regarding her brother openly. 'Well, is it?'

'You should get yourself a boyfriend,' Ken said, passing her a brandy, 'and leave me to my own devices. I care about the girl.'

'You fall in love every week, Ken, don't tell me this is a novelty for you.'

He refused to lose his temper. 'Ruth is different – '

'They are all different! It's their very difference which makes them all so similar.'

'You should try to get to know her, Joanie. Talk to her.'

The perfect eyebrows rose. 'Really, Kenneth, I can't see what I have in common with a jumped-up adventuress.'

'Can't you?' he said, walking out.

It was late afternoon and Ruth was just making some last-minute phone calls when Geoffrey Lynes walked in. 'How many are coming tonight?' he asked, sitting down without being invited.

'Two hundred and six at the last count, but still rising.'

'You'll never cope.'

'Oh, I think I will, Mr Lynes.'

'You can call me Geoffrey,' he said stiffly, his mouth spitting out the words like grape pips.

'Thank you, Geoffrey.'

'Not at all, Ruth,' he said, delighted to see how he discomfited her. 'Do you need any help?'

'No, Thank you. I've got all the help I need.'

'You're doing a good job,' he continued. 'Ted Morrison and I think you'll go far. We're pleased with your progress. It would be a shame to jeopardise all that hard work now.'

Ruth jerked up her head. 'I don't follow.'

'I believe the cinema still does business with Ken Floyd ...' Ruth said nothing, forcing him to continue, '... and I did hear that you put off another customer to accommodate him.' She still said nothing, merely flinched at the word 'accommodate'. 'You see, Ruth, it looks horribly like favouritism – something about which I have always been worried. Unfortunately this often happens when a woman is running a business.' He seemed apologetic. 'I was talking to Ted Morrison about this affair, and he said that perhaps I had better have a little word in your ear. We don't want you to become a laughing-stock, do we?'

'So what exactly are you saying, Mr Lynes?' Ruth asked him coldly.

He noticed the shift in her manner and altered his own. 'Only that we have other people to cater for, besides your Mr Kenneth Floyd. You do see my point?'

'If you'd made your point any clearer we could have stuck a flag on it, Mr Lynes.'

He got to his feet abruptly. 'Good luck tonight, Ruth,' he said, walking out.

The fact that he had gone behind her back to Ted Morrison was the final straw. Changing quickly, Ruth welcomed the guests, and when everyone was firmly ensconced, rang Ken. He was at home, and sounded sleepy.

'Are you OK?'

'Fine, I had just dozed off in the chair, that's all. How's the preview going?'

Ruth skipped round the subject, realising, with disappointment, that he'd been drinking heavily. 'I've had some trouble with Geoffrey Lynes, he's making things difficult.'

'So? What's the problem? I've told you before, you've got options.'

'Like working for you?'

'Why not? The pay's good, you can do what you like, when you like, in the comfort of your own home.'

'What would I be running?' Ruth asked, baffled.

'Me.'

'Ken – what are you talking about?'

He sounded amused. ' "Come live with me and be my love," ' he paused. 'Are you still there, or have you fainted?'

Terrified of making a fool of herself, Ruth answered him cautiously. 'Is this a proposal?'

'Well, it's not a proposition if that's what you mean – although that will follow later.'

'I love you,' she said simply. And I'll make you happy, she thought.

'I love you too, Ruth. Now, go back and tell that cringing little sod Lynes, to stick his cinema, reel by reel, up his account book.'

The letter fell on the doormat just before six. Jack Gordon picked it up as he was about to leave for work. He recognised the handwriting and hesitated.

'Who's it from?' Lilian asked, holding out her hand for the letter. Jack passed it to her reluctantly. 'It's from Ruth,' he said. 'Maybe – '

'I don't want to read it!' she said, pushing it back to him. 'I don't want to read anything that girl has to say.' She moved back into the kitchen, her face set, the lips tightly clamped together.

'She's your daughter.'

'No!' Lilian shouted, her hand banging down on the table. 'She *was* my daughter – but not now. What she did was unforgivable.'

'She was ill – '

'You always sided with her, Jack Gordon! All her life. It was always you and her. Never me.' She stopped and bent down to poke the fire. A few flames spluttered into life. 'Well, she's gone now, and that's all there is to it.'

'You're not that hard, Lilian. I'll leave the letter here, in case you change your mind.'

Lilian turned to look at her husband. 'Take it! I won't change my mind ... now get off to work.'

No sooner had Ruth arrived at the office than her father rang. 'Hello, flower. I got your letter this morning. It's such good news. Congratulations.'

'He's asked me to marry him and I accepted,' Ruth said, hearing the pips going. 'Dad? Give me your number, I'll ring you back – '

The line went dead. A few minutes later he phoned back.

'Give me your number, Dad, in case we get cut off again.'

'I can't, love, I'm at work. Tell me, is he a good man?'

'Ken's not like Derek, he's more worldly, if you know what I mean. I want you to meet him, Dad. Can you come down?'

He paused. 'It's difficult, with your mother – '

'I know, but it's important to me. We're getting married on 4 April. Will you give me away? You could ask Mother to come too.'

'She won't, Ruth. You know that.'

'Dad, we're going to run out of time – please can you come and see me? We'll talk about the wedding then.'

He seemed evasive. 'I'll see what I can do, and I'll ring you back in the next few days.'

The pips went again. 'Ruth?' he shouted. 'Good luck.'

The line went dead.

He never managed to get down to London. Instead, he phoned Ruth a couple of times a week, asking about the wedding arrangements.

'Dad, I have to know if you will give me away. It's only a Registry Office but I want you to be there.'

'It's not possible. I'm sorry, flower, I hate to let you down.'

'Then don't!' she said sharply. 'Sorry ... oh, sorry, Dad. I didn't mean it – '

'I know, love, but I can't get down.'

There was nothing she could say to persuade him; her mother had the final word, as ever. Apparently Lilian was not about to forgive or forget, or wish her daughter luck for the future – a future which suddenly seemed frightening again. In fact,

Lilian's attitude so soured the remaining days to the wedding, that only the re-emergence of Nina helped to lighten the atmosphere.

'I don't know why you let that old cow get to you.'

'She's my mother,' Ruth said, folding some clothes for her honeymoon and putting them into a suitcase. They were going to Florence for a few days and then coming back to the house in Hampstead to live. Joanie kept talking about moving out, but had made no real attempts to leave.

'Ken's a nice bloke,' Nina said, rolling on her back on top of the bed and folding her hands on her stomach. 'Bit of an old smoothie, mind you.'

'Just because he's got money, you're biased.'

'Jealous, more like.' She turned her head and watched Ruth, noticing how excitable she was, how quick in her movements. God, I hope it works out this time, she thought.

'Is he still off the booze?'

'Dry as a tinder box,' Ruth answered.

'Then for God's sake don't strike any matches.'

Ruth ignored the remark. 'Do you think he loves me?'

Nina blinked. 'How the hell would I know? Hasn't he said anything?'

'He says he loves me,' Ruth replied, sitting down on the edge of the bed. 'But he could just be saying it – '

'To spare your feelings perhaps? And I suppose he's marrying you just to spare your feelings? I wish someone would carry me off to their Hampstead mansion – feelings or no bloody feelings.'

Ruth began to laugh.

'It's no laughing matter!' Nina continued, warming to the subject. 'He's a noble man to share all that money with a woman he doesn't really care for. You should be honoured.'

'OK – I've got the message,' Ruth said finally.

'Then remember it! Ken Floyd could have married anyone he wanted, God knows he's been footloose long enough. He's marrying you because he wants to. Remember what I told you that day in the flat? You're made for the high life, Ruth, grab it with both hands.' She sighed and changed the subject. 'Anyway, how many are coming to the wedding?'

'Ken's father, his friends, and Joanie ...' Nina winced, 'I've invited you obviously, then there's Inger, Sam, and Nicki. We wanted a small wedding.'

'Well, you've certainly managed it,' Nina replied, turning over on to her stomach and fingering her hair. 'I should get this done properly instead of colouring it myself, I'll be as bald as a grape before long. On the other hand, I could make a feature out of it. "The first singer and dancer with terminal alopecia." Do you think it would catch on?' Ruth hadn't been listening. 'Did you hear me? Oh, never mind!'

She sulked for almost ten minutes, picking at the fluff on the counterpane, her face in profile looking softer than it normally did. Always high-spirited, she seemed unusually cheerful since her return, eager to go out with Ruth or with Inger and Sam. They liked her and enjoyed her company, although Joanie loathed Nina with a passion.

'That friend of Ruth's ...' Joanie said to her brother one evening, 'she's – '

'Common,' said Ken, finishing her sentence for her.

They were eating breakfast in the dining-room with Mrs Harvey, the housekeeper, bringing in hot coffee and fresh toast, Joanie waited until she left before continuing. 'What does that mean exactly?'

'Ill-bred. Working class.'

'That isn't important – '

Ken raised an eyebrow. 'Isn't it?'

'All right, have it your own way. I don't like Ruth, I never have ...' she raised her hand to prevent her brother interrupting her, '... but she behaves like a lady. If she and Nina came from the same town and pretty much the same background, why is Ruth a lady and why is Miss O'Donnell such a slut?'

'She isn't a slut, she's just ... unorthodox,' Ken explained, trying not to laugh.

'She's a tramp!'

'She's an actress.'

'And there's a difference?' Joanie asked him.

'Listen,' Ken explained patiently. 'For all I care Nina can earn her money vertically or horizontally – it makes no difference to me. She was a friend when Ruth needed one, and that makes her welcome in my home.'

'Not too welcome, I hope,' Joanie said, biting into a piece of toast.

April the fourth dawned brightly, faded around eleven and poured down at twelve. Looking out of her bedroom window, Ruth wondered why it always rained at weddings, especially hers. She had chosen to wear lilac, and although her head was uncovered, she carried a small bouquet of flowers pinned to her bag. The night before, Ken had given her a pair of sapphire earrings to match the engagement ring he had bought for her. Eager to please him, she had finally taken off Derek's wedding band, putting it with the few other pathetic relics she had kept from her previous marriage.

Dressed and ready to go, Ruth paused, trying to gather her thoughts. This is going to be a new life, a new start. I've come a long way, she said to herself, I have a career and a new husband . . . Then, without warning, the familiar wave of panic welled up in her as she thought of Laurel and caught her breath.

Joanie was already at the Registry Office talking to some of Ken's friends and wearing a wide-brimmed hat and a cream silk suit. She smiled grimly at Nina, her eyes watching her as she approached Ruth.

'You look lovely. Can I have the bag when you've finished with it?' she asked, pushing a small gold cross into Ruth's hand. 'Always trust a Catholic to get sentimental at weddings,' she said, embarrassed. 'Well, go on, get on with it.'

It was Ken's father, Robert Floyd, who gave Ruth away in the end. Jack Gordon remained in Oldham, in the park, digging the dark earth as his daughter married. Ruth thought of him, and of her mother, seeing her in that hat shop, her lips pursed, her scissors snipping at the material on the wooden counter.

The service was very brief, and although Ruth thought she was calm, her voice sounded unusually high as they exchanged vows. Some small things stayed in her mind afterwards – like the sound of a police siren outside, the rapping of the rain on the windows, and how Ken's mouth was cool and tasted of peppermint when he kissed her.

It never occurred to Ruth to give up her job. Since they returned from honeymoon she had been going to work as before, knowing that even if she didn't need the money, she needed the stimulation. The situation was regarded as something of a novelty; Ken accepted it with tolerance, although the housekeeper, Mrs Harvey, was decidedly cool and sided with Joanie, who spent a great deal of time undermining her brother's wife. Although her jealousy increased daily, she made no attempts to move out and every hint from her brother fell on deaf ears.

At first Joanie thought the marriage would falter, that Ruth would not manage to hold Ken's interest, the differences in their backgrounds and ages levering them apart. But she misjudged her brother – in Ruth, Ken found someone young enough to be artless and vulnerable enough to need protection. Without realising it, she brought out the paternal instinct in a man who had previously seen women as merely something to amuse him, in and out of bed. Ruth's power was in her simplicity and her dignity, and the depth of that power was something Joanie underestimated badly.

Ruth, however, had no difficulty understanding Joanie's position. Having lived with Ken since the break-up of her second marriage, Joanie had enjoyed running an impressive house, entertaining his friends and ruling the Harveys with a rod of iron. Rich and indulged, she had done exactly what she wanted, without having to consider anyone else. But when Ken married Ruth, everything altered, and Joanie resisted. The position of first lady was what she was used to, and the sudden emergence of another to challenge that status, rankled on her.

So when Ken came home one night earlier than usual and found the house quiet, he wandered upstairs to Joanie's dressing-room from where he heard voices. He was about to knock, when something made him pause and listen.

'. . . nothing but a common shopkeeper, that's what she told me. Her mother runs a hat shop!' There was a pause before Joanie continued. 'It's absurd! Ken could have married anyone.'

'Did you want the navy silk for tonight, madam?' Mrs Harvey asked, her voice incisive, each syllable clipped.

Ken leant against the wall, infuriated. So Joanie was discussing his wife with the staff, was she? Breathing deeply, he continued to listen.

'Yes, I'll wear that. Put it over there for me, will you?'

He could hear his sister moving around, probably looking into the long cheval-glass, her handsome face set. 'It will never last, of course, I told him before the wedding that she was only after his money. The girl has no class, no real breeding.' Her footsteps paced the floor. 'Oh, I don't like this! Pass me the red crêpe de Chine instead.' Ken listened, his temper rising. 'That's better, much more like it . . . You see, Mrs Harvey, money is a powerful advantage, but it must be used correctly. You do see what I mean?'

'Yes, madam,' the voice replied.

'My father made a great deal of money. Money which, I might add, bought this house and these furnishings. My mother knew how to make a home, and how to impress people . . .'

Ken thought of their mother, a small woman with a good background and a vicious temper. She had sent him away to school when he was six, having dismissed him after he was born to the care of a nanny. The difference between Ruth and his mother was immeasurable.

'. . . she had presence. Not like this girl. Oh, she's made Ken happy, but for how long? It's just a novelty, no more. And she's working, can you imagine that? Working! When she doesn't need to! I can't imagine what his friends must be thinking.'

'That he's a very fortunate man,' Ken said, walking in and dismissing Mrs Harvey with a wave of his hand.

With a look of total unconcern Joanie faced her brother. 'You should always knock before entering a lady's dressing-room.'

138

'I would – if it had been a lady's dressing-room.'

She sat down, pulling on her shoes. 'How long have you been listening outside the door?'

'Long enough to hear what you thought of my wife. Long enough to realise that you discuss personal matters with Mrs Harvey.'

'This is damn ridiculous!' Joanie snapped. 'That woman has been with me for over ten years. What I choose to say to her is my own concern.'

'Not if it concerns me or my wife.'

'Your wife!' she said, walking over to the glass. 'That girl certainly has you in a state, I must say. She's put life in the old man, I'll give her that. Even Father remarked on it.' She paused, her eyes brilliant with spite. 'We had lunch and he said – '

'I don't give a damn what he said! You're both as hypocritical as each other.' He walked towards his sister and faced her squarely. 'Ruth has always been fair with you, Joanie. By rights, this is her house now ...' He paused, allowing time for the words to take their effect, '... but she's endured your backbiting and your jealousy, because that's what it is – jealousy – '

'Jealousy! Dear God, why should I be jealous of her?' Joanie snapped, turning away and fastening some pearls about her neck.

'You're jealous because she's young and because there is something fundamentally good about her.'

'She's a shopkeeper's daughter from Oldham! That's *all* she is!' Joanie responded viciously and then stopped as she saw the expression on her brother's face. 'I didn't mean it, Ken, really I didn't ...'

He stood rigid, looking at his sister. He remembered how she had watched Ruth bring her few prized possessions to the house. Small things with little value, other than being hers. Joanie had watched through the window, with a look of complete disdain, as a chair and some pictures were carried to the suite on the first floor. 'I want you out of here, Joanie,' he said at last. 'Get a flat. I want you out of my house.'

She faltered, 'But ... what about tonight?'

'What about tonight?'

'Some friends of yours are coming round for drinks.'

Ken frowned. 'Ruth didn't tell me about that this morning.'

'It was my idea,' Joanie said, terrified of the effect her words would have. 'I know how you like to see people now and again for a few drinks, so I asked them.' She stopped. 'You used to love surprises.'

Without another word Ken walked out.

The humiliation forced Joanie to stay in bed the following day, and she moved out within the month.

It was a wonderful summer, the house free from Joanie's presence, the garden heavy with flowers. Having finally managed to find an excuse, Jack Gordon came down to London, arriving at the house in Hampstead late afternoon. Mesmerised, he stood in the driveway and looked; he saw a white building on three floors with double front doors, flanked by two columns. Each window was bordered with drapes, and allowed only a marginal insight into the rooms beyond. To Jack Gordon the place was immense and unexpected; a house seen on the television, or in films ... it was not Ruth's home.

She saw him and ran out. 'Come on in, Dad, I'm so glad you're here.'

He walked with her, his feet loud on the polished floor, his hands clasping his hat. Ruth showed him round, watching his face as door by door opened on to yards of carpeted luxury, the sun pouring in through the windows and playing on the mirrors.

Finally, she showed him his bedroom and the adjoining bathroom.

'All for me?' he asked, his voice not much above a whisper.

'All for you,' she agreed.

'If your mother could see this, Ruthie ...' He trailed off. '... Oh, she would be so proud.'

She squeezed his arm and looked at him. He was the same as ever, although his hair was a little thinner. I've missed you, Ruth thought. 'How's Mother?'

'She's well,' he said, moving over to the window and looking out. 'Your garden's grand, flower, really grand. Does it take much work?'

'Quite a lot,' Ruth answered, turning back to her original topic. 'Does she ever talk about me?'

'No, love,' he said simply.

Shaken, Ruth changed the subject. 'How's the shop?'

'Rubbing along, I think. Although I don't go near the damn place myself.' He glanced over his shoulder. 'I'd never have believed this house, Ruth, never in a million years. For you to have all this ... it's wonderful.'

He stayed for three days and seemed to get on well with Ken, although Ruth noticed that her husband's drinking accelerated whenever they had company. After a few days, Jack Gordon left, and almost immediately Nina moved in saying her landlord had thrown her out. With ill-concealed impatience, Ken rounded on Ruth.

'How long is she going to stay?'

'I don't know. I can hardly ask her to leave, can I?'

'Why not? You managed to get rid of Joanie.'

The remark struck out at Ruth and left her reeling. Ken had never said anything cruel before and his savagery shocked her.

'That's not fair! And it's not even true.'

'No, I'm sorry, it wasn't,' he said, seeing the look in her eyes and kissing her lightly on the forehead. 'But this place isn't big enough for the two of us, so get your little friend out.'

Ruth nodded, knowing that she was pushing her luck. But every time she mentioned flat-hunting to Nina she veered off the subject like a runaway train. Her peculiar elation, so apparent at the wedding, had continued and she seemed almost light-headedly cheerful. Knowing the people with whom she mixed, Ruth wondered idly if Nina was taking something.

'Has nothing cropped up?'

'With regard to a flat, or to work?' Nina replied.

'Either.'

She was sitting in the kitchen eating toast, her dressing-gown crumpled from spending the night on the floor. 'Well, I've got an audition this afternoon.' She gave Ruth a sidelong look.

'But I haven't found a flat in Kensington yet.'

Ruth was surprised. 'I never thought you liked Kensington.'

'I didn't until you lived there, then I got to like it ... But everyone else likes it too, so flats aren't easy to find. Anyway,' Nina said easily, 'I can always stay a bit longer with you, can't I?'

As the days passed and Ken's attitude became apparent, Nina stayed out of his way and relied on Ruth to pacify him. And he frequently needed pacifying, as Ruth discovered. All Ken wanted was her complete attention; in return she would be spoiled and protected, her history a secret from the world and a bond between them. Having never been married before, Ken wanted his wife on his terms, and Ruth, knowing firstly how much she loved him, and secondly, how much she owed him, played the game.

It was a game Ken enjoyed immensely. Having been fascinated by Ruth's composure, he was also intrigued by the sudden outbursts of anger which showed a deeper nature. Living with her he became captivated, and waking early would watch her sleep, seeing the dark blonde hair on the pillow and the lie of her hand on the sheet. Touching her, he was surprised by his own gentleness, his own desire to protect her, and found that he resented other people encroaching on their life together. In short, Ruth obsessed him.

The difference in him did not go unnoticed. 'He's besotted by that girl,' Joanie said to their father when they met for lunch at the Belmont. 'Fixated.'

Robert Floyd watched his daughter and sighed. Jealous women were a pain in the neck, he thought, and Joanie was a jealous woman just like her mother. 'She seems a nice girl,' he said, deliberately provoking her as he provoked everyone.

'Nice! Is that what they call it! She had me thrown out of my own house. How's that for nice?'

Her father smiled; he loved stirring things up, it appealed to his mischievous nature. 'You've as many faces as a church clock,' his wife used to say.

'You should find yourself a husband,' he continued, knowing

how the words would dance on her nerve ends, 'and settle down. Married life certainly seems to suit some people.'

'It will wear off! She can't keep Ken's interest for long,' Joanie continued, trying to sound light-hearted.

With deadly precision, Robert Floyd answered her. 'I doubt it ... especially when the children come along.'

Ruth sat down heavily and leant back against the chair surprised at her own tiredness. She could hear birds in the garden and a branch rapping the window-pane as the wind made savage snatches at the trees. Behind her closed eyelids, Ruth's mind wandered as she drifted off to sleep.

'Are you feeling all right?' Ken asked anxiously, touching her face and waking her.

Ruth glanced round; the room was unfriendly, the dark garden peering in at the windows. 'I'm fine, I was tired, that's all.'

Sitting up, she ran her tongue over her dry lips. The room was cool, the fire nearly out. With a conscious effort, Ruth got to her feet and caught sight of herself in the mirror – a young woman, dressed in a short grey suit, her fine legs stylish in the fashionable boots. She gazed at herself, looking into the eyes of childhood ... the eyes which told her.

Terrified that she might be wrong, Ruth waited until she had seen the doctor who confirmed that she was pregnant and that the baby would be born in August. With a mixture of joy and anxiety, Ruth waited for Ken to arrive home. He returned late and was in a bad mood. Realising that he had been drinking, Ruth went up to bed and sat by the window, anger building up in her. He hadn't been drinking much lately, she thought, so why now? Unsettled, pacing around the bedroom, she cursed him. It should have been such a special night and he had spoiled it.

He came up much later, drunk and aggressive. 'What the hell are you looking at?' he bellowed, kicking off his shoes and sitting on the side of the bed.

Tight-lipped, Ruth watched him. 'I wasn't looking at anything.'

'Yes you were! What's the matter with you?'

Ruth was astonished by the change in him, his manner vicious, the usual gentleness gone. She turned her back on him. 'Oh, leave me alone.'

'Christ!' he shouted, tearing off his shirt. Ruth flinched, hearing a button clatter on the floor. 'Bloody woman!'

It was obvious that he wanted to pick a fight, but Ruth was too tired to respond and kept silent. The ploy only angered him more. 'Well, go on, say something!' he continued nastily. 'You usually have a few words to say on the subject of how much I drink.'

'You can do as you like – '

'OH, CAN I? CAN I REALLY?' he roared.

Ruth sat up in bed. 'Keep your voice down!'

He had taken off everything except his trousers; his face looked blotchy in the half-light. 'Why should I?'

'The Harveys will hear you.'

'So what? I pay them – if I want to shout in my own house I will. I CAN DO AS I PLEASE.'

Ruth put out her hand to him. 'Ken – '

' "Ken," ' he mimicked unpleasantly. 'Ken – what?'

'You bastard!' she said finally, throwing back the covers and getting out of bed to face him. Her patience gone, in its place was fury.

' "You bastard," ' he mimicked. 'That's not like you, not like you at all, Ruth. You never use bad language normally, do you? You're too ladylike. Perhaps something's upset you, is that it? Has something upset my little wife?' He caught hold of her right wrist and twisted it.

Wincing, Ruth tried to shake him off. 'Let go of me!'

'Say please,' Ken said, squeezing her wrist, his mouth cruel.

Immediately Ruth stopped struggling, and drawing herself up to her full height she said coldly, 'If you don't let go of me now, I'll leave you.'

He blinked slowly, but he didn't release her hand. She saw him hesitate and continued. 'You should sober up, Ken, or you'll live to regret this.'

'Why should I?' he asked, his voice slightly blurred, his

expression vicious. 'Give me one reason why I should.'

'I'm pregnant,' Ruth said simply.

The shock filtered through the drink and he let go of her arm, grabbing her instead and kissing her on the mouth. Disgusted, she pulled away from him.

'I'll get some coffee,' she said coldly, walking downstairs.

With rigid, automatic movements, Ruth made the coffee. Many things she had endured in her life, but physical violence had not been one of them. She wondered what would have happened if she hadn't kept calm, knowing that her scorn had prevented an even uglier scene. The kettle whistled and reminded her of the kettle when she was a child in Oldham – whistling the nights away, she thought.

'Drink this,' she said, passing a cup to Ken.

He took it from her and sat down at the kitchen table. 'I'm so sorry. God, Ruth, I didn't know you were pregnant ... I got drunk because of my father ... The old bastard wouldn't hear a word I said about the paper, and I had such good ideas.'

Ruth listened, but said nothing. Instead she looked down at his hands round the coffee cup, and at the bruise on her arm. A familiar sense of uncertainty welled up in her – she had thought she could rely on Ken. She had thought he represented security.

'Don't look at me like that!' he said suddenly, making Ruth jump.

'I'm sorry, I didn't realise I couldn't look at you,' she replied. Her voice was different, even to her own ears. It was strained and sounded the way it always sounded when she was hurt. Cold.

'I'll make it up to you,' he said, catching hold of her and resting his head against her stomach. 'I'm going to give this baby everything. Everything in the world.'

'Everything?'

'Everything in the world,' he repeated firmly.

When they went up to bed Ken fell asleep quickly, his mouth slightly open, his right arm around Ruth. At one o'clock she was still awake, and after rolling him on to his side, got out of bed and walked softly over to the window. It was a cold night.

Even through the window it looked cold, the breeze making the branches chatter and the clouds slice over the dark sky. Ruth could hear Ken breathing behind her and watched as a plane flew past, its red lights flickering.

She knew then that some voyage had begun; that the safe harbour she had taken for granted was something fragile and uncertain. Ken loved her, but he drank. His drinking made him someone frightening, someone unknown, and it distanced her. Sighing, Ruth looked out over the front garden. She had wanted to rely on him, but that was dangerous; from now on there was another life dependent on hers, a life dependent on her strength.

I gave Laurel away, she thought. I lost her, but there's another child now ... Alert to every sound, Ruth glanced over her shoulder, but Ken was sleeping soundly ... I failed my first-born, she thought, closing her eyes, but I'll not fail now. The words made no impact in the dark, but they settled in Ruth's head and strengthened her. During a long night, she grew stronger and more determined. The course was set and from then on her first thought was not for Ken, but for her child.

Eight

Four months later the doctor told Ruth she was having twins. The news was an extra bonus to Ken, who had been loving and thoughtful ever since their argument, but Nina was more phlegmatic. She was then securely settled in her flat in Kensington, only two blocks from where Ruth had been, and the change seemed beneficial. The boldness which was typical of her had mellowed, and her appearance, although quaint, seemed almost tame by comparison with how she had looked before.

'My God, if I hear one more word about those twins you're having . . . ' she said, throwing down her bag in the lounge and sitting next to Ruth. 'Ken is such a bore about it.' She pulled out a packet of cigarettes. 'Want one?'

Ruth rolled her eyes. 'No, and I don't want a couple of dwarfs either.'

'I went for another audition yesterday, at the Royal Court.' She smiled ruefully. 'They said they thought I had potential – somewhere else.' She laughed, but for once seemed hurt.

Ruth touched her arm gently. 'They've no idea. They can't see what's good and what isn't. You wait, something better will come along.'

'Better a live dog than a dead lion,' she said enigmatically. 'I don't know, Ruth. Maybe I'm not all that good.'

'Be patient. It's a tough business and it takes time to get to the top.'

'I'm not sure I want it that much.'

Ruth was surprised. Nina's whole life had revolved around the theatre and the ever-present seduction of fame. 'Are you serious?'

She smiled wanly. 'Maybe I'd like to settle down, like you.'

'Have you met someone?' Ruth asked, her curiosity alerted.

'No ...'

She knew Nina was lying; she'd seen the look too often when they were at school. 'Nina, tell me!'

'Not yet. I don't want to count my chickens before they're hatched.'

Ruth groaned loudly. 'Dear God, you sound like my mother.'

Mistakenly, Ruth thought that the news of her pregnancy might finally persuade Lilian to get in touch. Jack Gordon had been delighted when she told him, but although she asked him to pass the news to her mother, there was no response, and her letters came back unopened.

'Leave it for what it is,' Ken said. 'You'll only upset yourself and that's bad for you. She's a fool to hold a grudge that long.'

'Maybe she thinks I'm being disloyal.'

He looked up. 'How do you work that out?'

'Having other children, after giving Laurel away – '

His patience snapped: 'Ruth, that was the past. It's over. You can't go back. We can only take care of the children to come.' She smiled but watched carefully as he poured himself another drink.

The pregnancy was difficult and tired Ruth. Having money to buy maternity clothes, she indulged herself, and employed interior designers to make the bedroom beside their suite into a nursery. Anxious to restore Ruth's affection, Ken bought dozens of expensive toys, and his father sent small gifts and enquired politely after his daughter-in-law's health. Joanie, however, did not relent, and thought of the babies as a further example of Ruth's unkindness to her. They seldom spoke.

Regretfully Ruth was forced to leave her job in the cinema at the beginning of April. Too large to be of any real use and too preoccupied with the coming birth to concentrate on work, she handed in her resignation. When he heard, Geoffrey Lynes took the news with mock regret. 'So we're to lose you after all this time,' he said cheerily. 'Good luck.'

Ruth smiled coolly and shook his hand. 'I'll be back.'

He looked nonplussed. 'No one told me.'

'Really? Well, you have a word with Ted Morrison, and he'll tell you all about it,' Ruth said pleasantly.

She had to admire the way he kept smiling as he showed her to the door. 'So we'll be working together again?'

She nodded. 'After the twins are born I'll stay at home for a few months and then come back to work.'

His smile looked as though it had been glued on. 'I shall look forward to it,' he said, opening the door of Ruth's taxi to let her get in.

'Oh, and so will I.'

He was still smiling as the cab moved off.

Nina visited Hampstead often, her presence essential as Ruth became more confined to the house. Ken no longer dared to comment and even invited Nina to one of their dinner parties, passing her off as an eccentric actress friend.

'Ruth looks good,' Nina said admiringly.

Ken glanced over to his wife at the end of the table. 'She's blooming. That's what pregnancy does for some women.'

'My mother put on three stone and her hair came out in handfuls when she had Trevor,' Nina responded, unconvinced. Ken's face seemed bloated in the candlelight, his colour high. The mark of the drinker was on him, Nina thought, and for a moment he looked suspiciously like her father.

'I believe you're an actress?' one of the guests, Sheila Fielding, asked suddenly. She was sitting next to Ken across the table, her voice high-pitched, rattling along the table like bamboo on a hot summer night.

'That's right, I tread the boards.'

'How fascinating,' she said, without the faintest interest. 'Are you well known?'

'Not for acting,' Nina replied smartly as the woman turned away.

Watching the people round her, Nina sipped her drink. God, what a motley crew, she thought, solicitors, bankers, publishers ... there must be enough money round this table to pay off the national debt. She glanced towards Ruth – Ken was right, she was blooming, but there was also something different about her, and if she wasn't very much mistaken, there was also a decided coolness between her and her husband.

'... Harry said that you've been writing an article on Saigon – fascinating...' Sheila Fielding said to Ken, '... really fascinating, I call that.' She leant over to him, a dry ghost of a woman. 'Tell me all about it.'

'It's nothing much, Sheila.'

'Oh, I wouldn't say that,' she continued, her mouth incised like a cut into a side of beef. 'My husband seldom does anything interesting.'

Ken glanced at her evenly, but the flattery was having its effect and he seemed pleased. 'You're a good listener, Sheila,' he said, before launching into a long account of his last trip abroad.

From where she was sitting Nina saw how much he was drinking, saw his hand reach for the glass and clumsily catch hold of the stem. His mouth was only inches from Sheila Fielding's ear as she listened avidly, his hand resting on her arm, the fingers pressing into her flesh. 'You always were a very attractive woman,' he said, as Sheila leant back in her seat, her deep red dress crumpled like the petals of a burst rose.

'I think Ruth wants a word with you,' Nina said bluntly.

Ken glanced across the table. 'Now?'

'Yes, now.'

He got to his feet and walked towards Ruth, leaning on the back of the chair as he talked to her. Nina glanced over to Sheila Fielding and smiled. 'Have you known Ken long?'

'Over twenty years,' she said coldly.

'Twenty years! That *is* a long time. And in those twenty years didn't you manage to get him into bed?' she smiled wickedly. 'I mean, *before* he was married.'

'What the hell has that got to do with you?'

'Only this – Ruth is my closest friend, and you are a cow. If you don't get your claws out of Ken Floyd I will personally maim you. Anyway, I might not have to, your husband looks like a man with very little sense of humour.'

The woman blinked. 'How dare you speak to me like that –' she said, stopping short as Ken returned to his seat.

He glanced at both of them. 'How have you two been getting on?'

'Oh fine,' Nina said smiling. 'We were just talking about politics.'

The larger Ruth became, the more often Ken brought up the subject of a nanny. At first, she had resisted, but as he kept repeatedly bringing the matter up, she considered it. 'I know what you're saying, but I want to bring these children up myself.'

'I'm not saying that you give them over lock, stock and barrel, only that if you hired someone reliable you could enjoy them *and* have time to yourself.'

'You mean time for you,' Ruth said coolly.

He shrugged. 'I confess that the thought passed through my mind. I thought that if we got a nanny we could get about more, especially now that you've given up your job.'

'OK, maybe we could get someone in – but I don't want anyone too strict, or too young. I want someone responsible and someone who'll not try to monopolise them.'

'Then pick someone you like,' he said, kissing her and leaving for work. An instant later she could hear the bang of his car door and the noise of the engine starting.

All day Ruth toyed with the idea. Ideally the job of baby-sitting should have gone to her parents, Lilian in particular. One part of Ruth still wasn't used to employing people, and having come from a home which was poor, it seemed incredible to think of paying someone to take over the care of her children when she was perfectly capable of doing the job herself. But by the end of the day she relented, and placed an advertisement in an upmarket magazine.

There seemed to be no end of skilled nannies, all with references from various country seats, or smart, W1 addresses. Having a very clear idea of what she wanted, Ruth asked the applicants to phone first, thereby allowing her to sort the wheat from the chaff. Some were curt, some ingratiating, and some downright rude, implying that she was lucky to be able to consider their services. At the end of an exhausting afternoon,

Ruth shortlisted two and asked them to come round the following day.

Ruth was fortunate that she looked older than her years. Dressing conservatively, she always looked poised and made full use of the fact, carefully avoiding the dolly-bird/gold-digger image. Always aware of the great difference in age between her and her husband, she adjusted her manner skilfully with outsiders, expecting, and receiving, respect.

The first nanny was young and rather plain, her hair tied back too severely for the pale face. She seemed over-anxious, so much so that Ruth took pity on her and spent over an hour trying to put her at her ease. Apparently she was from Scotland and found London overwhelming, and from what Ruth could gather by reading between the lines, she was saving money in order to go back home at a later date. The second woman, Mrs Corley, was a plump, bespectacled woman with a slight Yorkshire accent which twenty years in London hadn't obliterated. She breezed in cheerfully, crossed her sturdy legs, and passed Ruth three references all of which praised her to the skies.

'Very impressive, Mrs Corley,' Ruth began, 'But I'd like to know why you are leaving your present position.'

There was no hesitation before she answered. 'The child I look after is now ten and going away to boarding-school, so there's no reason for me to stay on with the family.'

Ruth nodded and turned back to her notes. Mrs Corley was apparently fifty-three, but she looked younger, her smooth round face untroubled, her hair still full and dark. Behind the glasses her eyes were humorous and regarded Ruth openly as she questioned her.

'Do you like children?'

'Mrs Floyd, I've had to work hard all my life,' she explained. 'From early on I knew I'd have to pick a job I could enjoy.' She smiled. It was Lilian's smile, without the bitterness. 'So I chose to work with children. I've had four of my own, two boys and two girls, and I've looked after nineteen others. So I'd say, yes, I do like children.'

Ruth warmed to her. 'We have a housekeeper, who lives in,

and her husband, Mr and Mrs Harvey. I've had the room next to our bedroom decorated for the twins, but there are three rooms on the next floor which would be yours.' Ruth paused. 'I shall spend a good deal of time with the children so you shouldn't be overworked. I know some nannies want to have the children sleep in rooms close to their own, but I would rather they were next door to me ... I'm sorry if that sounds strange, but it's the way I want it.'

She seemed to understand perfectly. 'That's only sensible. You want to enjoy them while they're babies.'

Ruth nodded, thinking of Laurel. 'So if you would like the job – it's yours.'

She seemed taken aback. 'Do you want a decision now?'

'If you can manage it. You see, I trust my instincts, Mrs Corley, and they tell me that you would be the ideal person.'

She smiled warmly. 'In that case, I would like to work for you very much.'

They shook hands and she left soon after, arranging to move in a week before the birth to help Ruth prepare for the twins.

Meticulously, Ruth made plans, clamping off the memory of Laurel and the first months in London, shuttering off every feeling of guilt and living for the next children. Life had been good to her again, she realised, and she was not going to waste her second chance by dredging up the past.

As the births became imminent, Jack Gordon rang his daughter daily, his own excitement tempered by his antagonism towards Lilian. 'I'm sorry about your mum,' he said repeatedly. 'She's stubborn, flower, that's all.'

'It's all right, Dad, don't worry.'

He sounded tired. 'I'll come and see the babies just as soon as they're born. You can leave a message at work for me, and I'll be there. Do you need anything?'

'Only to see you.'

He seemed preoccupied and slightly cowed. Ruth wondered if Lilian was making his life difficult, or whether she herself was, by expecting him to go against her wishes. 'Dad, is everything all right? I mean, you and Mother are both well, aren't you?'

'Of course we are. Now don't go worrying about anything, you've got enough on your plate.'

The pips went.

'Dad?'

'I'll have to go, see you – '

The twins were born on the afternoon of 8 August. Ruth had been talking to Mrs Corley in the nursery when suddenly she doubled up and grabbed the side of the cot. They were born seven hours later, and Ruth saw them the instant they came into the world. There was to be no mistake this time.

Catherine was born first, followed two minutes later by Graham. She was perfect and long-limbed, and cried non-stop, waving her fists in the air frantically. Within half an hour Ruth shortened her name to Kate, and when she placed her brother beside her, Kate stopped crying and lay alongside him almost protectively. The pattern of her life was set from that moment. By contrast, Graham was born calm, regarding the world with regret, although when Ruth touched him he responded and clung to her fiercely.

There was no sign of Ken. Upset and embarrassed in a way she could not fully understand, Ruth watched the children beside her, smiling half-heartedly as her husband finally walked through the door. He stood watching her for a long moment, seeing the small face without make-up and the look of confusion in her eyes, then from inside his pocket he pulled out a string of pearls and fastened them round her neck. 'Pearls for tears,' Lilian would have said.

'Not bad, Mrs Floyd, not bad at all,' he said quietly.

Four days later a serene Ruth came home with her children, Ken picking her up from the hospital and carrying Kate to the car, whilst she held Graham. Her son was sleeping, his eyes firmly closed; by contrast Kate was crying lustily, her arms flashing around in the blanket like fish caught in a net.

'Does she cry all the time?' Ken asked.

'Not all the time, just most of the time.'

He winced. 'Hell fire! they're sleeping next door to us,' he said, peering at Graham. 'Why doesn't he wake up with all this noise?'

Ruth looked at the little face. 'I don't know. Perhaps he's so used to hearing her he can sleep through it.'

'I hope the same goes for me,' Ken added thoughtfully.

It was an idyllic time, that first summer with the twins. It was the year that man set foot on the moon; the year that the first human egg was fertilised in a test tube; and the year they abolished the death penalty. After the first week, Kate settled and became cheerful, smiling widely and indulgently at anyone who looked at her. She was dark, like Ken, and almost flirtatious with men, even at that age. Ruth loved her to desperation, as she did Graham, but his dour little personality was hard to understand, and his almost constant sleeping worried her. So much so, in fact, that when he was three months old Ruth took him to a specialist.

'He's perfectly fit and normal.'

'He seems ... too quiet.'

The doctor smiled at the woman in front of him. New mothers worried too much, he thought. 'A quiet baby would be considered a bonus to some.'

But Ruth couldn't shake off the feeling of dread and tackled Mrs Corley on the subject.

'You know about children, what do you think? Doesn't he seem a little too quiet?'

She looked at Graham carefully. Since the twins' birth Mrs Corley had become indispensable to Ruth, and although she knew nothing of her employer's background, instinct guided her and she willingly provided the mother figure Ruth lacked. 'He is quiet, certainly. But otherwise he seems fine. Don't worry,' she said, tucking him up in his cot, 'he'll come on in time. Boys take longer, that's all.'

But Graham continued to make Ruth anxious, and as Kate seemed to rush on and develop, her son appeared to be held back somewhere ... and she couldn't reach him.

It was early one evening, when Ken was at work and Mrs Corley was bathing Kate, that Ruth made the discovery which changed her life. Graham was lying in his cot, smiling up at her as she stroked his cheek and made noises. Sleepily he closed his eyes and Ruth leant over to turn off the lamp by his cot. Catching it with the back of her hand, it fell off the table and crashed to the floor. Ruth jumped, startled, and glanced towards the baby. He hadn't moved.

Her stomach lurched. Slowly she leant forward into the cot and clicked her fingers. Graham's eyes remained closed. Panicking, Ruth repeated the process by his right ear and then by his left. Nothing. Graham's eyes remained closed and he slept on. Her whole body shaking, Ruth banged on the table, hammering with her fists, her eyes fixed on the baby. There was no response. Her eyes wide with fright, she shouted, clapping her hands, her voice high-pitched, hysterical. But he never moved.

Graham was deaf.

The noise brought Mrs Corley rushing into the room. Ruth caught hold of her arm and pulled her to the cot. 'Look!' she said, clicking her fingers by Graham's ears. 'Look – he's deaf!'

Mrs Corley watched him and then sighed, putting her arm round Ruth and guiding her out of the nursery. 'We better ring Mr Floyd.'

'Graham's deaf!' Ruth kept repeating as they made their way downstairs. 'My son is deaf!'

'There might be some explanation – '

'What explanation!' Ruth shouted.

Mrs Corley answered her firmly. 'Come and have a cup of tea, Mrs Floyd. It will calm you down.'

The words had their effect. Ruth nodded and followed her into the kitchen, sitting down obediently. 'I knew it, I told that doctor.' She pushed her hair back from her forehead, her eyes looking round wildly. 'It's my fault.'

Mrs Corley passed her a cup of tea. 'Drink that. It will do you good.'

'He's deaf...' she said, after taking a sip. 'Damn that doctor! I'm his mother and I *knew* something was wrong.'

Mrs Corley sat down opposite her. 'We'll have to phone Mr Floyd.'

The words swung round Ruth. Carefully, she put down the teacup and sat up in her seat. 'No, I don't think so, I'll tell him when he comes home.'

'But –'

'No!' Ruth continued, her mind made up. This wasn't Ken's problem; besides, he would only use it as an excuse to get drunk. Graham was her child, and her responsibility.

'We'll get help for Graham. I don't believe that there's nothing to be done for him.'

Astonished, Mrs Corley watched the young woman in front of her. Within a couple of minutes she had seen Ruth change from a hysterical mother into a coolly determined woman, her voice altering from the high pitch of panic to calm reason. The transformation impressed her.

'Thank you for the tea, Mrs Corley,' Ruth said, getting to her feet. 'I'll be with Graham if you want me.'

When Ken was told he went into shock, Ruth's composure unsettling him still further as he paced up and down the lounge. 'Graham can't be deaf! He can't.'

'Ken, it's going to be all right. We'll sort it out.'

He wasn't listening to her. 'That bloody doctor! I asked him when they were born and he told me they were healthy.'

'They *are* healthy. Graham is deaf, that's all.'

He spun round to face his wife. 'You're taking this very calmly. Why?'

'What's the point in both of us getting hysterical?' she asked. 'Graham is our child and we'll get help for him.'

'I can't understand your attitude, Ruth. It seems that you don't realise the seriousness of the situation.'

She got to her feet angrily. 'I don't realise! I *knew* something was wrong before any of you did.'

'You just sound so bloody uninterested.'

'I sound what?' she asked, her voice low. 'What the hell would you know about it? This is the first time you've ever been a father.'

'Well, listen to the bloody expert on motherhood!' he countered unpleasantly. 'You got rid of the first one soon enough.' He saw Ruth flinch and blustered, 'Oh, God, I never meant to bring that up – I never meant.'

'I was ill! I didn't know what I was doing,' Ruth said, her voice icy. 'Damn you for what you said, damn you to hell!'

That night Ken got drunk. Even upstairs, Ruth could hear him banging around in the lounge and shouting. Picking up the twins, she went up on to the second floor and woke Mrs Corley. 'I'm sorry to disturb you, but ... ' She trailed off, uncertain what to say. 'I've got problems at the moment and I wondered if I could stay up here with the twins.'

Mrs Corley could hear Ken downstairs and didn't hesitate for an instant. 'Come on, dear, come on in. I'll make us a drink.'

Uncomfortable and out of place, Ruth sat on her settee, Kate on her right side, and Graham in her arms.

'It's difficult for some men to come to terms with things, especially when it concerns their children. Your husband can't understand what's happened.'

'He won't find the answer engraved on the bottom of a gin bottle,' Ruth said bitterly.

Mrs Corley was sympathetic. 'Things will seem better in the morning. You'll see, these things sort themselves out – ' her conversation was interrupted by a banging on the door. Startled Kate began to cry, and before Ruth had time to react, Ken walked in. He stood watching her, obviously embarrassed, his heavy features almost ugly with a combination of contrition and self-pity. 'Come down with the kids, please, Ruth. I won't hurt you.'

'I don't expect you to. You don't have to hit me to make your point.'

'I didn't mean what I said,' he continued, weaving slightly in the doorway.

'I'm surprised you can even remember it.'

'Ruth, I love you.'

She turned away, sighing. 'Mrs Corley, could you bring Kate down to the nursery for me? I'll take Graham.'

Moments later, they were settled in their cots.

'Thank you,' Ruth said simply, embarrassment making her diffident.

'It's nothing, Mrs Floyd. Nothing at all.'

Back in her own bedroom, Ruth watched her husband. He was already asleep, lying almost fully clothed on the bed with his arm across her pillow. Angrily she pulled it away, but he didn't wake, and when Ruth woke the next morning in the guest bedroom, he had already left for work.

At ten, he sent some flowers and a grovelling note which Ruth tore up and consigned to the fire in the lounge. Affecting a chilling coldness, she saw little of Ken that week, and although he tried to apologise, she ignored him and spent more time with the children, especially Graham. But although she avoided him, she remembered his words and swore she would prove him wrong. No one was going to take the children from her, she thought grimly, no one; and no one was going to make them miserable either. Ken was unreliable, a drinker, and her son needed help. From then on the only help they could count on was hers.

Without discussing it with Ken, Ruth took Graham to see Dr Benjamin Throop, an eminent specialist who had been highly recommended. He was thorough and sympathetic, and when he finished his examination he sat down to talk to Ruth, his gaze repeatedly returning to Graham who was sitting on her lap.

'You see, Mrs Floyd, this is a rare condition and one which causes impairment in the limbs over a period of years. The deterioration occurs in slow stages, but it can accelerate at certain times – especially under stress.' He paused, watching the young woman in front of him. She seemed composed, competent, the kind of mother most able to deal with a severely handicapped child. He continued evenly. 'Mentally, your son is bright. This often happens in these cases, the patient is intelligent but hampered by an inadequate body. I'm afraid that Graham will need constant care – all his life.'

All his life ... all his life ... Ruth kept hearing the words repeating in her head.

Dr Throop continued. 'Graham could live to be twenty' – she flinched – 'or seventy. No one can be sure, but the way that medicine is progressing at the moment ... '

Her throat tightening, Ruth looked at Graham and hugged him, wondering how that clever little brain was going to react to a dumb and uncomprehending body.

'If you need help, Mrs Floyd – '

'I can manage,' Ruth said, getting to her feet. Her legs felt weak under her as she walked to the door.

'Well, if you do ever need help, please contact me again.'

She held Graham all the way home, stroking his cheek and tickling him under the arms to make him smile. He seemed happy. Later, she fed him and then laid him in his cot to sleep, Graham watching his mother as she bent over the cot.

'I love you ... ' she said gently, 'and I'll make you better, you see if I don't. You'll live, Graham, you'll have a long life ... ' She stopped, her voice breaking. 'I promise you, you'll live, and you'll be handsome and strong ... We'll surprise the lot of them. They don't know what we can do, do they?'

Graham's eyes followed hers.

'We'll show them, won't we?'

He smiled at her, like a conspirator.

Although Ruth had not spoken to Ken, he came home that night early and sober. There was a fire burning in the lounge as he sat down at her feet, resting his head on her knees. Her face was pale, the grey eyes bright in the firelight. Her stillness shocked him.

'Are the babies in bed?' he asked.

'For the last hour now. You could go in and have a look at them.'

He nodded. 'Ruth, I can't tell you how bad I feel about the other night ... about what I said. I didn't mean it. I didn't mean to get drunk ... I love that child. It's been murder without you,' he continued. 'I've missed you ... I don't want us to be unhappy.'

'Neither do I.'

Alerted by the strangeness of her voice, Ken looked up at

her. He saw a woman he loved and was frightened of losing; she saw a tired man, whose attractiveness was teetering. If he carries on drinking, she thought, he'll end up like any other middle-aged alcoholic.

'Why do you do it?' she asked softly.

'I don't know.'

'Well, you'd better sort yourself out quickly, Ken, because Graham's in trouble,' she rushed on, wanting to share some of the pain. 'He's suffering from a disease which stops him developing properly. His limbs will be frail and he'll need a wheelchair, and he'll always be deaf although he's not mentally handicapped and should be brighter than most children.' She touched Ken's cheek with her fingertips. 'He needs us. So if you can't help me – then get the hell out of it now, because I can't carry both of you.'

She saw the effect her words had; saw how he closed his eyes and shook his head slowly. Don't fail me, please, she prayed. Please don't.

'I won't drink again, Ruth, I promise you. We'll fix this, all of it,' he said, burying his face in her hair. She held on to him tightly. 'Graham will have the best that's possible.'

'He'll need us all his life,' Ruth said softly.

'Well, he's got us all his life, so that's one problem no one need worry about.'

He stuck to his promise like a wasp to the side of a jam jar, even giving up social drinking when they invited friends round. The shock of Graham's condition altered both of them, making Ruth harder and Ken thoughtful, although Mrs Corley took the news calmly, her support, as ever, constant. Able to deal with casual enquiries as to Graham's condition, when her father rang Ruth hesitated and gave herself away.

'What's the matter, Ruth?'

'Nothing. I ...'

'Are the children all right?'

She broke down easily. 'Oh, Dad, it's Graham. Graham's so ill ...'

*

'It's the little boy. He's handicapped.'

Lilian laid down the dishes on the table and looked at her husband. 'Handicapped? How?'

'He's deaf and he won't be able to walk.'

Putting her hand up to her mouth, she sat down clumsily in front of the fire. The kitchen had not changed, even the clothes-rack hung suspended from the ceiling as before.

'How's Ruth?' she asked finally.

Jack sat down beside his wife and put out his hand. Automatically, she took it in her own. 'She's really upset. Gone into herself, you know, like she used to when she was a child.'

Lilian nodded.

'I can't get much out of her, nor Ken. He's a good man, but he's shocked by all this.'

'Are they sure about the boy?'

'The doctors seem certain – '

'Doctors!' Lilian exclaimed, letting go of Jack's hand and getting to her feet. 'What do they ever know? They said my mother would be dead in a fortnight after that first heart attack, and she lived three more years.' She took off her apron, exasperated. 'Doctors! There'll be something to help that child, you mark my words.'

Smiling, Jack Gordon went off to ring his daughter.

While Lilian made the first tentative reconciliation by letter, Nina returned from her latest tour and, having heard the news, decided to spend some time at Hampstead. Knowing that Ken wasn't enamoured of her, she came round in the daytime and left early to go to the theatre, where she was appearing in an Agatha Christie play. Both Ruth and Mrs Corley came to rely on her visits and looked forward to the clip clop of her heels on the steps leading to the front door.

'Hi, kiddo,' she said every time she saw Graham. 'How's the man of my dreams?'

Without fail Graham laughed, although he couldn't hear her and responded only to her expression. She then hoisted him on to her skinny hip and walked around with him. 'So how's my favourite drunk?'

'Very funny, Nina,' Ruth said, pushing past her and looking for some clean nappies. 'Ken's not drinking – I've told you.'

'Just checking,' she said cheerfully, kissing Graham on the cheek loudly. 'How often does Graham see the doctor?'

'Every month.'

'That must cost a packet,' she said and then changed the subject. 'Do you remember how you said you'd be going back to work?' Ruth nodded. 'You won't now, will you?'

'Honestly, Nina, does that seem likely, with these two?'

'I just wondered,' she said, idling over to the window. 'This producer offered me a part on Saturday. Said I could go to the top.'

'But?'

She grimaced. 'Got it in one! I mean, it's all right sleeping around for fun, but business – that's crude.'

She sang to Graham, played with Kate and pushed them miles in their pram, stopping every time someone admired them.

'This woman came up the other day and asked me if they were mine. I could see that she'd already checked my hand for a wedding ring, so I said yes, they were mine, and not only that but they had different fathers.' She grinned at the memory. 'Moved off like a bat out of hell.'

She kept the house alive, lifting everyone's spirits and regaling them all with tales of the theatre. For once, the show in which she appeared kept afloat, and on a rare evening out, Ken and Ruth went backstage to surprise her, congratulating her on her performance which was surprisingly good. She was obviously uncomfortable, her make-up greasy and her hair sticky with lacquer. Away from the lights she looked tiny and doll-like, her confidence make-believe.

'You were good,' Ken said sincerely.

'Sure I was good.'

Ruth butted in. 'I enjoyed it, Nina. You were great. I can brag about you now and talk about my famous friend.'

She grinned up at her. 'You great beanpole – didn't I tell you I'd be a star?'

But when the spring came round Graham deteriorated, and by his first birthday he was sickly and fading. Ruth's father noticed the difference and came down to visit, bringing home-made food from Lilian, although her concern remained distant and never extended to a visit. Ruth watched her son, the worry causing her to lose weight, her nights spent in the nursery, her days occupied solely with him. Throughout the long months, they waited, all of them refusing to say what was uppermost in their minds – that Graham would die. But in October, he rallied, putting on weight and beginning to take a real interest in the world around him. Ken was delighted and took it as a personal reward for his continued sobriety. Nina was equally certain that her intervention had been the solution.

'I've lit so many candles for that kid I'm getting photo-phobia.' She peered down at him and stuck out her tongue. Graham laughed. 'He appreciates subtlety, though, I'll give him that.'

Then one afternoon, just as Ruth had fed them, the doorbell rang. Remembering that it was Mrs Harvey's day off, Ruth wiped her hands and went downstairs to answer it. In utter amazement, she found her father standing there.

'Well, what a surprise! Come on in, Dad, you look cold.'

He hesitated, noticing the dark shadows under Ruth's eyes and the strain in her actions. Graham's illness was taking its toll.

'I brought someone, love,' he said, glancing towards the gate.

Ruth hadn't seen her standing there, hadn't seen the tall, slim woman who waited. Her face devoid of expression, Lilian gazed at her daughter without making any movement towards her. In the cold wind, Ruth hesitated on the front door-step, then slowly, she began to walk towards her mother. Lilian still did not move, even as Ruth came within feet of her and stopped. The wind was blowing into their faces as they looked into each other's eyes, and then suddenly Ruth ran forward.

'Oh, Mum,' she said simply, the tears running down her face.

Nine

Lilian looked older of course, but strong and straight as a ramrod. She kept her appearance and tinted her hair, even applying a little make-up. For a woman who had never been out of Oldham she looked as though she could have gone anywhere and been at home. Ruth was proud of her.

'Mother, I'm so glad to see you.'

She smiled brittly and pulled back. 'And you, Ruth. You look very ... well.'

'Come in,' she said, suddenly embarrassed.

Walking round the house, Ruth could see how her mother stared, and watched her father's pride as he pointed out the various rooms. 'This is the lounge, dear. What do you think?'

Lilian walked in, and glanced about her. 'You've done well,' she said stiffly.

'I was lucky, that's all.'

She glanced over her shoulder. 'Can I see your children?' she asked, avoiding the word 'grandchildren' as though they had nothing to do with her.

Aware of the uneasy atmosphere, Ruth obediently took her mother to the nursery. Kate was on the floor playing with a toy mouse, and Mrs Corley was sitting beside her with Graham on her lap. She looked up as they walked in.

'Mrs Corley, this is my mother,' Ruth said, watching the two women as they shook hands.

Lilian's attention soon wandered. 'So you're Catherine?' she said, turning to the little girl, who looked up and grinned hugely. Lilian's response was automatic as she bent down to pick up her granddaughter. 'She's wonderful, Ruth. A wonderful child. You must be proud.'

Inexplicably moved, Ruth smiled and pointed to Graham. 'And this is my son.'

166

Again Lilian acted without thinking and, giving Kate to Mrs Corley, she lifted Graham into her arms. 'They said you were poorly, well, you look like a fine boy to me.' The baby blinked at her. 'It's hard, isn't it? Being held back.'

With a flash of insight, Ruth understood immediately what her mother was saying; just as she understood that Graham's illness had been the catalyst to unite them. Lilian saw in her grandson's dilemma, her own. As Ruth's son was caught by illness, she had been trapped by circumstances. It made for a powerful bond between them.

So the first reconciliation took place, although at five o'clock Lilian insisted that they had to leave.

'But if you go, you'll miss Ken,' Ruth said, crestfallen.

Lilian looked at her daughter with that same expression she used when Ruth was being tiresome as a child. 'We have to get home, Ruth, it's a long way.'

'So why go? Stay here, there's room for you both.'

'No, I don't think so,' she said coolly. 'Not this time.'

Defeated, Ruth drove them to the station and stayed until she saw them on to the train. Her mother kissed her, but did not look back, unlike her father who waved until he was out of sight, his arm out of the window, his hand silhouetted against the sky.

In a way Graham's misfortune helped all of them, although the most dramatic effect was upon Kate. She had always been an amenable child, accepting the fact that Graham needed more attention without resenting him. Instinctively compassionate, she soon became his protector. And he allowed her to be. Tirelessly running around after her brother, she was often fretful when Ken played with her later, and seemed ill at ease when separated from Graham. Aware of their unusual bond, Ruth watched the twins closely, making sure that her son did not manipulate Kate too much. Because, just as the doctor had predicted, Graham proved to be highly intelligent, and whereas Kate was tolerant, Graham could soon fall into a towering rage if he was denied something. Because of his handicap, Ruth found it difficult to discipline him although she knew he had to be controlled. Fortunately Mrs Corley was very firm with him, while at the same time making sure that Kate never saw her scolding Graham.

Inger came over regularly. She had a handicapped brother herself and passed on tips and advice which were welcomed by Ruth, if resented by Ken.

'She's not a flaming doctor.'

'I know that, but she's had practical experience and that counts for a lot.'

He looked impatient. 'I don't want amateurs round my son.'

'But *we're* amateurs, Ken. Graham can't live in a bubble. He has to learn how to adapt the best way he can at home. Otherwise he'll rule the roost because he knows exactly how to play each of us against the other.'

But even though Graham was difficult, Ruth loved him, admiring the way he struggled against his handicap and recognising his frustration at his deafness. He inherited Jack Gordon's deep brown eyes and would sit resolutely in his push-chair, watching Kate in the garden. Ruth knew that he wanted to run, that his sister's easy movements jarred on his nerve edges like rain on a tin tray; but he was too young to comprehend his situation and resentment took the place of understanding.

Ken felt particularly badly because the tragedy affected his son. Had it been Kate, he would have been protectively indulgent, whereas with Graham he was alternately impatient and then overwhelmingly sympathetic.

'Perhaps that doctor was wrong. I mean, perhaps we should take him to see someone else.'

Ruth sighed and put down the paper she had been reading.

'He's seen three doctors and they all say the same. There's no point going to anyone else. Besides, he seems to be coping well at the moment.'

'If you're happy then – '

Ruth smiled at him. 'I'm happy.'

He seemed preoccupied and wandered aimlessly around the room for a while before settling down in the chair next to Ruth's. 'I've been thinking. We don't seem to spend much time together any more. What with the children . . . and Graham.'

She waited for him to continue. 'And I was thinking that we ought to go away and enjoy each other again. You know, spend some time just indulging ourselves. Just the two of us.'

Ruth balked at the words, but she could see his point. Since Graham's illness had been diagnosed she had spent very little time with Ken. Her life now revolved around the children and left only the late evenings free for her husband.

'Have I been neglecting you?'

He shrugged. 'Well, it's just that I wondered if you thought I was part of the staff.'

'Sorry,' she said simply, knowing he would continue.

'Listen, Ruth, I understand your position, but I need you as much as they do ... maybe more, in some ways.'

'Oh, Ken, how could you say that!'

She expected him to laugh but he didn't. 'Things get difficult at work, Ruth, I get lonely, feeling left out. A man needs his wife.'

A warning bell went off in her head. 'What are you saying?'

He looked across at Ruth. Her hair was lifted off her face, her forehead high and smooth. She's turning into a beauty, he thought suddenly. 'Look, I'm not making a confession and I'm not sleeping with anyone else. God knows, I want you too much to do that.' He touched her shoulder with his fingertips and then added. 'But I can't say what might happen if you keep leaving me to my own devices.'

He said it as a joke, but Ruth knew him well enough to understand what he really meant – 'Spend time with me and love me, or I'll find someone who will.' It would have been no use whatsoever to try and reason with him, she knew that. The answer was simple – if she was to keep her husband, she had to please him. The decision was hers.

So they went abroad, leaving Kate and Graham with Mrs Corley and Ruth's parents, who were going to stay for a while. Inger also promised to drop in and Ruth knew without asking that Nina would never be away. She had said as much.

'Get off and enjoy yourself. I'll have these little monsters tamed by the time you get back.' She shifted Graham on to her other hip. 'You won't know them in a month's time.'

'That's exactly what I'm afraid of.'

She was tickling Graham and making him laugh with the peculiarly soundless gasp of a deaf child. Watching them, Ruth unexpectedly resented Ken's attitude and the way he had forced her hand.

'What's the matter?' Nina asked suddenly. 'You thinking of murdering someone?'

'I was thinking of Ken – '

'Say no more.'

Ruth sighed. 'I was thinking that he shouldn't have twisted my arm to go away on this trip. And for a month, as well. It's too long to be away.'

'He wants you to himself,' she said, obviously amused. 'One whole month of Ken – boy, what a break!'

'He shouldn't be so dogmatic,' Ruth continued, tossing some things into her handbag, unreasonably irritated.

'He's doing his "me Tarzan, you Jane" bit. You should be flattered.'

Ruth swung round on her. 'But they're his kids as well as mine! Why doesn't he care as much as I do?'

'Ken is a man,' Nina explained patiently, 'and men like to lead steady, pleasant lives. They don't want to be force-fed on problems all the bloody time.'

'I know you're right, Nina. I'm just worried about leaving the children.'

'They'll be here when you get back,' she said, adding wickedly, 'possibly unrecognisable, but they'll be here.'

Ruth left the following day, trying to be light-hearted as she kissed the twins goodbye. As they drove off, Mrs Corley was standing on the doorstep with Kate clinging to her apron and her arms around Graham. His eyes watched Ruth go.

But the trip served its purpose, and within a few days Ken was loving and thoughtful again, having dismissed the children to the back of his mind as he spent all his time with Ruth. As she relaxed, she basked in his attention, agreeing to his every suggestion and revelling in the way they made love, the night sounds coming through the open windows, the air playing along their bodies.

Letters came to the hotel in Florence almost daily. Some from Lilian:

> Dear Ruth,
>
> Hope you are having a pleasant time. The children are well and your father is taking them to the park this afternoon. Mrs Corley thinks they should get more exercise, but I'm not sure about Graham – still, we'll talk about that when you get back. That friend of yours, Nina, has been round to see the children. Don't you think she spends a little too much time here?
>
> > Love,
> > Mother.

and some from Nina:

> Ruth,
>
> By now that old trout, your mother, will have written and said all about how I'm monopolising – (have I spelt that right?) – the twins. I'm not, I just like to see them and take them out. She seems to think that she's the only person who can look after them and stands guard over their cot at night like Bela Lugosi over a haemophilliac. She's a pain in the blasted neck, if you ask me.
>
> Are you enjoying yourself? And have you regained that first flush of wedded bliss? And was it with Ken? How is the old man anyway – still off the bottle?
>
> My show closes next week so I'll be back 'resting' on the end of the dole queue ... Don't worry about a thing, all is well and the twins send their love.
>
> > See you soon, kiddo,
> > Nina.

'Another letter from Nina,' Ruth said, sliding it across the table to Ken. They were sitting on the balcony outside their room, the sun making patterns on the stone floor.

'She's never away from the kids, she must be a glutton for punishment,' he said, reading the page and turning over. 'Can't spell either.'

Basking in the heat, Ruth put her head back and felt the sun on her face. 'You're going to burn,' Ken murmured, his hand stroking her back.

'Mmmm.'

'Ruth, let me put some more lotion on.'

Sleepily she nodded, feeling his fingers move over her skin. Then, just as she fell to sleep, her mind wandered over to Hampstead and she imagined she was nuzzling Kate's hair and holding her son on her lap.

The holiday provided Ruth with a break she would never have taken otherwise. When they returned the children were pleased to see them, and her parents left the day afterwards in high spirits. In short, the separation had been good for all of them. So good, in fact, that when the phone rang early the next day, Ruth found herself almost irritated by the intrusion.

'It's good to hear you again. How are you?'

She didn't recognise the voice.

'It's Ted, Ted Morrison from the cinema.'

'Ted!' she exclaimed, having a sudden vision of him, smart in his business suit and inevitable bow-tie. 'How are you?'

'I'm well, overworked as usual, but otherwise in the pink. How are things with you?'

'Fine – couldn't be better.'

'And the twins?'

'They're lovely, Ted. Graham has some problems, but we'll sort it out.' She smiled. 'It's good to hear from you.'

'Well ... I'd been meaning to get in touch ... you know how it goes.' He was obviously embarrassed.

'I should have rung you, Ted. It works both ways, you know.'

There was a momentary pause. 'Ruth, I want to ask you something. You're quite at liberty to say no, I'd understand if you did. No hard feelings, and all that – '

'What is it?'

'Well, the fact of the matter is this. The man who took over the running of the cinema when you said you weren't going to come back last year had to go. He wasn't suitable.'

'He left before you had time to train anyone else?' Ruth asked, incredulous.

'Well, it was unavoidable,' Ted replied, lowering his voice. 'He'd been helping himself to the profits, if you follow my drift.'

'Oh,' Ruth said simply. 'What do you want me to do about it?'

'You see,' he said soothingly. 'I know that the twins are still small, but perhaps you could just come in and tide us over. You ran the business so well, you could pick it up in no time at all. We'll make it worth your while.'

The money didn't matter then, not as it had done when she first worked there. 'Is there any alternative?'

'Only if we let Geoffrey Lynes take over.'

'And how would that go down with the clients?'

'Not well ... so you see my problem. I'm not going behind his back; Geoffrey is a fine man with a wonderful head for figures, but he's not too good with people, and that's what matters in a job like this . . . Could you consider it?'

Unaccountably, the idea appealed to Ruth. A chance to work for a limited period would give her a different outlook on things, she thought, and was probably better than hanging around the children all day. Besides, she told herself, it was only temporary. 'I'll do it.'

'Wonderful – '

'Just a minute! I said I'll do it, Ted, and I will, but only on my terms. I don't want any interference from anyone, and I'll come to you if I need anything – no one else.' She was thinking of the disruptive Geoffrey Lynes. 'And I want to start work at ten-thirty and leave at five. Someone I choose can fill in for me in the evenings.'

He paused. 'All right. Anything else?'

Ruth smiled, her confidence soaring. 'Yes, there is. I want a better office, the room next to the conference area on the first floor would do.'

'You've got it. When can you come in?'

'Monday.'

'Thank you, Ruth,' he said, obviously relieved. 'You won't regret it.'

With a giddy feeling of excitement Ruth put down the phone, her hands shaking. Until then she had not realised how much she missed work and would never have admitted that she was bored at home all day. It would have seemed disloyal somehow. Her conscience nudged her suddenly. She had wanted to be the perfect wife and mother, but ... She got to her feet and moved round the study, looking at the endless books on the shelves. Row after row, all lined up like toy soldiers. There had never been any books in Carrington Street, she thought. If she had stayed there she would never have met Ken, or had his children, or lived in this house.

But she would have had Laurel instead ... The thought disturbed her and made her restless. Maybe she was pushing her luck, expecting to have everything – a family and a career. She walked to the window impatiently – but it was there for the taking, wouldn't she be mad not to grab at such a chance? The afternoon crept on and she still hesitated, thinking of Ken and his reaction. Before they married he had been interested in her work, enjoying her company and the fact that she made him laugh. Then he had thought that women without jobs were idle and boring ... Ruth wondered uneasily if the same applied to wives.

By the time he was due home Ruth had bathed the twins and was doing Graham's exercises to strengthen his legs – the ones which made him cry and reddened his skin – when she heard the door open downstairs.

'Ruth?'

'I'm up here. With the children.'

He took the stairs two at a time and swung Kate up into the air, making her squeal. 'Good day?' he asked, kissing the top of Ruth's hair.

'Interesting.'

He sat on the edge of the bath. He looked prosperous, almost complacent. 'What happened?'

'Ted Morrison rang.' He stared blankly at Ruth. 'You remember – he was the man who hired me for the job at the cinema.'

'Oh yes – I hope he didn't want you back.'

Ruth winced and began to comb Graham's hair.

'Well,' Ken said impatiently. 'What *did* Morrison want?'

'Oh, nothing.'

His eyes watched Ruth's face. 'He *did* want you to go back, didn't he?'

'It would only be temporary,' she said quickly, 'and you've always said I should go back to work some time, and that I could only talk about the children.' Ruth glanced away. They hadn't argued for months and she had no desire to start again, or worse, annoy him enough to send him back to the bottle.

'Well, what do you want to do?' Ken asked finally.

'I thought it might be a change for a while ... broaden my outlook. Besides, I was good at my job.'

He shrugged and touched her face. 'Will there be time for me? If you're out and about meeting all kinds of people – '

'It's just a job.'

'For how long?' he asked, wanting to please her, but aware that his instincts were to keep her at home. If I let her go she'll get bored with the idea, he thought, but if I stop her ... He hesitated, understanding Ruth well enough to know he couldn't stop her if she had made up her mind. The same cool determination which had first fascinated him now made him pause. 'Welcome back to the rat race, Ruth.'

The following week Ruth began work, arriving early at the cinema, her mind turning back to the days when she had first worked there. A cough startled her.

'How are you, Ruth?'

She turned to see Geoffrey Lynes, looking much altered. In three years he had aged a decade.

'I'm well, Geoffrey. And you?'

He smiled bleakly, sitting down in the seat next to her. 'Not too bad. I was ill, you know.'

'No, I didn't. Was it serious?'

'Parkinson's disease,' he said bluntly, looking up to see the reaction on Ruth's face.

'I'm sorry.'

He nodded. 'It's not that bad, really. One gets used to anything,' he said, glancing at her. 'It's good to see you again.'

'Ted Morrison rang me and asked me to help out for a while until you hired someone else.'

'There was never anyone like you,' he said quietly, continuing in a different vein. 'We've made some changes, but the show still goes on.'

Ruth smiled half-heartedly, aware of the fact that she pitied him, and he knew it. 'Why don't you show me these changes then, Geoffrey?'

'Yes,' he said, getting up slowly. 'Come with me.'

It seemed incredible to Ruth, but most of the bookings were from the customers she had first contacted; people who kept returning to the cinema because they were comfortable there. Out of every ten bookings only four were new film companies or private showings. Eagerly she began work, pausing at four in the afternoon, after missing lunch. The excitement of the place was contagious and Ruth slipped back into the routine as though she had only been away for a weekend. Ted Morrison called in once, and then left, obviously relieved, but Geoffrey Lynes hung around most of the day, drifting idly like a schoolboy watching a summer fête.

Ruth did, however, find time to ring home, and twice put in a call to Ken but each time he was engaged. At five-thirty, half an hour after she should have left, Ruth was talking to a politician who wanted to hold a press conference the next week.

'You're doing a wonderful job,' Ted Morrison said kindly, materialising at Ruth's elbow and pointing to his watch.

'Damn!' she replied, pulling on her coat and making for the door. 'Incidentally, Ted, thanks for the new office, it's a great improvement.'

He smiled and pulled his left earlobe thoughtfully. 'No

trouble at all. If you choose which colours you would like, I'll get it decorated for you.'

Ruth turned, 'I don't think I'll be here that long.'

And she actually believed it, then.

'Does she know?' Nina asked Ken over the phone.

He turned round and glanced over his shoulder. 'No. She hasn't the slightest idea.'

'Are you sure?'

'Positive. You worry too much.'

Nina was not convinced. 'Listen, Ruth's no fool, she'll sense something's different if you're not careful.'

A moment later, Ken rang off.

But Ruth never did guess that Ken had arranged a party for her twenty-eighth birthday, inviting friends, business acquaintances, and family to come to the house. That night, thinking that everyone had forgotten, Ruth came home alone. The house was in darkness as she made her way upstairs, yawning, and stopping to look in on the twins. They were in bed; Graham moving slightly in his sleep, Kate, quiet and still. Ruth was in the shower when she found the bracelet stuck into the bar of soap. It was gold, inset with sapphires, and matched the earrings and the brooch Ken had given to her when they were married. Quickly she dressed and clasped the bracelet round her arm.

'You look good,' Ken said behind her. He was leaning against the bathroom door, his hands in the pockets of his dinner jacket.

'Naturally – how could I look otherwise with all these jewels?' Ruth kissed him, laughing, and then pulled away. 'Stop it! You'll ruin the dress.'

'You're right. Listen, I want to take you out but I've got some phone calls to make. You finish getting ready and I'll come and get you.'

Agreeing readily, Ruth went up to see Mrs Corley who was watching television. 'Do you mind if I join you?'

'No. Come on in, you're always welcome.' She looked at the young woman in front of her. 'How lovely you look.'

'Ken bought me this,' Ruth said, extending her arm to show

her the bracelet, her ears alerted to the sounds of movement
below. Looking at Mrs Corley she smiled, and raised her
eyebrows. 'Has he arranged a party?'

'Something like that.'

There was a great deal of car door banging.

'And I'm not supposed to know?' Mrs Corley nodded. 'Then
I'll play along with it,' Ruth said, sitting down and watching television until Ken came upstairs, his face flushed with
triumph.

'Are you ready? We should be leaving for the restaurant.'

He led Ruth downstairs, watching her feigned surprise when
she saw everyone in the hall. There must have been sixty people
there, some of whom Ruth hadn't seen for years. Spotting her
mother and father, Ruth was just about to walk over to them
when Nina appeared, planting a kiss firmly on her cheek.

'If that's left a huge red gooey mess, I'll kill you.'

Nina pulled a face. 'Happy Birthday to you too.'

The house was soon full of noise. Inger talking to Lilian and
Sam propped up against the bar, his beard and long hair
looking oddly out of place amongst the tuxedos. As Ruth
greeted people several of Ken's colleagues congregated
together, watching her.

'You've got to hand it to him, she's quite a looker,' one said,
as his eyes followed Ruth, noticing the short black cocktail
dress and the long blonde hair.

'The old man never thought it would last – neither did
Joanie,' the man laughed drily. 'I bet she never thought she'd
be upstaged by a girl young enough to be her daughter.'

'Where is she now?'

'Abroad somewhere,' the man said, pausing. Ruth had tossed
her hair back from her face and the light caught the sapphires
in amongst her hair.

'Look at those earrings! They must have cost old Ken a
packet.'

'You have to pay to keep a woman like that at home,' the
other man answered, laughing.

Unaware of the conversation around her, Ruth enjoyed
herself, relaxing and drinking too much, so when Nina started

to give an impromptu performance of her latest role, she turned away laughing as Ken raised his eyebrows.

Over the last few years their marriage had veered perilously close to divorce, although every time, Ken promised he would stop drinking and Ruth believed him. Bruises came to be something commonplace; a drinking bout ending violently, Ruth's arms kept covered for days afterwards. The most unlikely things could set him off and the threat of his drinking hung over her for weeks until she forgave him; too proud to admit that the marriage was failing, too reliant on Ken to consider giving him up. The pity was that when he was sober he was another person, good company and good-natured. But his insecurity showed itself at odd times, and never when Ruth expected it. Going back to work she had anticipated opposition, but he gave her his full backing and when Kate went to preparatory school, encouraged Ruth to continue full time.

'But what about Graham?'

'He has enough of your time.'

'But he needs that time. He'll feel neglected.'

He pointed to the nursery door where Graham was being fed.

'You can't spend the rest of your life just waiting for Graham to walk or say something.'

'That's not fair! He can't help being handicapped.'

'No. But you can.'

She moved away and he caught hold of her arm. 'Ruth, you enjoy your work and when you're home the kids appreciate you more. Don't fool yourself that you could give it all up, you can't. You're ambitious, admit it.'

He was right; and she knew it.

During the last two years Graham's temperament had changed, becoming so violent that at times he was impossible to control. His lack of hearing exacerbated his frustrations, and though Ruth tried to soothe him it was usually Kate who calmed him down. The situation seemed hopeless for months, and then, as he sometimes did, Graham rallied, his personality becoming more docile as his fifth birthday came around.

But if Graham tried her patience, Ruth recognised her daughter's qualities. With admiration, she watched her with Graham, saw how she slapped him if he was out of control or encouraged him when they played together. And, astonishingly, he accepted her actions without any of the resentment he showed to Ruth or Mrs Corley.

Unfortunately his condition did not improve, and it was bitter for Ruth to hear that nothing could be done for her son.

'He is profoundly deaf, I'm afraid,' Dr Throop said evenly, 'and his legs will never be strong enough to make walking possible.'

'But he understands everything that's going on. I show him objects and he knows what they are, and he's beginning to write.'

'Graham is not stupid, merely handicapped,' Dr Throop explained. 'He requires a great deal of time and patience and now that he's getting older he might benefit from a stay at a clinic.'

Ruth took in her breath sharply. 'No one is taking this child away from me!'

'I'm not suggesting that. I merely thought that if Graham were to attend the clinic during the day he would benefit,' Dr Throop continued calmly. 'He would only be there during the day. The staff are qualified in dealing with patients like your son. They don't become emotionally involved and they'll get the best out of him. Believe me, if you love him you'll let him go there.'

If she loved him!

'All right, doctor, I'll take your advice. If you would be kind enough to arrange it for me.'

And so a month later Graham began at the clinic in North London. He hated it from the start, his little hands clutching at Ruth as she passed him over to the nurse in charge, his eyes following her to the car and watching as she drove out of the gate. But in the weeks which followed he did progress, and when Kate came home from school he tried valiantly to explain what he'd been doing, pointing out what he'd written or drawn.

Gently she'd go over it with him, their heads bent over the table, Graham's slightly large and unwieldy, Kate's small and neat, her long hair tied back in bunches.

His fragility crept up on Ruth unawares. She would be playing with him to make him laugh, when suddenly he would stiffen and his mouth would open in surprise because she had hurt him accidentally. When she hugged him, he would relax, but Ruth's heart would race for minutes afterwards in panic.

'His writing is so much better,' she said, childishly pleased with his progress as she pushed the book over to Ken.

'Damn sight better than Nina's ever will be,' he countered drily.

But when she caught sight of Graham struggling to reach something, it took her all her strength not to rush in and hold him, pushing the rest of the world away. In Ruth's eyes Graham was suffering, enduring a punishment which was, by rights, hers. In her son, she saw how she had failed Laurel, and it made her over-protective towards him.

And as she cosseted her son, she worried about her marriage.

Nina had been abroad frequently, writing to Ruth and itemising her conquests, most of which seemed to be either dope-raddled Bohemians or European aristocracy – if she was to be believed. In a rash moment she moved to Hollywood to try her luck, sending back reports of dirty dealings and casting couches. She even began to read seriously, possibly because of the influence of one of her lovers, and told Ruth all about the intricacies of T. S. Eliot's *The Waste Land* in numbing detail.

Missing her, Ruth turned to Inger for company, but she seemed placid by comparison and besotted by Sam.

'You worry too much,' she said, cutting up some peppers and throwing them into the sink to rinse. 'You worry about Ken, and Graham, and now your job.'

'I can't help it, it's my nature.'

'You could do yoga.'

'I could take up macramé as well – but I'm not going to do either,' Ruth countered drily.

She sighed and began to chop the vegetables.

'Doesn't anything ever worry you, Inger?'

'Now and again.'

'Like what, for instance?'

She pushed away some hair with the back of her hand. 'Sam.'

'Good Lord! Why worry about Sam?'

She smiled over her shoulder towards Ruth. The sun fell through the blind and made patterns on her hair. 'I love him.'

'And he loves you.'

She turned back to the sink. 'After his fashion,' she said.

In time, the relationship between Lilian and Ruth improved. Worried about Graham and unsettled with Ken, Ruth came to rely on her mother more and Lilian visited often, leaving Ruth's father to fend for himself. Ruth could see that her mother was growing older, but every time she tried to persuade her to abandon the hat shop, she wouldn't hear of it.

'Ruth has her own job and I have mine,' Lilian explained to Jack when she returned home. 'Just because mine's in Oldham, it doesn't mean it's not important to me – '

'She didn't mean that. She just wants you to enjoy the children. You know how often Ruth's asked us to go and live down there so we could be nearby.'

She frowned. 'And that's another thing. Doesn't it strike you as odd how often she invites us down?'

'Oh, for God's sake!' Jack shouted. 'The girl can't do anything right. When she doesn't ask you, she's in the wrong, and when she does, she's in the wrong too. She can't win.'

'It's no good losing your temper with me, Jack! That marriage isn't what it should be.'

He sighed and picked up his paper to indicate that the conversation was over. But the words blurred in front of his eyes and his attention wandered. All wasn't well with Ruth, he realised that too.

'We could go and live down there,' Lilian mused out loud.

Jack put the paper down. 'Do you want to?'

She shook her head and leant down to the oven. 'No, I

don't think so, I know where I'm comfortable.' She smiled indulgently. 'It's enough for me to see how well Ruth's got on.'

Ken was forty-nine by this time, and although he didn't look his age he seemed much older than the other fathers. Feeling out of place, he responded irritably.

'I look like Kate's grandfather standing outside the school gates. Why the hell are all the other dads so young?' He ran his fingers through his hair. 'It's bloody infuriating.'

'You look good to me.'

'Well, from an old lady like you that's quite a compliment,' he replied, his humour too sharp for comfort.

Ruth learned to fear the gin bottle most of all, holding her breath when they went out and someone offered to buy Ken a drink. Having always struggled with his weight he became heavier when he was on the wagon and it annoyed him. 'These damn suits don't fit! I'll have to go and see that tailor again.' He threw down a pair of trousers. 'I can't eat a damn thing without putting on weight.'

'You're chunky.'

He swung round. 'I don't want to be "chunky", thank you! I'm not a lorry driver.'

'I'm sorry ... ' Ruth stammered uneasily. 'It's just that I like you however you look.'

He kissed her fingers, all anger gone. 'What a right old bastard I am, how do you put up with me?'

But Ruth did put up with him and kept a careful check on how she looked, knowing that Ken bored easily and that being his wife might not be enough. She loved him, and spent time with him away from the children, dancing around his feelings. It was like having a third child. And as for Laurel ... she came into her mind when none of the others had any claim on Ruth's time, drifting into her thoughts when she was working or locking up the cinema at night. Sitting alone in her car, Ruth would wonder where Laurel was and if she looked like Kate, thinking of Derek and his kindness, of the house up on the Coppice and the way he waved to her without looking round. Ruth doubted if Derek would have liked Ken, although he would have loved Kate and been endlessly sympathetic with Graham. And sometimes, when she dreaded going home in case Ken was drinking, Ruth thought back and couldn't remember Derek ever being drunk or violent . . .

Resilient as she was, the doubts were insurmountable only when Ken was on one of his binges, or when Robert Floyd called to see the children, his attitude mischievously disruptive. Playing one off against the other, he would needle his son by defending Ruth, and then change sides, subtly goading his daughter-in-law about the state of her marriage.

Weary and disillusioned, Ruth carried on, totally absorbed with her own problems until one morning someone jolted her out of her small world and into theirs.

'Ruth, you have to help me,' Inger said over the phone, her voice almost hysterical. 'He's gone.'

'Who has?'

'Sam . . . he left! Said he was bored with me and wanted her.'

'Sam's left you?' Ruth asked, incredulous.

'HE'S GONE!' she screamed.

'Inger, where are you?' There was no reply. 'INGER! Where are you?'

'At the flat . . . I thought he loved me, but he loves her . . . You could stop it, Ruth. You could stop it!'

She was incoherent.

'Stop what? Oh, Inger, please calm down and tell me what's happened.'

'Sam's run off with your friend, Nina!'

Ruth shook her head. 'You're wrong, she isn't even in the country – '

'I know, she's in America! That's where they met up. He said he was going over to visit his parents and instead . . . I can't tell Nicki.'

Suddenly Ruth remembered Nina's insistence on getting a flat in Kensington, near to where they lived; and she remembered Nina talking to Sam at the party, her face tilted up, looking into his. It wasn't difficult to think back, remembering Nina as a child, the engaging liar, the show-off, the kid from the backstreets who never really wanted to leave, if her actions were anything to go by.

Dully, Ruth wondered how she could have betrayed Inger ... and deceived her.

Ten

If Ruth was stunned by the news Ken didn't even look surprised when she told him. 'I was expecting it.'

'Why?'

He undid his tie and sat down. 'The way Nina looked at him, the way she acted whenever his name was mentioned.'

'I never noticed that.'

He smiled cynically. 'My dear girl, you never see anything unless it has an arrow pointing to it.' Stung, Ruth kept silent, and watched as he poured himself a large gin. 'I told you years ago about Nina. I've always said she was out for anything she could get, and didn't give a damn about who she walked on to get it.'

Ruth rose to her defence. 'OK, what she did was unforgivable, but people make mistakes. Besides, Sam's already on his way back home.' She paused, feeling a reluctant sympathy for Nina, who had been deserted as soon as Inger had spoken tearfully to Sam. The wandering boy on his way back to his wife, she thought ruefully. 'I said I'd look after Nicki until everything's been sorted out.' She glanced over; Ken was drinking steadily. 'It was a stupid thing to do, to try and break up a marriage – husbands usually go back to their wives in the end.'

'But not always,' Ken said savagely, raising his glass.

Due to Ruth's efforts the cinema flourished and she became known in the business, her previews and openings always well attended with the pick of society, media, and a sprinkling of titled heads adding newsworthy glamour. Seeing the potential, Ted Morrison decided that the company should expand its interests and, after consultations with the board, discussed it with Geoffrey Lynes. 'Where were they thinking of opening another centre?' he asked cautiously.

'Knightsbridge. There's a building available which might do nicely. We would like Ruth to run it, of course.'

'Of course,' Geoffrey answered wryly.

'She's come a long way,' Morrison continued. 'She's got class and people like that, especially since she married Ken Floyd.'

Geoffrey blinked slowly. 'How do you make that out?'

'Money. The Floyds have real money, and that adds something to her success.' He paused and pulled at his earlobe, 'Mind you, I did hear that they weren't happy.'

'Is he drinking again?' Geoffrey asked eagerly, too eagerly. Morrison glanced over the desk. So that was it, he thought, the man's in love with Ruth. Automatically, he filed the information away for future reference.

'Yes, Floyd's well and truly back on the bottle,' Morrison continued, and then paused. 'Do you think it will affect her work? I'd like your opinion, Geoffrey.'

He hesitated. It was the first time in years that Geoffrey Lynes had power over Ruth. Resentment welled up as he remembered how she'd rejected him, how she thought she was too good for him . . . How strange life was, he thought. Suddenly the tables were turned and she needed him. In fact, her future depended on his answer . . .

'Geoffrey?'

'Sorry, Ted, I was just thinking.' He paused, savouring the moment. 'No, I don't think it will affect her work. Ruth is too much a professional to let personal matters sway her judgement.'

Wonders will never cease, Ted Morrison thought drily.

When Morrison approached Ruth she was ecstatic, and after talking terms with him she said, 'It sounds good, but I'd like to think about it and talk to my husband. I'll let you know tomorrow,' she concluded, getting to her feet.

All the way home she ran it over in her mind, relishing the thought of having her own cinema. She had come a long way since being an usherette, she thought wryly, and she had changed. Now she made her own decisions, relying on herself more and more; the need for success was vital to her – but so was her husband.

When Ruth walked in, Ken was sitting in the lounge and called out to her, 'Come in and tell me what happened at work.'

'The company want to open a new centre in Knightsbridge,' she said, taking off her coat and sitting down next to him, 'and they want me to run it.'

'That's marvellous.'

'Mmmm.'

'You don't think so?'

Ruth shrugged and pulled off her earrings. 'Yes, I suppose it's a good idea, and I'm flattered. But I'm not sure whether I want to take it on.'

'You don't have to work, I've always told you that. But you're better working, it suits you.'

'Why?'

'Oh, I don't know!' he snapped. 'Listen, it doesn't matter a damn to me if you work, or you don't. We don't need the money so it's only worth while if you want to do it.' There was impatience in his voice. 'They obviously think you're special.' He paused. 'You've come a long way.'

'So you wouldn't mind if I accepted?' Ruth asked carefully.

'No, not at all,' he said, his expression unreadable. 'Good luck.'

After turning the matter over in her mind for most of the night, Ruth made her decision, and the following day accepted the post.

'Well, what do you think of it?' Ted Morrison asked, opening the door of the cinema and letting her walk through.

The building was compact and old-fashioned. Previously it had been a theatre, until hard times struck in the sixties and anything off the Haymarket floundered and closed its safety curtains for the last time. The auditorium was small and deep green, the walls brocade and the ceiling emerald and gold. It was like being trapped, drowning, in seaweed.

Ruth shivered. 'God, it's grim.'

Ted pulled at his left earlobe and looked around. 'That's because it's been empty for so long.'

'No. It's all this ghastly green, it's too depressing. We could get rid of all of this and restore the mouldings . . .' Ruth looked about as she talked, '. . . then get some new doors and make the rooms upstairs into comfortable lounges, like the old Edwardian salons.'

Ted smiled. 'So you think it could have possibilities?'

'Of course. It's just a matter of bringing out its best points.'

Ruth worked frantically for the next month, glad of the help her mother gave by coming down to stay for a while. Impressed by Ruth's success, Lilian did everything to keep the house running smoothly, whilst Ruth made sure she was always home before Ken returned from work.

The workmen were good, but appalling time-keepers and required frequent monitoring, Ruth spending precious time on the phone trying to chase them up, before dashing back to Piccadilly to keep a check on the other centre. Realising that she needed help, Ruth employed a male secretary, Bill Pascoe, who told her where she should be, with whom, and why.

The decorations were finally completed on 12 February; the walls hung with hand-painted wallpaper, the curtains draped, the plaster-work glowing with its new gilding, and the upstairs rooms welcoming and glamorous. Aware that she had indulged herself, Ruth loved the place, and asked Ken and her parents to the opening. Ken declined, and, for once, Jack Gordon tried to persuade him.

'You don't know what you're missing, Ken,' he said cheerfully. 'I reckon this place will be a roaring success.'

'I'm certain it will,' he responded coldly.

'Are you sure you won't come?' Jack asked again, aware that he was begging him for his daughter's sake.

Ken turned away. 'I don't think I'll have time. Ruth isn't the only one who works in this house.'

The day after the opening, Ruth's parents left, and Ken never made time to see the new cinema. After the first fortnight, Ruth stopped asking him. Their marriage seemed destined for one of its unsteady phases and, for once, Ruth was disinclined to worry. She decided that if Ken wanted to be petty, he could get on with it; in fact, their relationship had deteriorated so far that when Ruth came home and found him drunk in the lounge she wasn't even surprised.

Mrs Corley helped her to get him up to bed and Ruth was just about to go for a shower when the doorbell rang. It was eleven-thirty. 'I'll go,' Ruth told her, having dismissed Mrs Harvey as soon as she saw Ken's condition. 'It's probably a mistake anyway.'

The wind was banging on the door and as she wrenched it open a cold draught blew past her. On the step a small, bedraggled figure stood with its back facing the door. Ruth knew who it was before she turned round.

'Nina.'

She had cut her hair short, and although it was February she was wearing only a jacket and skirt. She looked frozen. 'I've no money – can you pay off the taxi?'

Ruth looked down the drive to where the cab waited. 'Give me one good reason why I should.'

Nina tucked her hair behind her ears and smiled. 'Because you care about me,' was all she said.

After paying the driver Nina ran back, closing the front door softly and looking at Ruth. 'Sorry.'

'For what you've done, or what you are about to do?'

'You know ... Sam.'

Ruth turned away, her voice cold. 'You betrayed Inger and you let me down.'

'What the hell are you so annoyed about? It wasn't your marriage!'

'Not this time,' Ruth said sharply.

Nina was stunned by the remark, but recovered quickly. 'Oh, for God's sake! Inger got her flaming husband back. Anyway ...' she continued, 'Sam dumped me, didn't he? Left me in the middle of bloody California surrounded by nothing but orange trees and lentils.'

'So why did you stay on after he left?'

'Seemed like a good idea at the time. He'd paid up the rent

for the next three months so I thought I might as well take advantage of that fact. I also thought I might find some work out there.'

'But you didn't?'

Her eyes blazed. 'Yes, I got all the starring roles – after I changed my name to Dustin Hoffman.'

Ruth smiled reluctantly and moved into the kitchen, Nina following. She seemed tired, her body tiny and achingly fragile.

'How's Ken?'

'Drunk.'

Nina pulled a face. 'Temporary lapse or permanent stupor?'

'God knows – I don't.'

She was thoughtful for a moment, sipping the coffee Ruth had made for them. It was as if she had never been away.

'Apart from Ken being drunk, is everything all right between you two?'

'I can't tell,' Ruth said, glancing down. 'He seems to have changed since I took on the new cinema – '

'What new cinema!'

She explained briefly, to Nina's obvious amusement. 'Quite a jolt to the old masculine pride, hey? You want to watch it.'

'Maybe I should take some tips from you, as you're such an authority on relationships.'

Nina winced. 'Ouch!' she said, glancing over to Ruth. Money and success, she thought, don't keep a good temper or a man.

'I'm sorry,' Ruth said stiffly, 'I didn't mean to hurt you.'

'Really? Well, I'd hate to be here when you apply your mind to it.'

They fell into an ungracious silence.

'Didn't you meet anyone else in California?' Ruth asked finally.

'No one nice.'

'Where are the nice men, Nina?' she asked, suddenly exasperated. 'Where are they all? You think you've found someone, let down your guard and then ... Oh well,' she said softly. 'Let's hope someone will turn up for you.'

'Turn up or sober up,' Nina said brightly, raising her mug.

'Here's to tomorrow, may it be stuffed full of opportunities.'

They toasted each other like cavaliers.

Ken woke up with a hangover and a bad temper, Ruth grateful that the house was large and that he wasn't aware of their guest. By the time he left she was stiff with tension, although the re-emergence of Nina was a bonus for the twins, especially Graham, who felt a special affinity with her. After a few minutes he lost his reserve and was watching Nina, totally mesmerised.

'I like your chair,' she said, bending down and taking off the wheelchair brake. 'It's just like being a racing driver.' Gleefully she rushed him round the room making engine noises. 'VRMMM, VRMMM,' she shouted, whizzing him past the cooker and round the serving unit.

Graham's face whitened with astonishment and he made one of his strange, open-mouthed gasps of laughter.

'Again?' she asked, mouthing the word so he could understand. He nodded eagerly. 'Right, here we go!'

Watching them, Ruth saw her son's hands clasp and unclasp and his eyes crinkle up as he laughed. The wheel spun on his chair and made little rubber-tyre tracks on the kitchen floor as they raced round.

A minute later Nina collapsed into a chair, breathless. 'Enough,' she said, gasping and snapping the brake back on. 'More later.'

Graham nodded, satisfied.

'Will he be in this thing for life?' she asked Ruth.

'They say so.'

'Bit of a bore,' she said, leaning over and tickling him. Kate watched her solemnly from the back door. 'Never mind, old boy, you can still make money from a wheelchair. Look at Paul Getty.'

Ruth frowned. 'Paul Getty could walk, Nina.'

'Yeah, well, I know that ... but he didn't *have* to.'

After an exhausting day at the cinema, Ruth came home the following day about six and walked into the kitchen to get herself some milk from the fridge. Nina was sitting at the table, painting her nails. 'I think I've got a new flat.'

Ruth turned to face her. 'That was quick. Where is it?'

'Holland Park. Not the best area, you understand, but good enough until I can raise some money and buy a place.'

'Do you want a loan?' Ruth offered.

'No. I hate borrowing money, especially from you.'

'That's stupid. I've got it and I don't mind.'

Nina frowned. 'That is hardly the point. Besides, if you're having problems with your other half the last thing you need is me underfoot. Anyway, he's never liked me.'

'That's not true – '

'Yes, it is!' Nina insisted, screwing the top back on her nail varnish. 'He thinks I'm a bad influence on you. I can see it in his eyes. Oh, he's always polite, but it's that kind of creeping politeness you give to your bank manager just to keep life sweet.'

'He's been odd lately.'

'Maybe it's just that you're only noticing it now.'

'Nina!'

'Sorry.'

'I'm worried about him,' Ruth said, bending down and picking one of Graham's books off the floor. 'I try to talk to him about his drinking, but he just cuts me off. He won't discuss it, or see a doctor ... he just pretends it's something that happens now and again when he's under pressure.'

Nina thought of her father, thought of the sleazy, cramped rooms in Rock Street, the smell of boiled potatoes and the stack of beer bottles in the outside bin. 'All drunks are liars. My father used to come in reeling, and swear blind that he'd only had two pints. Pole-axed, he was, and he'd grin like a bloody organ-grinder's monkey and insist on his mother's eyes that he'd never do it again.' She sat down and began to straighten the stocking on her left leg. 'He made me sick. I always said I'd never get involved with a man who drank, and worse, one who lied about it.'

'I thought Ken would change,' Ruth said, smiling at her own naïvety, 'but he's getting worse. He drinks more, gets irritable with the kids, and ...' she paused and Nina looked up. She had seen the marks on Ruth's arms and was astute enough to realise that no one walked into doors as often as she claimed to.

'He what?'

Ruth stiffened in her seat and glanced away. 'He needs help. I've got to sort this out, or we're going to be in deep trouble. I can feel it, Nina, and I'm scared. I love him, but lately everything's seemed to be fading. You know how you have a photograph taken and at first all the colours are bright and clear?' She nodded. 'And then after a while they begin to darken and the outlines aren't clear any more? It's like that with us. I don't feel a part of him; and I don't feel that he's really interested in us any longer – either myself or the children – and I don't know what to do about it.'

The atmosphere changed. Although it was early afternoon, the kitchen seemed altered, becoming huge and impersonal – anybody's kitchen – yard on yard of bright tiling, all shined by Mrs Harvey, all kept clean and sterile. Like love, Nina thought suddenly.

'You'll have to get him to talk,' she said.

'Do you think it would help if I gave up my career?'

Nina shook her head violently. 'What the hell for? To sit at home and worry all day? To tie yourself to him and the kids?' She frowned. 'Ask yourself why you would be doing it – for what? They're growing up and Ken's got his own job and his own interests. If you ask me, he's got it too easy.'

'So why doesn't he see it that way?'

Nina's eyes were hard; she hated to see Ruth suffering, hated to see another impending disaster. She's been punished enough, she thought violently. Enough is enough. 'Why does anyone think they've been short-changed, Ruth? I don't know, I'm not a blasted clairvoyant and I can't read his mind.'

'I'm sorry,' Ruth said, withdrawing rapidly. 'All this must be very boring for you.'

Nina pulled a face at her. 'God! You sound so grim when you do that!' she said, tapping the back of Ruth's hand. Her nails were varnished deep pink. 'Listen, I'm not unsympathetic, but I see it differently. Ken has money and a great family –

OK, I know about Graham, but he's a smashing kid – and he's *still* hitting the bottle. Maybe you could do better for yourself.'

'Better than Ken?' Ruth asked, incredulous.

'Why not? He might be the kind of man for whom nothing is enough. He might resent his son's handicap; he might resent the time you spend with the twins; or with your career; I don't know, but if he can't be happy with everything he's got, then heaven help both of you.'

Unsettled, Ruth leant back in her chair. The world she had so assiduously built up seemed to be crumbling round her. 'Nina, could you stay on for a while? I need a friend at the moment.'

Smartly, Nina got to her feet. 'Not bloody likely! I'm not getting involved in anyone's marriage again – not even yours. You can come round to my flat any time, but I'm not staying. You have to sort this one out for yourself.'

'You always were a hard-hearted bitch,' Ruth said softly, smiling despite herself.

'You'll come through. You always do. But don't ask me to referee.' She winked suddenly. 'Charm the man, seduce him, there's lot of life in the old dog yet.'

Willing to do anything to save her marriage, Ruth greeted Ken warmly when he came home later that night. He was on edge, quick to criticise and trying to find any excuse to start an argument.

'What happened at work today?' Ruth asked, sitting on the arm of his chair and massaging the back of his neck with her hands.

'Not much.'

'Nothing exciting?'

He looked up at Ruth, bemused. 'I was at the paper, not the Playboy Club. What the hell exciting should have happened?'

His expression was hostile, all affection gone for a moment. Puzzled and afraid, she tried to humour him. 'I've been thinking – perhaps we should go on holiday for a break. Just the two of us.'

'I'm amazed that you could pull yourself away from your job and your children.'

'Our children, Ken.'

'Sorry, I forget that sometimes.'

Infuriated, Ruth jumped to her feet. 'Well, you shouldn't! They're yours as well as mine.'

He looked incensed, his heavy features reddening with anger.

'They don't need me! You're a mother and father to them – they don't require anyone else. You earn your own money, you run the house, you do all Graham's exercises – '

'Then why don't you, if it hurts you so much?' She faced him, her eyes cold. 'You've never been a proper father or husband.'

'My dear Ruth, you don't need a husband, you don't even need a man. You're a walking bloody machine, you run two jobs – not one. Oh no, that wouldn't be enough for Wonder Woman – and are constantly, grindingly besotted by your children, and we all know why – because you can't forget about the first one and you've spent the rest of your life trying to make up for it.'

'You bastard!' Ruth screamed. 'You always bring that up when you're trying to hurt me.'

He ignored her and continued. 'I'm surplus to your requirements now. I've done my bit. Not bad really, for a middle-aged stud, two kids. Not bad at all.' He poured himself a drink and added nastily, 'Well, you've got your kids now so don't expect anything else.'

'Our kids! Our kids!' she shouted, her hands clenched. 'You should be grateful, you never had any children before you married me.'

'Looking at my son maybe that was a good thing.'

The words savaged Ruth, the colour draining from her face as she struck out, hitting Ken on the side of his head with her fist. She caught him off balance and he reeled back and slumped into the chair clumsily. 'Go to hell, Ruth,' he called after her as she ran out.

Robert Floyd was sitting in his office five floors above the scrabbling streets. The room was large but sparsely furnished, its stark windows looking out to Regent's Park, a couple of abstract paintings and a modern glass-topped desk providing the only decoration. He sat behind his desk, thinking. At seventy-one, Robert Floyd was balding, thin to the point of frailness, and as mischievous as ever. 'How's Ruth?' he asked, his voice innocent.

Ken looked over to his father and shrugged. 'Things aren't going too well – '

'She's a good-looking woman, and smart. Someone was talking about her the other day, saying how she was making quite a name for herself. I bet Ted Morrison can't believe his luck.' He glanced over to his son and wondered about him. Not for the first time, Robert Floyd realised that Ken was a dolt. 'So, what is the matter?'

'She spends too much time at work or with the children. Especially Graham. I know he's handicapped, but . . .'

Poor Ken, his father thought slyly, he probably thinks it's a judgement on his virility. 'She's their mother, what do you expect?' Robert answered deftly. 'A good mother too, especially with the boy.' He thought of Graham, and how the deep brown eyes fixed on his. A strange child . . . a changeling, his old mother would have said.

Ken got to his feet, walked over to a concealed bar and poured himself a drink.

'That never helps!' his father snapped. 'You should stop drinking and count yourself lucky. You've had it cushy all your life, no money troubles, no worries – you should grow up. Christ, you've got it made, if only you knew it.'

Immune to his father's advice, Ken swallowed his drink and looked out of the window, remembering the conversation he had had with Ruth the previous night.

'Perhaps we should get some help,' she had said gently.

'You mean marriage guidance?'

'Well, why not? It could help.'

He had smiled sardonically. 'How very working-class of you, Ruth.'

'Well? What the hell are you going to do about it?' Robert Floyd asked, interrupting his son's thoughts.

'I'm going to take her on holiday,' Ken replied, putting down his glass and walking out.

It was not difficult for Ken to persuade Ruth to go away with him. She listened to his reasoning, coolly remote, cloistered off somewhere in that secret place he could never penetrate. She listened and agreed, also hoping that they could dredge up the old feelings from somewhere out of the mud of their bitterness. But even under the sunshine, well fed and tanned, they had little to say. People looked at them and admired them, rich and handsome, a lucky couple, they thought, not aware of the long pauses in conversations, the petty irritations, and the actions which, like the symptoms of an illness, heralded the death of love. When they walked together, they were moving apart; when they talked, they spoke in different dialects; and when they made love he was making love to any woman, and she to any man.

They returned even more divided, Ken walking in and hardly exchanging two words with the children. Ruth could have endured his moods, but the twins were becoming confused by the tension. At a loss to know what to do, Ruth challenged him. 'Ken, I know we haven't been getting on lately, but I still love you, and I'm quite prepared to give up my career if that would help.'

He got up from where he had been sitting and poured himself a large gin. What good would it do if she gave up work, he thought bitterly, she would just spend the rest of the time with the damn kids. He gulped at his drink, remembering her as she had been when they married; vulnerable, reliant on him . . .

'Ken?'

'Yes?' he said wearily.

'Don't you care about me any longer?'

'Ruth, this isn't going to work out, you know.'

Startled, she glanced over to him. 'What isn't?'

'Our marriage.'

'But we've only been married for seven years,' she said, panic in her voice.

He emptied the glass and refilled it, irritated by the look on her face. Why did she have to look so helpless now? All he'd ever wanted to do was to protect her and love her . . .

'We've been happy before, Ken, we can be again.'

'No ... it's gone.'

Ruth shook her head. No, this can't be happening to me, she thought, it can't. 'What's gone? Tell me, please!'

'We don't love each other any longer.'

Ruth walked over to her husband and laid her head on his shoulder. He didn't move. 'But that's not true, it isn't! I've just told you I still love you ...' She could feel his body tighten as he drew away. 'But you don't love me any more, do you?'

He said nothing and drained his glass a second time. Ruth knew that before long he'd be incoherent.

'Ken, is that it?'

Without replying, he turned away from her. I loved you once, I was obsessed by you, he thought. 'You're right, I don't love you any more.'

Ruth sat down heavily, her head swimming. The room was hot and heavy and on the table by the window was a bowl of early roses, their scent heady and provocative and somehow cruel.

'Why?'

'I don't know. You're a good-looking woman, with lots going for you – '

'Please, spare me the farewell speech!' she said suddenly, her pride making her cold. 'Do you give all your ex-ladies the same line?'

He shrugged. 'I can't be what you expect of me. I'm too old to change now. I thought we could make a go of it, but I was wrong, and I'm sorry. I need more time to myself.'

'When people marry they don't usually do it for solitude,' she said bitterly.

'As I said, I can't change.'

'Or won't!'

He turned round, the gin slopping in his glass. 'All right, I won't. Does that help?'

Against her better judgement, Ruth pleaded with him. 'Listen, Ken, we've had rough patches before and come through them. Let's have another go ... please.' Sick with anxiety, she was terrified of being alone with two children;

afraid of the loneliness and the guilt; and frightened of falling back into her past. 'Please, Ken, please.'

'I'm sorry, I can't go on any longer.'

Ruth said nothing and so he continued. 'You can keep the house, you'll need it for the children, and I'll make sure you have enough money – '

'I don't want it.'

He sipped at his drink. 'Don't be stupid, take what you can get and put it in trust for the twins.'

She nodded. This is not happening to me, she thought, this is only a dream, it's not real.

'Look after yourself,' he said, turning to go and then, changing his mind, he walked back to her. With long-forgotten tenderness he cupped her face in his hands, trying to see the girl he had fallen in love with; the girl in the cold night outside the restaurant who had needed him.

'Don't you love me at all?' she asked quietly.

His hands dropped to his side and he turned away.

'Where are you going, Ken?'

'Oh ... I've got somewhere.'

'I hope you'll be happy with her.'

He blinked, surprised that she had guessed, and stung by the sudden hatred in her voice.

'Who is it?' There was a flat silence. 'Ken, who is it?'

'Sheila Fielding.'

Ruth had an image of her – a brittle ghost of a woman dressed in a crushed red gown. The material had been like rose petals. 'She'll hurt you,' Ruth said coldly, moving away from him towards the window. 'She's not right for you, not right at all ... We're not finished, we could try – '

He flinched, wanting it to end, wanting to be away from her. 'No more. Goodbye, Ruth.'

Her old fight returning, she swung round. 'If you walk out of here now you forfeit the right to see the children again. Ever. If you go, I want maintenance for them until they're eighteen, money to cover all medical expenses for Graham for life, and an uncontested divorce.'

He smiled tightly. 'You were always a hard bargainer.'

'You don't know the half of it,' she replied sharply, waiting for him to smile and stay – to say it was a mistake, that he couldn't possibly leave. But he said nothing. Instead he finished his drink and walked out. It was twenty past eight – the Hour of the Angel.

Two minutes passed. Ruth stood in the hallway, the whole quiet, impressive house climbing up around her. Her head banged, her hands clenching and unclenching, her lips tightly clamped together like her mother's. I've lost, she thought, the panic threatening to choke her. I've lost. I shared this house, these children with a man I loved, and I lost him ... I've lost, she thought again, blindly turning round and round, her feet spinning on the hall floor.

Then she stopped. The panic faded, and in its place was cold, implacable fury. Steadily, she climbed the stairs, passing the nursery, passing the myriad rooms all sumptuously decorated, all inviting, all empty. Outside Ken's dressing-room she paused, and then opened the door and walked in. He had taken some of his clothes already. At least three suits were missing, but the others were still hanging there, row on immaculate row. His vanity suspended on a coat hanger.

It took her only a second to find the scissors and then she began, grabbing at his clothes, slashing them, ripping them, pulling them on to the floor as she tore at them, the sweat pouring off her, low cries of pain and anguish coming out of her in groans. Time after time she dug the scissors in, tugging, ripping, shredding, tearing at the clothes, lacerating the material until they lay in ribbons, only shreds of cloth, unrecognisable.

Panting, Ruth stopped and looked at what she had done, her breath coming in gasps, her hair falling over her face and sticking to her forehead. Then slowly, carefully, she rehung the ruined clothes on their hangers and closed the wardrobe doors without a sound.

Eleven

Disturbed by the heavy rainfall, Lilian could not sleep. She
turned over several times, but Jack was snoring softly, his
mouth open, one arm thrust over the edge of the bed. The rain
pelted down, striking the tin roof of the coal shed outside and
spitting against the bedroom window. Lilian opened her eyes
and looked up at the ceiling. The street lamp filtered through
the curtains and made vague outlines round the foot of the
bedhead, the large mahogany wardrobe, and the dressing table.
She looked at each of them, her mind going back to the time
before she was married, when she lived with Grandma Price
in Mapleshaw Road.

The rain continued unremittingly, as it seemed to do so
often in Oldham. Ruth always hated the rain, she thought,
remembering how she used to shelter under the tarpaulins in
the market stalls. Ruth, her daughter. She sighed and thought
of her as a baby, thin and sickly, crying in her pram, when she
used to dress her and put her out in the sunshine. But never
for long; within minutes the pram covers would be mottled
with soot from the chimneys, even the baby's face scattered
with black specks, like beauty spots in a Hogarth portrait.

She had really loved Ruth then, when she was dependent
on Lilian for everything. She had not been a good baby,
too fractious, but she had soon passed from babyhood into
childhood and altered. Lilian thought of her daughter –
remembered her as though she was actually seeing her – Ruth
reading her comics in the hat shop, silent and self-contained.
And then later, when she went to school, she would come by
afterwards to do her homework in the back room. Lilian sighed
and turned over, hearing Jack's breathing and the insistent
rain.

I should have loved her more, she thought suddenly, aware

of a surrogate anxiety; knowing by instinct that there was something deeply wrong. Ruth is my only child, I should have loved her more. I should love her more *now*. But how? Lilian thought back to the time when Laurel was born, and the guilt ached inside her – I should have taken that child and looked after her, she said to herself. I should have done what was right. The tears filled her eyes unexpectedly and she swallowed. I'm getting older now, she thought, I should be closer to Ruth, she's my only child. For an instant, all the suppressed feelings of so many years welled up in Lilian; all her actions crowded round her in that silent room, and as she lay there she could not stop thinking of her child and wondering . . .

At eleven o'clock that night, Ruth arrived on the doorstep of Nina's flat. The bell drilled out three times before she answered, her voice impatient. 'Yes!'

Ruth hesitated. 'Did I call at a vital moment?'

'You could say that,' Nina said, inviting Ruth in and going back into the bedroom. Voices came through the closed door, one angry, one soothing. Embarrassed, Ruth stood awkwardly in the lounge until Nina re-emerged, a dressing-gown wrapped tightly round her. 'What's the matter?'

'Ken's gone,' she said flatly, aware of the man in the next room.

'Fishing? Or for good?'

'This is no time to joke!'

'You're damn right,' Nina responded deftly. 'I've got someone here who thinks this is very unfunny.'

Ruth glanced towards the bedroom door and dropped her voice. 'Ken has walked out, bag and baggage, or maybe I should say – to a bag and baggage.'

'Huh?'

'He's gone to Sheila Fielding.'

'Stupid sod,' Nina said reflectively.

'I asked him for a divorce. It's over,' Ruth said, sitting down on the settee; her hair was messy and most of her make-up had worn off. 'I haven't told the children or my parents.'

'Your mother's going to love this. Mind you, she's probably

guessed – she can sniff out trouble like a pig finds truffles.'

Ruth ignored the remark. 'Should I go through with the divorce?'

Nina was prevented from replying by the emergence of a thick-set, middle-aged man, rapidly doing up the buttons on his waistcoat. He glanced at Ruth and then at Nina. 'I'll phone,' he said simply, letting himself out.

'I'm so sorry,' Ruth said, glancing up to see Nina smiling broadly.

'This is incredible! It's just like one of those Brian Rix farces. Enter the distraught female, and exit stout party, half dressed ... Oh God, let's have a drink,' she said, pouring them both a generous measure, the sound of the bottle on the glasses loud and intrusive. The room was getting warmer, a strange lethargy settling on Ruth.

'Ken's gone.'

'I know. You said.'

Ruth nodded, exhaustion dragging on her limbs. Physically and mentally spent, she leant back and sipped her drink. 'I don't know how to cope, Nina.'

'The same way you did when you first came down to London.'

'But I was on my own then. I didn't have the children.'

'Then count your blessings,' she said sharply, leaning forward in her seat. 'You do have children now, a big house with no money troubles, and a job. OK, so your life's not perfect. So you've no fella? So what? You will have, in time, you'll find another man – '

'I don't want another man,' Ruth said woodenly. God, she thought, why am I so tired? I've never felt so tired before.

'Does that mean you don't ever want another man, or that you want Ken back?'

'I don't want him back, ever! He's hurt me for the last time ... and I don't want another man either.'

'So you say.'

'So I mean!' Ruth snapped back, dragging herself upright in the chair. Nina watched her and could see her colour change; could see the fight coming back into her.

'Yeah, well, we'll see.'

'Listen, Nina, I've lost two men and a child. I loved Derek and he was killed; I had Laurel adopted; and now Ken's left me ... I can't take any more!' Ruth said sharply, her face reddening, her eyes fierce. 'I can't.'

Instead of offering sympathy, Nina was mercilessly cruel. 'You want to look ahead, not back. Sure you've lost Derek and Ken, although he was a dead loss anyway, but you've got to stop harping on about Laurel.'

'SHE WAS MY CHILD!' Ruth shouted, outraged, and galvanised into retaliation. How dare she, she thought, how dare she tell me what I should think and do?

'So what if she was your child?' Nina said coldly, getting to her feet and standing over Ruth. 'She's growing up just fine without you. You've got two other kids; you should count yourself lucky and stop moaning on about the one that got away.'

Ruth got up and faced her, her hands clenched into fists, her voice dark with fury. 'You wouldn't say that if you'd had any kids.'

'Oh, for Christ's sake! What makes you think you're the only woman who's ever been pregnant? I got rid of two babies I didn't want – and I don't regret it.'

'You did what?'

'Don't give me the big shocked act, Ruth! I don't want children because I'd be a useless mother. I've been at the receiving end of a woman who didn't love her kids, and who didn't give a damn for them. My parents couldn't have cared less for me if they'd found me in a packet of Cornflakes! I wouldn't want any child of mine to feel that way.'

'But how could you do it?' Ruth continued. 'Don't you ever feel guilty?'

Nina put her hands on her hips. 'Yes, sometimes,' she replied icily. 'Sometimes I look back and wonder whether I've deprived the world of an infant prodigy, another Beethoven or Noël Coward. Yes, I feel guilty! But I'd have felt a damn sight worse having a child I didn't want, without a father or a stable home to bring it up in.'

'You could have got married.'

'To be like you? To live to suit other people? Why should I? No! I'm all right as I am.'

'Well, I'm not!' Ruth said heatedly.

'So what are you going to do about it?'

The words bounced around the room. What *am* I going to do about it, Ruth thought, remembering Laurel, remembering her own slide out of reality, ducking under the protection of sickness and confusion . . . No, she thought, not this time. This time I keep a hold of myself for the children. I'm not prepared to lose, she thought violently. Damn them all! I won't lose!

'I'm going to get a divorce, then I'll look after the children and carry on with my career,' she said coolly.

Nina saw her rally, saw the vulnerability fade under a veneer of complete composure. Mesmerised, she saw Ruth physically pull herself up, shoulders back, her eyes calm. She watched and admired her. 'Well, you better get on with it then.'

'Besides, I can't *make* Ken stay with me. He'd go another time, or drink himself stupid. But he'd go nevertheless and I'd have to face this ten years from now when I wouldn't be able to start again.' She paused; the future didn't seem so frightening now that she had made up her mind. 'But I still love him.'

Nina's heart shifted. 'It fades, like a sun-tan.'

Ruth smiled grimly. 'You always were an unfeeling bitch.'

'And you were always so eager to please, so eager to say the right thing and to do the right thing.'

Ruth bristled. 'That's not true. I wasn't!'

'Yes, you were. You went to work for your mother just because they made you feel so bad you couldn't refuse. Then you married Derek to get away and felt guilty when he was killed, and you've never forgiven yourself for Laurel. I think that you believe all this is some sort of punishment – '

'Oh, I don't punish myself enough, Nina. I'm a fake, really,' she said, her voice deadly. 'I always wanted everyone to like me, so I was no trouble, made no noise, didn't get under their feet . . .' she moved away, resentment pouring out of her. ' "Be a good girl, Ruth," my mother said . . . Oh, I was always a good girl! Good girl for Mother, good girl for Father, good girl for Derek!' She jerked up her head. 'And why? If I'm honest for once in my bloody life I did it because I wanted them all to love me and take care of me. First my mother made all my decisions, then my father, then Derek ... I never made a decision for myself. Even when I came to London, George Armani or you were there to pull me out.' She stopped, self-hate in her voice. 'And then I married Ken. Why?'

Nina shook her head, unable to answer.

'I'll tell you why – I married Ken because he was rich and because *he would take care of me.*' Ruth stopped and pushed her hair back from her forehead, her eyes vivid and cold. 'Well, it stops here. From now on, I take control of my life and my children's. I'll never lean on anyone again.' She paused and looked directly into Nina's eyes. 'I can get by on my own – without anybody's help and without Ken.'

'Oh, stuff him!' Nina responded brightly. 'He was a right berk.'

Ruth woke the following day with a dull growl of unease in her stomach, remembering that Ken had gone and knowing she was on her own. For several minutes she lay looking up at the ceiling and was just about to rise when Kate rushed in, her little chubby arms thumping on the bedclothes until Ruth pretended to be annoyed and grabbed hold of her. She shrieked with pleasure, and when she was quiet again asked, 'Where's Daddy?'

Ruth touched her hair with her lips. 'He's gone ... he's not coming back, Kate. It's just you and me and Graham, and Mrs Corley, of course.'

It was a harsh way to tell her but Ruth did not want her to think he was going to return. She had warned Ken that if he left them he wouldn't see them again. And she meant it.

'Why did he go?'

'He had to,' Ruth said clumsily, not realising that the explanation wasn't enough for a seven-year-old. 'Because ... he didn't love me any more.'

She looked startled, her grey eyes tearful. 'Oh, Mummy!' she said, flinging herself into Ruth's arms and crying. 'I love you,' she murmured between sobs, '... and Graham does.'

Silently Ruth clung to her.

Mrs Corley took the news calmly. She listened and readjusted her glasses, and then began to get Kate ready for school. No judgements were passed and she offered no advice. When Ruth finished, she straightened her apron and began to fold some sheets.

'Well, Mrs Floyd, you know I'll do everything to help you and the children.' She smiled, instinctively kind. 'Graham's ready to do his exercises now ... if you feel up to it.'

Gratefully, Ruth nodded and followed her into the playroom where her son's exercise table stood. Graham was already there, sitting in his wheelchair, watching them. Having kept the news of Ken's departure from him, Ruth was surprised by the expression on his face. Bending down, she looked into his eyes, her father's eyes. 'You can't hear, Graham, but you understand more than anyone, don't you?'

Slowly, the child smiled.

Two weeks after Ken had left, Ruth informed her solicitor, Harold Ibrahim, that she wanted a speedy divorce on grounds of adultery, and that Ken no longer had any access to the children. He listened, stroked his patent leather hair with his small hands and smiled. 'My dear Mrs Floyd, I do think that possibly you are being a little hasty – '

'I want a divorce.'

Taking a deep breath he fiddled with the diamond ring on his little finger. There was a clock on his desk and a window which looked out into a courtyard. 'Of course, of course,' he said, using the same tone of voice that Ruth used for her mother, 'but this business of forbidding him to see his children – '

'He knew the terms when he walked out. He accepted them. He can write for news of them, or phone, but he's not to see them. I told him quite emphatically what I wanted from him ... and what I didn't.'

Harold Ibrahim blinked and looked at the woman in front

of him. She had always seemed so pliable before, he thought, even though she was doing very well in business. A woman with great style, someone had said. 'Your husband may contest it,' he continued evenly.

Ruth shook her head. 'No, Mr Ibrahim, he won't. Ken didn't want the responsibility of his children or his wife. He wanted to be a free agent.'

Harold Ibrahim nodded; the words sounded familiar – bitterness and divorce made easy allies. 'Very well, if that's what you want. I'll take on the case for you, Mrs Floyd, and after I've contacted Mr Floyd's solicitors ...' he wiped his palms on his hair again, '... I'll be in touch.'

So the divorce mechanism sprang into life like a sleeping lion nudged with a cattle prod. Within weeks Harold Ibrahim settled terms with Ken's solicitors, telling Ruth that the hearing would take place after the New Year. She heard the news and felt only relief; having at last taken responsibility for her own life, Ruth was grimly determined to live it her way.

At work, she told Ted Morrison what had happened and he was supportive and, thankfully, incurious. Geoffrey Lynes was another matter. He didn't exactly gloat, but his manner veered from compassion to familiarity all too readily. Pride made Ruth imply that she had thrown Ken out, but it became obvious to her that they all knew he had run off with someone else. For Ruth, the humiliation was almost as hard to bear as the pity.

'It's strange, isn't it, the way life turns out?' Geoffrey Lynes said one morning, his thin frame leaning against the door of the auditorium at Piccadilly.

'Really, Geoffrey,' Ruth answered, her voice steady, 'what do you mean?'

He scratched idly under his chin. There was a gap between his neck and his shirt which emphasised the weight he'd lost.

'Well, you began here, and now you're back full time, just like the old days.' He continued to scratch. 'Life's just odd, that's all.'

Knowing that she should have thought of some rejoinder, Ruth was left tongue-tied and outraged, as he walked off.

As each day passed Ruth spent more time at work, returning only when the children came in from school and she would play with them. But when they'd gone to bed the evenings seemed so lengthy that she found herself walking aimlessly around, switching the television on and off, or working on documents she had brought home. She did see Nina every few days, but knew it was unfair to expect anyone to listen to an eternal litany of moans, and Inger, irritatingly complacent now that her erring husband had returned, was little comfort. So, as the business at the cinema increased, Ruth altered her routine, staying with the children until bedtime and then getting the car out, directing it towards Piccadilly or Knightsbridge, and going back to work.

The company were delighted by Ruth's industry, offering her as much help as she needed, and laying on extra staff for the numerous functions, all of which Ruth supervised and attended, unescorted. She didn't have to be. There were always men attracted to her, but Ruth refused to get involved, keeping herself aloof – a demeanor some found intriguing.

As time progressed, Ruth's secretary, Bill Pascoe, became a splendid aide. Being of uncertain sex and the possessor of an evil tongue, he vetted everyone and tipped her off long before Ruth would have got the victim's measure. He appeared to know everyone in London, and everyone they had slept with, fought with, and lent money to. 'Watch this speaker tonight, Mrs Floyd ...' he said, pushing a drawer shut in the filing cabinet, and turning his small, tight body towards her. 'He was drilled out of one firm of solicitors for sharp practice, and believe me, that takes some doing.'

'Thanks, Bill, I'll watch him.'

'Oh, and you know that woman you interviewed to join the catering staff?' She nodded. 'Worked at the London Croft House and got fired for stealing.' He straightened his jacket. 'Just tipping you off...'

'I'm grateful to you. Many thanks.'

He looked rewarded by the compliment and left, although as Ruth watched him go, she wondered how loyal he was and what he had said about the situation ... 'You know that Mrs Floyd? Well ... her husband ran off, leaving her with two kids, one of whom is crippled.'

Wincing at the thought, Ruth slammed some papers down on her desk, turned off the light and went home.

The only person who still disrupted Ruth's home life was Mrs Harvey. Having always distrusted her, Ruth knew that she still resented Joanie's departure, and, although she could not prove it, Ruth was certain she still kept in touch with her original employer. Without being outwardly rude, Mrs Harvey felt no kindness for Ruth, and made her feelings apparent by a form of controlled animosity.

'I've done a list for you, Mrs Floyd,' she said crisply, her voice precise and quick as she pushed the paper across the hall table.

'That looks fine, thank you,' Ruth replied, watching as the woman walked away.

'I hate her,' Kate said suddenly.

'Kate! You mustn't say things like that,' Ruth replied quickly, aware of her own animosity towards the woman. 'Anyway, what time is your friend coming?'

'Four,' Kate replied, glancing over to the clock in the hall. 'Naomi's mother has a red car,' she continued happily, 'and a dog like – '

The doorbell interrupted her and she rushed over to answer it, greeting her small friend like a seasoned hostess. Amused, Ruth watched her as she showed Naomi to her seat at the table and chatted on easily.

'Where's Graham, Mum?'

Ruth was carrying some cake to the table and stopped beside their guest. 'I thought you might like to have tea with your friend on your own. I've made us something to eat in the other room.'

Kate's expression was one of genuine surprise. 'But we want

you to eat with us – both of you.' Ruth glanced at the little girl beside her. Naomi appeared to be totally unconcerned. Kate continued. 'I've told her all about Graham. She wants to meet him, don't you?' she asked the child, defying her to say no.

The girl nodded obediently.

'Please bring him, Mummy ... please.'

Graham was in the lounge playing with some Plasticine when Ruth walked in, sat down, and forced him to lip-read her words. 'Kate wants us to eat with her and her friend, Naomi,' she said, waiting until she was sure he understood. When he nodded, she continued. 'Is that all right?' He nodded again and she pushed him through to the kitchen.

Dressed in a navy and red jumper, his legs covered, Graham stared at Naomi. His thick, wavy, dark hair had fallen forward into his eyes while he'd been working and his hands were stained with red dye.

Smoothing his jumper, Ruth explained carefully. 'Graham is deaf, so you have to look at him and speak clearly then he can read your lips. He's only just learnt how to lip-read, so you must speak slowly.'

Kate glanced at her friend. The girl was peculiarly quiet.

'Clever, isn't it?' she said, beaming. 'I bet you've never met anyone before who can *read* what you say.'

The child remained dumb. Kate persevered. 'He's my twin, you know, and he makes smashing monsters with that Plasticine stuff.' She glanced over to her brother and smiled. Warmly, Graham responded. 'And he goes to this special place ... he can do sign language ... I can do it too, and Mummy, but Graham...'

On and on she continued, extolling Graham's virtues, and the more unresponsive the girl became, the more she talked. Sensing her frustration, Ruth watched as her little face reddened and she began to eat, ignoring Naomi and looking over to her brother as though she was seeing someone she hardly knew. Eventually, her school-friend responded, although she avoided any reference to Graham and even managed to keep her back to him. Kate was non-committal and unusually sulky, and when Naomi's mother came to collect her it was all Ruth could do to force Kate to wave goodbye at the door.

'What's the matter?' she asked when they'd gone.

'She didn't like Graham.'

'Yes she did, Kate. She was just embarrassed, that's all.'

With a look of complete astonishment, Kate looked up at her mother. 'Why?'

It was a good question, but what was the answer? Ruth thought. Perhaps it was because people are cruel and thoughtless and hurt other people; because the world will maim you if it can.

'Because people don't know how to behave when they come across someone who's different. They're frightened ... they don't understand.'

Kate looked towards the kitchen. The door was open and she could see Graham sitting calmly in his wheelchair, waiting. Ruth turned and followed her gaze, seeing her own son, crippled and bound to a chair, and realised what her daughter was thinking.

'Oh, Mummy ...' Kate said simply, and burst into tears.

Grieving with her, Ruth whispered, 'Listen, we love him and that's enough. We don't need anyone else, do we?'

Kate sniffed and shook her head.

'That's right, you mustn't be upset. We don't need anyone. Just you, me and Graham – and Mrs Corley. We'll show them all, won't we? Just us.'

As she spoke, Ruth realised the truth of her words. Forced into a long-overdue maturity, she welcomed other people's reliance on her, finally understanding that her years of dependency had been only a prelude to her private coming of age. With new insight, Ruth looked around her, saw the carpets, curtains, paintings, china – saw everything valuable and precious, everything worlds away from Carrington Street. There was nothing shabby here; no clothes-horse, no soot on the washing, no slap of the evening paper on a tile floor, nothing to indicate Ruth's beginnings.

On her own, Ruth moved around the empty hall, and then, laughing, her arms stretched out beside her, she lifted the bright oval of her face to the sunlight falling from the window above.

*

'Perhaps she should have tried harder,' Lilian said, folding up the sandwich papers and tucking them into the side of her bag. The train lurched uncomfortably out of Manchester, the buildings watching its staggering exit out to the countryside.

'I don't know how you can judge ... not knowing the circumstances.'

Lilian glanced over to her husband. He looks the same as ever, she thought. I've aged, and he stays permanently forty. She sniffed and looked at her hands thoughtfully; small, square hands with short nails. A give-away to anyone, she decided, folding them on top of her bag.

'I don't have to know the circumstances, Jack, I just know that this is her second marriage and it hasn't worked out – '

'Derek died! That was hardly Ruth's fault. If he hadn't been killed they would still be married.'

'You think so?' Lilian asked icily.

With a gesture of frank impatience, Jack Gordon turned to face his wife. Dressed in a navy suit and coat, she looked well groomed and smart and still quite young – if it hadn't been for the sour way her mouth set when she was angry. It was set now in a line, her eyes burning with criticism.

'Why do you have to say things like that?' he asked wearily.

'Things like what? I never *said* anything, I just implied that – '

'Ruth wouldn't still be married to Derek, if he'd lived.'

'Well, would she?' Lilian asked him, exasperated, and dropped her voice so that the other people in the carriage could not hear her. 'Think about it, Jack, think about where she is now. That huge house, money, staff – she was even in the London paper the other week, something about a big important politician giving a talk in the cinema. There was a photograph too, I showed you.' She raised her eyebrows. 'Now, you tell me, do you think Oldham would have been enough for her?'

Jack may have been mistaken, but he was sure that under the sharp bite of the words, there was some real admiration. 'She loved Derek,' he replied stubbornly.

The train shuddered to a halt. In the silent carriage, Lilian dropped her voice to a whisper. 'I'm not saying that she didn't love him – only that she's a very ambitious girl and she knows what she wants.'

'Now, hang on – '

Lilian interrupted her husband impatiently. 'No, you hang on! I know that girl. She's a good girl in some ways, but she's always wanted to get on. She did when she was a child, and she's never changed. You can't blame her, she's clever and she wants all she can get from the world – even if it costs her her marriage.' Lilian glanced out of the window, a thin sun trickled along the glass and struck the side of her face. 'No one can blame her really for wanting to move on. Love's not everything, after all.'

The words danced in Jack's head and skipped on his nerves. She's talking about herself, he thought dully, she's talking about us.

All the time Ruth's parents stayed with her, Lilian made no reference to the impending divorce and left the comforting to Ruth's father.

'You've not had much luck, flower, have you?' he asked, when Lilian was in the garden with the twins, Graham bundled up against the cold and Kate running over the lawn and flailing her arms around her like the sails of a windmill.

'The marriage was no good any longer, Dad. Ken was drinking too much and we were making the kids unhappy with all the arguments ... besides, he was seeing another woman.'

Her father looked away, embarrassed. 'I'm sorry.'

'I know. So was I, for a time,' Ruth said, straightening up in her seat and watching Graham through the window. 'But I've got the kids, Dad, and that's the important thing. I couldn't risk their happiness. I owe them that.'

'But they're Ken's children as well.'

She shook her head. 'No, not any more. He doesn't feel the same tie to them as I do.' She glanced over to her father. 'You know what I mean, Dad ... after Laurel.' He nodded and lit his pipe. The smoke clogged up the atmosphere in seconds.

'He was a stupid man to leave you,' Jack said, pointing with his pipe towards the garden. 'Still, you've got me and your mother if you need help.'

'I know ... I know.'

But if Ruth's father found it easy to come to terms with the divorce, it alienated her mother. During the days which followed, Ruth looked up several times and caught Lilian watching her. Embarrassed, she would smile quickly, but Ruth became uncomfortable, wondering if her mother was remembering Derek's death, the days after Laurel's birth, and the trauma which estranged them for years. Ruth did not know for certain, but when they left a few days later she was overwhelmingly relieved.

It was the beginning of a period of savagely cold weather when late January frosts bit into the windows and laced the pathway up to the house. On one bitterly cold evening, Ruth was talking to Kate when Graham interrupted, making his rough sounds which meant he wanted to talk. Deftly he moved his hands and described his psychotherapist, a young woman called Bella, who had been assigned to him.

'She's funny ... and told me about her brother in the army ...' He paused to think, and then remembered the sign he wanted, 'She's got a dog which won a prize at a show ...'

Totally immersed in his story he was unaware that Ruth was watching him and had noticed a difference in his actions. Not wanting to be too hopeful she regarded him for a long moment and then turned away, glancing back immediately to see if it was just an effect of the light; but it wasn't – Graham was moving his leg. It was hardly noticeable, but there *was* a slight movement. Ruth could see the rug judder and felt her heart thump in her chest. After Graham had finished his story she moved out into the corridor, and leant against the banister heavily. He's not crippled, she thought ... I knew it, I always knew it. Her breath came unevenly, her excitement making her dial Nina's number wrongly.

And then, as though someone had turned off a light, her euphoria vanished and she suddenly missed Ken; missed being

216

able to tell Graham's father the news; missed saying, 'Look, we knew he'd make progress,' and missed having someone there who would put their arms around her and be happy with her. For an instant Ruth was so deflated that she could hardly make the call and only Kate's laughter upstairs forced her to dial the number again.

'Graham's moving his leg!' she said without preamble.

Nina gave a great whoop of delight. 'Well, kiss that boy for me, and tell him that his aunt thinks he's a champion.'

Grinning wildly, Ruth glanced up the stairs. 'God, it's marvellous – do you think he'll ever be able to walk?'

'How do I know? But I don't see why not, two years ago everyone was saying he would never be able to use his hands properly, and they were wrong then.'

'If you could see him – '

'Do you want me to come over?'

'Aren't you seeing the Greek?'

Nina laughed shortly. 'He went back to the wife about the same time the show's run ended and I asked him for a loan.' She changed the subject deftly. 'Well, do you want me round, or not?'

'Yes, yes! Get a taxi. I'll treat you.'

She arrived twenty minutes later, dressed in a very long double-breasted black coat with a large, fox-fur hat.

'My God,' Ruth said drily, 'the Russians have landed.'

Grimacing, Nina walked in. 'Don't make cheap remarks, Ruth, this was Zorba's parting gift.' She pulled off the hat and threw the coat on to the hall table. 'OK, where is this miracle child of yours?'

As she opened the nursery door, Graham swivelled round clumsily in his chair to face her, smiling broadly. 'Hi,' he said simply, although the word was barely recognisable.

'Hi, yourself,' Nina responded, kneeling down in front of him, Graham watching her mouth carefully as she talked.

In the half-light his eyes looked darker than usual and there was an unusual calmness about him. After a few moments, Nina asked him to make a model for her, knowing that as he concentrated on the task she could scrutinise him for any sign of movement. Watching both of them eagerly, Ruth stood by the fire, her hands clenched. Steadily, Graham moulded the Plasticine whilst Nina waited, smiling every time he looked up towards her. His legs remained immobile – not a flicker of movement.

'He did move!' Ruth said, her voice almost tearful with frustration. 'I saw it! I did!'

Nina made a low sighing noise. 'Sure – maybe it was a one-off, maybe he'll do it again tomorrow.'

Overwrought, Ruth's anger flared suddenly. 'You don't believe me, do you?'

'Of course I believe you,' she said quietly, glancing back to Graham and adding, 'because he's moving now.'

They both froze and watched as Ruth's son shifted his position in the wheelchair and his left foot twitched. Ruth leapt forwards and snatched the rug off his legs. Graham looked up at her, startled.

'Graham – try and move your leg.' He appeared not to understand. 'Graham – move your leg! Do it!' Ruth repeated, more sharply. Nina watched her, surprised by the tone of her voice.

He tried to move, and nothing happened. Quickly, Ruth pushed up the left leg of his trousers and massaged his calf muscle. Under her fingers, she could feel it respond and tighten.

'Graham – try to move your leg!' she insisted.

A curious mixture of willingness and defiance flickered in his eyes, an expression Ruth hadn't seen before. She jerked his leg sharply, making Nina jump forward and clutch hold of her arm.

'Careful with him!'

Impatiently, Ruth shook off her hand, ignoring her, her hair falling forward over her face, her eyes almost yellow in the firelight. 'Graham! Move your leg!'

Resolutely he tried to move. Again, Ruth felt the muscle flicker and caught hold of her son's chin, pushing his head back and looking into his face. 'I love you, damn you! I love you, and you *must* move your leg.'

Disturbed by the tension, Nina tried to intervene. 'Now, just a minute –'

Ruth swung round on her. 'No! Don't tell me what to do – don't you dare! This is my child.'

Stung, Nina moved back. The firelight played on the walls around them, throwing huge shadow images of Ruth bending over the hunched body of her son, his wheelchair massive against the nursery wall.

'Look at me and watch what I say,' Ruth continued, her eyes never leaving her son's face. 'Move – your – leg.' The muscle tensed and relaxed, without movement. Ruth watched. Again, he tried and again there was no perceptible movement. Transfixed by the scene in front of her, Nina watched them both, seeing Ruth as she bullied her son, willing him, pouring every ounce of her own strength into him. 'Come on, come on! Graham, you can do it!'

On the third attempt, his face white with effort, his left foot jerked.

'Oh God!' Ruth said, crying, and grabbing hold of her child, and pulling him to her. 'I love you, Graham. I love you.'

Unaware of Nina's unblinking scrutiny, Graham smiled at his mother and nodded, the palms of his small hands sticky with exertion.

The phone rang minutes afterwards, Ruth leaving Nina with the children and running to answer it.

'How are you all?' asked Robert Floyd, who had been in frequent touch since Ken's hasty departure. Ruth did not know whether he was spying for his son or simply curious, but, as the children's grandfather, she welcomed him.

'Graham's just moved his left leg.'

'Wonderful! Will he be able to walk?' he asked, interest apparent in the thin voice. Over the phone, Robert Floyd sounded his age.

'I don't know. It's too soon to say.'

'But he might?'

'Yes, he might,' Ruth agreed. 'Ken should have been here to see this.'

'He's a fool,' his father said. 'I told him not to leave you, but he wouldn't listen. Never would, even as a child. Bloody idiot.'

For an instant Ruth was tempted to ask where he was, but resisted. 'I'll see Dr Throop tomorrow at the clinic,' she continued. 'Maybe he'll be able to tell us some more. I'll ring you tomorrow night, if you want.'

Robert Floyd smiled down the phone. 'Do that, Ruth,' he said, putting down the phone in his office where he stayed late thinking about the paper he had established. What a waste of time, he thought, smiling grimly, just for Joan and Ken; she was in America somewhere and he was in bed with Sheila Fielding. He got to his feet and poured himself a drink, wondering how Ruth's children would turn out. He liked Kate, thought her amusing, but Graham was another matter – he had seen that look on other people's faces, a look of mixed emotions, frustration and jealousy. It was a look Robert Floyd had encountered many times in his life, and it made him wonder.

The phone rang and interrupted his thoughts. 'Dad?'

The old man grinned mischievously. 'Ken! How are you?'

'Fine,' he replied. 'Have you heard anything from Ruth?'

There was only the faintest pause before he answered, 'Not a word, Ken. Not a word.'

After Ruth put the phone down, she turned to see Nina watching her. 'Who was that?'

'Ken's father.'

Nina raised her eyebrows. 'Is he still in touch?'

'He calls about three times a week to see if we're all right,' Ruth answered, walking downstairs with Nina following her. 'I can never quite make him out. He's a creepy kind of man, and I wonder if he's feeding the information to his son ... but he still bothers to phone, which is more than Ken does.'

They walked through into the lounge where Mrs Harvey had lit a fire and turned on the lights. Above the mantelpiece a large Empire-style mirror reflected the two women.

'When's the divorce?' Nina asked, taking the drink Ruth offered her.

'Next month. The hearing's on the 28th, and the decree absolute follows six weeks later.'

'Any regrets?'

Ruth turned away and drew the curtains. They felt cold in her hands and the night was frosty, with a high moon.

'Some ... but not many,' she said, sitting down and curling her legs under her. Her mind was on Graham, not Ken. He had moved his legs ... he was going to walk ... 'I've had enough of men,' she said abruptly.

'Likewise.'

Ruth smiled. 'Don't tell me you're mending your ways – sticking to the paths of righteousness and clean living.'

'No,' she said. 'I'm just off men, that's all.'

Ruth laughed loudly, the sound rich and heavy, nuzzling into the furnishings of the sumptuous room. She's changing, Nina thought, she's coming into her own at last.

'How long are you off men?'

'Oh, until the next one comes along, I suppose,' Nina replied, grinning wickedly. 'I never had much will-power, you know.'

'You were wise not to marry.'

She shrugged and kicked off her shoes. 'Really? I could have done with some maintenance now and again. But I can't stand the thought of being stuck with one man and not able to pick and choose.'

Ruth raised her eyebrows. 'That's a man's way of thinking.'

'Maybe ... I've been lucky because I can go where I like and with whom I like. OK, so I don't have any stability and I get dumped sometimes, but it suits me.'

'Do you ever see Sam?' Ruth asked.

'No, not since Inger pulled that "I'll have you back, Sam, warts and all" trick.' She smiled archly. 'I know what I did was wrong, but I thought I loved him at the time – I really did.'

'We are a couple of dopes,' Ruth said, smiling at her. 'We can't find one decent man between the two of us! All those girls we were at school with weren't any better looking or any more intelligent, and they're all married and settled. What the hell is the matter with us?'

Nina drained her glass and got up to refill it. 'Search me. I'll tell you, I don't think there are any real men around any more.'

'They're all married or divorced,' Ruth added.

'Or queer.'

'Yes, or queer,' she agreed. 'I'm not so sure I'd mind that any longer.'

'You would if he started wearing your frocks,' Nina added drily.

Twelve

The divorce was granted that spring, leaving Ruth still a young woman with a large house and two children to take care of. She never saw Ken after the night he left and he never wrote or contacted her by phone, not even to enquire about the children. Apparently he had cut his losses and run, making a break for it with Sheila Fielding. The news passed like a bush fire through London, many people taking great pleasure in the failure of the marriage, no doubt passing the good news to Joanie, sulking in America. But Ruth heard nothing of this. Drawing back into her work and her children, she steered clear of wedding invitations and dinner parties where she would have to attend alone, and became something of an enigma.

There were more important matters to concern her. After Graham's incredible progress the clinic altered his exercise routine to encourage his muscles to develop. Finding them more painful, Graham became hard to cope with, his temper snapping easily. Kate controlled him with a mixture of patience and good-natured bullying, and because of the tie between the two children, he usually quietened and listened to her. But at seven he was no longer a baby, and as his strength increased, daily battles took place on the exercise table.

'Listen, I know he's difficult,' Ruth said evenly, 'but punishing him might not be the answer – '

Mrs Corley interrupted her. 'I don't want to punish him all the time, but I must control him.' She stood up to Ruth adamantly. 'He's a very bright child, and he plays me up sometimes.'

Ruth considered her words and thought of Graham, seeing him through Mrs Corley's eyes. Yes, it did seem possible that he would manipulate her, he was clever enough for that. She glanced back to the woman standing in front of her, knowing that her answer would decide if Mrs Corley was going to stay with them, or leave.

'You are absolutely right,' she began carefully. 'I know they are very firm at the clinic,' the words stuck in her throat, '. . . perhaps we should begin to change our attitude at home.' Mrs Corley relaxed and smiled warmly at Ruth, her faith restored. 'You do as you think fit, I have every confidence in you.'

The clinic also decided that some firm action was called upon to stop Graham from developing into a violent, uncontrollable child, and worked out a series of lessons for him which were demanding and forced him to use his quick brain. By making him work hard mentally they reasoned that he would become less inclined to be physically disruptive. The method frequently worked, but on occasions Graham could be exceedingly violent and dumbly uncommunicative. He had inherited characteristics from both of his parents; from Ruth, charm and a quick brain; from Ken, impatience and a violent nature.

After one particular battle, Ruth sat down, exhausted, in front of her son. He was silent, his hands on his lap, his head down. There was a small mark on his bottom lip where he had bitten it and several scratches on the backs of his arms.

'What's the problem?' she asked him, lifting up his head so that he could read her lips. There was no response. 'Graham, you are my child and I love you. You must tell me what is worrying you. Tell me.' Again, he made no effort to explain. 'Aren't you happy at the clinic? Aren't you happy here with us?' Slowly he shook his head. 'You're *not* happy?' Ruth asked quickly. He shook his head violently. Seeing his impatience, Ruth put up her hands and stopped him, holding his head still. 'Graham, tell me what's worrying you.'

He hesitated, defiance blazing out of his dark eyes. Then, slowly and agonisingly, he explained in sign language. He felt wrong, he said, using the sign emphatically so that there was no doubt about his feelings. With a hollow feeling in her stomach, Ruth started to speak, but he interrupted her, saying that he felt stupid, and that all the other children at the clinic were silly and didn't like him.

'But you're not stupid, Graham, you are very, very clever – all the doctors tell me that.'

He signed to Ruth that he wanted to talk, touching his lips with the ends of his fingers. Her heart shifted with pity.

'You can learn to do that, if you really want to. I'll help you. You know I will. Just tell me what will make you happy.' Suddenly angry, he banged his hands down on the arms of his chair. Ruth jumped back, watching as he signed to her. Apparently when he tried to talk, the children who weren't deaf laughed at him.

'Oh, Graham,' Ruth said, taking his hands in hers. 'That just means they're even more stupid than you thought. I'll help you to talk properly and then no one will laugh at you any more.'

He looked at her and nodded. His face was serious.

'But you have to do something for me as well,' Ruth said slowly. 'You have to be patient and not lose your temper ... I know it's difficult, but you'll have to try. Will you do that for me?' He nodded, his dark hair falling over his forehead. 'It's a hard old world, isn't it, Graham?'

A slow look of understanding came into his eyes; the look he had had since he was a baby; the look only they understood.

'She'll go mad when she hears,' Geoffrey Lynes said, pacing round the boardroom in Piccadilly. 'She thinks that new cinema is her baby.'

'I can't help that,' Ted Morrison replied, equally irritated, 'it's the bloody board's fault. "We have to concentrate on our company image,"' he parroted. 'Bloody idiots! They can't see how profitable the place is.'

'I don't understand it, we're making a fortune.'

Ted Morrison sat down, pulling his left earlobe as he talked. 'They said that they didn't mind keeping the cinema here in Piccadilly, but the Knightsbridge place had "travelled too far from the company image to be allowed to continue".' He paused, remembering the words. 'In short, they want to sell it.'

'Sell it!' Geoffrey Lynes repeated. 'God, I'm not going to be around when they tell her – '

'When *we* tell her,' Ted Morrison corrected him. 'We have been given that unpleasant task.' He swivelled round in his chair. 'After what she's done, after all the work ... she made it a talking place.'

'That's probably what they don't like,' Lynes said bitterly. Despite his old antagonism towards Ruth, he was struck by the injustice of the situation. He thought he would have liked to see her brought down a peg or two – the lovely Mrs Floyd cut off at the knees – but when he thought of her he saw her only as the young girl with the scarf tied round her hair, all those years ago, in Piccadilly. 'Who's going to buy it?'

Ted Morrison shrugged. 'Who knows? Some snotty city kid out to make a fast buck; some stodgy cinema chain.' He sighed. 'What a bloody fiasco.'

Resigned to the unpleasant task of telling Ruth, they made their way over to the Knightsbridge premises in a gloomy mood. Bill Pascoe approached them as they walked in.

'Good morning, gentlemen. Can I help you?'

Geoffrey Lynes gave him a suspicious look. 'Not really. Where's Ruth?'

'Mrs Floyd is in the projection booth,' he said, raising his eyebrows. 'Perhaps you would like to wait here.'

Ignoring the suggestion, both men made their way to the booth. It was in semi-darkness, two huge 35mm projectors arranged in front of the portholes through which they could see the cinema, and the fifty or so guests waiting for their film. Ruth was working, head down, her hair drawn back in a French pleat, her eyes fixed on the open projector in front of her.

'Is that you, Henry?' she asked without looking round.

Geoffrey moved towards her. 'No, it's me, and Ted Morrison.' He looked round; two reels of film lay on a table next to Ruth. 'What the hell is going on?'

'Henry has let me down,' she said. 'I have to get this film running.' She glanced up. 'Pass me the sound tape, Geoffrey – no, not that one, that one.'

He passed it to her, watching, fascinated, as she threaded

both reels, film and sound track, clicked the switches into place and then turned on. The film flashed, and then threw an image on to the screen below, the audience clapping in anticipation. Heaving a sigh of relief, Ruth straightened up and wiped her hands on a white handkerchief. In the semi-darkness she seemed more slender than ever, her large wide eyes steady, her mouth curved in a smile of greeting. She was changing, Geoffrey Lynes thought. There was a curious contained sexuality there which he had never seen before.

'Well, gentlemen, what can I do for you?'

Ted Morrison glanced round. 'Dear God, do you have to do this often?'

'Only now and again, when something goes wrong.'

'I didn't know you could work the projectors.'

She smiled indulgently. 'Oh, Ted, I know this place inside out. Every corner, every light – otherwise how could I run it?'

The two men exchanged glances. Ruth saw the look and was about to say something when a tall, burly figure walked in.

'Mrs Floyd, my car broke down. I'm so sorry.'

'It's all right, Henry, I've set them up,' she said easily. 'You carry on now, will you?' she said, walking out with Ted Morrison and Geoffrey Lynes following her.

Outside, she turned to them. 'So what is going on?'

'Nothing,' Geoffrey Lynes said, although Ted Morrison interrupted him immediately. 'We want to sell this place.'

'We do?' Ruth asked, still smiling.

'Not us, the board, they decided that they want to keep the Piccadilly cinema, but they want to sell this one.'

'But it's making a fortune – ' Ruth began.

'That's not the point. They're worried about the company image.'

Infuriated, Ruth walked to her office, the two men following her. They can't do this, she thought, they can't. 'So, what are they planning to do?' she asked, sitting down and crossing her legs.

'Sell it.'

'To whom?' she enquired, her voice colder.

'They haven't found a buyer yet.'

'They made their decision very rapidly, considering they didn't have someone ready to buy.'

'It's the new man on the board – Harringshaw. He's a whizz-kid.'

'Steven Harringshaw,' Ruth said to herself. The two men exchanged glances. 'So he's making a clean sweep of it, is he?'

'He said that he wanted you to continue with the Piccadilly cinema ...' Ted Morrison trailed off, silenced by the look on Ruth's face.

'That was good of him,' she said, her voice tight with anger. 'I think I'd like a word with Mr Harringshaw.'

Startled, Geoffrey Lynes interrupted her. 'Oh, I don't think he's about to change his mind, Ruth.'

'I sincerely hope not,' she said, smiling.

It was a very cold morning, unusually so for that time of year, frost on the pavement and a thin skimming of ice on the roof of the buildings. Far too early for her appointment, Ruth paced about outside, waiting to see the small, dandified figure of Harold Ibrahim drive up in his silver Mercedes. She had phoned him the night before, saying it was a matter of some urgency that she see him first thing in the morning. Always eager to do business with Mrs Floyd, Harold had agreed. Impatiently, Ruth walked up the street, her heels clicking on the pavement, her hands dug deeply into the pockets of her fur coat. A car drew up, but it wasn't Harold. Taking a deep breath, Ruth continued to walk past the bare trees, hearing the sound of a clock striking in nearby Fleet Street. Seven-thirty. She glanced at her watch and was pulling up her collar when Harold's car came into view. He parked and approached her, smiling.

'Good morning, Mrs Floyd. This is a very early hour to meet. I hope I didn't keep you waiting long. Unfortunately my secretary does not come in until nine, so there was no one here to let you in.' He unfastened the door and stood back to let her pass into his office. 'Well, what can I do for you?'

'I want you to arrange something for me.' Ruth paused, her voice composed, her heart hammering. 'I want to buy the cinema I now run in Knightsbridge.'

Harold blinked, but otherwise expressed no surprise. His hair was as deeply and artificially black as ever, its shine giving it the appearance of a varnished door. 'This is a very unusual step, Mrs Floyd. One I hope you have considered at great length.'

'I have enough money to meet half the amount they are asking.' She paused, thinking of the conversation she had had with Steven Harringshaw the previous afternoon. 'But in order to raise the remainder I will need to mortgage the house and use it as collateral.'

Harold sighed. 'Is that wise?'

'It is my house.'

He nodded. 'Indeed. Mr Floyd signed it over to you, lock, stock and barrel. But this is a gamble – '

'Only if it fails.'

'Only if it fails, yes. But can you be certain it won't?'

Ruth was prepared for this. 'There's no way it can fail. I have all the contacts, all the bookings for the next eighteen months, and I run the place now anyway. It would just mean that I owned it, instead of running it for someone else.'

'But can you guarantee its success?' he asked, impressed by the courage of her decision.

'Oh, how can anyone guarantee anything?' She smiled winningly. 'I want to own it, and put my mark on it. It will be more successful when I have full control.'

'I should advise you against this. Your house is paid for, you owe nothing. You have money in the bank. Why risk a loss?' Why indeed? he thought, intrigued by the woman in his office. He could remember Ruth Floyd when she was just married, quiet and reserved, deeply reliant on her husband. A pretty woman, but not one destined for great things – or so he had thought then.

'I intend to buy that cinema, Harold, whether you arrange it for me, or not.'

Harold Ibrahim had no intention of losing profitable contact with any member of the wealthy Floyd family. Patting his immaculate hair, he said, 'In that case, I will organise everything for you. I'll speak to your bank and then put in a bid with – '

'Mr Steven Harringshaw,' Ruth said calmly, watching as Harold wrote down the name in his file.

'And what about insurance?'

'Geoffrey Lynes is the financial director of the cinema, as you know, and I assume that he will continue to work with me, although obviously I won't speak to him until I know if my offer has been accepted. If everything goes to plan, he'll organise that side of the business.'

Painstakingly, Harold Ibrahim made some more notes, blotted the paper, and recapped his pen. Behind him, the morning was beginning to soften, the first frosts evaporating in a thin sun.

'Thank you for everything,' Ruth said, getting to her feet. 'And don't worry, this will be a huge success.'

Harold walked to the door with her. 'I'll be in touch within the week,' he said, changing the subject. 'I've been hearing stories about your cinema in Knightsbridge. You're becoming well known.'

'People seem to like the place.'

'Rich and powerful people seem to like it,' he said astutely. 'That's what makes the difference. There's no point aiming to be popular with the wrong clientele.'

Ruth shook hands with him warmly. 'You must come and have a look round,' she said. 'The next time there's something special on, I'll give you a ring.'

'I would be enchanted,' Harold said, opening the door on to the morning chill.

Ruth made her way back to the office with a light heart and an even lighter head. It was a gamble, she knew that, just as she knew she would never have dared to undertake such a risky adventure if she was still married to Ken. Alone, and taking responsibility for her own life, Ruth had become aware of her ambitions. Ambitions which did not fade, but grew every time she was written about; every time her cinema was used for a special event. There was no way she could fail, Ruth thought. If, God forbid, the cinema did make a loss, she had the house as collateral, and property was always rising in price. Instead of seeing it as a risk, she thought of it as a way to make a great deal of money for herself; and when she made it for herself, she made it for her children.

Nina came round that night, although Ruth had not told her about the cinema. She walked in and froze. 'When did that come?' she asked, pointing to the Burmese kitten Ruth had bought for the children only days before.

'That's Barnie. He's good company for the kids,' Ruth explained, 'and besides, Graham's very fond of him.'

Nina remained unimpressed. 'I don't like cats. We had one at Rock Street, it got run over by one of the tyre lorries going up by Tommy Fields.' She looked at Barnie. 'Cats are lousy things, they have fleas and mites.' On cue, he rubbed against her leg. 'Damn thing!' she said, shooing him off. He watched her with a kind of controlled malevolence from under the settee.

Ruth smiled. 'Graham talks to him – '

'Does he answer back? ' Nina asked flippantly. 'A talking cat,' she continued. 'That's one up on the neighbours, even in this area. Maybe I should borrow it, my agent could find work for a red-headed actress and an Oriental tom.' Ruth gave her a bleak look. 'It was just a joke!' Nina said, changing the subject quickly. 'Anyway, how are things? You should be going out with someone by now. You've been alone too long.'

Ruth sighed. 'I don't want to meet anyone,' she said thinking of the cinema and wondering when she would know if it was hers, or not. 'I'm in no hurry.'

'You're thirty-one this year.'

'So are you – ' Ruth replied coolly, 'and you haven't even been married yet.'

Nina stuck her tongue out. 'Sticks and stones ...' she said, pushing the cat off the settee and sitting down.

'I heard from Inger this morning,' Ruth said evenly. 'She's pregnant.'

Nina pulled her face. 'Well, that's one way of keeping Sam at home.'

'What a thing to say!'

'Oh, stop pretending to be so shocked, Ruth, you know that's what you're thinking.'

'She wants a girl.'

'So did Sam,' Nina added wickedly.

It was almost ten days before Ruth received the decision. The cinema, Harold Ibrahim told her over the phone, was now hers.

'Congratulations,' he said cheerily. 'I hope you are an enormous success.'

Breathing a deep, satisfied sigh, Ruth answered, 'It will be.' She paused, smiling to herself. '*I* will be.'

Geoffrey Lynes took the news with all the grace of a wild game hunter looking down the barrel of a shotgun held by the lion he had originally been chasing. In short, he had been beaten at his own game. 'You've bought this cinema?' he asked, incredulously.

'Yes, why? Does that matter to you?'

He coughed violently and Ruth passed him a glass of water. The Parkinson's disease was making his hands shake again. 'Sorry about that. It's this damn cold, I can't shake if off . . .' he explained, embarrassed.

Tactfully glancing away, Ruth sifted through the letters on her desk. 'I would like you to stay on. Will you stay and work with me?'

'As what?'

'Financial director. What else?' She could sense his resentment and toned down the irritation in her voice. 'We've worked together very well in the past. You would just continue in the same vein.'

'Hardly,' he said, continuing before she had time to speak. 'Now that you own this cinema, won't that make it difficult to run the premises in Piccadilly?'

'Why?' she asked, taken aback.

'Division of loyalties.'

Ruth smiled. 'I spoke to Steven Harringshaw. He wants me to continue running the Piccadilly cinema for him at the same time as I'll run this one – '

'For yourself,' Geoffrey finished.

'Yes,' Ruth said coldly. 'Is there something wrong with that?'

'It will take up a lot of your time.'

'I have time.'

'So I heard,' he said, regretting the words immediately.

'What does that mean?' she asked, her face set, her voice hard.

'Well, you're divorced and there's no other man in your life,' he finished, looking away. God, she could make him uncomfortable, he thought. Over the years she had always had the ability to make him feel inadequate just by the expression on her face.

'And having no man in my life is a serious matter, is it? Perhaps I am only buying this cinema as a substitute for a husband, hey?' Ruth's eyes were dead, cold, unfathomable. 'Maybe you should tell me if this is a drawback. I wouldn't want to be an embarrassment to anyone.'

Geoffrey withered under the attack. 'Your life is your own.'

'Yes, it damn well is!' she said, walking round the desk to face him. 'I'm doing what I want for the first time in my life. I have no one to answer to, no one to depend on, and no one to tell me what to do. This is my cinema now, Geoffrey, and if that worries you, you're free to leave.'

For several seconds, neither of them spoke. Geoffrey looked at Ruth and saw a different woman. There was no hesitation in her voice or her manner; she had presence, and, more importantly, she knew it. 'It's not a problem,' he said stiffly. 'I'd like to work with – for – you.'

'With me, Geoffrey,' Ruth said, sitting down again and acting as though everything was perfectly normal. 'What's happening today?'

There was only the slightest pause before Geoffrey answered. 'I had a phone call from a banker concerned with the Carter project,' he said, still smarting from their exchange. 'He said he wanted to talk to you about the hire charges, so I told him to come here around ten-thirty. He sounded foreign, very excitable, talked a lot.'

'I can hardly wait to meet him,' Ruth said drily.

Mr Dino Redici arrived at ten-fifteen, Geoffrey Lynes showing him to Ruth's office. Smiling hugely, he grabbed hold of her hand and ground it into his own. 'So charming to meet you, Mrs Floyd,' he said, sitting down. 'I've been looking forward to this little chat.'

Unaccountably flustered, Ruth smiled and looked at her desk, pulling out the papers on the Carter project. Her visitor watched, his long legs crossed, his narrow tanned face a study of good humour. A clever man, Dino Redici had done his homework and knew that Ruth Floyd was admired for her looks as much as her ability. He also knew that she was alone and bringing up two children; that she was wealthy; and that she remained distant. Information from another source said that she possessed an address book which was the envy of many in London. Not easily impressed by men or women, he studied her.

For her part, Ruth found herself immediately fascinated by the man, experiencing an intense physical attraction she had never felt before. Eminently masculine, he was obviously easy with women and had the advantage of all men who wear clothes well – he had style.

'We are so pleased with everything you've done,' Dino Redici continued, aware of the electricity between them.

'It was nothing,' Ruth replied carefully.

He smiled, the skin creased deeply in his narrow cheeks. 'In my country we know how to say thank you.' He brought out a cigarette case and offered it to Ruth. She declined. 'Very wise, bad for the complexion.'

'So I believe,' she replied, her voice cool.

'You are good at your job,' he said generously, 'and you pronounce my name perfectly. Most people say Redici, as if it has two "c"s. How did you know?'

'It rhymes with Medici – '

He leant back, grinning broadly. 'Excellent – Lorenzo de' Medici – wonderful, wonderful man,' he trailed off into Italian, waving the cigarette round in his hand. 'Excuse me, I forget myself. Would you like to have dinner?'

'No,' Ruth said without thinking.

'Are you sure? You seemed hardly to consider the matter.'
He smiled, massively amused. 'Perhaps it was the *way* I asked.
I shall try again,' he said. 'Would you like to have dinner?'

For some reason unknown to her, Ruth accepted.

He took her to a well-known restaurant, and between courses
told her a series of Italian jokes which lost more than a little in
translation. His manner was volatile, larger than life, a trait he
cultivated, playing the red-blooded Italian to the hilt. But by
the end of the evening, she knew no more about him than at
the start, and recognised, under the extrovert exterior, a very
clever man. Her instinct put her on her guard.

'Have you been to Italy, Mrs Floyd?' he asked politely, as
they drank coffee.

'Call me Ruth. And yes, I visited a couple of times with my
ex-husband.'

He gestured extravagantly for the waiter to refill their glasses.
'I knew you were married to Ken Floyd. Then I asked around
and I found out that you have two children,' he said, making
the word sound like 'cheeldren'.

Ruth immediately drew back, her friendliness evaporating.

'You know a great deal about me. What about you, are you
married?'

He rolled his eyes like a fruit machine. 'No wife, no children –
no hope!' Again, another assault of laughter. 'I have six
brothers and two sisters – all in Italy. They think I'm crazy to
come here. "It's too cold in the winter,"' he said, mimicking
a woman's falsetto voice. The man on the next table blew his
nose. 'But I came and I like it, and so I've stayed.'

'And you're in banking?' Ruth asked.

'I dabble,' he said, playing his job down although she knew
he was important – her own spies had told her so. But she did
wonder how a staid English firm came to terms with such a
rabid extrovert, and was impressed by his position and his
rapid move up the ranks.

'You should have one,' he said to Ruth, ordering another
sweet.

'Really, no, thank you anyway.'

He looked disappointed. 'You can't be worried about your

235

weight,' he said. 'English women worry so much about the inches, Italian women are slim and beautiful and then ... blow up and become old ladies. Fat old ladies!'

The words were said light-heartedly, but his expression when he looked at her was intimate and made her bluster.

'I'm not worried about my weight, but I don't like sweets much, even though my children would have loved one of those.'

He leant forward eagerly. 'Good. We'll take them out on Sunday and buy them one.'

The shutters closed down at once. Dino saw Ruth pull back, saw her reaction, her coolness at any suggestion of familiarity. He saw it and, stimulated by the challenge, pursued the matter. 'They would like it, believe me.'

'I'm sure they would, another time.'

'No, not another time,' he said, his expression immovable. 'This time.'

Ruth felt cornered and did not like the sensation. She had come a long way since Ken walked out and had no desire to be hurt again. Coolly, she answered him. 'I don't think it would be a good idea.'

The black eyes watched her for a moment and then Dino tapped the back of Ruth's hand with his spoon. 'Trust me, I don't hurt people.'

'I don't intend to let you,' she said coldly.

'You are a clever woman,' he said. 'You are respected, rich, and willing to gamble, if buying that cinema is anything to go by.' He paused. 'Gamble on me, I could make you happy, and I won't hurt you.'

Ruth hesitated, and when she did speak her voice was low and threatening. 'You better not hurt me, or my children, Dino ... or I swear to God you'll regret it.'

He looked surprised and then laughed, the handkerchief in his top pocket waving like a white flag.

Dino Redici was quite a person to live up to. He talked faster, laughed louder and came to quicker decisions, his every action as enthusiastic as a child's. A total extrovert, he was adamant that he was going to have a good time and that anyone with him would do likewise, whether they liked it or not. He was a comic figure, a joker who had the last laugh on everyone. Clever, cunning and passionate, he saw in Ruth something he admired and wanted; something he was determined to possess.

They did take the children out that Sunday, and from the instant they met Dino they responded as though they had always known him and were merely welcoming him back. It was incredible for Ruth to see Graham hoisted out of his wheelchair and thrown bodily over Dino's shoulder, the immaculate suit crumpling under the weight; and Kate was similarly captivated, recognising in Dino a soul-mate who was as interested and excited in everything as she was.

Ruth, however, was not as easy to win over. The sexual attraction she felt for Dino intrigued and alarmed her. Having never wanted a man before, she found herself day-dreaming about making love, and surprised herself by her own depth of feeling. Confused and reluctant to be out of control, Ruth alternated between rejecting Dino and then, when he deliberately drew back, longing for him.

Knowing him to be an intelligent man, she wondered, in fact, if he wasn't perhaps a great deal smarter than even she took him for. But if she worried about the speed with which the relationship was moving, the children were landed, hook, line, and sinker within weeks. Mrs Corley won over almost as quickly.

But the suddenness of his devotion worried Ruth. He was too volatile, too eager, wanting everything today, not tomorrow, and she wondered if his interest would extend from weeks to months. Certainly it seemed unlikely to continue for years. Wanting him, she continued the relationship, but at the same time keeping a tight rein on her emotions. She had been deceived before, she remembered, recalling how excited Ken had been about the children – before the novelty wore off and the hard truth set in.

Her prudence was hampered, however, by the children. Knowing how much they liked Dino, Ruth was reluctant to dampen their enthusiasm, but they were children, she reasoned, and needed protection almost as much as she did. So that night

Ruth tackled him over dinner. 'Dino – '

He interrupted her immediately. 'That sounds serious.'

'What does?'

'The way you said "Dino". My mother used to say it like that when she was angry about something.'

She smiled half-heartedly. 'I was just going to say that I appreciate all the attention you're giving the children, but they might get to like you too much, and depend on your always being there.'

She stopped, embarrassed and surprised by her own clumsiness.

'Go on,' he said, demolishing half a bread roll.

'Well, they might ... I mean, you've been very good to them, and to me, of course ... but they are children and see things differently.' She trailed off and turned her attention back to her soup.

'Ruth, you are such a worrier. You worry about this ...' he said, slapping some more butter on the bread, '... and that ...' he continued, the roll crumbling under the onslaught, '... when there is nothing to worry about. I know what I'm doing.'

Her head jerked up, a thin trickle of anger in her voice. 'Well! That's just great, isn't it? *You* knowing what *you're* doing. But where does that leave me?'

'Oh, you have a temper!' he said, smiling widely. 'I wondered. All this cool English poise I kept seeing – I thought there had to be some real feeling bubbling underneath.'

He smiled, his voice low, intimate. The familiar rush of feeling washed over Ruth. Discomfited, she lowered her voice. 'I don't like to be kept in the dark. I don't know how serious you are.'

A piece of roll dropped from his hand. 'I told you, trust me.'

'I trusted my ex-husband – '

'Ah, but he drank. One can never trust a drunk,' he said smoothly, watching her, noticing the colour in her face and the way she kept moving her hands. She's unsettled, he thought, and nervous.

'All right, Ken was a drunk. But I trusted my first husband, and he died.'

238

'Not to spite you, I think,' he said, grinning broadly.

'I loved Derek,' Ruth retorted, stung by his levity.

'So?' he said, his smile fading, his eyes pitiless. 'I've loved women, but they also left ... Life goes on.'

His attitude made her pause. More softly, she added, 'If I got too involved with you and something happened ...' Unable to continue, Ruth laid down her spoon and glanced away. There was a party going on at a nearby table with a huge birthday cake, its candles flickering.

Dino followed her gaze. 'You see that cake?' he asked. 'That has been made for someone's birthday, with a particular number of candles to indicate how old they are. Before tonight they had fewer candles, and next year, they will have more. That fact should not affect how much they enjoy the cake.'

Ruth glanced back at him, an expression of cool amusement on her face. 'I'm sure that's very profound, but I don't understand a word of it.'

He laughed loudly. 'The English have no conception of fate.'

'And the Italians have no conception of responsibility,' she countered drily.

'Trust me,' he said, dismissing the subject and turning his attention to the next course.

And so Ruth did begin to trust him, seeing him most days, and when they didn't meet, he phoned her and held long conversations in the early hours when he had insomnia. 'I can't sleep,' he said, sounding as fresh as a sparrow.

Ruth rolled over and turned on the bedside lamp. 'Well, I can. Dino, please, don't ring me so late again, I have to go to work in the morning.'

'I was thinking,' he continued, ignoring what she'd said and launching into some intricate idea he had been chewing over. 'Well, what do you think?'

'I think I should get some sleep.'

He sighed down the phone. 'Did you miss me today?'

'Yes, I missed you,' Ruth answered, imagining him.

'You never say so unless I ask you first! You should tell me. You're always holding back. Relax. I tell you how I miss you and you tell me not to call you at night! Any normal woman would appreciate the gesture.'

Ruth snapped awake. 'Any *normal* woman! Listen, if you don't like me the way I am, then that's your loss, not mine. I'm not changing for anyone.'

He laughed down the phone. 'All that passion under that chilly exterior,' he said, hugely amused. 'You pretend to be so much in control, Ruth, and you're fooling yourself.' He could imagine her fury, and smiled. I have the measure of her, he thought, all I have to do is wait.

'I'm going back to sleep.'

He was not prepared to let her go so easily. 'We must take the children out on Sunday – I'll think up something exciting.'

Ruth flinched. 'Dino, don't go to too much trouble, they're only seven, after all.'

'Nothing's too much trouble, Ruth,' he said, ringing off.

In the weeks which followed Dino's affection intensified. For the children, it was paradise, like having a father and an older brother all rolled into one. He could understand them without effort and held long conversations with Kate as she poured out her heart to him. Graham was a little harder to win over, but when Dino began to take him to galleries where he could see and touch the exhibits, he was captivated. They needed a father; Ruth realised that, but she thought that Dino was too unreliable to want the role. Daily, she saw their attachment to him growing, and daily she avoided any discussion about their relationship. She refused to acknowledge how much she wanted him, and he stood on the sideline, waiting.

'I can't believe it, a cinema! She must be mad.'

'Steady on, Ken,' Robert Floyd said, trying to calm his son, while at the same time hugely amused by his reaction. 'Ruth knows what she's doing.'

'How the hell did she pay for it?'

'With money, I expect. That's how people usually pay for things.' He leant back and added slyly, 'Anyway, what's it got to do with you? You left the woman.'

Ken flinched on the other end of the line. He had broken up

with Sheila Fielding, and returned to his bachelor life – wine, women, and more wine. 'I like to know she's all right.'

'Bullshit!' his father said curtly. 'You're curious, you bastard. You want to know how she's getting on, now that she's doing well. You struck out there, boy, you really did.' He paused, wondered whether or not to add the *coup de grâce*. The temptation was too strong to resist. 'She's even got a new man in her life.'

Ken winced, and then reached for his drink. 'Who?'

'Dino Redici. Some banker. Sharp as a tack.'

Jealousy scratched at Ken Floyd as he struggled to keep his voice steady. 'Is she going marry him?'

'Why not?' Robert Floyd answered, delighted to inflict some punishment on his recalcitrant son. 'After all, she's a free woman, thanks to you.'

The Knightsbridge cinema went from strength to strength. Ruth obtained a drinks licence and it became a meeting place for the rich, famous, and infamous. Society hostesses, politicians, singers, actors, and various titled heads all flocked to where they could meet a stimulating variety of people, all equally willing to be seen and talked about. The atmosphere of the place amused Ruth as it changed into an intimate club, the cinema still used for films, but also for talks and impromptu performances. Playwrights began to show select previews of their plays there, inviting a tiny audience of the most influential and powerful to attend. When the news leaked out, large sums of money exchanged hands so that outsiders could gatecrash the proceedings. But try as they might, every one of them was foiled as Bill Pascoe bounced the various intruders.

And it made money, big money; money which Ruth put into the bank and invested, money which she began to enjoy, relishing the freedom it gave her, and the power. With a flourish, she rewarded Bill Pascoe by increasing his salary, and offered a substantial increase to Geoffrey Lynes.

'Why?' he asked, sitting down in her office. On a whim, Ruth had had the place decorated to be more in tune with the cinema; the walls were panelled, the windows hung with velvet curtains, her desk a valuable antique. It was more like a study in a country house than an office in the middle of London.

'Why?' she repeated. 'Because you've earned it. It's a way of saying thank you for your support.'

Geoffrey smiled thinly. 'Buying loyalty?'

'You are a surly sod,' Ruth said coldly, watching his face colour as he glanced away. 'Take it or leave it, Geoffrey, the money's yours if you want it.'

He took it, grudgingly, remembering how he had hired her originally, remembering how she had needed the job. He took the money, and burned.

If the news met with mixed reactions in some quarters, it rapidly became very hot gossip in Oldham, Ruth's mother being constantly besieged in the hat shop and cross-questioned. 'What a thing to happen, Mrs Gordon, your girl getting on like that. She's almost famous.'

Glowing, Lilian patted her hair into place and smiled. 'I always knew Ruth would go far.'

The other woman smiled back. 'Well, she certainly has, and no mistake. Got to the top, so she has ... And who'd have thought it, when you think back to her trouble.'

The lid of the cash-box snapped down. 'That's all behind her now,' Lilian answered curtly. 'She's made a real life for herself now – and no one should forget it.'

Stung, the woman left without another word.

When she had gone Lilian leaned against the counter, her legs shaking, as pride and jealousy fought for the upper hand in her mind. She had seen Ruth's steady progress, and her setbacks, monitoring them from a distance, and commiserating, her sympathy always more fluent than her praise. Realising that she was suddenly tired, Lilian sat down and looked about her. The shop had hardly changed, a new counter and some curtains the only concession to advancement. Despite Ruth's frequent attempts to give her parents money or help, Lilian resisted, accepting only those things which could be thought of as presents.

She pulled back the curtain, looking into the back room. The small table stood there, and the tiny oven, the kettle perched on top. Her eyes glanced round – row on row of hat boxes and stacks of materials fought for space on the shelves, along with several polythene bags full of feathers, net, and other trimmings. Lilian sighed and thought of Ruth's house; the space, the money, all the furniture and china Lilian would have loved.

A rush of envy choked her – she had always wanted to get on, Grandma Price had always encouraged her, but it wasn't to be. In the end, it was Ruth's destiny, not hers. Lilian sighed and got to her feet, bending down to look into the small mirror on the counter. Automatically, she powdered her nose and refastened her right earring, turning, with a smile on her face, when she heard the bell ring on the shop door.

It was a warm, leafy evening in late summer when Dino invited Ruth to his flat in a wide road in Richmond. Ruth walked round admiring the décor, the great splashes of colour and the mass of paintings. It was opulent and luxurious, the bedroom sporting a massive, four-poster bed. Ruth looked round and smiled. 'My God, this looks like something out of the "Amateur Seducer's Manual".'

Laughing, Dino rubbed the side of his nose with his forefinger. 'You don't like it?'

'Well ... it's beautiful, but very much the bachelor pad,' Ruth answered, smiling archly over her shoulder. 'How many ladies have you brought back here?'

It was the first time she had ever seen him discomfited. He glanced away and then showed her back into the lounge, pouring Ruth a drink and settling himself down into a huge, soft, leather chair, his feet dug into the silk carpet in front of him.

'I'm sorry, did I offend you?' Ruth asked finally.

He was curiously subdued as he answered. 'No. I was wrong to bring you here.'

The atmosphere cooled several degrees. Sipping her drink, Ruth's mind raced. She had made the decision the previous night, knowing that she wanted Dino and that she wanted a relationship with him. Even if it was only physical. With overdue insight, she finally admitted that for all her success she had never experienced deep sexual satisfaction – a fact which had never mattered until she met him. Now it had assumed paramount importance, disturbing her work and her equilibrium. She wanted the man sat next to her; wanted him as she had never wanted another man.

'Ruth, I should take you home now,' Dino said, rousing her from her day-dream.

Embarrassed, and not a little annoyed, she finished her drink and followed him to the door. In silence, he drove her home, and when she glanced over to him his face was set, his mouth tight. Confused and frustrated, Ruth stared straight ahead and when the car pulled into her drive, got out without a word.

Her heels clicked on the stone steps as she walked up to the door.

'Mummy? Where's Dino?' Kate asked, running towards her.

Ruth sat on the bottom of the stairs, her hands clasped. 'He's gone home.'

'Why?' she asked petulantly.

'He ... wasn't feeling well.'

Her face was sulky; she obviously thought her mother was to blame. 'But I was looking forward to seeing him so much –'

'Oh, shut up, Kate!' Ruth shouted.

She sprang to her feet, startled, and then ran upstairs, crying loudly. Hearing her bedroom door bang, Ruth flinched, unfastened her jacket, and made her way into the kitchen.

The room was hot and scrupulously tidy, each thing in its place, and every dish sparkling. Ideal homes, she thought bitterly, pulling up the blind and opening the back door for some air. Persistently, her mind kept running over the conversation she had had with Dino, looking for the reason why he had reacted so oddly. It made no sense, she thought, banging her hands down on the table. She should never have become involved, she had been doing fine on her own, just her and the children.

Savagely disappointed, Ruth snatched open the fridge door and poured herself a glass of milk, dropping two ice cubes into it, and rubbing a third over her forehead to cool herself. The wood pigeons cooed softly from outside and a bee sidled around the cooker looking for a place to land. Continuously she questioned herself as the bee settled on the window-ledge and basked itself in the sunlight, its wings flickering, its body round and heavy.

Mrs Harvey came in soon after. 'There's a phone call for you.'

Ruth's heart missed a beat. 'Who is it?'

'Your mother.'

'Tell her I'll ring back later, would you?'

The woman nodded and walked out.

By nine, it was apparent that Dino Redici was not going to ring or explain. The hot evening began to melt into night, Kate refusing to talk to Ruth, and Ruth too upset to try and cajole her. Following the usual routine, she took Graham through his exercises and then sat down with her head against the back of the chair, her eyes closed. By ten the night was smouldering, the heat crawling in from the garden and nuzzling into the rooms. But still he didn't call. An hour later, Ruth touched up her make-up and when the clock struck the half-hour, she left, the sticky air clinging to her as she opened the car door. The roads were quiet, the theatres not yet emptied for the night. Ruth drove along, her hands hot on the steering wheel. But anger made her a bad driver and in exasperation, she pulled in at the kerb, deciding to walk the rest of the way to the cinema.

She realised that she loved Dino; realised it just as she realised that he was wrong for her; her timing, so perfect in business, failing her emotionally. Her shoes tapped along the pavement, her hands clenched. She thought of Derek, Ken, Dino ... thought of the men she had loved, and shuddered in the hot air, her head sticky and thumping with the heat. It might even thunder, she thought, looking up to the treacherous sky. On she walked, the heat dragging at her, her mouth dry, thinking of the cinema, thinking that at least she could work there and forget what had happened for a while. It was entirely her own, each brick hers, each piece of furniture chosen by her. Feeling suddenly optimistic, Ruth walked on. Work was reliable, she realised, dependable, the only constancy in a shifting world.

Turning the corner, her senses were alerted. She stopped and then suddenly began to run towards the next block, towards the cinema, towards something she knew had happened and did not dare to admit to herself. Her feet pounded on the street, echoing down the darkness and running towards the light she could see round the next corner. Then she turned, and stopped.

High into the black sky the flames curled, licking the darkness, their heat and colour boiling the night. Ruth gasped and leant against a wall to get her breath. Up went the flames, up towards the heavens, taking her cinema with them, savaging the curtains, the couches, the wallpaper, blackening everything she had chosen with such care, destroying everything she had built – and owned.

Her eyes stinging with tears, she walked towards the burning building. A fireman turned, saw her approach, and put out his hand to stop her. 'Don't go any closer, luv, it's dangerous.'

She looked at him as though she didn't understand.

Baffled, he said, 'Keep your distance, luv, you don't want to get burnt, do you?'

Ruth glanced into the man's eyes and then smiled wryly, while behind her the flames curled upwards to the unfeeling sky.

Thirteen

'Ruth?'

It was Dino, his voice subdued. 'Listen, I'm sorry for what happened, I've just heard.'

Her voice chilled him. 'What exactly are you sorry about – the fiasco last night, or the fire?'

'I treated you badly – ' he said quietly, 'but I don't usually go out with women like you. Women with children – '

She cut him short. 'You knew I had children when you first asked me out. Don't use that as a get-out.'

'You misunderstand me – '

'I doubt it.'

'What are you so angry about?' he shouted suddenly.

She laughed, but the sound was odd, without humour, the pain obvious. 'I've just seen all my hard work and most of my money go up in flames on the same night that you made a fool of me – and you ask why I'm angry.'

'I wanted time to think about our relationship.'

Ruth was close to tears. 'You told me once you would never hurt me or my children . . . Well, I know you're a lying bastard, but they don't – it's not fair to treat them that way.'

'I care for you deeply and for the children.'

'You have a great way of showing it!'

'Ruth, I behaved badly – '

'Oh, for God's sake!' she shouted, beside herself. 'What do I care any more?'

He tried to calm her, she seemed close to breaking point. 'Hear me out. I did the wrong thing bringing you back to the flat, I . . . was playing a game with you, Ruth.' He breathed in deeply. 'I wanted to make love to you and I knew I'd have to get you to trust me first. So I waited until the time was right . . .' The words punched her. He'd read her so well, known exactly how to manipulate her. 'I treated you like every other woman and expected you to behave like them.' He paused. 'Then, when I got you to the flat, I was ashamed. Forgive me.'

'What the hell does it matter?' Ruth asked, her tone bitingly cold. 'Nothing you say now matters. I should have realised anyway. Put it down to my naïvety.' She laughed bitterly.

He was stunned by the words. He had expected anger, not defeat. 'Listen, you can rebuild the cinema. It will be the same as before, maybe better.'

She laughed again, and he winced. 'I've just spoken to Geoffrey Lynes, Dino. Apparently he was a little ... careless.' She paused, the words cheated her. 'He didn't insure the cinema ...' Dino sucked in his breath. 'There was something about it not being fully covered ... I've lost a fortune!' she said sharply. 'Now tell me everything will be all right. Now tell me, Dino ...' her voice broke. 'Tell me everything will be all right.'

Robert Floyd was enjoying himself. Sitting in his spartan office he lit a cigar, leant back in his chair and thought about the phone call he had just received. He had known about the fire, of course, he had too many spies around London to miss it; but he hadn't known about Geoffrey Lynes. He coughed suddenly and flicked some ash off the cigar, staring at it thoughtfully and remembering that the specialist had told him to stop smoking. Specialists, he thought wryly, they tell you to give up everything just so you can die a year later.

Ruth's predicament appealed to him. He had spent his life setting people one against the other, in business and private life. His wife against his mistress; his son against his daughter; and now Ruth against Ken. The thought thrilled him, nurtured his mischievous streak. Poor old Ken, fifty-odd, and still acting like a kid, while Ruth clawed her way up and took gambles.

Some of which did not come off. Like the cinema. He smiled again; oh yes, he was going to enjoy their little chat. He liked Ruth. Class and guts, he decided, were a rare combination in a woman and if that woman happened to be the mother of your grandchildren ... The intercom sounded, announcing Ruth's arrival.

'Send her in,' he said cheerily.

She looked good, he had to give her that, she wasn't about to look penniless, even if she was on her uppers.

'How are you, Robert?' Ruth asked, sitting down opposite him and pointing towards the ashtray. 'I thought you weren't supposed to smoke.'

'That's what they tell me,' he agreed, pulling on his cigar. 'But I say live dangerously ... and bugger the consequences.'

Ruth raised her eyebrows. She knew the old man in front of her wasn't going to come to the point quickly; he was enjoying himself too much. No, she had to work for it, beg for it – but she had resigned herself to that fact as soon as she had decided to ask him for help. She was banking on his nature, that quirky, malicious temperament which would revel in the piquancy of the situation.

'How's Kate?' he asked. Kate was his favourite, the one person on whom he did not play tricks.

'She's very well and learning how to swim.'

'That's good. It could be useful if she found herself in the deep end any time.'

Ruth flinched. You bastard, she thought, crushing her pride and continuing. 'Graham's making progress too, he's more placid now.'

'You fuss that boy,' Robert Floyd said quickly. 'He depends on you too much.'

'He's handicapped. He needs me. After all, he has no father.'

The words swung between them. Round one to you, Robert Floyd thought, amused.

Aware that he was waiting for her to continue, Ruth wondered how much to tell him ... especially about Geoffrey Lynes. She did not know if he had acted deliberately, if his behaviour had been premeditated, a result of his illness, or simply resentment. But she *did* know how jealous he was; how he had loathed to see her rise as he descended. Any man would have balked at the turn of fortunes.

'Ken heard about the cinema,' the old man said, interrupting her thoughts. 'He was ... surprised.'

249

'Really? I'm amazed he had time to think about it, he's usually so busy.'

Robert Floyd smiled widely, enjoying himself. 'Well, it's lovely to see you, Ruth, and hear about the children – '

'Oh, let's stop playing games! I need money to rebuild the cinema.'

He blinked. 'My money?' Ruth nodded. 'My dear girl, why should I lend you money?'

'Because I'm a good businesswoman. I made that cinema into a show place and I can do it again – '

'It burned down!' Robert Floyd said, his eyes bright with pleasure. 'Why?'

'My financial director slipped up,' Ruth said bluntly. 'He arranged everything perfectly at Piccadilly, So I naturally assumed that he would do the same for the new cinema.'

'Really?' he replied, making the word sum up all of Ruth's stupidity and negligence.

'All right, he let me down! But it was *my* house I used as collateral, not yours; and *my* money!' Her face was set. 'I'm not asking you for a hand-out. I'll pay you back – '

'I haven't said I'll lend you the money yet. I didn't get rich to throw my money away on gambles.'

'Oh, do as you like, Robert!' Ruth said suddenly, aware that she had no intention of crawling to the malicious old man in front of her. 'I have a job at Piccadilly, I won't starve.'

'But you don't want the job at Piccadilly as much as you want your own place. You want to be boss – '

'Not enough to beg from you!' she snapped, getting to her feet.

Robert Floyd hesitated and lit another cigar. 'You're a proud woman, Ruth. Pride can be expensive. I should, by right, tell you to sod off.' He turned his winter eyes on hers. 'But I like guts and . . . I'll lend you the money. After all, it's still in the family – even if it means you'll be working for me,' he added, as an afterthought.

Ruth looked at him and forced a smile. You think you own me, she thought. Well, you're wrong, no one does. 'Thank you, Robert,' she said formally.

'I'll ring Ibrahim and get things in motion,' he said triumphantly. 'Incidentally, what are you going to do about Geoffrey Lynes?'

Ruth paused. 'I'm not sure, yet.'

Nina rang just as Ruth arrived home. 'I just heard about the cinema. What happened?'

'It burned down . . . I wasn't properly insured.' The enormity of the situation hit her afresh. 'I've lost a fortune.'

'But why wasn't it insured properly?'

'Geoffrey Lynes – '

There was a low moan down the line. 'I was about to ask if anyone was hurt, now I'm hoping he went up in the flames.'

'I don't know if it was deliberate . . .' Ruth trailed off, suddenly weary.

Hearing the note of despair, Nina rallied. 'A fire! Just like *Gone With the Wind*! Atlanta burning, and Vivien Leigh. All we need now is a Rhett Butler – '

'I've got one,' Ruth said, smiling grimly.

'Who?'

'Robert Floyd.'

There was a moment's silence. 'Joke?' Nina asked.

'No joke. I need money to rebuild that place and I intend to have it. Robert Floyd is lending it to me.'

'Why?'

Ruth's patience snapped. 'Why do you think! To get the place going again.'

'But if you've lost money, why borrow? Why not just settle for the Piccadilly cinema until you've raised the money yourself?'

'I want it *now*!' Ruth said, close to real anger. On the other end, Nina flinched. This was the other side of Ruth, the implacable side, the side which forced Graham to talk; which had forbidden Ken to see the children; the side which made her indomitable and somehow almost frightening.

'Suit yourself,' Nina said airily, changing the subject and trying to depress her own feelings of anxiety. 'How's Dino?'

'Like every other man.'

'What happened?' she asked, listening as Ruth told her about the previous night. When she had finished, Nina said, 'So, what's the problem? He wanted to seduce you, so what? He came clean in the end. Actually, it's rather romantic ... in a sordid kind of way.'

'He lied to me!' Ruth shouted. 'He conned me – '

'Oh, for Christ's sake! Every man cons every woman except his mother. You should let me meet him, I'd give you an outsider's opinion.' She paused, 'Anyway, I know it's none of my business, but why didn't you borrow from him?'

'I don't want to ask him. I don't want to rely on anyone.'

'You're relying on Robert Floyd.'

'That's different! He's the children's grandfather, he's part of the family.'

'So it's not serious between you and Dino?'

'Nina! I have a business to run ... I can't be bothered with all that.'

'Can you be bothered with dinner?'

Ruth smiled. 'Yes, I'd like dinner.'

'All right, we'll make up a foursome tomorrow.'

'You do know someone respectable, I hope?' Ruth asked, smiling.

'I'll turn over some stones and see what I come up with.'

'You might like Dino,' Ruth added, her own attitude softening. 'He has a good sense of humour.'

'That's an advantage. What does he do again?'

'He's in banking,' Ruth answered.

'Robbing them, or running them?'

'Very funny. He happens to be very well thought of.'

'So was Mussolini,' Nina added, drily.

They met in a small, select restaurant on the river. Ruth and Dino arrived early and spent half an hour in uncomfortable small-talk, neither of them certain what the other was thinking, both of them slightly uncomfortable in each other's presence. They were just drinking their second Martini when Nina walked in with a fleshy, middle-aged Israeli.

Dino leapt to his feet and kissed her hand. 'I've heard so much about you,' he said. 'You're charming.'

'And you're tall,' Nina responded, sitting down and glancing over to Ruth. She was wearing a white dress which showed off her fair skin and the hot red of her hair.

Dino leant forward in his seat towards her. 'I believe you're on the stage.' She nodded. 'Are you in a show at the moment?'

'No, I'm resting. I do more resting than an invalid.'

Dina bellowed with laughter and she watched him intently, her eyes never leaving his face. Once or twice she laughed to accompany him, while her companion, Bertie, drank steadily, overcoming his shyness in an alcoholic euphoria, his hand clasped around the stem of his glass like a gorilla with a stick of bamboo. 'So she said ...' a gust of wheezy laughter before the punch line, '... but on him it looks good!' Dino listened, translated the words into Italian and burst out laughing.

Nina glanced over to Ruth. 'Where in God's name did you find this great stick insect?'

'He's fun.'

Dino was busily telling another joke. 'He's tapped! And as for dressing well, I could hear that suit coming.'

'Listen, Nina, he's good company,' Ruth insisted, rising to his defence, 'not like that Jewish bagel you brought.'

'Bertie has some important contacts,' she said coldly.

'I knew there would have to be something to recommend him.'

There was another explosion of laughter from across the table. 'That man,' she continued, looking at Dino, 'is incredible. I've never met anyone who's so ... immature.'

'He's won the children over.'

'Aren't they a little old for him?' she added spitefully.

But Ruth didn't care what Nina thought and was soon enjoying herself immensely, her mind temporarily taken off the problem of Geoffrey Lynes and the burnt-out cinema. The more Bertie drank, the giddier he became, laughing so much that he couldn't eat, his dinner jacket strained across his stomach like a ship's sail in a gale.

'Nina is a beautiful name,' Dino said, his attention wandering. 'It reminds me of a Russian heroine ... names mean such a lot, don't you think?'

'I suppose. What does Dino mean?'

He smiled, giving her the benefit of his perfect teeth. 'It's short for "Giovanni" – my mother nicknamed me this when I was small.'

'I'm called Herbert,' Bertie said suddenly.

They all looked at him.

'So why shorten it to Bertie?' Nina asked.

He shrugged clumsily, his napkin falling off his lap. 'I dunno, I just hate Herbert, that's all. It reminds me of all the fat men I've ever known.'

The two women exchanged glances.

'This,' Dino said, tapping Bertie's stomach, 'is the fruit of success ... you are a Bacchus amongst men.'

Delighted, Bertie raised his glass to him. 'And you are a prince. I know class when I see it, and you ... have class.'

Nina took a long drink from her glass. 'I hate to break up this mutual admiration society – but could somebody ask the waiter to bring us some coffee? I'm choking.'

By eleven, Nina's aversion to Dino had been overcome by his careful attentions, and she was soon regaling him with stories, her head bent towards his, her face animated – '... and when they asked me to do Camille,' Nina continued playfully, 'I couldn't ... I just couldn't ...'

Bertie leant forward. 'You should, you would have made a memorable Camille.'

'Do you think so, do you really think so, Bertie?'

Dino was quiet, watching them. 'Oh yes, I'd have backed your Camille any day.'

Nina was glowing like a lighthouse when Dino leant forward, offering Bertie a cigar. 'I know Martin Corman,' he said casually. It meant nothing to Ruth but she could see that it impressed Bertie, 'and I believe he's starting to cast for a new show next year.'

'How did you hear about that?' Bertie asked, immediately sober.

'I have big ears and a long memory,' Dino said smoothly. 'Well, am I right?'

'So far as I know.'

'Perhaps there would be something for Nina there?' Dino

254

suggested artfully. 'Martin said he was looking for new talent, and anyone who provided that new talent might be in a position to benefit ...' He trailed off, and puffed on his cigar for a moment. 'Of course ... I could be wrong.'

They all knew he wasn't.

Apparently this was the way Dino Redici liked to do business, acting like an irresponsible child and fooling everyone until the moment came for him to say the right word, in the right ear, at the precise moment when it could do the most good, or cause the most harm. Aware suddenly of Dino's power, Nina's attitude altered and she listened to him more carefully, always ready to change sides and ally herself to the winner. When the evening drew to a close, Dino kissed her on each cheek and shook Bertie's hand.

'So I'll tell Martin he'll be hearing from you?' he said, smiling widely.

'Of course. Yes. Well ... it's been fun,' Bertie said, hailing the first taxi and bundling Nina and himself into it quickly, obviously eager to get away.

'Greasy little man,' Dino said smoothly as they moved off.

It was very late when they arrived back at Hampstead. Ruth immediately went upstairs to see the twins and was in Graham's bedroom when she heard Dino's footsteps behind her. Turning round, she beckoned him closer. He walked over to the bed and looked down.

'He's fast asleep,' Ruth said, watching her son. Graham's hair had flopped over his face and his hands clutched the blankets.

'He doesn't look a great deal like you.'

'I know. He's like my father.'

They were both standing over the bed. Easily, Dino slid his arm around her shoulder. Ruth froze and then moved away. He watched, puzzled by her response. 'What's the matter?'

'I don't want to,' she said clumsily, wanting him to go.

'Want to do what?'

Impatiently, Ruth pushed back her hair and walked out in

to the corridor. There were no lights on, the only illumination coming from the hall below.

'I've too much on my mind at the moment, Dino ... I'm not good company.'

Suddenly irritated, he snapped at her. 'What's the excuse tonight? Business or the children?'

She was stung by the remark and began to walk down the stairs. He followed and caught hold of her arm, making her flinch and shake him off. 'Don't do that! I want to be on my own ...'

'For ever?' he asked, his voice cold. 'You better make up your mind, Ruth, because I want to know where I stand. You can't expect me to hang around on the sidelines permanently.'

'I don't want to talk about this tonight.'

'Well, I do!' he shouted. The sound drifted down and echoed in the dark hall.

Startled, Ruth turned to him. 'I have just lost my cinema, my money, and I have had to beg a loan from Robert Floyd.' She was shaking with fury. 'And you want to know how I feel about you? And you have to know *tonight*!'

'Yes,' he said simply. 'You're not the woman you think you are, Ruth. You want that cinema, because you want the power. OK, build the cinema! Bigger and better than ever ...' his voice was rising again, his face taut in the half light, '... build it for your children, spend your life piling brick on brick, and pushing pound on pound in the bank, and then ask yourself when you're older if it was worth it.' He shrugged his shoulders, exasperated. 'You'll break my heart,' he said, carefully, 'but I still want you.'

'I told you – I'm tired!' Ruth said coldly.

His temper close to breaking point, Dino turned and walked down the stairs away from her.

Cursing under her breath, Ruth moved into the bedroom and threw down her bag on the chair, pulling off her earrings. She turned round sharply as she heard a noise behind her. Dino stood in the shadowed doorway and without saying a word, caught hold of her tightly.

Threatened, Ruth shook off his arms. 'Why don't you go?

I've told you I don't want you to touch me!'

He paused. The bedroom was in darkness, the only light provided by a weak moon coming through the window and swamping the wall against which they stood. Fascinated by her response, Dino watched her, her face shadowed. 'What is it?'

'I want you to go home,' she said, her mouth dry.

He touched her arm and she moved back against the wall.

'Don't do that! Take your hands off me.'

Frowning, he thought back, remembering her softness earlier. He was certain she wanted him as much as he wanted her. She had been tender, gentle, and welcoming as the evening wore on, her every action drawing him closer, inviting him to make love to her. And now she was reacting like this – it made no sense. With an ironic smile, Dino pushed his hands deep into his trouser pockets.

'Feel safer now?'

Ruth's back was to the wall, the palms of her hands flat against the paintwork. She could not see him clearly in the dim light, but she could hear his breathing. Regular, unlike her own.

Trying to remain in charge of the situation, Ruth smiled uneasily and pushed away from the wall to pass him. Immediately he leant forward to stop her, his mouth on hers. For an instant Ruth froze and then responded, her body against his. After a moment, he pulled away from her, his voice disembodied, throaty.

'If I can't use my hands, we have a problem.'

She glanced into his face, although in the half dark it was impossible to read the expression in his eyes.

'You see,' he continued, 'if I can't help, then you'll have to take your own dress off.'

The words were said softly, invitingly, and they mesmerised Ruth. With a feeling of intense excitement, she unzipped her dress and stepped out of it so it fell to the floor.

The dim light made her alabaster, ghost-white, her hair falling around her pale face as she moved. Dino watched, and then smiled as she stood in front of him.

'Perhaps, if you wouldn't mind ...' his eyes were dark, unreadable. 'You see, I would undress myself, but ...' he shrugged, '... without hands, I am somewhat handicapped.'

As she unfastened his tie, Ruth began to smile, and then, glancing up at Dino who was also smiling, she began to laugh. Suddenly aware of the absurdity of the situation, both of them started laughing, Dino still keeping his hands in his pockets as Ruth tried hopelessly to take off his shirt and trousers. At last, laughing uncontrollably, Ruth fell back on the bed, Dino beside her.

The moonlight struck the side of his face and the smile faded on her lips. Gone was the humour and the clowning, now she was only aware of his closeness, his body, and how much she wanted him to make love to her. Gently, he kissed her mouth, her forehead, and then, as she closed her eyes, her eyelids, his mouth moving back to hers with more urgency as she responded, holding on to him.

'Permission to use my hands, Mrs Floyd?' he asked, his voice low.

Ruth moaned gently. 'Permission granted.'

The following morning Dino rose just as the light was crawling under the curtains and across the floor like a cat stalking a bird. Waking, Ruth turned over and looked at the clock. It was four forty-five. Instantly she fell back to sleep, dreaming of frogs which were swimming in upturned top hats, and Graham, running like a normal child. When she woke again it was seven-thirty and Dino was in the bathroom, singing under the shower.

'Quiet!' Ruth hissed through the glass door. 'The children will know you're here.'

He smiled widely and continued to sing.

'Dino!' she snapped, banging the door with her hand.

He turned off the shower. 'Good morning.'

'Good morning,' Ruth repeated as he kissed her forehead and left a wet imprint of his hand on her shoulder.

'Did you sleep well?'

'Yes,' she answered, watching him dry himself. 'You didn't though, did you?'

He turned round, surprised. 'Oh, I always wake early, I can't sleep for more than four hours.' He tapped his forehead with his index finger. 'Crazy.'

Surprised that she felt so comfortable with him, Ruth watched as he dressed and looked round for his tie.

'Is this what you're looking for?' she asked, passing it to him.

He snatched it from her hand and flung it round his neck in a pantomime gesture. 'I feel happy,' he said simply, smiling at Ruth.

'So do I.'

'I'll see you tonight?'

'You can come for dinner, if you want.'

He pulled on his jacket and sat down on the edge of the bath next to her. 'We should live together.'

'Really?' Ruth said, light-heartedly. 'Your place or mine?'

'No, I'm serious. If you want we could even get married.'

'No. Definitely no!' she replied, leaning back. 'Thank you, Dino, for the offer, but I'm not marrying again. I've tried it twice and it didn't work out. I don't want to risk it ... or risk losing you.'

'And I thought you were a gambler,' he said softly, lifting Ruth's hair and kissing the back of her neck, 'but if you won't marry me, we should live together. I'll buy a big house for all of us and we'll be happy.'

Ruth straightened up, her hair falling back into place.

'Dino, this is my house. I'm proud of it, I like the headed notepaper and the Hampstead address. I've earned it, every brick and every piece of furniture.' He tried to interrupt, but she stopped him. 'When I came to London I was on my own.' She paused, but did not tell him about Laurel. 'Crummy hotels, crummy jobs, and long months when I relied on Nina keeping me sane. There was nothing out there for me – and when Ken came along I took a chance, and because everything had been so damned hard before, the thought of being some rich man's wife didn't faze me for one minute ... besides, I loved him.'

He looked at her carefully.

'I'd nothing to lose then, I could only go up. But I'm older now. And whatever they say, people don't get braver, they get scared, because they know what the world can do to them. I look at Graham and feel so wretched, wondering if I did something to harm him, or if I could help him more. And then I think of Kate and pray that she'll have an easy life, a life of private schools and nice clothes and a happy marriage.'

'Ruth – '

She carried on quickly, wanting to say everything, wanting to make him understand. 'You see, I love you – so much, that it would be folly to marry you. I don't want you to die or leave me for some other woman, or sleep in another room. I won't live that way!' She stopped and took in a deep breath. 'I've had some bloody awful times, but I've got over them and now I'll rebuild my cinema, because no one can stop me ... I want the best for my children, and I want you to stay with us.' Gently, she took hold of his hands. 'Don't ask me to give up this house. Don't ask me to change. I am what I am, and what I have, I keep.'

'In that case,' he said smiling, 'I'll come and live with you.'

'The cinema's burned down!' Lilian said, as Jack Gordon put down the phone.

'It's all right, Ruth says it can be rebuilt.'

'But the money ...' Lilian's voice trailed off. 'At least it was insured.'

She saw her husband's hesitation and jumped on it. 'It *was* insured, wasn't it?'

Jack shuffled around uneasily. 'Well, Ruth said that Geoffrey Lynes – '

'I knew it!' Lilian said, taking off her apron and filling the kettle. 'I always told Ruth not to trust that man. But she's always been headstrong and now look where it's got her.'

'She's rebuilding the place!'

Lilian turned on the gas. 'With what?'

'She's borrowed the money from Robert Floyd.'

Lilian's mind turned over the words; she remembered the old man – thin, yellow-skinned, smoking a cigar, and using a stick to lean on. Crafty as a monkey.

'Why Robert Floyd?'

'I've told you, so she can build a new cinema.'

'What for?'

'Don't be stupid! It was hers, she has to rebuild it.'

Lilian folded her apron and then poured some boiling water on to the tea. 'I think she tried to run before she could walk, if you want my opinion. Perhaps she should hold back her ambitions for a while.'

Jack looked at his wife and raged at her inwardly. The expression he had seen so often was on her face, a mixture of sympathy and triumph. For a moment, he prayed that Ruth would rebuild the cinema and that it would flourish – if only to see that look wiped off Lilian's face.

'Anyway,' she continued spitefully, 'why didn't she borrow the money from that Italian fellow? I thought they were as thick as thieves.'

'Dino Redici,' Jack answered evenly, 'she seems to like him a lot.'

'Ruth seems to like very strange people. I'm sure I don't know what she's up to.'

Jack picked up the evening paper and opened it, knowing that Lilian would drone on, with or without an audience, her judgement vitriolic, her tongue merciless.

'She should think about those children more. What about their futures?'

'Ken pays maintenance, and all Graham's medical bills. You know that. Ruth isn't putting them at risk.'

'Ken Floyd has been a great help,' she said, softly. 'They may even get together again – '

'For God's sake! He had another woman. He left her!'

Thwarted, Lilian's temper snapped. 'Well, what can you expect? She wants too much of her own way. She always did.'

Picking up his hat and coat, Jack walked out. He made for Oldham Edge, standing in the stiff breeze and looking over the moors, seeing the mill chimneys and Shaw, lurking in the incline. The air smelt good to him up there, had done ever since the days when he used to bring Ruth, when she was a child.

He smiled to himself. She had always been special – having

her mother's sense of style, without the bitterness. And he had loved her. Not as much as he did now – now he was proud of her, enjoying her triumphs as though they were his own, following all her ups and downs, feeling all her heartaches, seeing her develop into the woman she was. He turned up his collar against the wind and screwed up his eyes. Far away, he could see the rows of houses, tiny in the distance, like Carrington Street, and Grandma Price's, all identical, not like Ruth's house ... Ruth's house, Ruth's children, Ruth's career – he thought of them all, savouring the pleasure they gave him, and then he turned and walked back to the sooty streets.

It was November when Dino finally moved in, to a loud welcome from the children and Mrs Corley, although Mrs Harvey was another matter. Her daily notes became shorter and her conversation with Ruth, brusque to the point of monosyllabic. Knowing that she had to tell her parents, Ruth hesitated, dreading her mother's reaction and her certain disapproval. Unusually cowardly, Ruth told her father first and asked him to relay the news.

'Just tell me that you're happy,' he said.

'Very happy. He's good for me and he cares for the children better than Ken ever did. They could be his own. It's going to last this time, Dad.' She said the words with certainty; having found a man who satisfied her, physically and mentally, she was determined to keep him.

'I'm so glad for you, flower, but your mother's going to create, you know that.'

'I know she is, but I don't want to get married again. We're happy as we are.'

'Listen, your life is your own,' he said firmly, 'like I've always said. You must do what you think is right, and let all the other silly beggars sort themselves out.'

Ruth smiled down the phone. 'Thanks, Dad. Can you tell Mother the news?'

Well ... I can't say I'll enjoy it, but if you want me to, I'll tell her.'

'Then you could both come down and get to know him,' Ruth said eagerly.

'Just let her get used to the idea first, that's all.'

It took nearly nine months for Lilian to get used to the idea. She kept in touch from a distance, using her numerous chest infections the way old soldiers use war wounds to avoid doing anything they don't like. Conversations between mother and daughter continued unabated, but Lilian's attitude remained cool and judgemental.

With Robert Floyd's money, work went ahead to rebuild the cinema. Day after day Ruth was on the phone, assuring customers that the premises would reopen within months, hanging on to her reputation as she hung on to the bills. Frequently irritated by what he took to be an obsession, Dino still listened to Ruth's plans, advising her and protecting her the only way she would accept – at a distance. Arguments flared up quickly and savagely, only to be forgotten in bed later, their sex life providing the unbreakable bond between them.

And there was always Nina to provide the light relief. Whether it was due to Dino's intervention, or whether it was purely chance, Nina managed to land a role in the new show and came to see Ruth frequently to read her part. Unfailingly patient, Dino listened and passed on names of useful people he knew, warning her against others. 'You should be careful,' he said seriously, 'these people aren't respectable.'

'Then we should get along fine.'

'Nina,' he said wearily, 'you should be more ... demure.'

She smiled winningly. 'As in *De More I See You?*' she asked, breaking into song.

And when Ruth worked late into the night, Dino shared the early hours with her. Always a bad sleeper, he would sit and read, glancing up to see Ruth's eyes closing as she toiled over the cinema plans. He found it easy to confide, and sometimes in the early mornings he would waken Ruth, talking through the silent hours, sharing his dreams with her and encouraging her to share her own. In time, the magic of the cinema even captured him, and he began to understand what motivated her, and that the fear of failure was the spectre which made her run.

But Ruth never told him about Laurel, knowing that it was the one thing for which he would not forgive her. As an Italian, he believed that children were God's gift, and to reject such a gift was tantamount to murder. So Ruth hugged the secret to herself, warning Nina and her parents against making any chance remark.

Lilian, however, had other things on her mind. 'You should marry, it's not respectable.'

'Mother, we're living in the nineteen-seventies, people don't care any more.'

Lilian sniffed. 'You should think of the children, instead of yourself.'

Ruth bristled and changed the subject.

Aware that Dino Redici was everything she had hoped to find, Ruth had a perfectly good reason not to marry him. She was too afraid of failure, of the dark shapes at night and the memories which hounded her dreams. She remembered too well the hotel in Bayswater, the late night shops with their doomed clientele, the smells of cabbage boiling and mist on cold November mornings. And such thoughts made her resist a marriage which might lead to funerals, or drunken rages, or doors banging closed in the early hours.

And in Ruth, Dino found someone whom he admired, and someone whose sexual appetite matched his own. Cool and refined, Ruth impressed him by her very English demeanour, her passion only apparent at night. He found the paradox of her nature compelling and although he would storm out and return to his flat when they had a particularly violent argument, the next day usually found him back at Hampstead, where she was waiting for him.

Then the afternoon after Nina's show opened, Ruth came home and slumped into a chair in the lounge, her eyes staring ahead, her hands resting on her stomach. Alarmed, Dino came over to her, crouching down next to her chair.

'What is it?'

She knew the feeling well, and sighed. 'I'm pregnant.'

'A baby?' he asked, incredulous.

Ruth burst out laughing. 'That's generally what women give birth to, Dino.'

Infinitely gentle, he turned her hands over and kissed the inside of each palm.

When he was asleep that night Ruth watched him for a long time, the thin dark face against the pillow, the fine arm over the white sheet. Fourteen years on she was going to give birth to another child. Fourteen years after Laurel ... Ruth tried to picture her daughter – she would be a young girl now, she thought, maybe going out with a boyfriend. Suddenly tearful, Ruth turned over in the bed, trying to sleep. But the feeling of unease did not pass and ground into her dreams, waking her, clammy and tired, at three.

Dino was already awake and pulled her to him. 'What's the matter?'

'I don't know.'

His voice was low, disembodied in the dark. 'Don't worry, everything will be perfect.'

Instinctively, Ruth's hand moved to her stomach and rested there. A flutter of alarm made her panic. 'There's something wrong, I know it!'

Firmly, he soothed her. 'Ruth, nothing is wrong. This is a new start for us, a new beginning.'

The words drummed into her head like a bird trapped against a window-pane.

PART THREE

Renewals

_____ Fourteen _____

FLORENCE

Kate had grown up quickly. From being a child one day she had become tall overnight, long-legged, long-necked, with a deep fall of dark hair and that fine-boned look of breeding which reminded Ruth of her mother. At twelve she gave the impression of a girl four years older, and when she spoke her voice had a peculiarly husky tone which she had inherited from her father.

'Mum, I'll bring Graham through if you're ready,' she called out through the window of the lounge to where Ruth was sitting with Dino. 'Shall I?'

'If you would, Kate ... and answer the door, will you?'

They were about to celebrate the twins' birthday. Fleeing from London and the smoggy sun, they had made tracks to Dino's villa in Florence, perched high up over the city, the garden hotly scented and the walls parched under the overblown sun. He had invited his family to join them, his mother heading the table like the matriarch she was, and his brothers and sisters gathered round, brown-skinned and smelling of lemons. Not to be outdone, Ruth had invited her parents, hauling them off from Manchester on their first flight out of England. Lilian had been nervous, sitting next to Ruth on the plane with a smile of grim determination on her face. When they had landed she walked out into the sunshine and paused for a moment, looking up to the blue sky and pulling off her hat as she took her husband's arm.

Kate brought Ruth's thoughts back to the present as she pushed Graham out into the sunshine, the wheels of his chair making faint tracks on the stone floor.

'Hello, darling,' Ruth said, leaning across and kissing him. 'We're all ready for dinner.'

He responded by smiling and waving at Lilian, who had been spending a great deal of time with him. Courageously, he stammered a brief thank you for his presents and when he finished they all clapped, Dino passing him a glass of wine.

'You'll make an orator yet, Graham,' he said, turning to translate for his mother who spoke no English.

'Here you are, Graham,' Kate said, pushing a plate across the table to her brother. Deftly she flicked away a fly with her hand.

'He should eat more,' Dino said for the third time that day. As thin as ever, he found it impossible to believe that anyone could exist without massive intakes of food.

'He eats what he needs,' Ruth said sighing. 'He can't move around like the rest of us, so he doesn't need the same amount.'

Unconvinced, Dino rubbed the side of his nose with his forefinger, his white suit luminous against the white walls behind. His skin, which was always tanned, was even darker, the lines deep, and as he talked he waved a white crust of bread in his hand like a flower.

'You look wonderful,' he said, kissing Ruth's bare shoulder. His mother's eyes followed them. 'I love you.'

There was a hoot of laughter and he turned. Several of his relatives had heard him and were pointing, the men raising their glasses.

'So you heard me!' he said defiantly. 'Well, I'll say it again!' He got up and bent over Ruth, grinning. 'I love you,' he repeated as she laughed, pulling the brim of his hat over his eyes.

It was a lustrous afternoon, the sun stroking everyone as the breeze cooled their skins. The table was covered with food, the small wicker baskets of bread piled high. Wine was drunk in large quantities, although Lilian only tasted hers and scolded Ruth's father when he asked for a refill. When the time came for the twins' birthday cake to be cut, Graham began to cough, his breath coming in irregular gasps. Jumping to her feet, Ruth pushed him into the cool house and fetched an inhaler from a drawer in Dino's desk. Graham was then half out of his wheel-chair, one hand up to his throat and the other scrabbling on the arm of his chair.

Clasping the inhaler he breathed deeply several times, the look of panic fading in his eyes.

'Are you all right now?' Ruth asked, her own heart pounding.

He nodded, passing the inhaler back to her. 'Fine,' he stammered, the word almost unrecognisable to anyone except mother.

'You should keep that in your pocket in case you have an asthma attack,' Ruth said, stroking the thick hair and watching his fingers tremble on top of his thin legs. 'You promised me you would.'

He smiled slowly, their secret smile, and leant his head against her stomach, his breathing gradually returning to normal. Ruth had spent most of the night with him, sitting by his bed and listening to his breathing accelerate from normality to a series of gasps which made her rigid in her seat. They had been in Florence for a fortnight and he had been mercifully free of attacks until then, although Ruth put this one down to the excitement of the birthday party. Sitting with him quietly she thought back to the first time it had happened.

It had been ten months after David was born. One night, after Ruth had finished playing with the baby, she found Graham white-faced and silent in his wheelchair. Knowing instinctively that he couldn't breathe, she loosened his shirt collar and began to rub his hands. The chair rattled under him. Panicking, Ruth slapped him and he gasped, his breath returning as his hands clutched Ruth's, the fingernails sharp against her skin. When she finally managed to settle him in bed, she went downstairs and rang Dr Throop at the clinic.

'I don't understand it. Nothing like this has ever happened to Graham before. It looked like an asthma attack.'

The doctor was sympathetic. 'This can happen with your son's condition. I'll have a look at him tomorrow, unless you want me to come now.'

'No, I'll manage. He's been so difficult lately, it might upset

271

him more if you came over.' She sighed deeply, 'Why do you think this happened?'

'As I said, it may be due to his condition ... or he may be bringing it on himself to get your attention.'

Ruth was indignant. 'He was choking! Why would he want to do that?'

'To get you away from the baby,' came back the reply.

Ruth had always underestimated Graham's intelligence, making the same mistake for which she despised others – judging him mentally handicapped because of his physical defects. Repeatedly, he manipulated his mother to gain her attention, to restore the total commitment he had enjoyed before David was born. He wanted to restore her complete devotion, the same devotion which he received from Kate. In fact for many years Ruth was so occupied with her son that her daughter brought herself up, giving unfailing support to her mother in their mutual care of Graham.

So for several years Graham was blissfully happy. He had three females running around and taking care of him, and was exempted from the discipline a father would have enforced. Ruth was persistent with his exercises and his speech, tirelessly forcing him, but otherwise her son was her blind spot. Ever careful of Graham's feelings, when Dino moved in she was terrified that his condition would deteriorate and watched him carefully for the first few months, but after he discovered that Dino was as loving and supportive as Ruth was, Graham seemed to settle.

The arrival of David, however, affected him more profoundly than anyone had foreseen. His asthma attacks became an almost daily occurrence, and the clinic was convinced that the only way to help Graham was for him to stay with them full time.

'I can't do that,' Ruth said stubbornly. 'He'd think we'd abandoned him.'

'I agree,' Dino replied. 'His place is with the other children at home.'

'But Dr Throop thinks otherwise. He says Graham is a special case –'

Dino laughed drily, '*All* children are special cases. My sister had asthma and coughed all the time – then suddenly she fell in love, got married and she's fine.'

'I think Graham is a little young for marriage,' Ruth responded, with a wry smile.

'But he's not too young to know how to manipulate you,' Dino answered sharply. 'He can't ruin everyone else's life just because he wants your whole attention. He has to learn to fit in with the rest of us.'

'He gets confused, angry – '

'Anger doesn't kill people!' Dino shouted. 'Believe me, I know.'

When Ruth talked to Nina, she was in agreement with Dino, although she was for more drastic measures.

'I'd shove the little swine into that clinic for two weeks and bugger off to Florence, that would cure his temper damn quick.'

'Oh, Nina!' Ruth said, exasperated.

She shrugged her shoulders and leant towards the fire in the lounge. 'He's been spoilt, by you, Kate and Mrs Corley. Now that there's a new baby he'll ruin everything for you unless you put him firmly in his place *now*.'

'I can't, he's only a child.'

'So was Stalin once.'

Ruth walked into Graham's room later. He was drawing at a side table, hunched over the paper, his eyes fixed ahead of him. Ruth's heart lurched uncomfortably as she moved over and touched his shoulder. He turned calmly, as though he already knew she was there.

'Graham, what's the matter? We used to be such friends, and you used to tell me everything. Can't I help you now?'

He watched Ruth's lips carefully, but when he glanced back to her eyes he was defiant. 'There's nothing wrong,' he said in sign language.

'But there is!' Ruth insisted, pushing the drawing to one side and perching on the table. 'Something's making you unhappy.'

273

For an instant he seemed about to confide. The cold hostility in his eyes wavered and he let the pencil drop on to his lap. For a child of nine he seemed tired and already past his childhood.

'Tell me, Graham.'

'Can't,' he replied.

'Yes, yes you can!' Ruth said firmly. 'You can tell me anything, because I love you.' She lifted his chin up and smiled at him. 'You're my first son, and that makes you very precious.'

The firm line of his mouth relaxed.

'When you were little, I used to worry so much, but then you tried so hard to learn how to talk ...' Ruth stopped, her voice breaking. 'I was so proud of you. And now you're growing up you make me even more proud every day.' He was watching, reading the words. 'Do you know something? No one could replace you. No one.'

Smiling deeply, Graham's slim fingers closed around Ruth's hand, the touch of his warm skin the first contact he had offered her since David's birth.

For several days afterwards there was a peace between mother and son, Ruth's words calming Graham down considerably, his anger hardly in evidence. Showing him the baby, he was less resentful and even made the odd attempt to hold him, although Ruth noticed Kate's watchful eye and how she was always near at hand to return David to Mrs Corley when Graham tired of him.

'Hold him carefully, Graham,' Kate said, lifting the baby on to his lap. 'He's only little.'

'I am careful,' he signed.

'Not careful enough!' she responded briskly. 'You have to support his head.'

She continued talking, but her eyes seldom left her brother and her hands fluttered around David like autumn leaves. Her maternal instinct floundered between the two of them. On one side, she loved Graham deeply and protected him, but on the other side she knew that David needed defending as well. Carefully she fussed each of them in turn, and when the baby was sleeping her attention was turned back to Graham.

'He's very angry about the baby, isn't he?' she said when Ruth was making dinner.

'Who is?'

'Graham, of course. He's angry. He thinks we don't love him any more.'

Slowly, Ruth began to chop some carrots. 'Is that true, Kate?' she asked thoughtfully. 'Does he really believe that?'

She nodded. 'He said that no one cares about him any more since David came along. He said that they only really cared at the clinic.'

Unreasonably angry, Ruth turned on her. 'That's not true! Time and time again I tell him how much I think about him, but he won't believe me. He's so damned unreasonable! He always thinks he's hard done by.'

As ever, Kate rose to his defence. 'He's ill.'

Ruth took in a deep breath and looked down at her daughter. 'I know that! But he's always going to be ill. He's got us and we love him – that should help.'

Kate seemed close to tears. 'It's not fair! He can't hear and he can't walk properly and people think he's funny. It's not fair!'

'Kate, I know you love Graham, but we've got to be firm with him. He has to learn to live with us, and not expect the whole family to be on call just for him.'

'You don't care!' she shouted, running to the door. 'You like David better 'cos he's normal.'

With that parting shot she ran out. Infuriated, Ruth flung the knife into the sink, where it clattered noisily. When she turned round, Barnie was watching her from the back door.

'And what the hell are you staring at?' she asked angrily.

The atmosphere became so tense that Ruth actually began to feel guilty if she played with David, finding herself tied to Graham with a chain as heavy and unwieldly as Marley's ghost's. With childish ruthlessness, Kate decided that her mother should be made to feel badly, and spent a long time talking to Graham when Ruth was involved with the baby, in order to underline her neglect. Surprised by her attitude, Ruth

275

found herself excluded from the twins' confidences, and after a week was angry and annoyed.

'It's bloody ridiculous! As if I haven't got enough on my mind with the cinema,' she said to Dino one night. 'They're children and they're making me feel like an outsider.'

He smiled and stretched out his long arms in front of him.

'All children are politicians,' he said enigmatically.

'Brilliant! That's a great help, Dino.'

He smiled again and began to wind up his watch. The action grated on her.

'When I was little in Italy, we behaved like this. We led my mother a great dance whenever she had a baby. We were all jealous of the new child. But in some ways it's a good thing – it works out the pecking order for the children.' He glanced over to Ruth. 'There's no need to worry. When David is a little bigger he'll fend for himself.'

'I'm not waiting until he's a little bigger!' Ruth said sharply. 'I don't like atmospheres, and I don't like the children to think that they can get away with this sort of behaviour. I know that Kate feels she has to protect Graham – she always has done – but this is too much. Besides, Graham takes advantage of her.'

He fastened the watch back on his wrist carefully. 'Ruth, leave it a little longer. Things will work out.'

Ruth took his advice reluctantly, but her grinding unease continued. She woke unsettled and found herself tense throughout the day, watching David for any signs of handicap, talking to him and moving her hands in front of his eyes to check his reactions. To all intents and purposes, David was perfectly normal, but Ruth could not relax and her fear made her draw back from Dino.

'It's just a reaction to Graham, that's all,' Nina said when he rang her for advice.

Dino glanced over his shoulder before he continued. Ruth was nowhere in sight. 'She's behaving strangely. Neurotically.'

Nina raised her eyes heavenwards. 'Ruth gets like that when she's worried. She's got a lot on her mind,' she said, trying to make light of it. 'Besides, she's probably worried about the cinema on top of everything else. How's it doing?'

'Fine. They're getting bookings again, but not enough to pay off Robert Floyd yet. Not by any means.' He frowned. 'I keep telling her I could get the money, but she won't hear of it –'

'She wants to do it her own way.'

'By owing money to Robert Floyd? Dear God!' Dino said, his voice rising. 'It's not good business to rely on a man like that, it's stupid. I keep trying to advise her.'

Don't we all, Nina thought ruefully.

'Ruth never wants advice. She listened to everyone and did everything they said when she was a kid, and now she likes to do everything her own way.'

He was unimpressed. 'She spends too much time at that cinema. All day, and half the night, working. Then she comes back here and worries about the children. Some way to live!' he said, infuriated.

Nina heard the tone of his voice and winced. Don't blow it, Ruth, she thought. Don't blow this one. 'Give her time, Dino, David's still very young, after all, and that fire shook her up badly.' She paused. 'She needs you.'

'Then why doesn't she tell me that?' he asked angrily.

It was a wet, uncomfortable day. March winds rattled the doors and Barnie howled endlessly to go out, returning minutes later to leave dirty paw marks across the hall and up the stairs. Ruth collected Graham from the clinic and returned home where Dino was amusing Kate in the kitchen, a smear of Marmite along his top lip as a make-believe moustache. When Ruth walked in pushing Graham's wheelchair, he was in the middle of a piece from the *Marriage of Figaro*, his long arms waving the bread knife in front of a delighted Kate.

'What the – ?' she said, stopping in the doorway.

He stopped singing. 'Evening, darling,' he said, planting a kiss on Ruth's cheek and picking Graham up. 'What a day!'

'It's bad outside too,' she said frostily.

Dino frowned at Graham in mock distress. Apparently there was no animosity between him and the children. 'Are you tired, Ruth?'

Her annoyance turned to sarcasm. 'Good Lord, why should I be tired? I've been looking after David, running around London, doing the shopping, and collecting my son from the clinic, all in the midst of a gale force wind. Now why should I be tired?'

Without a word, Dino put Graham back into his wheelchair and nodded to Kate. She understood him immediately and pushed her brother out of the kitchen, pulling the door closed behind her.

'Having a good time, were you?' Ruth asked bitterly, turning to unpack the groceries. 'I'm glad someone is. I had a cancellation at the cinema today, and that bloody man, Pascoe, has asked for a week off.' She slammed down some tins, her hand shaking. 'There was also a message from Robert Floyd waiting for me, which, I might add, I did not return.' Her voice was thin with tiredness. 'The cinema's got to start making money, it has to!'

Dino walked over to her and ran his forefinger along her arm. 'What's the matter really?'

'Nothing's the matter!' Ruth shouted hoarsely. 'My kids can't stand me any more and it feels like the end of the world, and ...' Stupidly, she burst into tears.

'Sshhhh. It's just that you're tired coping with the baby – '

Ruth was not about to be placated. 'No, it's not that! I've had children before ...' she trailed off, afraid that he might read something in her eyes. 'I feel like something awful is going to happen,' she said, pulling away from him and beginning to put the groceries in the fridge. 'Where the hell is Mrs Harvey anyway?'

Dino was baffled. 'It's her night off. It always is on a Thursday.'

'Oh, yes ...' Ruth said more quietly, '... I forgot.'

'Listen, you need a break. We could go away for a holiday – '

Her eyes were sharp with anger, her mother's eyes. 'With a cinema to run! And in the middle of term! I can't just uproot Graham and Kate and clear off somewhere. It's not possible.' She looked at him closely. 'And wipe that bloody stuff off your mouth, you're not a child!'

She had gone too far. Dino's face altered from good humour to aggravation. For an instant, he almost hated her. 'Don't shout at me! I'm not a servant and I won't be shouted at. Talk to me properly and we'll discuss things, but otherwise,' he pointed to the door, 'I'm going out.'

Ruth saw the change and instead of calming him, pushed him even further away from her. 'In that case, get out!' she said coldly. He paused for an instant and then left.

As she heard the car pull out, Ruth pulled off her coat and sat down wearily. Upstairs, she could hear Mrs Corley calling for Kate, and the bang of the lift door as it reached the first floor. A few minutes later, a radio began to play and the pipes began a slow thumping as the water was drawn for the first bath. Dumbly miserable, she laid her head down on her arms, her stomach shifting with unhappiness and anxiety. Incredibly, she dozed, waking at eight-thirty and making her way upstairs. Mrs Corley was on the top corridor, her arms full of clean sheets.

'How's David?'

'He's fine,' she said, surprised by the question, and noticing Ruth's high colour and creased clothes. 'Why?'

'Oh, nothing . . . I fell asleep in the kitchen, of all places, and I've just woken up.'

'Don't you feel well?' she asked, reaching up and feeling Ruth's forehead. 'You've got a temperature. You should be in bed.'

She shook her head vigorously. 'No, I don't want to go to bed yet, I've got some work to do. Where are the twins?'

'Watching television.' She glanced at her watch. 'They've got to be settled just as soon as I've moved these things.'

Gently Ruth touched her arm. 'Let me do it.'

A film was ending as she walked in. Kate turned to her and then frowned, obviously disappointed that it wasn't Mrs Corley.

'Come on,' Ruth said, with forced cheerfulness, 'time for bed.'

Stiffly obedient, Kate went to Graham and took the brake off his chair, turning it in the direction of the door. Seeing his mother, he smiled warmly. Kate, however, was not forth-coming and was eager to go to bed. Reluctantly Ruth turned out her light and closed the door, going on to Graham's room and talking to him for a while. He was quiet and oddly amen-able, as though he was trying to please her. Finally, Ruth bent to kiss him on his forehead.

'Sleep well, Graham. I'll see you in the morning.'

Although Ruth had found it easy to sleep on the kitchen table she could not even doze in the comfort of her own bed and lay motionless, her eyes wide open. The wind had picked up speed and an angry shower pelted the window like children throwing stones. The bedroom seemed curiously unfriendly and over-large, the pieces of furniture grinning at her like guardsmen. Disturbed, Ruth turned off the main light and switched on two lamps instead, pulling back the curtains to look out on to the drive for Dino's car.

Cars passed on the road, but none stopped. Repeatedly, Ruth visited David's cot as she waited, peering into the closed and sleeping face, watching his movements, and checking his breathing. Because of her disquiet Ruth had wondered if he was ill; wondered if she might find him still and moon-white, his breath gone. Her hands clammy with panic, she walked down to Graham's room and then Kate's, monitoring her children in the still night.

Hearing her wanderings, Mrs Corley woke and made her way down to the first floor, pulling a dressing-gown over her stocky figure and a hair-net over her curlers. 'Mrs Floyd?' she called down the dim corridor. A shape moved in the half light. 'Is there anything wrong?'

Ruth materialised in front of her. She was agitated, her hair loose over her shoulders, her face drawn. 'I'm just worried, that's all. I don't know why ... It doesn't make sense.'

Surprised by her appearance, Mrs Corley asked, 'Can I get you anything?'

Ruth shook her head. 'No, I don't need anything. I'll go back to the bedroom ... I've got some work to do.'

'You should get some rest, you don't look well,' Mrs Corley

said firmly — children and work, work and children, she thought, that woman will kill herself if she's not careful. 'I'll take the children to school tomorrow — you have a lie-in.'

'We'll see ... I'm sorry I woke you.'

Mrs Corley touched her arm lightly. 'No trouble, Mrs Floyd,' she said, moving off.

The night ground on. There was still no sign of Dino, and Ruth still hadn't been able to sleep. Agitated and tearful, she tried to work, but her mind wandered and, infuriated, she flung the papers to the floor and lay down on the top of the bed. The wind began to die down, the sounds less mournful as the moon crept out from behind clouds. In between the curtains the silver light sighed in and, eventually, Ruth slept. She dreamt of Laurel. She wasn't tall, as Ruth was, she was slim and tiny and her eyes were the same colour as Derek's. In her dream she was playing in the patch of garden on the Coppice, the lawn only the size of a dinner napkin. From an upstairs window, Derek called to her and she lifted her hand. Then as Ruth watched, Laurel shrank to the size of a baby and instead of being on the grass she was suddenly in her cot, a child again. When Ruth touched her she was as cool as an alabaster dove, but as she tried to lift her, other arms moved into the cot and pushed Ruth aside.

Startled, Ruth jumped up, fully awake. Initially, she thought she was still dreaming, but in fact there was someone knocking faintly on the bedroom door.

'Come in.'

It was Kate. Tiny and pale she hovered in the doorway like a ghost child.

'Kate?' Ruth whispered, her voice riding the dark air.

'It's Graham ...' the child said simply, 'Graham's hit the baby.'

The words galvanised Ruth into action as she ran over, kneeling in front of her daughter. 'What did you say?'

'Graham hit the baby,' she repeated, clinging on to Ruth's nightdress as her mother moved towards the door. 'David's all right ... Mrs Corley doesn't even know.'

Ruth hesitated, wanting to go to her son, yet knowing that Kate wanted to be comforted. In the dim room, she picked up her daughter and sat down on the edge of the bed. She was cool in Ruth's arms, so cool that her mind slipped back, thinking of her dream, thinking of Laurel. Ruth knew what it had cost Kate to tell her what had happened; knew how she loved her brother and how she must have wanted to protect him, to cover up for him again.

'When did he do this, Kate?'

'Mrs Corley had bathed David and was getting some clean sheets for the cot when Graham . . .' Kate paused, uncertain of the words, only certain of her betrayal, '. . . he never saw me, I was by the door . . . he thought I was in the playroom.'

Ruth slipped back into her dream, remembering all the strange arms reaching into the cot for her child.

'Graham hit him through the bars of the cot . . .' Kate continued, her voice high. 'David cried and Mrs Corley came back . . . but Graham had moved then and she never thought . . .' Kate stopped and looked at Ruth. 'I didn't want to tell on him . . . but he shouldn't have done it.'

Her eyes staring into the darkness, Ruth sat with her arms tightly around Kate who was crying. 'You did the right thing to come to me, sweetheart,' she said, her voice calm. 'Graham was very wicked to do what he did, and there is no excuse for it.' She took in her breath. 'He must be punished, you do understand that, don't you?'

Kate looked away from her mother and began to pick at the cord of her dressing-gown. 'But he'll know I told you.'

Ruth squeezed her tightly. 'How could he know? You told me that he didn't know you were there. So how could you possibly know what he's done, let alone tell me?'

She stopped crying, her voice more firm. 'What are you going to do?'

What am I going to do? Ruth thought. What am I going to do? The words went round and round in her head like a child's toy mobile in a breeze, although the answer was obvious and she knew it. Taking Kate's hand, Ruth moved into the corridor. The place was in darkness, except for a trickle of moon which striped the dim hallway. Silently, she settled her daughter in bed and walked to the nursery.

David was sleeping, his right hand poking out of the bars, the fingers curled into the palm. He looked peaceful and his mouth was slightly open, his breathing steady. When Ruth picked him up he only moved slightly once before slipping back into sleep. Carefully, Ruth undressed him on her lap, examining his arms and legs for marks. There was nothing visible. Slowly, she turned him. He mewed suddenly, like a kitten. At the base of his spine was a bruise, the size of a hen's egg, and red, deepening in parts to purple. Cold with shock, Ruth re-dressed him and leant back in the chair, her hands stroking his head.

Downstairs, the front door closed almost silently. Only the creak on the third stair told her that Dino was home and was making his way upstairs. A minute later, his thin, tanned face appeared round the door. He frowned and came in, pulling up a chair and rubbing his nose against David's neck.

'I'm sorry,' he said. 'I went back to the flat, got myself a drink and then went to bed. But I was lonely . . . I kept thinking about you and the children and . . . so I came home.'

'I'm glad . . .' Ruth said, reaching out and touching his cheek with the tips of her fingers, 'because we've got a problem. Graham hit the baby. Kate told me only a little while ago.'

He stiffened. 'What?'

'Graham hit the baby – '

'Dear God! Is he all right?'

Ruth nodded. 'This time.'

They both looked at David, their child. Ruth knew what he was thinking because they were her thoughts also. With a courage she did not think she possessed, Ruth had made the decision for both of them. In the cold night as she waited for Dino to come back, she had settled the matter, and when the decision was made, had felt nothing except a dead sense of loss which consumed her.

'Graham must go to the clinic, Dino. He must live there for a while . . . until he realises that he can't hurt this child.'

He said nothing, merely nodded. When he looked away his eyes were dull.

283

'He has to go, otherwise he'll keep hitting David until one day . . . you understand that, don't you?'

'Yes.'

Ruth rang Dr Throop in the morning and told him what had happened. He seemed relieved that she had made the decision so rapidly and insisted that she was doing the right thing for both Graham and the baby. Ruth's mouth was set as she put down the phone. Her son, she thought, her child, the one she realised guiltily that she loved the most, was leaving. The thought crystallised in her brain, the pain rocking her.

'Wake up, Kate,' she said softly.

The child turned and opened her eyes. Already, she knew. 'Mummy?'

'I'm taking Graham to the clinic. He has to stay there for a little while.'

Kate looked at her mother, a sense of guilt welling up in her because she had told on her brother, and he was going away . . .

'Kate,' Ruth said firmly, seeing the reaction, 'it's not your fault. Graham has to go.'

They exchanged a long look.

'Can I come with you?' she asked simply.

Graham was still sleeping as Ruth touched his shoulder. He turned, waking slowly, looking at her with her father's eyes. Ruth's heart ached. Carefully, she washed and dressed him, and then they ate breakfast together in his room. Ruth thought he suspected what was happening, but said nothing. A cold breeze slapped against the window, the sound angry to Ruth's ears although Graham could not hear it. She watched her son, his head bent, cutting his food, watched the tiny legs under the rug, and the way he smiled at her. She smiled back, treacherously, moving the tray and sitting down in front of him.

'Graham, I know you hit the baby,' she said slowly. His face seemed at first surprised and then resigned. I love you, she thought numbly. 'That was wrong of you. I know that you've been unhappy for a while here with us and that you feel at home in the clinic. Graham, you have to go there for a while – '

He grabbed for Ruth's hands and held on to them, his mouth trying to form words. 'No – Mummy! I – won't – do – it – again.'

The words caught in her throat, her hands tight in her son's. Why did you do it, she thought. Oh, God, Graham, why?

'Yes, you will. Graham, I don't want to hurt you but it's the only solution.'

He was panicking, his words becoming indecipherable. 'Mummy!'

Unable to speak, Ruth tried to withdraw her fingers. She kept thinking of Laurel, of the child she had given away; kept seeing her in this little boy who was begging her to keep him.

'Mummy! I – want – to – stay – home.'

Crying, Ruth grabbed him and kissed him repeatedly, her lips against his skin, her eyes closed. Then she quickly drew back, holding his chin and talking slowly so that he understood.

'Graham, I love you, and I will always love you, whatever happens. But what you did was wrong and you must go away until you can come home and live with us happily. When you're ready to come back, and sorry for what you've done, I'll come for you.'

He wriggled in the chair. 'Let – me – stay,' he gasped.

She thought for a moment he was going to have an asthma attack, as his breath altered and he stiffened in his chair. Then he stopped struggling, relaxing back into the seat with his head bowed. Silently, Ruth wheeled him out into the car. Kate followed. Neither of them spoke on the twenty-minute journey to the clinic.

'He'll be fine,' Bella said, smiling at Graham kindly, having been obviously forewarned of his arrival. Graham did not respond. 'Don't worry about him, Mrs Floyd, he'll be safe here ... We'll call you,' she said finally, looking at Ruth who hesitated by the front door. The wind blew across the flat lawns and caught hold of their clothes, making rough snatches at the gravel.

Bending quickly, Ruth leaned over her son and kissed the top of his head. Graham did not move, but his hands clenched the arms of the wheelchair tightly. Her legs felt weak under her as she moved back to the car, Kate watching her from the front passenger seat. For a moment, Ruth leant against the bonnet with her eyes closed, and then pulled open the door, turning to see the wheelchair with its little passenger being pushed across the few remaining winter leaves.

'Graham ...!' she shouted helplessly after him.

But he couldn't hear her.

In the years which followed Graham was in and out of the clinic every time they had trouble controlling him. The stays were never very long, but they served their purpose and made him realise that the family could no longer be at the mercy of a child. On that first occasion after he had injured David, Graham remained at the clinic for a month. The days taunted Ruth, telling her repeatedly that she was an unfit mother ... and for her, it was due punishment for Laurel.

When Ruth finally collected him on a sunny April morning, she wheeled him out to the car, his little face white and thinner than before, his hands instinctively reaching out to her. She bent down and lifted him, smelling him against her lips and feeling his tears on her cheek. His breath seemed to burn her.

'Graham, Graham ...' she repeated over and over, seeing him smile as she strapped him into the car seat. All the way home Ruth talked, turning to look at him when the lights were red.

'I love you,' she said, laughing when he nodded.

Dino looked forward to his return enormously. Emotional in the extreme he had spent as many nights pacing the floor as Ruth had, rushing for the telephone to see what the news was; how Graham had slept, how he had eaten, if he was still crying ... They went through his exile with him, and when his punishment was over they were as chastened as he was.

'He's very difficult,' Dr Throop said evenly on the morning they took Graham home. Ruth was talking to Bella outside, Dino walking down the corridor with the doctor. 'He veers between being placidly uncommunicative and violent. He actually frightens some of the other children, and although the older ones tried to bully him, he seems impervious to threats.'

'Bully him?' Dino said, aghast. 'How can you let such a thing happen? You're not fit to run a clinic!'

Immune to abuse, Dr Throop continued calmly. 'Graham is intelligent enough to know that he can make his life easier by being amenable – it's only when he can't understand something, or when he's homesick, that he resorts to violence.'

Dino stopped walking and looked at the man next to him. 'But he's all right now? He can cope?'

'Until the next time,' Dr Throop answered calmly.

Gradually, Graham learned how to live within a family again, accepting, if not loving, David. Surprisingly, the greatest effect was on Kate, who grew up the instant they left Graham at the clinic for the first time, and as the years passed she seemed to become very much the older sister/mother figure.

So they passed into their thirteenth year, celebrating their birthday in the cool, Florentine house on top of the hillside where Ruth was sitting with Graham after his asthma attack. David was crying in the bedroom, having woken from his afternoon nap.

'Kate, can you get David for me?' Ruth called out to her daughter as she sat with Graham. His colour was returning to normal, his breathing steadied.

'Better now?' she asked. He nodded. 'Well, that's good, because you're just in time to cut the cake.'

The sun was losing some of its heat and along the railings of the balcony the red geraniums glowed hotly against the white paint. A couple of birds flew overhead and made patterns on the floor and Ruth could hear her father laughing with Dino as she pushed Graham's chair out.

'Hello again,' he said, smiling broadly. 'How do you feel?'

Graham smiled and nodded. 'OK,' he stammered.

Lilian leant forward. 'Should he be out in this sun? Isn't it too hot for him?'

'He's fine, Mother,' Ruth said, trying to keep her voice calm. 'It's good for him.'

'I don't know if it's good for him – all that sun on his head.'

'Mother, I should know –'

287

Dino interrupted them. '"Happy birthday to you!"' he began, standing up and conducting everyone else as they joined in the singing.

They ate and talked until the light faded and Dino's family went home one by one. His mother was the last to leave with his brother, and as the old lady kissed Ruth on both cheeks, the light from the door made her skin glow like topaz.

'Mother says thank you,' Dino translated, even though by this time Ruth understood a fair amount of the language. 'She also thinks we should get married, she thinks living together is immoral.'

'Tell her I wouldn't love you any more if we were married.'

He translated for her and she frowned, raising her eyebrows and walking off with Dino's brother.

'Is she very disappointed in me?' Ruth asked, her arm through Dino's.

'No more than I am.'

'What does that mean?'

He rummaged for a cigarette and lit it, blowing smoke into the soft night sounds. 'It means why don't you marry me?' He glanced at Ruth seriously. 'You're getting older, this might be your last chance.'

She laughed loudly and he frowned. 'Does that mean no?'

Ruth nodded. 'For now at least.'

He inhaled deeply and the cigarette tip glowed savagely in the dark air. '*Lasciate ogni speranza voi ch'entrate!*' he said.

Used to his quotations, Ruth smiled. 'What does that mean?'

'It's Dante, *The Divine Comedy* – "All hope abandon, ye who enter here."'

'I see,' she said. 'Well, what about – "This here young lady, she knows wot's wot, she does."'

He frowned. 'What's that?'

'Sam Weller, from Dickens's *Pickwick Papers*.'

He laughed and slung his arm around Ruth's shoulder. 'And do you know "wot's wot"?'

She paused and added seriously, 'I know when I'm lucky and that's everything.'

*

'Another boy! Is he normal?' Joanie asked her brother over the phone. Her voice swung like a pendulum over the Atlantic.

'Don't be spiteful,' Ken said briskly. Over the years he had put on weight, his drinking accelerating rapidly. After a particularly bad binge he would admit himself to a clinic to dry out, but his abstinence never lasted. Neither did his women. They came and went, and as he grew older he could not decipher one from the other. Only one face remained clear, and that belonged to Ruth. As the years passed, he thought more, not less, about her – and the obsession returned.

'It's just that she seems to keep bouncing back,' Joanie continued bitterly, '... even that blasted fire didn't keep her down. I wonder who paid for those renovations?'

'Does it matter? It's not your money,' Ken said, bored with the subject. He knew that Ruth had struggled to get the cinema rebuilt and although he didn't know who had lent her the money, he realised that the house had been used for collateral and that she worked harder than anyone he knew.

'She's done well, she's a success.'

Joanie sniffed. 'She got lucky. She married you *and* your money. She hadn't a bean before that. She wasn't used to money – '

'But she certainly made it work for her, didn't she?'

Joanie was stung. She had expected Ken still to feel bitter, even more so, now that his ex-wife was climbing back.

Deftly, she changed the subject. 'How's Graham?'

Ken smiled wryly; she always mentioned his son when she wanted to underline his inadequacies. 'He's been in the clinic again. I spoke to Father and he said he's been hitting the new baby.'

'Happy families,' Joanie said, her good humour restored. 'Perhaps the child would feel more secure if its mother could persuade the father to marry her.' She paused, pretending to think for a moment. 'Mind you, would you take on a woman with three kids, a white elephant of a cinema, and loans up to her ears?'

Ken thought of Ruth, of her hair, that stunning coldness of

her voice, and her courage. 'Yes, I'd take a woman like that on,' he said quietly.

David was little trouble, taking after his father although he was more placid by temperament, his mass of Italian curls needing cutting every few weeks. He inherited his father's love of music and sang out tunelessly whenever the radio was turned on, humming away in his high chair as Mrs Corley tidied up the playroom.

'He's good, isn't he?' Ruth asked her.

'Good as gold. The best baby I've ever had to look after.' She looked round. 'Mind you, you deserved one that was no trouble after everything that's happened.'

Ruth sat down and began to fold some nappies. 'I worry about Graham, you know. I wonder . . . how long he'll live.'

She nodded briskly. 'He'll be all right.'

'But if he outlives me, who will look after him?'

'Kate will, of course.'

'But that's just the point – why should she?' Ruth said sharply. 'She has her own life to live and she'll have her own family one day, why should she want to take her brother on?'

Mrs Corley took the nappies from Ruth. 'You should stop fretting about things. What will be, will be. Life never follows the paths you want, no matter how long you think about it and plan things. Graham will come out all right, you'll see.'

Carefully, Mrs Corley tidied away the children's clothes. She was even more stout than before, her hips expansive, her chin fleshy, her strong arms capable. Never a person to worry, she lived every day in total acceptance of what was to come, and made no plans. Because it was so alien to her nature, she marvelled at Ruth's stamina, at the body blows she had received over the years, and from which she rallied, every time. But she knew that the worry about Graham had taken the hardest toll. Ambitious and determined, Ruth was permanently concerned about business, but those matters she could control; only her son ate into her, their particular love binding them closer, as he constantly tried her.

Fifteen

Nina was back. Ruth had not seen her for a while because she had spent much of the previous two years touring abroad, writing her usual incoherent letters. The last had come from New York, New York, with a vulgar picture of an Andy Warhol painting on the postcard and a cryptic message:

> Ruth and family,
>
> Coming home next week – 23 November – to do show
> in London. Great news – for both of us. You and me.
> I got a mention in the paper here, some critic seemed
> to think I had 'it'. Asked me out on the strength of
> 'it' and left later, without 'it'! So now I've had it! Wot
> a laff! Nothing changes, New York's London without
> Eros – or is it the other way round? See you soon now.
> Lots of love to the kids, and Caruso. Happy times
> are coming –
>
> > Nina

Ruth read it to Dino and he laughed. 'We'll have her over for dinner when she gets back. Give her a ring and arrange it.'

'I don't know where she's living now. She might have given up the old flat before she went on tour.'

He flicked the postcard over. 'She could stay here,' he said generously.

November the 23rd turned out to be a hot day; not warm, hot. Freak weather, everyone said, ripping off their winter woollies and pouring into linen suits. Dino came home at lunch-time and stretched out in the garden on a sun lounger, his long form basking gratefully in the unexpected sun. Beside him, David was listening to the radio while Barnie kept creeping up on Dino's prone figure and jumping on him every time he fell asleep.

'I'm home,' Ruth shouted through the window, watching as Dino flung his son over his shoulder and ran in.

Neither of them was expecting Nina to visit on her first evening home, so when the doorbell rang and Kate answered it Ruth was astonished to see her standing there.

'Well, I'll be – '

'Damned,' she finished cheerfully, kissing Kate and looking at her approvingly. 'You're getting pretty,' she said, 'and *tall*. Like your mother.'

Kate smiled. 'Are you staying?'

'Sure. Your mother invited me.'

'Did I? You never replied to my letter, Nina,' Ruth said, walking over to her and giving her a quick hug.

'Didn't I? I was sure I had.' She beamed. 'Still, I can stay, can't I?'

By the time she'd got into the kitchen Graham had been brought down by Mrs Corley in the lift. He pushed open the doors and wheeled towards her.

'Well – and how's my favourite delinquent?' Nina asked cheerfully, leaning towards him so he could read her lips. 'You caused a lot of trouble, didn't you? Are you behaving yourself now?'

'I'm a good boy,' he stammered.

'You're talking better, too,' she said, pushing him into the kitchen. 'Something smells delicious.'

On and on she rattled, talking to the twins and Dino, before turning her attention to David, whom she hauled out of his high chair like a cork out of a bottle. Her hair was still red, but golden red, her make-up natural, making her appear younger. She was wearing beige culottes with a silk jacket and a pair of very expensive boots, and in her ears she wore a large pair of pearl and diamond earrings which could have blinded anyone at ten paces.

'You look good,' Ruth said.

'You too.'

'Really? I was wondering about my hair.'

She looked at it closely. 'I can see your point.'

'I should have known better than to ask,' Ruth said, drily. 'We got the postcard; after I had it translated it was very interesting. What's the good news for both of us?'

She was jiggling David up and down in her arms. He looked delighted and poked a finger in her ear. 'Ouch!' she said, turning back to Ruth. 'Something vital, absolutely vitally important! But I'm not telling you now. I want to save it for later.' She looked innocently at Ruth, wearing her 'I need a favour' look.

'I've invited someone to dinner – here – tonight – with us. Do you mind terribly?'

'Who?'

'He's a friend,' she said evasively.

'Serious?'

'Could be.'

'Married?'

She pretended to be shocked. 'Do you think I'm that kind of woman?'

'Why? Have you changed?'

She laughed loudly and tickled David.

Tony Milton arrived an hour later, leaving his Jaguar in the driveway and ringing the doorbell as though he was checking the wiring. When Ruth answered he shook hands and then took off his coat, piling it on to the hall chair with his bulging briefcase.

'Evening,' he said pleasantly, with a strong Birmingham accent. 'You have a nice home.'

He was all of fifteen stone, dressed expensively but with slightly flashy taste. A little of his soft flesh draped over the side of his collar and made white rubber gloves out of his hands. Years ago he would have been attractive, but now his dark hair was thinning a little, and his eyes were two blue sapphires at sea in the surf of white skin.

'Nina and you go back a long time,' he said, smiling as Ruth showed him into the lounge.

Dino sized him up immediately. 'What business are you in, Mr Milton?'

'Call me Tony, everyone does.' He glanced over the back of the settee. 'You French?'

Ruth could see Dino stiffen. 'Italian,' he said coldly.

Tony looked over to Nina. 'Like Frank Sinatra, hey?'

The pre-dinner drinks were not a success. While Nina and Ruth found time to catch up on the previous months, the men held staccato conversations behind them. Tony's grasp of the English language being somewhat tenuous, he struggled manfully with his vocabulary, making a point and then suddenly throwing everyone into confusion.

'... I was saying to this man, you could make money on this deal with me, us and a few other people could make up a conjugation.'

Ruth looked at him with an expression of cool puzzlement.

'You mean a conglomerate, idiot,' Nina said quickly. 'He was talking about life after death the other night and said that he didn't think God was impotent ... ' she began to laugh, '... instead of omnipotent. I nearly died.'

Ruth raised her eyebrows. 'Since when were you Shakespeare?'

'Ever since I met him,' she said, glancing over to Tony with a look very close to affection. 'He's nice though, isn't he?'

'Dino or Tony?'

'Tony! You know what I mean.'

Ruth looked at her seriously. 'Is this love, Nina?'

'Well ... something close.'

'But, isn't he a bit, you know, a bit ... rough?'

'As a bear's arse,' she said laughing. 'But he's the kindest man I've ever known.'

It turned out that Tony had been 'lucky in business'. He'd been born in Birmingham, brought up by his grandmother and bought a shop at twenty. The shop had flourished, and he'd bought another, and another ... and the rest was history. He was in the hardware trade, which branched out into do-it-yourself.

'... So I always say to people if you want something doing you "do it yourself"'!' he laughed loudly. 'There's a lot of money in it, a lot of money.' He turned back to Dino, slinging his plump arm over the back of the settee. Ruth expected to hear the seams rip. 'You should know, you're in banking.'

'But not in hardware,' Dino answered grandly.

'No, well ... I do OK though.'

'I'm sure you do, Tony,' Ruth said, giving Dino a bleak look. 'How did you meet Nina?'

'In New York. I was over there on business, good business, I might add, I made a lot of – '

'Tony, get back to the point!' Nina said impatiently.

'Sorry – I met your friend in New York, she was in a show and I saw her and thought, "I've got to meet that lady" – so I went back after they'd finished and asked her out and we've been irreparable ever since.'

'Inseparable!' Nina shouted, laughing. 'It's OK, everyone, it's only really bad when he's nervous.'

Out of the corner of her eye Ruth could see Dino refill his glass.

With very little in common, the two men struggled through the meal while, heartily amused, the women left them to it. It was at the end of dinner, as Dino was relating some banking investment scheme, that Nina finally told Ruth her news.

'Tony's got sackfuls of money. Carts of the stuff. He doesn't know what to do with it.'

'So?'

'Well, he's bought this property in London, near Leicester Square, and he was talking about selling it on. It's an old cinema, half converted, once was part of some mansion place but now it's half-cinema and half-house ... and Tony doesn't want it.'

'Yes?' Ruth said cautiously.

Nina rolled her eyes. 'I told him that you managed a cinema in Piccadilly and that you owned one in Knightsbridge. Well, actually, I didn't have to tell him that, he'd heard about the fire.' She grinned wickedly. 'I said that yours were high class – not your usual choc-ice and a grope in the back seat dive – and that you might like to buy it from him, as no one else would really want it, it being such a dump and all. And as you are a friend of mine I would look upon it as a favour to me if he kept the price cheap.'

'How much?' Ruth said bluntly. 'It would have to be dirt cheap. I don't have any money left now, not after the fire, and I've only just paid off Robert Floyd.'

'Listen, it was only a suggestion, you do what you like. But I thought that you might prefer to dump the Piccadilly place and work solely for yourself. After all, Ruth, you're not going to starve, are you? Dino would always lend you the money.'

'Listen, I like the idea ... ' Ruth said, her mind already running over the proposition, 'but it would be a gamble.'

'So since when have you been afraid of a gamble?' Nina asked, dropping her voice. 'You're working for that company flat out, and for what? A salary? Why not invest in the cinema you've already got and this one, and build up your own places, instead of putting money in other people's pockets?'

'I want to do it – '

'So what's holding you back?'

'Dino,' Ruth said flatly. 'He never says anything, but I don't know if he would like my becoming even more involved in work.'

'You *are* involved. You run two cinemas now, the only difference would be that if you bought this one, you would be running your *own* cinemas. No one else in London could touch you.'

Ruth thought for a moment. 'I could go bankrupt.'

'You could,' Nina said, shrugging, 'but you won't. You could have folded after the fire, but you got yourself going again. Think about it, Ruth.'

She knew she wasn't going to need time to think about it; Ruth's expression had taken on the look Nina recognised, the look she used when she was encouraging Graham, the look she employed whenever she had decided on something.

'I'll think about it. Thanks, Nina. I'd have to look at it and talk to Dino.' She smiled brilliantly. 'God, it's tempting, but it's a risk – it could fail.'

'That's what they said to Columbus.'

Ruth smiled coolly. 'I never knew he ran a cinema.'

'Well, he never made a go of it – he was away a lot.'

Tony Milton collected Ruth the following day, taking her to view the cinema, and introducing her to everyone on the site as 'Mrs Lloyd'. The premises were small but promising, capable of seating only fifty people, and full of the kind of intimacy which seduces customers. Fired with enthusiasm, Ruth was pleased to see that under the grime the building was sound. It would be another showpiece, she decided, a club as well as a cinema. Aware that she wanted the place, and wanted it desperately, Ruth assumed an expression of composure and turned to Tony with an indifferent air.

'This is a stupid time to buy a cinema, Tony. You know that. The boom is fading now. No one goes to the cinema as much as they used to.'

He smiled, the sapphire eyes disappearing under the milky folds of skin. 'Don't snow me, Ruth! I know what you're up to, you want me to drop the price. Listen, I'm prepared to do a deal because a lot hangs on this for me. You talk to Milo – '

'Dino.'

'Yeah, Dino, and see what you think. Here are the keys. Get him to have a look and then make me an offer.' He winked broadly. 'Something I can't refuse.'

'Like free tickets on the opening night, you mean?'

He looked shocked. 'No offence, Ruth, I was just kidding, just kidding, that's all.'

Because some of the electricity had been turned off, the cinema was gloomy when Ruth returned later that evening, the foyer grimy and dull with shadows. Standing with her arms folded, she waited for Dino's reaction.

'No!' he said simply. 'It's a stupid idea. What the hell would you do with another cinema?'

'I'd still only be running two. I would give up my job at Piccadilly and work here and at Knightsbridge.' She looked around. 'I'm going to call it "The Belvedere".'

'That means "a fine prospect" in Italian,' Dino said evenly. 'But there was also a famous statue called the *Apollo Belvedere* – after the god who drowned,' he finished sharply.

Ruth glanced at him. 'You don't like the place?'

'I don't like the whole idea!' he shouted. Ruth flinched, waiting for him to continue, to work off his annoyance in typical style. 'You're mad! You've just managed to pay off that leech Floyd and you're going to start again – what for?'

She straightened up and faced him. 'For me! And for my children! That's what for. I want to do this. I want to own more, to build more, to expand – '

'You want an empire, you stupid woman!' Dino said, his voice hard. 'You have enough – '

'Enough for whom?' Ruth countered, her own voice as controlled as his was passionate. 'Not enough for me. I am my own woman, and I want what I can get. Not what you want, not what my mother wanted – what I want. And I want this place.'

'Enough to jeopardise us?'

She winced at the words. 'In the end you are all the same, aren't you? Ken wanted me to spend all my time with him, not the children, not work – just him. Because I wouldn't adapt he left me.' She paused, her eyes brilliant in the half light. 'And now you're offering me an ultimatum – why, Dino? You fell in love with me when I was running a business, what's changed? Do I have to stand still for you to keep loving me?'

'It's too much for you!'

'No! You're trying to hold me back and I won't be.' Her voice was incisive, definite. 'I won't change for you.'

'I don't ask you to change – ' he said, his voice hard.

'You do! You ask me to limit myself, and that would change me.' She shrugged her shoulders. 'I want this place. Besides, it's a good price.'

'That all depends how much you're prepared to pay for it.'

'Oh, don't be so damned cryptic! Say what you think.'

'I think that at this moment I loathe you,' Dino said darkly. 'I think you're selfish and irresponsible – '

'I could make it a success.'

'It could fail!'

'Thank you for the vote of confidence,' she said bitterly, turning away and walking across the floor. His eyes followed her. She moved with her head erect, her shoulders back, determined, cool, remote. Burning with anger, Dino watched her tap the walls and pull at the torn wallpaper, her actions as graceful as ever, the actions of a young girl, not a businesswoman.

'I'm not trying to tell you what you can or cannot do.'

Ignoring him, Ruth continued to walk around, running her fingers along the dusty window-ledges and shaking the curtains.

'You can't tell me what to do,' she said, her tone glacial.

'I despise you!' Dino said violently. 'I hate you when you're like this, it cheapens you –'

'Why?' she asked, turning.

'It makes you hard,' he said, angered, 'and you're not hard.'

Ruth's mind slipped back to Laurel and she smiled bitterly.

'Don't make me choose,' she said, looking across the dim room to where Dino was standing. 'Love me enough not to make me choose.'

He heard her and at first he was so astonished that he could not respond. Hadn't he loved her enough? Backing her, supporting her, accepting her on her terms, not his?

'I love you more than anyone else could! I love another man's children, I love our child!' He was angry, almost out of control. 'And if we're talking about love, Ruth, why doesn't your love extend to marrying me? You see, I wonder,' he said cruelly, 'if you want to keep your options open, in case someone better comes along?'

She moved over to him and slapped him hard. For a second she thought that he would strike her back, but he didn't, he simply smiled ironically.

'All that anger. I do love all that anger,' he said, catching hold of her hand and turning it over to look at the palm. 'In this hand you have the world – if only you knew it.' He looked round, 'Do you really want this place?'

Ruth nodded.

'Then buy it. I'll help you – though I don't know why. I only know that whatever it costs me, my life would be worthless without you.'

Ruth told Ted Morrison that week. She was straightforward

with him and explained that she was buying another cinema and would be leaving after a month. He looked sorry rather than angry.

'Well, I suppose I can't say I'm surprised. I expected that you'd leave us one day.' He pulled at his earlobe. 'I have to admire your courage though, buying another place.'

'I can only lose,' Ruth said, smiling calmly.

'Well, I wish you good luck, and I hope it's a success for you. Are you thinking of taking any staff with you from here?'

She shook her head. 'No, it wouldn't be fair. I'll hire my own when I get settled.'

'What about Geoffrey Lynes?' he said suddenly.

The question caught Ruth off guard. Morrison saw her falter and continued rapidly. 'He's about to get failed on his medical examination and prematurely retired.'

'So?'

'He's just been told about being made redundant. He's got Parkinson's disease, as you know, and the company won't make any exceptions – even in his case.'

Ruth's voice was cold. 'And I'm supposed to?' she asked. 'Why? He damn near ruined me. Because of his negligence I nearly lost my home. Because of him I've worked day and night to pay off debts and get the Knightsbridge cinema back on its feet.' She thought of Robert Floyd and took in a deep breath. 'Geoffrey Lynes brought me to my knees – why should I care what happens to him?'

Morrison watched her, impressed by the sheer strength of character which struck him across the desk. He knew that Ruth had fired Lynes, and he also knew that no one would ever discover whether his oversight had been a mistake or a deliberate act of revenge.

'He's in a bad way.'

'So was I,' Ruth countered.

'Did he try to ruin you?'

She smiled wryly. 'Only he knows that.'

'But he couldn't harm you again, could he?' Morrison said evenly. 'He would hardly dare. The question mark is still hanging over his head after all this time, he could never dare to risk another ... blunder. Besides, he's too ill to try it.'

She knew what he was really saying. In the end, if Ruth chose to hire Lynes again and keep him powerless, her revenge on him would be all the more humiliating.

'He'll manage. He has a pension.'

'He has a good brain,' Morrison countered. 'You know that. Besides, he's desperate, he'll dance to any tune you play. You could use him, Ruth. If you put him in a position without authority you could utilise his know-how, without endangering yourself.'

She shook her head. 'He would refuse, he'd think I was taking revenge. Humiliating him.'

'If he really let that cinema go up in flames, he deserves his punishment.'

Ruth thought about Morrison's words as she walked into Geoffrey Lynes's office. He was watering a bedraggled ivy, and looked up, shocked to see her.

'Ted has just told me that you've been made redundant ... I've bought a new cinema, Geoffrey.' She remembered how he had interviewed her, how she had waited for his decision, how he had lorded over her. 'Do you want to work there?'

His surprise was obvious as he turned to face the window. A light shower began to tap dance on the chilled glass.

'I've been here for twenty-six years. Twenty-six years!' he repeated, rubbing his hands together. 'Since I was twenty years old. "A good company man, Lynes," they used to say. Dedicated to my work, I was.' He rubbed the back of his neck. 'Never married, you know, I never found the right woman and then I got too old to even bother looking – too old and too shy. What a waste.'

He spat out the last words, his voice bitter. 'All that time spent here when I could have married and had a family. All those evenings of getting home late and all those weekends alone ... '

'Geoffrey – '

He interrupted Ruth abruptly. 'What! What are you going to say? Should I be grateful to you for taking me on your staff again? You think I tried to ruin you, don't you?' His eyes betrayed nothing. 'Well, I remember you when you were no one – marrying that drunk Ken Floyd who dumped you with his kids and now living with some Italian and having his ... ' he stopped and blew his nose. 'God, I don't know what the hell is the matter with me.'

Ruth looked down at her hands, her heart hammering with anger, her voice cold.

'You know, Geoffrey, it will do you good to get it all off your chest now, because I don't want you to be harbouring grievances and plotting behind my back – although if you ever do, I'll ruin you, I'll take you to the highest court in the land and bleed you dry,' she continued smoothly. 'You obviously think I'm some upstart who got lucky, now I'll tell you what I think about you.'

He glanced away, his hands shaking.

'I think you're a self-righteous, jealous bastard, who should have been knocked into shape long ago. I think you're spiteful and cold, but I also think that you're good at your job, and I know you need a favour ... If you want to come and work for me you can. Your responsibility will be limited because I don't know whether I trust you' – his eyes flickered, but he said nothing – 'but I know you won't dare to try anything again. Besides, I'll be watching you every minute ... Take it or leave it, Geoffrey, it's the best – the only – offer you're likely to get.'

He shifted in his seat uncomfortably without looking at her. There was a choice, he could retire on a pension, or take her offer and work until illness prevented him from continuing. With Ruth, he would have something to fill his days, days which lately had seemed hostile and endless. She didn't trust him, she had said so, but she didn't have to. He was too old and too ill to resent anything any longer.

'When do we start?'

'I want to open in the New Year,' Ruth said calmly, without a hint of triumph. She now had him on his knees, where he had had her ... But had he tried to ruin her? She wondered for the thousandth time. He had never denied or admitted it, and she had never asked him.

'At the end of January, hopefully, which means we have to

get the place ready and in top order by then.' She glanced at him. He was too thin, his colour poor, his actions the actions of an old man.

'We have to work hard, very hard ... Are you well enough?'

He replied without hesitation. 'Tell me what you want me to do.'

They took it from there.

The phone rang – it was Nina. 'Thank God you said you'd buy the cinema. Did Tony ask a fair price?'

'More than fair,' Ruth replied. 'He asked a very silly price actually. I was wondering if the whole edifice was going to crumble down on our heads and crush us to death in the middle of a private viewing. Why? I've been trying to get hold of you for a week to tell you what happened.'

'We went away, and Tony wouldn't tell me about it. He said I had to ask you.'

Ruth was bemused. 'Well, you can take it from me, he asked a ridiculous price and it's all settled.'

She laughed suddenly. 'In that case – I'm getting married!'

'What!'

'I told Tony that if he was serious he would offer you the building real cheap, as a favour to me. He'd been proposing for months and I'd turned him down. So then he said that he'd only do it if I married him as a reward ...' She laughed again. 'And I was terrified you'd tell him he was asking too much!'

'But that means he's lost money on the deal.'

'Yeah – but it's romantic, isn't it? Besides, I've told you he's got more money than you could shake a stick at.'

'So when's the happy day?'

'In the New Year. As soon as we can.'

'Are you having a big white wedding?'

'Do me a favour! I don't speak to my family any more and he doesn't even know who his are! We'd be hard pressed to find a dozen people we'd want there. You and Dino and the kids come though, won't you? Oh, and your parents.'

'You can't stand my mother!'

'I know, but I like your dad and I think I should ask them.'

'Well, if that's what you want,' Ruth said. 'Anyway, who's giving you away?'

'I never thought of that. Maybe your father could, or Dino?'

Ruth smiled. 'I'll ask them. Church or Registry Office?'

She was quiet for a moment. 'Once a Catholic, always a Catholic ... church, I suppose. Neither of us has been married before so they can't turn us away. I care about him, you know. The big, silly sod.'

They married in early January, as the snow fell outside in leaf-sized flakes and made feathers along the church windows. The service was short and poignant, the smell of incense over-whelming in the cold air. Ruth's parents came down for the service, and her father gave the bride away, walking proudly up the aisle with her on his arm. Nina wore a mink coat and a small mink hat, her red hair just showing around her ears. She looked pert and happy and when she turned to smile at Tony she was obviously in love with him. The feeling was mutual. He was dressed like a large, over-stuffed panda, his skin white with the cold and his dark suit a little too tight and a little too sharply tailored. They exchanged rings and he dropped his, scrambling around on the icy marble floor looking for it. With a look of undisguised amusement, Nina turned and raised her eyes to Ruth.

They held their reception at the Dorchester, where Nina had laid on an astonishing amount of food and champagne.

'Well,' she said, raising her glass to Ruth. 'Here's to you and me. Who'd have thought that I'd end up marrying a rich man and that you'd have your own cinemas?'

Ruth smiled at her. 'Just get back for the opening, that's all.'

'Would I miss it?' Nina replied.

But she did. Apparently they were busy soaking up the sun somewhere in the back of Arabia, or China, or wherever the postcard said that week, because it changed every time she wrote. The places changed, but the sentiments were the same, her luck and happiness travelling well to England.

'You're expanding again!' Robert Floyd said over the phone.

'I heard this morning. You do like to gamble, Ruth.'

'It's not a gamble, it'll be a huge success, you can rely on it.'

'I don't need to, it's not my money this time,' he countered maliciously. 'How's Kate?'

'She's well, I'll bring her over to the office later in the week,' Ruth said, knowing how the old man liked to see Kate, and also knowing that his affection did not extend in the same way to Graham. 'How are you?'

'Thriving,' he said emphatically, puffing on a cigar. In fact he was still struggling after a bad case of flu, his irritability and spite the only things keeping him going. 'I've heard it's going to be quite something.'

'I'm calling it "The Belvedere",' Ruth said evenly.

'Jesus Christ! What a name to give to anything,' Robert Floyd said, laughing mightily. 'You've got style, Ruth, I'll give you that.'

He was still laughing when he put down the phone.

It was raining in Oldham, the sky forbidding dark, the lights on in the kitchen where Lilian was baking.

'I spoke to Florrie Collins this morning,' she said to her husband. 'She's very poorly. Very bad indeed. It's the weather, all this damp, it can't be doing anyone any good. Besides, she never dresses properly, never keeps herself warm. I saw her without a coat the other day, so what can you expect?'

Jack looked up over the top of his paper. 'She was never strong. What's the matter now?'

Lilian bent down and lifted a cake out of the oven. The heat warmed her face, and made her skin pink. 'It's her heart,' she said, looking over to Jack. 'Pass me that cloth, will you? She asked after Ruth and wanted to know all about the cinema. Just curiosity, I suppose, like most of the Nosy Parkers round here.' She pushed back some hair with her hand. 'Anyway, I think we should go to the opening.'

Jack Gordon hid behind his paper, smiling. Since Ruth had bought the cinema Lilian had alternately raged at him and bragged to the neighbours. There were two versions; firstly, Ruth was getting above herself, and secondly, she was just trying to get on. It depended on Lilian's mood which account she favoured.

'You want to go then?'

'We should,' she said firmly. 'For moral support. It's the right thing to do.'

Jack smiled ruefully. 'She'll be pleased to see us. Anyway, I like to see Dino and the children.' He paused, thinking of Graham.

'Well, what do you think, Jack?' Lilian snapped. 'I was talking to you.'

'Of course we should go,' he said firmly. 'Ruth's done us proud, and no mistake. She's a credit to us.'

Lilian sniffed. 'Yes, she is. And she's doing well for those children.' Her mouth set. 'Not that we haven't always done right by her – '

She stopped suddenly. Jack saw her flounder and pretended to read as Lilian bit her lip, remembering Laurel and wondering where she was.

Sixteen

LONDON
Four years later

Ruth and Nina had arranged to meet in a small restaurant in Kensington, and Nina, delighted at the prospect of something to do, swore to arrive early. She was late. She was so late that Ruth ate half a bowl of peanuts and read the paper twice, without noticing the man who came in and sat down at the next table. When she finally looked up, he was watching her.

'Ken,' she said flatly.

'The same . . . you look good.'

Ruth said nothing and he shrugged. 'I know what you're thinking – I've aged.'

But it wasn't age which had caught up with Ken Floyd. He was fifty-nine then, but looked younger. The years had been kind, but the drinking had altered him. Around his eyes, the flesh was puffy and slightly pink, and the grainy skin had coarsened and looked pock-marked. He had kept a full head of hair, but despite the expensive suit and the easy manner, he looked florid and crude.

'So, what are you doing now?' Ruth asked, looking round for Nina.

'This and that,' Ken said evasively. 'I never liked work, you know.'

'I remember,' Ruth said icily.

He glanced at her and smiled. In the warm light of the restaurant she was almost flawless, growing finally into that beauty he had always anticipated. Sitting with her legs crossed and her hair swept back from her face, Ruth looked at him curiously. Across the table, Ken Floyd saw the woman he had once married, and wanted her.

'Take a seat,' Ruth said sarcastically as he sat down at her table.

He ignored the remark. 'You know, I was only thinking of you the other day – and now we've met. Strange, isn't it?' Ruth said nothing and he continued. 'It's good to see you again after all these years. You never remarried, why?'

'You spoiled me for anyone else,' Ruth said drily.

He laughed, a cynic's laugh. 'Still bitter, darling, after all these years?'

'Ken, I don't want to talk to you, so why don't you go?'

He hesitated, aware that he was intimidated by the woman in front of him. Having built many a fantasy around Ruth, he was surprised and hurt to find that she was uninterested in him – in fact, if he wasn't mistaken, she disliked him. The knowledge made him spiteful and he struck out.

'I was with someone for a time – oh, not Sheila, that fizzled out only a year after I left. She went back to Harry.'

'Poor old Harry.'

Finishing his drink, he signalled for the waiter to top him up. 'No, this girl was young and pretty and she made me laugh. She was a lot like you.'

The words had no effect on Ruth. She was embarrassed, nothing more.

'There was never anyone like you.'

'No, when they made me they broke the mould,' she answered coldly.

'I met a few other ladies, but nothing permanent.' He paused, trying to sound nonchalant, the question burning his lips. 'Are you with anyone special? I heard tell that you had some crazy foreigner in tow.'

Ruth turned her eyes on him and his stomach lurched. 'The crazy foreigner is a damn sight better man than you'll ever be.'

'So why don't you marry him?'

'You know why.'

He smiled sloppily. 'Still in love with the old man?'

Suddenly uncomfortable, Ruth regarded her ex-husband coolly for a moment, and then said, 'Ken, I don't want to deflate your ego, but I don't love you, I merely want to make

308

sure that you pay for walking out on us. If I remarry, you won't be forced to keep paying maintenance or the medical bills for Graham. You deserve to be bled white, and do you know why?'

He didn't know her then, there was nothing of the girl who had obsessed him in this formidable woman.

'You haven't answered the question, Ken, but I'll tell you anyway. You should be punished because you never gave a damn for your children or for me. You haven't even asked after them – you've told me all about *you*, but never even enquired about your own children.'

'I hear all about them from my father. Besides, I keep getting the bills – I know they're OK.'

Ruth shook her head in disbelief. 'Don't you care about them?'

He slumped in his seat clumsily. 'OK! OK! How are they?'

'If I told you I'd only be wasting my breath.'

He swallowed some more of his drink and leant forward on the table. His eyes were faintly bloodshot and his hands were clumsy round the glass. Ruth watched him, despising him and yet pitying him at the same time. She resented the fact that he had had all the advantages in the world, and abused them; but she could still remember his tenderness when they first married and it tempered her.

'There aren't so many medical bills for Graham,' he said thickly. 'Is he better?'

'He's fine, still crazy about his computers.'

'What about Kate?'

'She's decided to train to be a physiotherapist. She's a great favourite with your father.'

He leant back and smiled, the drink taking effect, its mock bravery making him belligerent. 'In that case everyone's just hunky-dory. So why all the fire and brimstone?'

'You don't understand, do you?' Ruth asked, still baffled by him. 'All these years have passed and you've never seen them, or written to them, or sent cards on their birthday. I mean, both anniversaries fall on the same day, you wouldn't even have had trouble remembering the dates.'

He looked suddenly spiteful. 'Listen to me, Ruth. It was part of the divorce settlement that I never saw or contacted those children – '

'Do you really think that would have stopped anyone who really cared?' she asked bitterly.

'Oh, I give up!'

'Yes, you always did.'

Glancing away, Ken smiled at someone at another table. 'It's strange, Ruth,' he said, turning back to her, but I'm not a young man any longer. I'd been thinking that I should see my kids and get to know them.'

Ruth thought he was trying to annoy her and refused to rise to the bait.

'A father should be in touch with his children –'

'Over my dead body,' she said resentfully.

'Oh, you'd rather have that bloody Italian bring them up?'

'He's done fifty times more than you would ever have done,' she snapped, 'and probably more than most fathers.'

Ken changed his tactics. 'Still, you wouldn't begrudge me some time with my children – after all, you've had another one with this guy. A boy, wasn't it?' Ruth said nothing and waited for him to continue. 'Mind you, you never had trouble with kids, did you? Quite the doting mother – apart from that first little slip-up.'

Ruth flinched, just as he had hoped she would. Having believed for years that she still harboured some feeling for him, her revulsion hurt him deeply and made him vicious. At that moment all Ken Floyd wanted was to punish Ruth, to make her suffer as she had made him suffer, to repay her for his humiliation. He chose to forget that he had been the one to leave.

'Let's look at this logically, Ruth. If I chose to take the matter to court and fight dirty, I could merely cite the fact that you gave away your first child and they would be sure to grant me access to my children.'

Ruth froze in her seat, her mouth hardly able to form the words. 'You wouldn't dare!'

'Oh yes, I would.'

'Listen to me, Ken,' she said carefully, trying to keep the panic out of her voice, 'you agreed to the terms of the divorce because you had no interest in your children. They were a bore to you. You paid for their upbringing and Graham's medical bills and that was enough to assuage your conscience. Don't come the loving father routine now, it won't wash.'

He smiled and finished his second drink. Determined now on his course of action, he continued resolutely. 'I want to see them! You either agree amicably, or we'll go to court. The choice is yours.'

Ruth sat motionless, trying to collect her thoughts. His attitude shocked her, as did his obstinacy.

'Why do you want to see them? Why now?'

An expression of regret came into his eyes and he put down his glass. For a second Ruth could see him as he had been, but when he looked up again his eyes were humourless and cold. 'I've been – '

Nina interrupted them before he could explain, walking over to the table and facing Ken.

'Hello, you old bastard. Still drinking yourself into the grave?'

He looked up and smiled. 'Why, if it isn't Mary Poppins. What made you crawl out of bed so early in the day?'

She smiled back brilliantly. 'Only the possibility of seeing you, Ken. But it's better than I thought. I could hardly imagine, in my wildest dreams, that you would end up the raddled old drunk you are. My father would love you.'

'Really? I'm surprised you know who he is.'

Nina's smile widened. 'You're in my seat. Move yourself.'

Slowly, he got to his feet. 'You always were a scrubber,' he said unpleasantly.

'Sure, and you were always a drunk. I reckon that makes us about even.'

He walked off unsteadily, paying his bill at the door and moving out into the cold afternoon. Nina watched him and turned to Ruth. Her face was expressionless, her eyes cold and unwelcoming.

'Where the hell have you been?'

'Shopping. Why, what's the problem?' Nina asked, jerking her finger to the door. 'What's laughing boy been saying?'

'He wants to see the twins.'

'What!' she said, putting down her handbag and undoing her coat.

'Exactly. He said that he wants to see them and that if I oppose it he'll go to court and tell them about Laurel.' Ruth shivered, as the old ghost crept up on her. 'You can imagine what that would do to Dino ... or Graham for that matter.'

Nina thought for a minute. She had expected something like this to happen, that one day Ruth's past would come back to torment her. Secrets, she realised, remained secrets only so long. Watching Ruth's progress, she had followed the articles in the papers and seen the photographs in the society magazines ... and she had held her breath.

'Let him see them,' Nina said casually, trying to cover the unease she was feeling. 'You can't stop it, Ruth, and besides, they're grown up enough to come to their own decision about him. They know he left the lot of you ... what sort of man does that make him?' Ruth looked unconvinced. 'Listen, those kids of yours aren't stupid, they'll have him sussed out in no time. Let the old fool see them, it'll do him no good.'

'But why now? Why does he want to see them now?' Ruth asked her frantically. 'We only met by chance, it was a fluke ... if I'd never seen him today he'd never have thought about contacting the kids.'

Bad timing, Nina thought wryly.

'Perhaps he would, and perhaps he wouldn't ... who knows? You did see him though, and that's what matters. Leave it up to Graham and Kate – they'll give him his marching orders.' She glanced at the menu and back to Ruth, the matter decided. 'Anyway, why the lunch? You pregnant again?'

'Don't be crazy. It was Tony's idea, he asked me to talk to you ... he thinks you're spending too much money.'

Nina's eyes widened in astonishment and then she smiled and beckoned the waiter to come over to the table.

'Champagne, please,' she said sweetly.

*

'That was stupid, even for Ken,' Robert Floyd said, irritated beyond reason, and grinding out his cigar in the ashtray on his desk. 'Bloody fool.'

Joanie smiled lazily and looked around the office. Nothing had changed in all the years since her father had begun his paper. The same bareness – barrenness, Ken had called it when they used to visit as children. No trimmings, sparse, like the man himself. Thin and barely fleshed. But he was getting old, Joanie thought suddenly, the tyrant was finally getting old.

'Ken wants to see his children. You know why.'

Robert Floyd shook his head. What love he had for his son was rapidly fading, especially now he was trying to disrupt Ruth's life again. Wanting to feel a closeness, particularly in the light of events, the old man found that Ken had once again distanced himself by stupidity.

'She's done her best for those children and he's trying to undermine it all. That's a cheap trick. Even for him.'

Joanie raised her eyebrows. 'You know why he did it.'

Robert Floyd swung round on his daughter, 'I don't give a shit why he did it! It was wrong,' he said, sitting down. Rain tapped the windows and made the room gloomy.

'He should have asked Ruth to let him see his children. She's not unreasonable – '

'She's bloody impossible!' Joanie said savagely, defending her brother even though she had been told only half the story and knew nothing of Laurel. 'If you recall, one of the stipulations of their divorce was that he was *forbidden* to see those children – '

'Ken was knocking off Sheila Fielding at the time,' her father reminded her. 'Frankly, I'm surprised he got off so lightly, I'd have taken him to the cleaners. Besides,' he added peevishly, 'don't think I haven't realised why you're defending him – it's your way of getting back at Ruth for throwing you out.'

Joanie sprang to her feet and walked over to the window. The heavy rain made the shapes blur, the park only a haze, a poor impression, nothing quite real. Greed made her keep her temper – she had seen how much her father loved his grandchildren and it worried her. Robert Floyd had made a fortune, and she wanted to be the one to benefit. So much so that she had returned to England to protect her interests.

'When all's said and done, Ken should tell Ruth the truth,' she said finally, turning on the lamp on her father's desk. The light pooled round them.

'I told him that,' the old man replied, smiling grimly, 'and do you know what he said in reply?'

Joanie shook her head.

'He said it wasn't the right time.' Robert Floyd sighed deeply. 'Trouble is, it's never the right time for Ken.'

The meeting with Ken played on Ruth's mind so much that she found it impossible to concentrate on anything for the next couple of days. Dino noticed the change in her and when she told him that Ken wanted to see the children he was furious.

'No! Never!'

Ruth thought about Laurel. Sudden pain filled her, like a stitch in her side.

'Dino, they are his children. Anyway they aren't children any more, they're adults. They'll make up their own minds about him.'

'No!'

Ruth sighed deeply and turned back to him. He was tearing up some letters angrily and little white flakes of paper kept falling on to the carpet.

'Once wouldn't hurt.'

'No!'

'They are *my* children! I can decide.'

He stopped tearing and looked at her coldly. 'What's this all about? Do you want to see Ken Floyd again?' He paced over to her, outraged. 'Do you still love him?'

'For God's sake!'

He threw the pieces of paper on the floor. 'Don't bring Him into this! You're guilty about something. I can see it in your face.'

Ruth flinched, startled by the words. 'Dino, listen to me – '

'No,' he roared. 'For years I've listened to you – now you can listen to me. I don't want Ken Floyd seeing the children.'

314

Ruth winced, powerless to explain, incapable of telling him about Laurel. 'He only wants to see them – '

He interrupted her. 'You loathe the man! So why are you letting him come back into your life?'

'Not my life, the children's.'

'It's the same thing! Don't insult my intelligence!' he hollered, pulling the curtains closed irritably. They swished among the rails like trains. 'I forbid that man to see them!'

'You can't! He could take the matter to court,' Ruth said, close to panic, seeing her secret exposed and worse, imagining Dino's reaction.

'I don't care if he takes it to court. We'll have a fight. I'm not afraid of Ken Floyd!'

Ruth turned away, horrified. 'I can't do that, Dino.'

Alerted by the change in her voice, he came and sat next to her. 'Don't be frightened. I'll get a friend of mine to act for us and we'll get a ruling in our favour. Ken Floyd agreed not to see them before –'

'I can't go to court,' Ruth repeated, her eyes dull, her voice emotionless.

'Why not?' Dino asked, amazed by her stubbornness.

'I just can't, that's all.'

A look of suspicion came into his eyes. Having never seen it before, Ruth was startled and glanced away.

'This makes no sense,' he said, running his hands through his hair. 'You explain to me why I should let this man see the twins again; explain why I should let him hurt you and the children?'

'He's their father,' Ruth said quietly.

'He was their father when he left them!' Dino said, jumping to his feet, 'something he's conveniently forgotten all these years! He's managed to live without them so far, so why this sudden urge to see them now! He's never been a real father.'

'He's paid the bills for them.'

Dino smiled bitterly. 'I never wanted him to do that! I told you that I would pay – but no, you kept accepting money from Floyd,' he said savagely, his mouth twisted with anger. In all their years together, Ruth had never seen him so enraged.

'You want to get your own back so badly you're prepared to beggar yourself and humiliate me. Why?' he pointed at her. 'Why? You're either too bitter to let him go, or you still love him.'

'I don't love him,' Ruth said wearily. He was going to find out, she thought, he was going to find out and then he would leave her. 'I stopped loving Ken the day he walked out.'

'So why do you hold on to him, Ruth?'

'I don't!' she replied, getting to her feet and pacing the floor. 'But he should pay for what he did to us!'

'For ever?' Dino asked wildly. 'No! It's stupid, pointless! You should look forward to our future and forget him. I have money, you have money – we have enough money to feed our kids and half the children in Rome – get rid of the man, once and for all, he'll only bring you grief.'

'I can't,' Ruth said simply.

Dino glanced out of the window to steady himself. David was in the garden, the cat watching him from the branches of a willow tree, the clouds hurling themselves against the pale sky. 'You're lying to me, Ruth. You've never lied to me before, so why now?'

Ruth said nothing, her head bowed, her hands on her lap. Seldom afraid, she was suddenly terrified, realising that she could lose the man she loved.

'I can't go to court, Dino, Ken will expose something that happened a long time ago and use it against me ... '

He turned slowly, but said nothing.

'You know that I was married very young and that Derek was killed.' Dino was silent, he didn't even nod to indicate that he heard her. She breathed in deeply and rushed on. 'I had a child, a girl. I had her adopted ... I was ill at the time, or I would never have done it – *could* never have done it. You know how I love the children.' Ruth glanced up, startled by the expression on his face. There was no tenderness there any longer, only a sense of betrayal. She knew then she should have told him when they first met, should have risked losing him then, rather than now, so many years later, when she loved him so much.

316

'Oh God, Dino, I couldn't tell you! I thought that you would hate me for it,' she said and reached for his hand, but he moved away from her. 'I knew you would never forgive me,' she said quietly.

He left the room without a word.

The air was chilly and seeped into his clothes as he walked, making him shiver. Blindly distressed, Dino kept moving past shops and houses, his heart banging, his hands clenched. Time stopped for him as he stared ahead and saw only the past – saw Ruth laughing and welcoming him, saw them making love, Ruth gentle and willing in the dark. He had longed for her, loved her, trusted her ... and he had told her once that she would break his heart, seeing even then some shadow, some secret part of her which would damage him. He crossed the road, not knowing where he was going, just walking, his feet hitting the pavement, his heart bursting. She should have trusted him, he thought, she should have loved him enough to trust him. Suddenly he stopped and looked up at the blind sky, his own pain making his body shake.

You'll break my heart, someone said. He flinched as the phrase repeated itself, hearing it over and over again ... without realising he was saying the words himself.

Ruth stayed in the lounge for nearly half an hour without moving. She was too shocked to cry and too exhausted to rouse herself. I've lost him, she thought ... but I have to go on living ... I have to. Unable to face Graham, Ruth passed his door and was just going into her bedroom when she heard the sound of his wheelchair.

She turned, forcing herself to smile. He nodded and smiled in return.

'What are you doing?' Ruth asked, surprised that she could talk and function normally. Or maybe she wasn't normal, she thought, maybe that was the explanation for everything. In sign language, Graham explained that the clinic had found some company which wanted to employ him. He seemed exhilarated, his handsome face animated and free from its usual sullen expression.

'Graham, that's wonderful,' Ruth said gently. 'When would you begin?'

They wanted him to start the following month. He would be working from home on his own computers and would be paid monthly. Ruth bent down towards him, taking him in her arms, his hair mingling with her own. Willingly he responded and clung to her, his strong arms pulling on her own, his breath warm against her cheek.

'Well done, Graham. I'm proud of you.'

He nodded, unusually emotional, his face only inches from her own.

Dino had not returned by seven, or eight, or nine o'clock. Ruth wondered if he had returned to his flat, putting a distance between them as he usually did when they quarrelled. But when she rang there was no answer and the evening dragged on relentlessly. When he hadn't returned at ten, Ruth roused herself, her bewilderment making her angry. Damn him, she thought, why won't he come back? They'd had arguments before, they'd get over this one. But this was different, she knew, this was about Laurel. Unable to wait in the house any longer, Ruth left, crawling down the dark streets in her car and looking for him, searching for his angular figure amongst all the others. She even went to his flat, staring up at the dark windows and ringing the bell uselessly. Leaning against the wall, she forced herself to think of where he might go ... and then remembered the church in Kensington.

It was quiet when she arrived, the night air hard as it pinched her skin, the street empty. Only an old man, half drunk and half senile, his coat marked where he'd wet himself, mumbled incoherently as she passed. Ruth carried on quickly, reaching the church and walking in on her toes, her heels raised off the stone floor. It appeared to be empty, but as she made her way up the aisle Ruth could see Dino's thin figure seated in one of the pews. She approached cautiously, and sat down beside him. He looked at her and she took in her breath. His eyes were dark, clouded, the pain obvious.

'Your head's uncovered.'

Ruth rummaged in her bag for a scarf and tied it clumsily.

'I keep telling you to wear something on your head when you come to church and you keep forgetting,' Dino continued, his voice curiously expressionless.

'I thought you'd be here.'

'I like it here,' he said, his eyes glancing upwards to the incense burner above him, its scent compelling, the red glow of the holder making a punch into the darkness of the ceiling.

'Dino, please talk to me.'

Impervious to her words, he remained silent, the atmosphere so hostile that Ruth jumped when a side door opened and admitted an elderly priest. He walked up the aisle past them, an old man, small and curled up like a leaf, his long gown rustling as he moved.

'You don't know how you hurt me ... you deceived me,' Dino said finally, glancing in Ruth's direction and then turning away again.

The priest coughed and lit a candle, placing it with the others in its tray. They blazed out against the cold stone and the marble columns and made patterns on the windows.

'I never meant to hurt you,' Ruth said softly. 'Never.'

He ignored her words. 'I never believed that you would have hidden anything from me. We've been so happy for so many years,' he looked at her and shrugged. 'Haven't we? ... I was.'

The sadness in his voice tore at her. 'I was happy all those years and I am happy now. You've always made me happy.' He said nothing. 'Dino, I'm sorry, I don't know why I didn't tell you – except that I was frightened of losing you.'

He was thinking of something else, his mind wandering. 'We had David –'

'We *have* David!' she said frantically. 'Stop talking in the past tense, we're not dead!'

'I feel dead!' he shouted. The words ricocheted round the church walls and drummed on their ears as the old priest turned round, startled.

'Forgive me, Father,' Dino called out as the old man walked into the vestry. 'Ruth,' he continued dully, 'you were my life. You were everything I ever wanted. Nothing mattered to me as much as you.' He touched her throat with his fingers. 'I

319

wanted you, loved you . . . ' he snatched his hand away. 'You've made a fool of me! You've lied to me . . . you've torn me apart.'

The tears burned behind her eyes. I have done this to him, Ruth thought, her own pain intensifying as she watched him suffer. I have done this to him . . .

'Dino, don't say that. We can still – '

'There's no point any longer!' he snapped, agitated beyond reason. 'What I thought was perfect and good is spoiled. *We* are spoiled.'

Ruth's fight returned as she heard the words. Used to struggling, she recognised the one glimmer of hope. He loved me once, she thought, and if he's suffering then he still loves me . . .

'We're not spoiled!' she said fiercely. 'Nothing in life is perfect, Dino, you know that. Nothing can be.'

But he refused to look at her and knelt down with his long hands pressed together, his eyes closed. Without thinking, she pulled at his shoulder and he turned, still on his knees.

'Have you no honour?'

The word stung her. 'Yes, I have honour! Enough to know when I'm wrong and enough to stand by the mistakes I've made. Don't pray to your God to forgive me, your God is not my God, and I can make my own apologies to Him without your intervention.'

With dignity Ruth rose to her feet, her face white as marble, 'I regret what I did, but I tried to compensate by loving the other children . . . I didn't tell you about Laurel because I knew you wouldn't forgive me. I was right.'

She pointed to the incense burner and the stained glass window. 'Look at these things, Dino. They're supposed to frighten us and make us fear hell. Well, they don't frighten me!' she said, her head erect, defying the gods. 'I've been through my own hell and found my own God, and I can't believe that He's here now, or that He is any part of you – otherwise you would have forgiven me already.'

She left the pew in the same moment that Dino rose and put out his hand to stop her.

Shaking her head, Ruth stepped back from him. 'I love you,

Dino. Each day, each night, each moment I've loved you. I've loved your child and loved your kindness. But I won't be patronised by you and I won't ask for your forgiveness! Don't make me beg – I won't beg for your love.'

Without another word she turned and ran out, her shoes clattering on the floor, her hands ripping off the scarf from around her head.

Ruth waited uneasily throughout a rainy spring for Ken to get in touch. He made no contact. Gradually, her fears subsided and she began to relax, although Dino was adamant – she was not to accept any further financial help from Ken Floyd.

'We have enough money. I want you to break all contact with that man,' he said firmly. 'The past is the past.'

The past is the past. The past is the past, Ruth repeated cautiously, wondering if Ken would think likewise. But when summer began, heavy-flowered and sultry, and they still hadn't heard, Ruth believed the matter to be settled once and for all. So she made an appointment to see Harold Ibrahim and tell him of the change in her plans.

'I don't want any more money from Ken, no maintenance, no medical bills for Graham. Nothing.'

Harold smoothed his patent hair and looked at Ruth. He smiled, his eyes sharp. 'You're being a little hasty, I think.'

'I don't.'

He smiled again and began to push the cuticle down on his forefinger. 'My dear lady, I really think I ought to advise you to hold out for what you can get – '

She smiled ruefully; holding out for what she could get had nearly cost her Dino. 'No, Harold, I've got all I want from Ken. He's paid maintenance for a long time, but I don't want it any more.'

Harold fixed his eyes on the cuticle, bit off an imaginary piece of skin and looked back at Ruth. 'Why?'

'I bumped into him a couple of months back,' Ruth said smoothly. 'We hadn't seen each other for years and when we talked he said he wanted to see the twins. He implied that he would see them by hook or by crook.'

Harold raised his eyebrows and smiled confidently. 'How very interesting. I don't recall that Mr Floyd was that keen to see his children before. He agreed willingly enough to give up his right of access.' He turned his attention back to his finger. 'How very odd.'

'He's getting older.'

'But no wiser, I would have thought.'

Ruth smiled half-heartedly. 'As you say, no wiser ... I just thought that if I released him from his commitment to us, he might simply fade away.'

Harold smiled and thought for a moment. The clock on his desk chimed delicately, fourteen hours already gone in the day.

'You do realise that he could easily contact the twins? They aren't children any longer – they're old enough to make up their own minds. We couldn't take the matter to court.'

Surprised, Ruth stammered, 'But Ken implied that he could take the matter to court and win custody –'

'Of adults?' Harold smiled patiently. 'The twins are no longer children. Ken Floyd is their father and as such he can see them if he chooses to. Just as they could see him – if they chose to. We have no control in this case, legally, over adults.'

Ruth sighed deeply, but her feeling was more of anger than relief. So Ken had lied to her, threatening her with the one thing she feared above everything – exposure. Her past picked over by strangers, her secrets revealed.

'I see,' she said coldly.

'However, if I were you, I would forget the matter. Mr Floyd is a capricious man, and he probably said all this merely to annoy you. We've had a very good run, you know. He's paid maintenance for years without any trouble – '

'He has the money,' Ruth said bitingly.

Harold smiled and looked at his finger again, 'As you so rightly say – he has the money. However, he did settle all Graham's medical bills without hesitation, so we should be grateful for that.' He pushed the file away to signal that the subject was closed. 'I'll inform his solicitors that you no longer require any financial support.'

Ruth nodded. 'Yes, that's what I want. I want to free myself from him, and then, hopefully, we'll never hear from Ken Floyd again.'

Angry as Ruth was, she did allow herself the faintest smile of triumph. With an ability to see the advantage in any situation, she realised that despite himself, Ken had done her a favour. By forcing her to tell Dino about Laurel she had admitted something which had haunted her for years. No longer would she have to worry about a chance remark from Nina, or Lilian making some reference to her first marriage. Humming under her breath, Ruth walked to the car.

But if Ruth was certain of the future, Dino was not. Being by nature passionate and loyal, he hovered uncertainly between alternate emotions of betrayal and love. He wanted Ruth, as he had always wanted her, but the dark past unsettled him, and made him wonder if there were other corners to her personality.

Confused, he temporarily distanced himself from Ruth, giving himself a breathing space, a chance to assess the situation.

'Do the twins know about Laurel?' he asked Nina over the phone.

She had been surprised when he called and even more surprised when he had described what had happened – Ruth had made no mention to her of their argument in the church, or of her reluctant confession. Recognising the impatience in Dino's voice, Nina tried valiantly to intercede.

'Kate knows, of course, but not Graham. Ruth has had too many problems with him over the years to tell him about Laurel. He'd never understand and he'd never forgive her for it. You know how jealous he is.'

Dino sighed down the line. 'I don't agree. Ruth should tell him, otherwise if he finds out by accident, he'll feel worse. Graham has a very unforgiving nature. He bears grudges.'

Nina prayed that the same could not be said for him.

'Ruth's on a hiding to nothing with this one – if she tells Graham he'll get jealous, and if he finds out he'll feel deceived ... ' She paused. 'Personally, I'd leave Graham in blissful ignorance. What he doesn't know won't harm him.'

'You might be right,' Dino said absently, his thoughts running on.

'You don't think Ken will be in touch, do you?' Nina asked.

His Mediterranean anger flared hotly. 'That bastard! Oh no, we have nothing to worry about on that score.'

And it seemed he was right. The summer continued uninterrupted, although the weather changed suddenly, collapsing with a spate of savage gales. Several slates were torn off the roof and Mrs Corley was ill with bronchitis. In a rare moment, Ruth let down her guard and told her mother that she had confided in Dino.

'You didn't tell him!'

'I had to, Mother. I had no choice.'

'How did he take it?'

How did he take it, Ruth asked herself. He seemed the same as usual, but then again, at times, he lacked a certain tenderness, a compassion which had always been spontaneous before.

'He's come to terms with it,' she said cautiously.

Lilian sniffed, sensing that Ruth was not about to confide anything else. Piqued, she decided to change her tack. 'You shouldn't be looking after Mrs Corley, Ruth. She should be in hospital.'

'Mother, she's been marvellous to me over the years; she's only got bronchitis, after all. She'll recover soon.'

She could feel the cold draught of disapproval wing down the line. 'If she went to hospital she'd recover more quickly. She can't have you running around after her. I'm sure you know what to do for the best, dear, but Mrs Corley *is* supposed to be working for you. You don't want to spoil her ... besides, I've had a bad chest now for years and I've had to cope alone.'

Ruth gritted her teeth. 'You have Dad to help you out.'

'It's not the same!' Lilian responded querulously. 'Your father has no idea how to look after anyone. I've been so ill sometimes I'd have loved the attentions of a daughter.'

'Mother, you know you only have to ask me and I'll come.'

She sniffed. 'I wouldn't dream of dragging you away from

your family and your job. I've always managed.'

Incensed, Ruth resorted to her mother's trick and changed the subject. 'You get too tired. You should give up that shop. You should have retired years ago, like Dad did.'

'Your father looked forward to his retirement from the day he began work!' Lilian replied bitterly, her voice sharp. 'All he does now is read, read, read. He should have been more ambitious.'

Ruth continued doggedly. 'Why don't you sell the shop? Then you could move near to us.'

Her mother's tone stiffened. It was all right to grumble about something, but another thing to alter it. 'I know where my home is. No, Ruth, I shall continue with the shop as long as I'm able. After all, it is mine, I wouldn't want to give it up. You must understand that?'

Ruth's mind shifted back to the past; she could feel the curtain in her hand which led to the back room; could smell the soot in the Oldham air and hear the grind of her mother's scissors on the counter. Lilian's Millinery . . .

'Yes, I understand, Mother. But come down soon, won't you? And give my love to Dad.'

'He's reading.'

Ruth sighed. 'Then tell him when he's finished.'

With formidable determination Lilian Gordon hung on to the hat shop, and although Ruth offered to buy her a better business, she resisted. Jack Gordon would have let his daughter do anything for him, but Lilian saw Ruth's help as interference and refused everything except small gifts or necessities. And every night, as it had done for years, the yellow blind came down on the window, the hats peering blankly out from their wooden poles.

Too many bad memories of Oldham forced Ruth to make frequent excuses over the years not to visit her parents. Possibly aware of how she felt, neither of them had pushed her, but when a business trip to Manchester cropped up, Ruth took the opportunity. After a long day's work, she drove over to Oldham, parking on Carrington Street. Uneasily she got out of the car and looked round. Each house was tightly closed, unchanged from childhood, with the same net curtains and scrubbed steps. Even the bread shop on the corner was the same, no hint of the years between, the faded sign turned to 'Closed', an advertisement for Vimto over the door. Ruth shivered and turned her coat collar up against the Northern air, bitter with the chill from the moors.

With curious hesitation, she knocked and her father opened the door, a book in one hand and his glasses in the other. 'Well, I'll be damned! Come in, flower, your mother's just gone next door.'

Ruth raised her eyebrows. 'But she can't stand Mrs Livesey.'

'Oh, I know that, but it doesn't stop her going round.'

The kitchen was tidy, as always, the fire blazing and an armchair pulled in front of it. There was an imprint on the cushion where he had laid his head and as Ruth looked up she could see the inevitable clothes-rack, empty for once, and hoisted to the ceiling.

'I was only just thinking about your girl,' he said, filling the kettle, 'and I said to your mother, "I bet Kate rings us tonight."'

Ruth smiled. 'And did she?'

'Just now. She said she was going to some publishing do with Robert Floyd. He seems to think a lot of her,' he said, putting the kettle on to boil and lighting his pipe. 'It's good to see you here, Ruth, it's like old times.'

'I was up in Manchester, Dad,' Ruth said shyly, '. . . and I thought I'd drop in and surprise you.'

He nodded. 'I'm glad you did, and your mother will be.' He smiled and turned back to the kettle, making them a cup of punishingly strong tea and laying it on the table with some digestive biscuits.

'How's Dino?' he asked with genuine interest. He liked the man and saw in Dino more of himself – a masculinity which had not been as apparent in Ken or Derek Collins.

'He's fine, and Graham's doing some work for Robert Floyd's paper. He seems to like it; at least, it makes him feel useful.'

'That's good,' he said, puffing on his pipe and filling the air with smoke. 'He's needed something to keep his mind occupied, being so handicapped.'

'He seems to be coping better at the moment.'

'Mmm, but he's a difficult boy. Your mother's favourite, you know.'

Ruth sipped her tea. 'She loved him from the moment she saw him, didn't she?'

'From the first moment,' he replied, looking momentarily abashed. 'Oh, don't get me wrong, your mother loves all the children – it's just that she feels closest to Graham.'

'And which one do you love most?'

He smiled. 'You couldn't put a cigarette paper between 'em for me. I love them all the same.'

Lilian returned half an hour later, pushing open the front door and calling out to Ruth's father. He winked and motioned for Ruth to keep quiet.

'There's someone to see you here, dear. A surprise.'

She walked in with an expression of resignation on her face, obviously expecting a customer or an unwelcome neighbour. When she saw Ruth she smiled automatically, but walked past without kissing her or even touching her arm. Affection suspended, as always.

'Well, well, this is a great surprise, as you said, Jack.' She turned to Ruth, taking off her hat and placing it on the table under the window. 'How is everyone? How's Graham?'

'He's fine, I was just telling Dad about him.'

She nodded and pulled on an apron.

'Are you going to cook tonight, Mother?' Ruth asked, astonished.

Her mother's expression flickered between unease and irritation. 'I have things to do.'

'I just thought . . . ' Ruth blundered, momentarily confused, 'you know, with my being here . . . I thought we could talk.'

She began to pile packets of flour, mixed fruit and eggs on to the working top, her thin frame moving around the kitchen rapidly. Ruth's father had already turned back to his reading.

'We can talk while I bake.'

Ruth sighed and sat down watching her mother, remembering the evening Derek had come to collect her for their first date, remembering him kissing her on the front step and the sleepless night she had spent wondering whether or not to marry him. It wasn't difficult to slip back to being a child there, to the cold settee and the smell of soap flakes and washing overhead. Ruth had wanted to be a nurse then, and instead she had ended up in her mother's hat shop, stacking the boxes in the back room.

'Ruth!'

'I'm sorry, Mother, I was just thinking.'

Lilian looked at her daughter and then pointed to Jack. 'All the time he sits there, reading, reading, reading. You'd think he had nothing else to do.'

'He likes to read.'

'I would like to read,' she said, stirring some dried fruit into the mixing bowl. 'I'm sure you'd like time to read, but the rest of us are too busy to even think about it.'

Ruth glanced over to her father. He obviously hadn't heard a thing she said.

'No ambition,' she continued, pouring a little milk into the mixture. 'Thank God you had ambition and did well for yourself.'

'It's just that he's got a different personality,' Ruth replied, defending him, aware that nothing had changed, that this conversation was at least forty years old.

'Different personality my foot!' Lilian pointed to him again and a drop of cake mixture fell on to the floor at her feet. 'Jack! What are you reading that's so important?'

He glanced at the cover. '*The Best Western Tales*,' he replied before going back to the book.

'*The Best Western Tales*!' she repeated, infuriated. 'I wouldn't mind so much if it was good literature ... but that rubbish.'

Bemused by the conversation, Ruth kept silent, realising as Lilian continued, that she was, in fact, teasing her husband. Feigning inattention, he would read and she would rail at him, her activity a virtue, his inactivity a stick with which she could beat him as hard and as often as she liked.

'I asked him yesterday to collect the meat from the butcher's.

328

"Don't forget, now, will you?" I said before I left for the shop. "Oh, no, dear, I won't forget," he said.' She scooped the mixture into a greased cake tin as she talked. 'But when I got home – no meat! Useless, that's what he is, utterly useless.'

'What happened?' Ruth asked, fascinated by this side of her mother's nature, a side she had never seen before.

'I sent him over there to knock the butcher up. It was only just gone seven and I've given that man a lot of business over the years ... Not to say that I can't get better meat on Park Road, but it's further to go and I get a bit tired at the end of the day.'

On and on she talked as Ruth drifted back to her childhood, to the days she stayed with Grandma Price and the nights when she watched her mother working on one of the numerous hats she made over the years.

'How's Dino?' she asked suddenly, pronouncing the word 'Dyno' although Ruth had corrected her a hundred times.

'He's well. Working hard at the moment.'

'I'm not prying – your life is your own, as I've always said ... but are you two ever going to get married?'

Ruth breathed in deeply. Before, Dino had always asked her, but lately he had not mentioned marriage and his omission suddenly nagged at her.

'Mother, why does it matter so much whether we marry or not?'

'Because David has his name and the twins have Ken Floyd's name – it just seems confusing, that's all.'

'I don't want to marry again,' Ruth said stiffly, watching her mother wipe around the edges of the cake tin.

'Well, as I say, it's your life, but it does seem odd. That's all.'

Feeling aggravated, Ruth turned to her father for distraction. 'Is that book good?'

He looked up, his finger poised on the line he was reading.

'Smashing. Do you want to borrow it when you go home? I could finish it tonight, if you do.'

'It's OK, Dad, but thanks anyway.'

The evening uncurled itself. Lilian made a fruit cake and a

dozen mince pies, and Ruth's father read every line and every word of his book with all the attention that Moses must have paid to the Ten Commandments. Sitting there, Ruth wondered what her life would have been like if she had stayed in Oldham, if she had kept Laurel and lived with her parents. Maybe marrying again; maybe not; maybe continuing to live in this same house, bringing up a child with all the irritation and interference Lilian would have been sure to give. The thought chilled her.

'Ruth, pass me that sugar shaker, will you?' Lilian asked impatiently. 'I was thinking about tomorrow,' she continued. 'If you like, I could meet you for a coffee in town, around twelve.'

Her voice was indifferent, but Ruth instinctively knew how much her mother wanted her to say yes.

'That would be nice. I'll pack in the morning and then after we've had a chat I'll carry on home.'

'Just as you please,' she said calmly, closing the oven door on her cakes.

They met in Blakeley's tea-room, Lilian was smartly dressed, having just left the shop, her dark grey suit immaculate, her expression faintly smug.

'You look wonderful, Mother.'

She touched her hair self-consciously. 'Well, you don't visit Oldham often and I wanted to look nice so I could show off with you.'

Ruth was touched. 'People will think we're sisters.'

She blushed and then picked up the menu brusquely. 'You always were fanciful, Ruth.'

That evening Kate was standing in the hall, talking to Dino. 'Graham's acting oddly,' she said, her throaty voice lower than usual. 'It's weird.'

'How oddly?' Dino asked, one long arm wrapped round the banister, his tie loosened.

'Just odd. I don't know, but he's different.' She shrugged. Dino listened to her carefully, Kate was always the barometer for Graham's moods.

'Do you think we should go and have a word with him, I mean, seeing that Mum's away?'

'Maybe . . . ' he said and then changed his mind. Graham's behaviour was always erratic. 'No, leave him to it.'

'But he wouldn't take his medicine, and when I came in earlier he was in the gym, beating hell out of the punch-bag.'

'Well, maybe he's just feeling low.'

'He wouldn't talk to me, or explain,' she said, obviously wounded by his lack of trust. Immediately, Dino caught hold of her and hugged her. He loved Kate, seeing in Ruth's child a warmth her mother too often suppressed; a warmth he looked for and at present found only intermittently.

'Listen, we all know how bloody-minded he can be. Leave him alone, he'll be fine.'

She looked apologetically at him. 'I'm sorry you had to come home to this.'

'That's all right,' he said, kissing her forehead, 'it's not your fault. Graham manipulates us all, you know.'

At that precise moment, Ruth walked in, putting her car keys on the table by the door. Seeing the anxious looks on their faces, her mind immediately turned to Graham. 'What is it?'

'Graham's being odd,' Kate said, smiling wanly. 'Could you go and see him?'

Ruth's first instinct was to rush upstairs, but the cool look on Dino's face stopped her. She had seen that look before – Ken had developed the same reserve when their marriage began to fail. Smiling broadly, she walked over to Dino and kissed him. The relief in his eyes was obvious.

'And how are you?'

'Neglected, rejected, lovelorn,' he said, equally aware of the atmosphere and wanting to retrieve their usual familiarity. 'I came home early and Mrs Harvey said you'd be late. You can't imagine what I went through.' He smiled, waiting for her response. 'I missed you so much, darling.'

'Maybe I should go away more often,' Ruth said cheerily, knowing it was the wrong thing to say the moment the words left her lips. Clumsily she had made light of his affection, pushing him away.

'Perhaps you'd better go up and see Graham,' he said, the disappointment thick in his voice.

Her son was in his wheelchair in front of the computer, rows and rows of numbers on the green screen, the sound of the tapping keys jangling on Ruth's nerve ends. Gently, she touched his shoulder and he turned.

'Hello.'

Nodding briefly, Graham looked back to the screen. Surprised and irritated by his lack of manners, Ruth picked up the electric lead which fed into the plug. Startled, he watched her.

'You should learn some manners, Graham. If you ever ignore me like that again, I will pull this out of the wall and wipe whatever it is that you have been working so hard on OFF the computer.'

He watched his mother's lips and understood her. A slow smile spread across his handsome face. 'Sorry,' he signed.

'So you should be,' Ruth said, easily placated by him, easily charmed. 'What are you doing?' she asked, pointing to the mound of papers on his table.

He told her in great detail, his mood lifting as he continued. Even to his mother's eyes, he seemed oddly exhilarated and a little too frenetic. Knowing that Kate had been having trouble with him, Ruth gave Graham his medication, expecting resistance. He took it easily, as he used to when he was a child.

Downstairs, Kate was waiting for the verdict. 'Well?' she asked.

'He seems all right. A little highly strung, perhaps, but nothing serious.'

She relaxed visibly. 'Thank God, I thought he was going to have an asthma attack earlier.'

'But he hasn't had one for months now.'

'That's what I mean.' She pushed her hands into her jacket pockets and glanced at her mother. 'He had me scared, I can tell you.'

'Graham has a habit of doing that,' Dino said coldly behind them.

*

As they had done so often in the past when words failed them, Ruth and Dino made love. At first the action seemed mechanical, too desperate to be loving, but soon the old feelings returned, their mutual passion restoring their closeness. In each other's arms later, they slept and then Dino made a booking for dinner at a small Italian restaurant, surprising Ruth when she came out of the shower.

'Good idea,' she said simply, pulling on a black velvet dress, high-necked, its colour unrelieved except for a heavy gold chain. Used to wearing her hair up, that night Ruth had left it loose about her shoulders to frame her face. Dino looked at her, and ached.

They were only half-way through their second course when Nina's voice interrupted them. 'Hi, can we join you?' she asked, pulling out a chair and sitting down. Tony followed obediently, his face flushed with food and wine, his colour radiant.

'You'll never guess who I saw today!' she began. 'Inger, of all people! She had that kid with her –'

'Nicki.'

'No, the girl. What's her name?' She thought for a moment and shrugged. 'Oh, I can't remember. Anyway, there she was coming out of the health food shop on the King's Road, wearing sandals!' She burst out laughing. 'Bloody sandals – no one wears sandals any more except monks.'

'But what was she doing there? They don't live in London now,' Ruth said, baffled.

'That's what I thought. Well, I was so curious that I waved and she stopped, giving me that holier-than-thou smile she's so good at, and told me they were living in Wales.'

'I thought they were in Ireland,' Ruth said. 'Sam hated Wales.'

'That's right! That's what I thought. Still Inger likes Wales.'

Ruth looked at Nina. 'And Inger always gets what she wants.'

She nodded. ' " 'Twas ever thus." '

They turned back to the men. Tony was in full flight, Dino's expression distant. 'So this man says to me – "Why should I trust you?" – and I said, "Listen, you never trust anyone, why

333

should you? I wouldn't" – so I set out the deal in front of him and he looks, and he says, "That's farcical." '

'Farcical?' Dino repeated lethargically. 'He said it was farcical?'

Tony frowned. 'Yeah, you know ... when it makes good sense.'

'Feasible!' Nina said, laughing and turning back to Ruth. 'Christ, he's such an idiot when we're with company!'

Alerted to the change in Dino's manner, Ruth glanced over to him, smiling, and looked away quickly as he winked, his expression comically lecherous. Nina continued to talk, watching her husband like a proud mother watching her plump spoilt child.

'Tony's a good man,' she said, leaning towards Ruth. 'You know, I used to want to be famous.'

'I wanted to be a nurse,' Ruth responded idly.

'It's not the same thing!'

Ruth shrugged, feeling high-spirited, frivolous – the things Dino loved in her. 'Oh, I don't know, it's just one theatre to another.'

Nina continued, intent on her own vision. 'I wanted the bright lights...'

'You get bright lights in an operating theatre.'

'... and flowers ...'

'Patients get flowers,' Ruth insisted, her eyes never leaving Dino's face. I love you, she thought contentedly.

'... and big, shiny cars.'

'Like hearses?'

Nina sighed and looked at Ruth. 'That's what I really wanted.'

'Are you disappointed?' Ruth asked, the words ringing with irony.

She didn't hesitate for a moment. 'Who, me? Hell, no. We both got lucky in the end, didn't we?'

Seventeen

Graham's manner was altering. Only subtly at first, but then more obviously, his secrecy paramount. He was alone more and more, and avoided eating his meals with the family, preferring to watch television or work from his own room. Late at night Ruth could hear the bleep of his computers, or the ponderous bumps and shuffles as he made his way to bed. He never slept a great deal and rose early, banging the lift doors as he made his way down to the ground floor to collect his letters. Relieved that her relationship with Dino had improved, Ruth was not prepared for any further trauma. Making allowances for her son's condition, she still stood back and let matters take their own course.

And yet, as ever, Kate suffered for her brother and saw herself to blame. 'He's so strange. I try to talk to him, but he just ignores me or continues working on those blasted computers!'

Ruth took off her reading glasses and rubbed her eyes. 'You know he's difficult, Kate, but he'll recover, he always does.'

'But he's cutting me off.'

'No more than me.'

'You don't understand!' she said, her husky voice rising with indignation. 'We're twins, and that makes the difference.'

'And he's handicapped – that makes a difference too.'

Kate walked out, annoyed.

Loved as Graham undoubtedly was by his sister, David never learned to trust him. Ruth doubted if he remembered Graham's violence towards him, but he had an inbuilt suspicion and avoided contact whenever possible. As a well-balanced, cheerful child he found Graham frightening and could not understand his swings of mood or the violent outbreaks of energy when he would work off real or imaginary ills by exhausting himself in the gym.

So one morning when David rushed into Ruth, incoherent and almost hysterical, her first thought was that Graham had hit him again.

'What is it? Tell me!'

'It's Graham . . .' he stammered. 'He's stuck!'

'What do you mean, he's stuck? What's that supposed to mean?' Ruth asked, although David had already turned and was running down the corridor.

He called over his shoulder to her. 'He's stuck! I heard a bang, but I can't open the door.'

Ruth ran to Graham's door and knocked. There was a muffled sound from the other side.

Panic seized her. 'David, get your father. Quick!'

In desperation she tried to push the door open herself, but there was something behind it blocking the way. She was still pushing when Dino arrived and hurled his weight against it, opening it far enough for Ruth to squeeze through. Graham was lying on the floor, his body against the door and his face chalk-white. Looking round frantically, Ruth rushed into his bathroom and found the inhaler, pushing it into his outstretched hand.

Dino called through the door to her. 'What's happening? Is he all right?'

'He's OK, he's had an asthma attack,' she replied, her voice shaky. 'Give us a minute and I'll let you in.'

Ruth knelt down, seeing Graham's familiar recovery signs, the colour coming back into his face, his breathing returning to normal.

'My God, Graham, you frightened me,' she said, although his eyes indicated total indifference as to whether she was frightened or not. 'Come on, let me help you get up.'

Catching hold of his arm, Ruth helped her son back into his chair. His skin was cold and tight under her hand, the power evident. As soon as they moved away from the door, Dino came in.

'Thank God you're all right,' he said in sign language. Graham watched him carefully. 'You *must* keep that inhaler on you – '

336

Impatiently, Graham reminded him that he hadn't had an attack for nearly a year.

'I know that, Graham, but you've had one now. You must take precautions – just think what might happen if we're not around to help out, or if you got stuck somewhere.'

The thought chilled Ruth and she leant against the table.

'It won't happen again,' Graham sighed, his hand movements quick and irritable. As Ruth stood behind him she could see a large, red bruise on the back of his neck where he'd fallen. For an instant, she nearly touched him.

'Leave us for a while, Dino,' she said, her eyes pleading with him to go. 'I'll be back soon.'

He nodded quickly, and left.

She made her son some coffee and sat down beside him at his work table, the main computer grinning at her like a jolly green giant from a child's picture book. Graham had leant his head back and was breathing slowly with his eyes closed, the cup in his strong hands and the steam rising upwards in the still air. Out of the corner of her eyes, Ruth saw a letter, half concealed, the writing familiar. It was Ken's writing.

She glanced back to Graham just as he opened his eyes. 'Do you feel better now?' she asked.

He smiled slightly and nodded.

'In that case I'll go to work. If you want me, ask Mrs Corley to ring the office and I'll come back.'

Dino was in the bedroom when Ruth returned and looked up as she walked in.

'Ken's been writing to Graham!' she said, her eyes blazing.

'What?'

'I said that my ex-husband has been writing to my son –'

'And *his* son.'

'You've changed your tune!' she said coldly. 'It's not that long ago you tried to forbid him to make any contact with them.'

He sighed. 'Ken is Graham's father. I was just stating the obvious.'

'Well, I know the obvious!'

His patience gone, he flung the towel he was holding on to

337

the floor. 'Why all the excitement? Can't we discuss this?'

'We never discuss anything! We argue!' Ruth shouted.

Breaking into Italian, Dino stormed off, slamming the bathroom door closed behind him. Ruth paused and caught her breath. There was a mirror on the bedroom wall and it reflected her image, her hair dishevelled, her expression hard. With a shock, she recognised herself and disliked what she saw.

Hesitating, she walked to the door, and knocked gently. 'Dino, let's not fight about it.'

'I don't want to fight with you,' he said, walking out to face her, his expression weary. 'But if you want my advice, you should talk to your son. Ask him why he never mentioned it to you.'

Ruth leant against the wash-hand basin. 'I don't know if that's the right thing to do. Graham will only clam up or lie to me ... I couldn't see the date on the letter, so I don't know how long this has been going on.'

Dino folded his arms. 'Has he written to Kate?'

'Not that I know of. No ...' she said firmly, 'Kate would have told me.'

'So why is he only writing to Graham?' he asked, turning to pull on his shirt. 'Have a word with Kate – she might know something.'

But she didn't, and was astonished and more than a little indignant. 'What did the letter say?'

'I don't know, I didn't have time to read it.'

She scratched her nose thoughtfully. 'Well, we can't judge until we know what it says, can we?'

'And how do you suggest we find that out?' Ruth asked coolly, 'I can hardly go in and ask Graham to borrow the letter.'

She shook her head. 'No. You'll have to read it when he's not about. When he's in the gym, or something ...'

'I hate doing that, Kate. It seems so dishonest.'

'He's hardly acting very honestly himself, is he?'

The next morning Ruth waited for the sound of the lift doors banging closed on the first floor and then jumped out of bed, running along the corridor and looking over the banister. She could see the top of Graham's head and watched him as he began to rifle through the post. Taking the opportunity, Ruth made her way to his room and found the letter. It read:

> My dear son,
>
> It was wonderful to see you last week after so long. I regret what happened between myself and your mother, but that is the way things turn out sometimes. You are a credit to me and the way you've coped with your handicap is truly amazing. I'm proud of you – I just wanted you to know that.
> I'll see you next Thursday, as arranged.
>
> > With love,
> > Father.

Ruth had been so immersed in the letter that she hadn't heard the lift doors banging closed, or the sound of Graham's wheelchair on the hall carpet. Transfixed, her heart pounding, she stood with the letter in her hand, watching as the handle of the bedroom door turned.

It turned and stopped. There was a shout from down the corridor and the sound of Kate running. Immobilised, Ruth waited, hearing Kate's voice as she spoke to her brother.

'Graham, can you help me with something?'

There was a silence. Obviously he was answering her in sign language.

'No, it won't take long. It's just that I can't pull the table away far enough to reach the book which fell behind it. Please help, Graham, you're a lot stronger than I am, and I need it before I go to the hospital.'

There was another pause, and then she said more calmly, 'Thanks, Graham.'

Ruth heard her move off, and the sound of the wheelchair passing down the hallway. Relief made her dizzy and she took a few deep breaths before replacing the letter and making her way back to the bedroom. Ten minutes later, Kate came in.

'Thank God you diverted Graham just then, I was – '

She smiled bleakly. 'I know, I saw you go into his room – and I saw him come back.'

'Did he know I was in there?' Ruth asked anxiously.

Kate shrugged and sat down on the bed. 'You never know with Graham. What did the letter say?'

'That your father was proud of his son and that he was coming here tomorrow to see him again.' Ruth walked towards the dressing table and began to rub some cream into her face, her hands still shaking. 'Why didn't Graham tell me that he'd seen his father, Kate? Why does he feel the need to hide everything from me?'

'He's not the only one who's hiding things.'

Ruth turned round sharply. 'What does that mean?'

'Well, think about it – Graham is deaf. He can't hear the doorbell ring. Mrs Corley is still too poorly to get out and about, so she didn't let my father in, which leaves only one person – '

'Mrs Harvey!'

She nodded. 'Mrs Harvey.'

Ruth settled the pot of cream down on the table-top. 'I always detested that bloody woman!'

'And my father hired her, or Joanie did. She worked for them first, and she obviously thinks that her first loyalty is still to them.'

'I pay her!'

Kate looked down at her hands. Her mother always saw things too definitely, something was this, or that. No shades of grey, no blurred outlines. It was a quality which made her skilful in business, but clumsy in emotional matters.

'That doesn't mean anything, Mum. In Mrs Harvey's eyes you ousted Joanie and then my father – she probably resents you.'

Ruth smiled bitterly. 'You're probably right. When I first lived here I was so young, and so inexperienced. She knew that. Not that she made things difficult, she simply never took the trouble to hide what she thought of me. I was an upstart in her eyes – and I obviously still am.'

'So, what are you going to do?'

Ruth thought for a moment, her grey eyes cold. 'I'll talk to the woman. With any luck she'll hand in her notice.'

It was a forlorn hope. Although she challenged Mrs Harvey that afternoon, she responded in her usual fashion, her winter face unfathomable. 'Mrs Floyd, I'm so very sorry if I have offended you. I was put in a rather difficult position, you see. Having been employed for many years by Mr Floyd I felt a certain loyalty to him, and when he arrived on the doorstep to see his son I naturally assumed that you approved.'

'But why didn't you tell me about the visit?'

Her back stiffened. 'I thought your son would inform you of that.'

'I see,' Ruth said evenly, allowing her dislike of the woman to become obvious.

'It won't happen again, madam.'

'It had better not, Mrs Harvey. I won't have disloyalty. You work for me and abide by my rules. You are no longer employed by Mr Floyd, and you owe him nothing. If I can't trust you, I shall have to let you go.'

Her eyes flickered momentarily. Ruth could imagine how she would relate the conversation to her husband later.

'I understand, madam.'

'I hope you do,' Ruth said icily. 'If Mr Floyd comes to this house again when I am not here, he is to be refused admittance. You will telephone me at work immediately and I will deal with the matter.'

'And if he gets in touch by letter, or phone?'

'All his letters are to come to me, likewise all his phone calls.'

'If that's all, madam?'

Ruth stopped her. 'Not quite. When he came here last week – was my son expecting him?'

There was only a momentary hesitation. 'I should think so. He was waiting in the hall when Mr Floyd arrived.'

Swallowing uncomfortably, Ruth turned away. 'Thank you, Mrs Harvey.'

Logic forced Ruth to be reasonable although, denied her mother's strength of character, Kate was less sympathetic. 'Why don't you see it for what it is? My father went behind your back, sneaking about and coming here to see your son. He never gave a damn for us for years, and now he wants to come back? No, damn him!'

'Kate, listen to me,' Ruth said, catching hold of her daughter's hands. 'Ken Floyd is your father.'

She shook her mother's hands off. 'Why do you let yourself be used like this?' she said wildly. 'He left you for another woman, left you to bring up two kids, run a business and keep this place going on your own!' She shook her head, enraged.

'He's getting older. He's over sixty, Kate.'

'I don't care if he's seventy – I hate him! And I shall always hate him!' she cried hoarsely. 'Even Grandfather can't stand him – so why should you defend him?'

'I'm not defending him! And I don't have to answer to you!' Ruth countered, her face white. 'I was married to that man and had his children. Much as I may dislike him, I have to try and sort this matter out, and hysterics won't help.'

'He never cared about us before . . .' Kate continued blindly. 'Besides, why did he only want to see Graham, and not me?'

Ruth sighed. Of course, she had never thought of that, had never realised how hurt Kate must be feeling, overlooked by her own father. More gently, she tried to explain.

'Perhaps he knew that you and I were so close that you would never have gone behind my back.'

Kate shrugged, the look of an injured child in her face. 'And maybe he wasn't interested in me.'

'That's not true! It's just that Graham is his son.' Ruth thought back, remembering Ken. 'Your father is a very weak man, Kate, and maybe he can understand Graham because he sees so much of himself in him.'

'How could he? He never saw Graham until the other week,' the girl responded bitterly.

Ruth was losing patience. She was doing her best to cope with the situation, but ever since Ken Floyd had re-emerged in her life, nothing had been the same ... now she was even arguing with her children.

'I don't know, Kate! I don't understand why Graham had to be deceitful, or why his father contacted him in such an underhand way.' She paused. 'But I'll find out tomorrow, once and for all. Your father's letter said he was coming to see Graham. Well,' she added with grim humour, 'he can see his ex-wife too.'

That evening Ruth stayed with Graham, watching him like a heron watches a garden pond. His duplicity didn't surprise her – in a way she had even expected it, knowing that he felt the world was against him and that his mother had betrayed him by having another son. But Ruth had thought that by her constant attention she could eventually convince him of her unchanged love. That was her first miscalculation – because Graham believed that his mother had abandoned him. Although an intelligent eighteen-year-old, he thought like a child emotionally. The usurping of his position by a new and perfect son, succeeded in alienating him further, and made him believe that he was now relegated to second place.

Constantly making allowances for Graham, Ruth could imagine her son's delight when Ken contacted him – at last there was someone who wanted him. Only him. That fact alone, she realised, would have been irresistible for Graham.

'What are you going to do?' Dino asked, the night before Ken was due to visit.

'I'll talk to him.'

'And then what?' he asked bleakly, his own disquiet flaring up. 'Are you going to talk to Graham? Are you going to try and stop him from seeing his father? If you do, you'll be making problems for yourself. Graham's no longer a boy. He's clever and bitter and very angry.'

'I know my son.'

He raised his eyebrows. 'Then you are very fortunate indeed.'

The morning that Ken was expected, Ruth rang the cinema and spoke to Bill Pascoe, telling him that she was not going to be in that day. Assuring her he could cope, he then asked where the film was for the showing that evening at Knightsbridge.

'With the projectionist,' Ruth said, coolly.

'He hasn't got it,' Pascoe replied, obviously relishing the situation. 'Henry said you had it.'

'Bill, I don't keep the films at home. I never have, you know that. Get back to him and ask him to find it. Then ring me and let me know that everything's all right.'

'It will be,' he said silkily. 'Don't worry, I'll ring you later. Bye.'

Graham was working on his computer all morning. The letter had not stipulated the time that Ken was due to arrive, so Ruth paced around the house all day, worried about the lost film and waiting for the doorbell to ring. By twelve-thirty, her nerves were raw.

Ruth spun round to find Mrs Harvey standing in the doorway of the lounge, watching her.

'Master Graham was wondering if you were staying home for lunch – and if you would like to eat with him?'

Momentarily wrong-footed, Ruth hesitated before replying. 'Tell him I'll join him, and bring something up for both of us, would you?' The woman turned to go. 'Oh, and Mrs Harvey, I'll answer the door today.'

She nodded and walked out.

It was a clever move on Graham's part. They ate their meal in his room, Graham seemingly relaxed, although Ruth knew that if the bell rang he couldn't hear it and could only guess at what was going on. But when they had finally exhausted every topic of conversation, he became irritable and edgy, no longer making an effort to speak and communicating in sign language instead, finally telling Ruth that he was going into the gymnasium to do his exercises.

'Do you want me to come with you?' she asked. He nodded briefly, misery making him dull. Ruth looked at him as he wheeled his chair into the other room, saw the strong arms, the dark eyes, and wondered if she was doing the right thing, or if she should simply walk out . . . Maybe he was entitled to contact his father after all, she thought wearily. The work-out was long and exhausting. Ruth could hear the deafening thud of the weights as they fell back on to their supports, and the clank of the press as Graham forced his thin legs to lift the bar. She turned away, embarrassed, and was about to leave when she heard the bell.

Ken was already smiling as she opened the door, his eyes registering surprise as he saw Ruth. With considerable aplomb, he made a mock bow to her and walked into the lounge, Ruth following him. Sun flooded the walls and mottled the silk carpet, and on a side table a bowl of lilac flowered against the polished wood, the smell faintly intoxicating in the warm room.

'Did Graham tell you I was coming?' he asked simply.

Ruth shook her head. 'No. But he should have. Or you should have told me yourself. I found out because I saw your letter – '

'That was convenient.'

His outrage infuriated her. 'Don't act the injured party, Ken! You should have come to me first and we could have sorted something out. Instead of all this ... intrigue. It's not fair to set my son against me.'

He sat down heavily. His colour was very red, the features losing their firmness in the coarse flesh. 'And you would have allowed me to see him, I suppose?'

'If I thought you really wanted to get to know him. Yes.'

Ken was surprised. So the old man had been right, after all, Ruth could be reasonable. But then the old man was always right about Ruth, having quite a soft spot for her. He could hardly blame him, in the sunlight her skin was flawless, her eyes as steady as they had always been.

'I want to see my son. It's important to me.'

'Why now?'

He glanced round, his eyes fixing on a large oil painting. 'God! What an appalling painting! What a very Catholic piece of devotion! And how out of character for you. Is that due to the influence of your lover?'

Ruth ignored the remark. 'Ken, we're talking about Graham, not Italian art.'

'Well, you always knew more about your children than

345

anything else,' he said nastily. 'Have you got a drink?'

She sighed and walked over to the drinks trolley. 'Gin, I suppose?'

'Not too much tonic, Ruth. Why ruin the taste?'

As she poured him a double, Ken watched her and said, 'Just a bit more ... you don't begrudge the old man, do you?'

She passed it to him and sat down on the settee, keeping a distance between them.

'You haven't aged, Ruth, well, not that much.' He took a long gulp of the drink. Her hair was darker than before, he realised, but it suited her, framed her face well.

'It's my worry-free existence,' she said drily, crossing her legs. He finished the drink and refilled his glass immediately with the familiarity of someone who knows a place well. She could remember him when it was his house, when she had been the stranger.

'Ken, why do you want to see Graham? And why only him? Why didn't you contact Kate as well?'

'It was my son I wanted to see – '

'You are incredible! Don't you realise how much that hurts your daughter?'

He continued dreamily. 'I was so proud when I saw Graham. He's managing so well, it's a shame that he's handicapped. He's so good-looking too – just like his father.'

He laughed loudly and Ruth winced. She had to make him realise the importance of the situation, quickly, before he drank any more. 'You can't fool around with Graham, Ken. He's not like other people. He can't cope with any kind of stress – it makes him ill and then he suffers from asthma. We know how to cope with him, you don't.' She paused, dreading the words. 'He could live another fifty years, or only two – no one is sure. But I want him to live as long as possible ... He can't cope with worry of any kind – and he requires constant love and support.'

Not certain that anything she said was being understood, Ruth got to her feet and walked to the window. Ken saw her, and blinked, the drink taking effect so that he thought momentarily that it was Joanie standing there.

346

'I don't want to keep you from your son, Ken. He's your child as much as mine and I don't want to hurt either of you. But you *must* be careful with him. You can't come back and then leave when you're bored with him. If you want to love him you must be permanent – otherwise you'll hurt him and possibly even kill him.'

She turned. Ken was staring at her with an odd expression on his face, the empty glass resting on his right knee.

'Graham is dangerous – as dangerous as a man skating on thin ice with a bomb in his pocket. I know that, I live with that, as do the rest of us in this house. We love him, so we cope. If you can honestly tell me you will be there for him when he wants you, whenever he wants you ... then you're welcome here.'

He said nothing and merely refilled his glass. Ruth saw the liquid slop around the edge and heard the hiss of the tonic as he poured it in.

'I need my son,' he said finally.

Ruth nodded. 'All right, but remember what I said, Ken.'

'I'll remember ... but I want to see him.'

'Go and see him then.'

He stood in the middle of the room facing her. For an instant Ruth thought he was going to say something but he stopped himself. He looked disorientated and almost pathetic, and after he drained his glass he walked upstairs past Mrs Harvey who was just coming into the hall.

'Mrs Harvey,' Ruth said, her voice ice-cold, 'Mr Floyd may visit Graham whenever he likes – but I wish to know about the visits if I'm not here.'

'Very well, madam,' she said, with a note of triumph. 'By the way, Mr Bill Pascoe is on the telephone for you. He said something about a film.'

Ken visited the following week, bumping into Kate by the gate as she was setting off for the hospital. She hadn't seen him since she was seven years old and stopped as he put his hand on her arm. She was wearing a pink dress, her long hair tied back from her face, her eyes shaded by a pair of sunglasses. It was a hot June day and the sun was peeling into the sky.

From where Ruth stood by the front door she couldn't hear what they said, but she saw Kate shake off his hand and walk away quickly. Ken gazed after her, his jacket over his shoulder and when he saw Ruth he smiled briefly, without humour.

'She's like you ... stubborn.'

'What did you expect? Did you think she'd rush into your arms crying "Daddy!"?'

He ignored the barb and walked past her into the hall. It was only eleven in the morning but he smelt strongly of gin.

'How's Graham?'

'Fine. He's expecting you. I'm off to the Belvedere, so I'll say goodbye now.' Ruth stopped and looked at him closely. 'Are you feeling all right? You look awful.'

'Just a hangover ... nothing to worry about.'

'You should stop drinking so much, Ken. It can't do you a bit of good.'

He turned away, touched by her concern, remembering it being given so often and so willingly in the past. 'You never could stop worrying about any of us, could you?'

Strangely embarrassed, Ruth left.

Dino resented his presence from the first, and Ken's visits caused endless arguments and made the atmosphere tense in the house. To avoid the two men meeting, Ruth arranged for Ken to come to the house when Dino was at the bank, and after their first brief encounter Kate made sure that she saw as little of her father as possible and avoided all reference to him. He also caused a deep rift between her and her brother, as Graham idolised Ken and talked about his father almost continuously.

'Dino looked a bit miffed when I saw him the other day,' Nina said when she met Ruth for lunch. 'He seemed pig sick about Ken.'

'He doesn't like the idea ... He's hopping mad about it, actually,' Ruth said. 'And Graham doesn't help, talking about his father all the time.'

She looked tired to Nina, her composure an effort.

'Is Ken still drinking?'

'As though there was no tomorrow.'

'Daft bastard,' Nina said thoughtfully, scooping up some lasagne with her fork. 'I wonder what he's up to – '

'Ken wants to see his son,' Ruth said interrupting her, the words as much to convince herself as her companion.

'Sure, sure, I know that,' Nina said, laying down her fork, 'but, unless my instinct's wrong – and I've never been wrong about a man yet – he has an ulterior motive.'

Dino thought along the same lines as Nina. Violently jealous of his own possessions, Dino saw his home and family invaded, and took Ruth's passivity in the matter as final proof of some remaining feeling for her ex-husband. He hovered uneasily between anger and frustration, aware that he was, in some way, lessening himself by accepting the situation.

'I don't give a damn what you think, Ruth. It's emotional blackmail,' he said, passing the toast over the breakfast table to David. 'He's just trying to ingratiate himself.'

'What's ingratiate?' David asked innocently.

Dino shrugged. 'It means that he's trying to win favour with Graham.'

'You mean, like crawling?'

'Something like that, David, yes,' Dino replied, his voice thin with irritation. 'I don't want him coming here more than once a week,' he continued, pouring some honey into his coffee. 'That's more than enough. David! Stop doing that.'

He was flicking crumbs at Barnie who was too old and too idle to move. He was ten then and staggered through every winter.

'Leave the cat alone, David. It's not fair,' Ruth said, her own voice more agitated than she had meant it to be. 'I think you're right, once a week is plenty,' she said, turning back to Dino.

'Do you think he'll keep the visits up, Ruth?'

'I hope so,' she said, seeing the look on Dino's face and adding quickly, 'for Graham's sake. I told Ken exactly what would happen if he didn't.'

Dino leant forwards and slapped David around the left ear briskly. 'I told you – leave that cat alone!'

Oblivious to the trauma he caused, Ken visited each week, after which Graham related meticulously what his father had said, always managing to imply that Ruth was somehow at fault and that he would have preferred to have his real father living with them instead of Dino. The manner of the visits altered too, the two men secreting themselves in Graham's rooms and developing an intense relationship which Ruth soon grew to resent.

Then on one of the first wet days of August, Ken told Graham that he was going on holiday, asking Ruth if he could take his son with him.

'Where?'

'On a boat I've got. He could have a great time.'

Her stomach lurched. 'He could also drown.'

'Ruth, you can't say no, he's looking forward to it.'

'You've told him already!' she said, disbelievingly. 'How could you, without asking me first? Now you've got his hopes up he'll never take no for an answer.'

With biting clarity, she wondered if that was his intention.

'You treat him like a kid, Ruth. He's an adult now. He's grown up.'

'But you're not!'

Ken flinched but remained silent.

'How could you possibly cope with Graham on your own? You won't have the facilities for him to do his exercises and you wouldn't begin to know what to do if he had an asthma attack.'

'Kate can cope,' Ken said simply.

Ruth froze, seeing her daughter taken over and monopolised by her father; seeing the children who had been her whole existence, slipping away from her. She breathed in deeply to keep her voice steady. 'Kate is training to be a physiotherapist. She couldn't take the time off, even if she wanted to.'

'I thought she might like to come with us. She's very close to Graham.'

Ruth's throat constricted. 'She doesn't like you, Ken! And she certainly wouldn't want to be stuck on a boat with you for two weeks. Besides, what sort of holiday would it be for her, looking after her brother?'

'Graham said they got on well,' Ken replied, suddenly enraged by the woman in front of him. After all this time, she still couldn't let her kids out of her sight. Well, now *he* wanted them, and he was going to have them.

'That's not the point!' Ruth said angrily. 'Kate has her own life to lead, she's not Graham's private nurse and companion.'

'I just thought – '

'Well, think again!'

But it wasn't that simple. Graham was set on the trip and when he told Kate and asked her to go with them she was too soft-hearted to refuse him.

'I'm not sure, Graham.'

He glanced over to his sister and watched her lips, reading the words and frowning. 'We would have a good time,' he insisted.

'I don't like my father,' she said emphatically. 'You may feel close to him, but I don't.' Kate glanced at her brother, seeing the dull look in his eyes, the rush of disappointment.

Ever wary of his feelings, she hesitated. 'Anyway, how long would it be for?'

Graham tried to keep the look of triumph off his face as he answered. 'Only a couple of weeks ...' he signed firmly. 'Just two weeks, Kate ... please.'

She nodded reluctantly.

'You should have said no,' Ruth said, when she heard.

'He would have been so hurt.'

'Kate, you're not here solely for your brother's convenience – besides, you don't get on with your father, just think what it would be like on a boat with him for two weeks.'

'But Graham's looking forward to it.'

'It's out of the question!' Ruth replied, turning away from her daughter and beginning to gather together some papers. Don't go, Kate, she thought blindly, don't go. 'Besides, how would Graham do his exercises?'

'My father's having some bars and apparatus put into the boat. We could take Graham's medication, and I can cope with his asthma if he has an attack.'

Ruth stiffened, so Ken had organised everything, had he? Holidays, equipment – all the caring in the world, after years of neglect. Her heart racing, Ruth clenched her fists, the nails digging into her palms. 'Do you want to go with them, Kate?'

She replied evenly, her husky voice firm. 'I want to give it a try, Mum. Just to see how things work out. I feel as though I should make the effort to get to know my father, and maybe if I go on this holiday I'll get to like him . . . and maybe I won't. Besides, Graham wants to go so badly it would break his heart if I refused.'

Unable to reply, Ruth began to organise her papers, placing them tidily in her briefcase for when she went over to the Belvedere later. She smiled to herself, suddenly comforted; at work she would feel better, it was always good therapy if she was upset. She clicked the locks on her case firmly. Children grew up, she knew that, they grew up and left to lead their own lives – she had expected it. It just hurt so much because it was Ken; because he was the one to take them away from her.

'Mum?' Kate said softly, worried by her mother's silence. She seemed detached, remote.

'You must go, if you want to, Kate,' Ruth said, picking up her briefcase and walking towards the door of the study. 'Just be careful, that's all.'

Two weeks later they set off, Ken collecting Graham and Kate with a look of triumph as he turned to his ex-wife.

Left to their own devices for two weeks, Dino and Ruth relaxed and enjoyed each other again. With relief, Dino stopped staying late at the bank, something he had done ever since Ken's re-emergence, and started to drop in at the cinemas, mingling with the customers or reading his papers as Ruth worked. Aware that she had stupidly taken him for granted, Ruth began to see Dino in a new light – he was, after all, still a bachelor who owned his own flat – and she realised, with overdue insight, that he was eligible and she was vulnerable.

But she did not understand Dino completely and did not know that he saw in her everything he wanted – the class, the elegance and the passion he had not found in other women. He loved her for her qualities, but resented her stubbornness. Quarrelsome and emotional, Dino was bound to Ruth by their child and their mutual and constant attraction, his temperament making allowances for the only woman he really desired.

Their relationship intrigued many, as did the various developments in their lives, and with rabid curiosity, Geoffrey Lynes followed events.

'I never thought you'd have Ken Floyd back – '

'He isn't back, Geoffrey. He merely comes to the house to see the twins ... and to take them on holiday.'

He was clutching a roll of film to his heart like a tin bouquet. 'Still, it must be strange having him around after all these years.'

'He needs to see his children,' Ruth said dully.

'He never used to need anyone.'

She looked up at the man in front of her coldly. 'You never liked him, did you?'

'No,' Lynes said, with considerable feeling. 'I thought he was a lucky man who had had all the advantages. I was jealous of him, I suppose.'

'But not any longer?'

'No ... I'm not jealous of anyone any longer.'

Ruth nodded and turned back to her papers.

Lilian, however, was violently opposed to the idea of the holiday, and voiced her opinion loud and long over the phone. 'You must be mad, Ruth! Not that I'd dream of telling you how to run your own life, I've never interfered in that way – but to let those children go off with Ken Floyd – '

'They aren't children, Mother, they're eighteen years old, and he's their father,' Ruth said, forcing herself to sound calm. 'Besides, they seem to be having a good time. Graham's not ill, and the change will do him good. He stays in the house too much, either working on those blasted computers or in the gym. It's not healthy.'

'He's not well – '

'He's handicapped, Mother, not an invalid! He should live a fuller life.' Mentally she distanced her son, preparing herself for what she took to be his inevitable departure. 'I've been thinking about it while they've been away ... Graham should be out and about, meeting people and doing something other than working. He's a young man.'

'And a restricted one,' Lilian added softly. 'Don't give him ideas, Ruth, otherwise he might think he can live normally when he can't.'

Ruth clenched the phone tightly. 'But maybe he could.'

'How? Get married? Have children? Graham can't even talk properly and he can't hear – how could he have a normal existence?'

'He could meet someone and fall in love,' Ruth said simply. The words danced round her. Maybe he could, she thought, maybe he could.

'If I were you I'd think very carefully about what Dr Throop says. We know that Graham could live to old age – or die unexpectedly. We've always known that. How could you risk his health by pushing him out into the world?'

'Oh, Mother, how could I risk his happiness by not pushing him?'

She sniffed loudly. 'Well, I have to go now. Your father sends his love to you all. Is David all right?'

'He won a swimming final at school today.'

'That's good. Having one strong, healthy boy should be enough for you.'

When she rang off, Ruth was shaking.

'Do you think Graham could have a normal relationship with a woman?' she asked Dino that night as they lay in bed.

Surprised by the question, he hesitated before replying. 'I'm not a doctor, how do I know?'

'But what's your instinct?'

354

'Graham's normal, he must have normal feelings and emotions.'

Ruth interrupted him. 'So he must get frustrated.'

'Do you mean sexually?'

'Yes, sexually,' Ruth answered. 'As you say, he's fit and strong and very handsome. He must miss human contact, especially female contact.'

Fascinated by the thought, Dino turned in the bed to face her. 'Has he said anything?'

'Graham? No, not a word. I'm just thinking out loud. Maybe some of his aggression is due to his physical frustration.'

'Maybe it is . . .' Dino answered, his mind running on. 'Could he have children?'

'Dr Throop says he's capable of fathering children.'

'But how would he go about finding a girl? He hardly ever leaves the house.'

Ruth thought for a moment, trying to imagine how Graham could experience some tenderness, some compassion other than her own. 'Kate has friends – nurses at the hospital.'

'And you think they'd want to go out with Graham?' Dino asked, incredulous. 'For God's sake, Ruth, he's crippled – '

' – and handsome and intelligent,' she concluded, rising to his defence. 'These girls work with people far more handicapped than my son, they're used to it.'

Touched by her concern, Dino laid his hand against Ruth's cheek lightly. 'I would tread very carefully. All Graham needs now is to be rejected by a woman.'

'But if she was the right woman – '

'*Quidquid agas, prudenter agas, et respice finem,*' he said, infinitely gentle. 'Whatever you do, do cautiously, and look to the end.'

She answered him softly, aware of his tenderness. 'I'll be careful, Dino.'

When the twins returned they appeared well and rested. Kate was a little thinner than usual but full of life; Graham was tanned, his white teeth almost perfect against the deep colour of his skin, his eyes clear and without their usual look of anger or suspicion.

'We had a marvellous time. I hardly got sea-sick at all,' Kate

355

said, turning back to Graham and repeating it in sign language.

He watched her and continued himself. 'Father said that we could do it again later in the year ... he was a good navigator ... we went to this island off Corfu and the sun was belting down ...'

They talked to Ruth for two hours and then dropped into bed exhausted. Graham didn't even look at his post and ignored the computers which stared back at him blankly. While he slept Ruth watched him, as she had done so many times. He was lying on his back, his strong arms on top of the covers, his hair untidy. She remembered the day that she discovered his deafness and the time he hit David ... and she prayed that his good mood would last, foreseeing a future for him that even she didn't really believe existed.

But Kate was beyond sleep; still excited, she was sitting up in bed when Ruth went in to her. 'I thought you'd be asleep.'

'I couldn't.'

Ruth sat down beside her, trying not to show her true feelings. 'How did you get on with your father?'

'I'm not sure. He was trying to be nice – but I don't feel close to him. Not yet anyway.' She pushed back her long hair from her forehead. 'He was marvellous with Graham though. Endlessly patient, and he even managed to learn some sign language so that Graham didn't have to keep writing notes for him.'

Ruth found to her astonishment that she even resented Ken's kindness and realised for the first time that she was jealous of him. 'And Graham? How was he?'

'He loves Dad, that much is certain,' Kate said easily. 'He thinks he's everything perfect in the world and God help me if I ever said otherwise!'

The smile that passed over Ruth's face was brief. 'How much was he drinking?'

'A hell of a lot. From morning to night. I'll never know how he kept upright.'

'Practice,' her mother said drily.

'It can't be good for him. Not so much, and not every day.'

'That's his problem,' Ruth said, kissing her daughter on the cheek, 'not ours.'

Throughout the months, Ken's visits continued. Graham's love for his father escalated, his weeks revolving around the meetings, his conversation dominated by the subject. And Ken seemed similarly committed, although after a while Ruth noticed an alteration in his manner, his devotion strange and highly-pitched. Unsettled, she tackled him.

'Is everything all right between you and Graham?'

'Fine,' he said, looking strained, the marks of recent weight loss obvious, although he still helped himself to a drink as soon as he came in.

'I know Graham looks forward to your visits. But you seem so committed to him.'

'Maybe I feel guilty for the way I left you all,' he said, glancing away quickly. 'Maybe I'm making amends.'

'No, Ken. That's not it. What is the matter?'

He sat down heavily, his suit jacket flapping open.

'Nothing.'

Ruth's initial irritation turned to curiosity. She had suspected Ken's motives for some time, just as she had built up a steady resentment towards him. It had been her own choice to let him into her family, but now she was determined to know what he wanted.

'Listen, I need an answer, Ken. Why are you spending all your time with us? Any why pick out Graham in particular? He loves you – you don't have to prove anything any more.'

Without answering, he poured half the contents of the glass into his mouth. His eyes were vague and his hands shook slightly.

'You drink too much,' Ruth said coolly. 'You'll kill yourself.'

He smiled ironically but said nothing.

'Haven't you got anyone of your own?' she continued, shielding her eyes from the light which flooded in from the window. 'I know you don't get on that well with your father – ' Ken laughed shortly. 'Well, what about Joanie?' she asked, but there was no response. 'All right, so maybe that's not a good idea, but haven't you got anyone else?'

He shook his head. 'No one.'

'But you could find someone. You don't look your age, and you could always find yourself a girlfriend – '

'I've had enough!' Ken said suddenly, slumping forward in his seat with his head in his hands. The empty glass rolled round his feet and came to rest beside the table leg. Ruth jumped back, too startled to say anything.

'I've had enough!' he repeated, looking at her, his eyes full of tears and his mouth slack. 'I can't go on – I just can't. I have to come here!'

He grabbed hold of Ruth's hands, pressing them to his mouth. His lips were hot against her skin.

'I have to come here, it's the only place left,' he said, becoming incoherent, the drink making his voice thick. 'I can't go anywhere else . . .'

Ruth tried to pull her hands away, embarrassed by his behaviour, her voice cool. 'Ken, I don't understand what's wrong with you,' she said, as his fingers clenched hers. 'Tell me what's the matter, please.'

Ken turned his head and tried to focus, his eyes clearing, although the tears still ran down his face. Repelled by him, and yet aware of an overwhelming pity, Ruth glanced away.

'I've got cirrhosis of the liver,' he said, and then laughed, the sound inhuman, like one of Graham's noises. 'I'm dying – that's the long and the short of it . . . and I wanted to come home.'

Ruth shook her head violently and stood up, clasping her hands together, her hair bleached by the bright daylight. 'No, it's not true! I don't believe it.'

'I've known for over a year now,' Ken continued. 'They said that if I didn't stop drinking I wouldn't last eighteen months. That's why I wanted to see the twins and get to know them, especially Graham because I never bothered to help him when he needed me . . .'

He began to sob, his head down in his hands, his hair untidy on the back of his collar.

'Ken . . .' Ruth said uselessly.

'Oh God, I'm so afraid . . .! I'm so bloody afraid to die.'

Ruth hesitated, standing in the middle of the lounge and watching the man in front of her. As Ken wept she realised her mistake in thinking that he had been a threat to her family. All the jealousy and bitterness she had endured had been for nothing; Ken couldn't take her children away, he couldn't do anything to her. He was helpless. Her resentment lifted with the realisation, and from that moment he altered in her eyes, so that Ruth saw him defeated, frightened, and alone like a child ... With a mixture of pity and relief, she took him in her arms and rocked him.

Eighteen

Ruth realised it was pointless to explain to Ken how cruel he had been. Having always been selfish and thoughtless, in his desire to contact his children it never occurred to him that his death would have a detrimental effect on them. His aim was simple – he was afraid to die and needed comfort. That fear obliterated everything Ruth had said about Graham and the effect trauma could have on his health.

Ruth told Kate immediately. Although she had never become close to Ken, the fact that he was her father made her grieve, her eyes filling with that age-old look of disbelief and bewilderment before she burst into tears, asking her mother repeatedly if the diagnosis could be wrong.

'No, I'm sorry, Kate, it's true . . . he hasn't got long to live.'

She looked steadily at her mother. 'Have you told Graham? Oh God, Mum, it'll break his heart.'

'I can't tell him yet,' Ruth said, wondering when she could, wondering how he would take the news. 'I'll tell him in a while.'

'Where is Dad?'

'At his flat.'

Kate looked away. 'Alone?' Ruth nodded. 'Is he going to stay there?'

'He has to go into hospital for treatment every few days, but otherwise he'll be there.'

'Oh, Mum,' she said simply.

'I know . . .' Ruth answered, catching hold of her daughter's hand. 'I know.'

Dino came home that night full of joy about some investments he'd made, his voice echoing in the hall, his good humour apparent. When no one answered him, he made his way to the study where Ruth and Kate were sitting. The room was inviting in the half-light, the lamps turned on, the rows of books piled round them, a fire burning. It looked comfortable and welcoming and caught him off guard.

'Hello, everyone ...' He looked at the two women. 'What's the matter?'

'My father's ill,' said Kate.

'How ill?'

'Very. He's dying, and he's on his own.' She stopped talking and looked up at the man who had treasured her, caring for her and loving her unconditionally. 'He wanted to come here – '

'To die?' Dino said coldly.

'Yes.'

'This is a house, not a hospital!' he answered, threatened by the look on her face. 'Your father drank himself stupid, so he can take the consequences.'

Kate looked at him, stunned. Her face was white with anger. 'How could you be so cruel? He's dying, how could you say such rotten things?'

'Kate, don't!' Ruth said, interceding between them.

But Kate wasn't listening to anyone. 'You've never been unkind before,' she shouted at him. 'Never! You've always been wonderful – better than any father ever could have been – so why act like this now? He needs us – he's got no one else.'

Dino stood in front of her. 'Whose fault is that? I know he's your father, but he was also Ruth's husband. Do you think I want her to see him die?' He glanced away, his frustration palpable. 'He made his own decision how to live his life so why should I pay for his mistakes? Why should any of us?' He stopped, anger dissolving into blind pity. 'Do you think I want you to see your father die? Or Graham to see that? Dear God!' he said suddenly. 'Has anyone told him?'

'I couldn't,' Ruth replied, turning her face to the fire, the heat burning her.

'Well, someone will have to tell him,' Dino said bitterly. 'I knew this would happen! I knew that Ken Floyd would be nothing but trouble! Now he wants to *die* here with his family around him! Why? What has he done to deserve that?' He pointed upstairs. 'And who's going to tell Graham?' We all know what it might do to him – so who's going to be the lucky one to tell him?'

'I will,' Ruth said softly.

'Damn right you will! Because I won't! And as for you – ' he said, swinging round to face Kate, 'you can have your father here and watch him die – but don't ask me to join you. He should be in a hospital, where he belongs!' He walked to the door and then turned. 'Just remember one thing, I love both of you . . . remember that when you're grieving for Ken Floyd – and ask yourselves if he could say the same.'

He walked out and ran up the stairs.

They could both hear him moving about as he packed his case, the sound of drawers banging as he hastily snatched up some clothes. Minutes later he came down, saying nothing to either of them, walking past the study and slamming the front door as he left. In complete bewilderment Kate heard the car pull out and looked over to her mother.

'Oh God! I'm sorry, Mum, I never thought this would happen . . . go and stop him!' she said, getting to her feet. 'Bring him home.'

'Which one?' Ruth answered dully.

Ken moved in the following day, going first to Graham's room and staying for over an hour. When he came out, his face was grey and he staggered upstairs without telling anyone what had taken place. To all intents and purposes a very sick man, he refused to stay in bed, and tried repeatedly to elicit some response from Graham who had retreated into his own world again. The familiar bleep from the computers started once more as he worked into the night, while above him, his father paced the floor and waited.

They all waited, David being the only one who was unconcerned. Being blessed with an easy temperament he simply thought that Ken was there as a guest and no one disillusioned him.

'How long is he staying, Mum?'

'I'm not sure,' Ruth said, glancing over to Kate.

'A day? A week?'

Ruth could see her daughter glance away.

'I don't know, David. Why?'

He smiled easily. 'Well, it's just that I wondered if my friend Tim could come and stay – '

'Not yet, David!'

He looked rebuffed. 'I only asked.'

Kate leant across the table towards him. 'Can't it wait? I mean, can't you go and stay at Tim's house?'

'It's not the same.'

'Yes it is!' Kate said, her voice rising.

'No, it's not!' David retaliated, glancing over to Ruth. 'You always said I could have anyone to stay – '

'You can – '

He interrupted her. 'So why can't Tim come?'

Kate had calmed down and answered him evenly. 'If you're allowed to have your friends to stay, why can't Mum? After all, it works both ways.'

David digested the information and then smiled. 'But after he's gone, Tim can come and stay then?'

'After he's gone . . .' Ruth said, as her throat tightened. 'After he's gone, Tim can come and stay.'

Sometimes Ken spent days reading, other times went into the garden and walked round. He tried valiantly to keep up his spirits but, having never been a brave man, he was hopelessly bewildered and often begged for reassurance.

'How are you feeling?' Ruth asked him one morning.

'Not so bad. I slept well.' He glanced towards her. 'Are you going into work today?'

She recognised the plea in his voice. 'Why? Do you want me to stay at home? I do have some things I could do here.'

He looked away, his bravery evaporating. 'I just thought . . . I'm sorry, I had no right.' A low shaft of sunlight fell into the room, cruelly cheerful. 'I can't go on much longer, Ruth.'

She smiled, a high summer smile; the smile Ruth used when Graham was ill, a smile to encourage the impossible. 'Yes you can. You're safe here, and besides we want you here.'

He interrupted her. 'No, it's not right, none of this. I shouldn't have expected to come here and invade your family.'

'The twins are your children too, Ken.'

His voice was flat, without emotion. 'I gave them up.'

'Yes, and I gave Laurel away,' Ruth said quietly, putting her guilt into words. 'We all make mistakes, Ken. Yours are no worse than mine.'

'And I let you go,' he said, lifting his hand and covering hers. 'I still love you,' he said, smiling bitterly. 'No, don't get me wrong, I'm not making some last-minute, dying-man, "run away with me" plea – I wouldn't do that to you. You're happy with someone else and that's how it should be. But I do love you.'

'Ken –'

'I'm not brave, I never was,' he said, interrupting Ruth again. 'Anything for the easy life, I used to say, although I never thought it would all catch up with me – that in the end I'd be dependent on you and on the kids.' He turned to her. 'I told Graham how ill I was – he was pissed off with me.'

'He'll come round in time.'

Ruth regretted the words instantly.

'In time? Whose time, his or mine?'

As the days passed, Ken developed a peculiar habit of clutching on to whoever was with him, almost as though he could hold on to the world physically. Death frightened him and he asked Ruth many times if she believed in an afterlife.

'I'm not sure,' she said, thinking of Nina's beliefs and how she used to shiver at her versions of hell. 'Maybe, maybe not. Dino would know.'

'He's a Catholic.'

'Ken, this is hardly the time to be a bigot!' Ruth said, amused.

He laughed loudly. 'I'll come back and haunt you for making remarks like that.'

'Really?' she asked, trying to turn his mind from the shadows. 'Tell me what you'll look like so I'll be sure to recognise you.'

He pretended to think for a minute. 'A poltergeist – I could break vases and move things and you'd never know where they were.'

Ruth shook her head. 'That's no good, Mrs Harvey does that already.'

He smiled. 'A ghost then, one of your honest-to-goodness ghosts. I could walk up and down the corridors at night and make noises.'

'No. I'd think it was Graham's computers. You'll have to do better than that.'

His eyes clouded over suddenly. 'I could come back and you'd never know ... I could be calling for you and you'd never hear me.'

His good humour broke and in its place was panic. His hands clutched at the sheets and he turned his face into the half shadow. Seeing his despair, Ruth rose quickly and sat on the bed next to him, her hand touching his forehead, soothing him.

'Ken, I'll always hear you. You won't be alone, I promise.'

He gasped and held on to her, his fingers biting into her arms, his head heavy on her shoulder. 'I'm so afraid to die ... so afraid.'

Ruth could say nothing, and simply laid her lips against his cheek.

'Ruth.'

'Joanie.'

The two women exchanged names uncomfortably, Joanie walking into the house imperiously as Ruth stood back to let her in. She glanced around the hall, her resentment barely disguised.

'You've made some changes.'

Ruth followed her glance. 'It's been a long time,' she said simply.

'Quite long enough,' Joanie replied, moving up the stairs.

With huge amusement, Robert Floyd watched her go, puffing on his cigar. 'How's Ken?' he asked.

'Worse, much worse,' Ruth replied, irritated by Joanie's manner and worried about Dino, who hadn't been in touch for days: 'The doctor said he can't go on much longer – ' She

365

turned, angered by her own lack of tact. 'I'm sorry, Robert. Forgive me.'

On the evening of 28 October, Ken suddenly deteriorated and asked for his son. Ruth went to Graham's room and explained the situation, saying that his father wanted to see him. He watched her lips and then glanced away. Ruth tried again. And again he turned away from her.

'Graham,' Ruth said angrily, 'your father wants you. He's dying.'

She watched as he gave his reply in sign language.

'He needs you!' Ruth said, infuriated. 'You know that, how can you be so cruel?'

His eyes were expressionless as he answered her.

'That's no excuse!' she replied coldly. 'Your father didn't mean to let you down ... he wanted to get to know you, and that's why he came back. Your father didn't intend to die and he doesn't deserve this.'

Behind him the computers bleeped resolutely.

'Graham, I'll ask you once again. Will you come and say goodbye to your father?'

Ruth watched his long hands and skilful fingers spell out his reply. 'I'VE ... SAID ... GOODBYE.'

For a long moment she looked at him in blind fury, her breathing rapid, her eyes blazing. Having never felt the need to strike her children before, Ruth hesitated, but then slowly lifted her hand. Graham watched her, his expression one of loathing, not fear, and then he turned back to his computer. With a sick heart, Ruth dropped her arm and walked out.

When she got back upstairs, Ken was lying in bed, his face yellowish and his breathing uneven. He turned as he heard her footsteps. 'Is he coming?'

Ruth shook her head.

'No matter,' he said, sighing and turning away. 'He's upset and he can't forgive me ... I would have been the same.'

'No you wouldn't!' she said, feeling his forehead and signalling for Kate to ring for the doctor.

He lost heart suddenly, although the doctor said that there

was no immediate danger and that a good night's rest might steady his condition. Later, Ruth sat down by the bedside, taking Ken's hand in her own.

He turned to her. 'Go to bed. I'll be all right.'

'I'd rather stay here for a while.'

He smiled slowly. 'Your place is downstairs . . . go on, please, I haven't the strength to argue with you.'

Reluctantly, Ruth got up and walked to the door. As she opened it he said, 'I made a right cock-up out of all of it, didn't I?'

Ruth rested her head against the door. I remember you when you were young, she thought, when you were healthy, and I loved you.

'You gave me a home, and a place in life . . .' she said gently, 'when I most needed it. We were happy, Ken, you know that.' The tears burned behind her eyes. 'No, you didn't make a cock-up of anything . . . Now, go to sleep. I'll see you in the morning.'

He saw her walk out, heard her footsteps and closed his eyes. For a long time he thought of Ruth as he first knew her, vulnerable, her unease making her cold at times. But not with him, with him she had been gentle. Smiling, he remembered her voice on the phone and in the dark, and knew with a sense of gratitude that she had been the one splendid obsession which had made life worthwhile.

But when Ruth went up to wake him the following day, the curtains were still drawn, and by his bed was an overturned glass. He lay on his back, his head half-obliterated by the sheet, one hand hanging over the edge of the bed, the fingers curled towards the palm. On top of the blanket was a bottle of gin with only the tiniest amount left in the bottom. The doctor told her that he had inhaled some of his own vomit and choked, too drunk to move. When she told Kate that her father was dead, she said it was due to a heart attack, pushing the gin bottle down to the bottom of the bin outside. When she told Graham, he seemed unmoved, his face never expressing the faintest trace of sorrow. In Graham's eyes, Ken Floyd had betrayed him – just as Ruth had done by giving birth to David.

The undertakers took him to the Chapel of Rest, dressing him in one of his business suits and combing his hair back from his face severely. That afternoon Ruth visited, hovering over him, aware of a biting grief which left her breathless. With infinite tenderness she bent down and kissed Ken's forehead. It felt like the wax candles in Dino's church and was cold to her lips. For over an hour she stayed with him, repeatedly touching his hands, trying to communicate with him, her words of tenderness halting, her voice breaking with raw pain.

Ruth phoned Dino as soon as she returned to the house. He was at the bank, his voice at first impatient and then softening quickly, his anger lifting as she asked him to come home. When he returned later that night he seemed subdued, holding Ruth to him tightly, his relief obvious.

But Ken Floyd stayed amongst them, walked along the corridors and in the rooms, leaving his memory in snatches when it would catch Ruth unawares, her composure crumbling under the repeated onslaught of her loss. She was walking into the bedroom when she suddenly felt his presence. Not a ghost, nothing so tangible, only his sense, a shadow of him. Ruth stood motionless for an instant and then panicked, looking around the room blindly, her eyes darting into corners, searching, her ears straining for a sound, any sound, which might be his.

'I can't hear you, Ken,' she said helplessly. 'If you're talking to me I can't hear you.' She stopped to listen and then continued wildly. 'I can't hear you ... Oh God, I can't hear you out there!'

They all attempted to recover in their own way, although Kate refused to talk about Ken for several days, feeling guilty for her antagonism towards him.

'I should have loved him more,' she said repeatedly to Robert Floyd, when she went to the newspaper offices to visit her grandfather.

'You couldn't have loved him more; Kate, he was a difficult man to love.'

She rose to her father's defence. 'No, he was just...'

'Difficult,' Robert Floyd finished for her. 'Do you miss him?'

'Do you?'

The old man bit back a peevish retort; now was no time for spite. 'He was my son, naturally I miss him.'

'He tried to make it up to us, both of us, Graham and me. But I never forgave him for what he did because he hurt Mum ... she had to struggle so hard.'

'He should never have left your mother, especially for that silly cow Sheila Fielding.' He saw the look on Kate's face and moderated his tone. 'How's Graham reacting?'

'Strangely,' Kate replied, thinking of her brother's constant work and of his withdrawal. 'He thinks Dad let him down.'

Robert Floyd smiled to himself; that was the first time he and Graham had agreed on anything.

'He loved Graham far more than he ever loved me,' Kate said suddenly.

The old man shook his head and glanced over to the phone where a light was flickering. Irritated, he snatched up the receiver. 'Take that bloody call, will you? I don't want to be disturbed! And don't put anything else through until I tell you.'

Kate's face was almost childish as she looked at him. 'Am I interrupting you? I could go.'

'No, stay with me. The rest can wait.'

'My father was really ill, wasn't he?' she said pathetically, begging for reassurance. 'I mean, he couldn't have lived, could he?'

'No, he couldn't have lived,' Robert Floyd answered, feeling his age, feeling the whole weight of an over-long life.

Kate nodded once. 'I just wondered ...'

'How is your mother?'

'I don't know,' Kate answered honestly. 'I really don't know.'

Ruth was coping, as she always did. With Dino's loving support and her work, she found it possible to cope with the trauma of Ken's death, although Graham continued to try her. Walking in to see him one evening, she found him crouched over the computer, his face pale with tiredness, his hands busy over the keys. When she touched his shoulder he turned, smiling.

Relieved by his good humour, Ruth sat down next to him. 'What are you doing?'

'Work,' he signed briefly and turned back to it. The keys clicked and the words came up on the screen; words, numbers, calculations, all there in front of him, all more real to him than the world outside. After a while he stopped and looked at his mother, signing to her.

'I'm sorry I was so cruel about Father's death,' he said, his fingers working confidently. 'I loved him ... and I thought he'd let me down.'

Ruth was touched by his confidence, seeing in it some spark of their old relationship. 'Graham, you have to understand something. Your father was a loving, but a rather selfish man, He loved all of us, in his own way, but he couldn't face any kind of responsibility – it frightened him. When he knew he was ill he wanted to make up for his past actions and he wanted you to know how much he loved you.'

He nodded briefly, and then outstretched his right hand towards Ruth's. She took it gratefully, the long fingers resting against her own.

'I'm ... sorry,' he said clumsily, the words just decipherable.

He changed from then on, becoming more gentle, the full brunt of his frustration and bitterness mellowing every day. Having worried that Ken's death would prove to be just another failure in Graham's life, Ruth was delighted to be proved wrong as he rallied and pulled himself back into the family. The change in him was so immense that Ruth literally thanked God, and turned her attention more to Dino, her affection accelerating as she relaxed, her mind for once not totally occupied with her son. The sober atmosphere which had curled around the house lifted, and a sense of humour returned.

Even Ruth's relationship with her mother seemed to be running more smoothly, and when she rang her from the Belvedere, she was in high spirits.

'Hello, Ruth. How is everyone?'

'They're all well, thanks. Actually, Graham seems very well, he's changed a lot. I think you'll notice a difference when you see him.' Her voice sounded faint on the line. 'Mother, can you hear me?'

'Just about. Can you speak up?'

'I'm at work. I just wondered if you and Dad were going to come to us for Christmas?'

'What?'

Ruth raised her voice. 'ARE YOU COMING FOR CHRISTMAS?'

'There's no need to shout! Of course we're coming.'

They arrived ten days before the festivities, laden with presents and a home-made Christmas cake which Lilian had carried faithfully all the way from Carrington Street.

'Mother, we could have bought one.'

'Not like this, we couldn't. Nothing to beat a really good fruit cake.'

Ruth looked at her and smiled. 'I'm glad you're here.'

Flushing, Lilian turned away. 'Well, I think I'll go up and unpack. Where's Graham?'

'In his room finishing off some work for his grandfather. Go and have a talk with him, will you, and tell me what you think?'

She came down into the kitchen soon afterwards, unbuttoning her jacket and straightening the collar of her blouse. 'That boy of yours seems much better. I think he's settled down at last.'

Ruth nodded. 'So do I. Oh, and it's Christmas, Mother, and New Year, it might be a whole new beginning for us.'

'You shouldn't cross your bridges before you come to them,' she said stiffly, starting to unpack the food she'd brought, 'and don't count your chickens – '

'Mother,' Ruth said coolly, 'I've waited for years to see my son happy and I'm going to enjoy every minute of it.'

In a rush of seasonal *bonhomie*, Dino invited twenty people for a pre-Christmas party, all of whom accepted with alacrity, hell-bent on starting the festive round of parties as soon as humanly possible. That Friday Ruth prepared everything with the help of Lilian and Mrs Harvey. The arrangement was not a success. What Ruth did, Lilian altered; what Ruth arranged, Mrs Harvey re-arranged. In the end, Ruth's patience snapped and after she exchanged a few sharp words with her mother, Lilian retreated to her room. The arrival of Nina didn't help.

'God! What a mess . . .! And you're usually so organised.'

'Why don't you keep your opinions to yourself, Nina!'

She frowned and pulled on an apron. 'OK, what do I do first?'

The food was finished with three-quarters of an hour to spare. Kate was completing the finishing touches as Ruth dressed to the accompaniment of Dino's whistling and David's radio from the room down the hall. She was nearly ready when there was a knock on the door and Graham came in. He was dressed up in a suit and tie, his handsome face smiling, and a rug over his legs.

'Graham,' Ruth said, walking over to him and touching his cheek. 'You look wonderful. Are you going to join us to-night?'

He read her lips and nodded.

'I'm so pleased,' she said, aware of a profound sense of well-being as she called Dino.

He materialised at the bathroom door, looked at Ruth and then at her son. 'Well done,' he said warmly. 'How would you like to look after the bar?'

It was a clever suggestion which would give Graham something to do instead of having him wander aimlessly round, waiting for someone to talk to him. Ruth looked at Dino over the top of her son's head. 'I love you,' she said.

'If that was for Graham he couldn't hear you.'

'And if it was for you?' Ruth asked softly.

'Then I got the message – loud and clear.'

The evening was a happy one. Geoffrey Lynes arrived on time with a bunch of flowers, and Ted Morrison and his wife almost collided with Nina and Tony on the step. When they came into the lounge Tony's face was set.

'What's the matter?' Ruth asked Nina.

'His suit's too damn tight! That's what's the matter.'

Ruth glanced at Tony and then glanced away. The buttons were dangerously strained.

'Undo the jacket buttons,' she said quietly.

'He can't undo the buttons because the shirt doesn't fit either.'

Ruth was trying hard not to laugh. 'Why didn't he try the suit on to see if it fitted before now?'

Nina looked at Tony and raised her eyebrows. 'Well, that would be the sensible thing, wouldn't it? I told him to do that and he said, "It's OK, I've tried it on." He had done – a month ago!' she said angrily. 'And in a month he's been to about three thousand business lunches and swollen up like a bloody pig's bladder.'

'Don't swear!' Tony said suddenly, lapsing back into silence as though the mere effort of talking strained the suit seams further.

'I'll say what I like!' Nina said defiantly, poking a finger into his paunch. 'But if you think I'm going to stand next to you all night waiting for you to go off, you've another think coming.'

Otherwise the evening went smoothly. At the bar Dino dived back and forth giving orders to Graham who was enjoying himself enormously. Having never before seen him in a crowd of people, Ruth was stunned by his good looks and surprised by his apparent poise. Her dreams for his future seemed suddenly probable, rather than impossible.

Even Robert Floyd seemed touched by the Christmas spirit, arriving late and smiling as he approached his granddaughter.

'Your mother looks well, Kate,' he said, glancing over to Ruth, 'she's got good taste,' he continued, looking round the hall which had been redecorated. 'I like the colour scheme, I always said this place was too dark. Yes, she's very discerning ...' he continued, glancing over to Dino and adding maliciously, 'in most things, that is.'

The last guests left at one-thirty in the morning, waving from the pavement and making the usual banal remarks about the stars. Ted Morrison kissed Ruth on the cheek and wished her a Happy Christmas, while Geoffrey Lynes hovered behind him, waiting for a lift home. From the lounge came the sound of music as Dino danced on happily with Kate, Graham tidying the bottles on top of the bar. Ashtrays overflowed with cigarette ends and the smell of pastry and cake wafted through the rooms like the spectre of Christmas Present. Kicking off her shoes, Ruth sat down in front of the fire, watching them. Warm and contented, the music singing in her ears, she fell asleep. When she woke later the twins had gone and Dino was sitting beside her, snoring softly, his head on her shoulder.

The following morning was Christmas Eve and the street outside was scattered with a faint sprinkling of snow like sugar on the top of a mince pie. The winter trees were still and along the roofs ice crystals flashed up into the December sun. Dino woke with a hangover and shuffled off to the bathroom like a Chelsea pensioner. Ruth turned over, smiling, as he came back to bed with a glass of Alka Seltzer.

'Good morning,' she said cheerfully. 'How do you feel?'

He lapsed into Italian and slumped against the bedhead.

'I could get you some breakfast.'

He grunted and rolled over, pulling the bedclothes around his head.

In the kitchen there were hardly any signs of the previous evening's festivities. All the china had been washed and put away and the glasses were lined up on the trays, sparkling and polished, sharp in the daylight. Ruth was just walking into the hall as the lift came downstairs carrying Graham.

He smiled and opened the doors. 'Good morning,' he signed.

Ruth bent to kiss his cheek. 'Did you sleep well, Graham?'

'Fine,' he signed. 'How's Dino?'

Ruth shrugged. 'On his way either in or out of a coma.'

Graham smiled again, his dark eyes watching his mother. 'Can you come up to my room? I have something to tell you.'

Intrigued, Ruth walked up the stairs as her son took the lift. The computer was already turned on, its acid-green face beaming at her, while beside the machine several pieces of paper were carefully laid out. Graham pointed to the screen and then said in sign language. 'Can you read the screen? It would be easier for me.'

Ruth nodded, mildly amused. He turned his wheelchair round to face the machine. The computer bleeped indifferently and the screen was ready. At the top Graham wrote:

DEAR MOTHER –
THIS IS VERY DIFFICULT FOR ME TO SAY.
BUT I HAVE THOUGHT ABOUT IT FOR
QUITE A TIME AND REALISE THAT YOU
NEED TO KNOW.

He glanced up at his mother and she shrugged, half smiling.

I HAVE HEARD FROM LAUREL.

Ruth read the words, shock coursing through her body, her eyes fixed on the malevolent screen.

I KNOW ALL ABOUT HER BECAUSE FATHER
TOLD ME ONCE WHEN HE WAS DRUNK. IT
DOESN'T MATTER THAT YOU DIDN'T
WANT TO TELL ME – I THINK I
UNDERSTAND – BUT SHE NEEDS SOME
HELP AND SHE ASKED ME TO ASK YOU FOR
THAT HELP.

Ruth read the words twice, her mouth dry, the sheer impact making her dizzy. Suddenly light-headed, she reached out for a chair and sat down. Laurel, she thought blindly, Laurel. My daughter, my child. Laurel.

SHE HAS A CHILD OF HER OWN, CALLED
JAMES, AND SHE'S DIVORCED. SHE HAS NO
HUSBAND TO SUPPORT HER AND SHE
LIVES IN YORKSHIRE.

Graham stopped typing. Ruth looked at the words, read them and then re-read them, her stomach knotting with confusion. Laurel married with a son? It didn't seem possible. She was still a child, wasn't she? Her mind refused to work

375

coherently and the words blurred and made no sense. Laurel
was how old? Ruth thought back and then remembered.
Laurel was twenty-two, old enough to be a mother and a wife.
Laurel, her daughter.

Suddenly threatened, Ruth glanced over to Graham, his
handsome head in profile, the eyes fixed on the screen. Why
had Laurel got in touch with him, she thought. Why Graham,
of all people? Cold and shaky, Ruth's hands clutched her knees
tightly. Laurel, she kept thinking, after all these years; after all
those years of trying to forget her, of dismissing her to the back
of her mind. Her existence was so far in the past it was hardly
real. She was only a phantom. Only a child, a baby Ruth had
had once, in another time, another place, a child called after
the tree in the park, the one her father showed her. Laurel.
The computer bleeped again:

SHE'S WELL AND JAMES IS WELL.

Quickly, Ruth caught hold of the wheelchair, turning
Graham round to face her. His eyes were moist with pity.

'Graham! Where is she? I want to speak to her,' she said
hoarsely. 'Please, tell me where she is.'

He read her lips and then glanced at his mother's eyes.
'Watch the screen,' he signed.

Ruth was beyond reason. 'No! No, Graham, you tell me!
Tell me in sign language. Where is she? Can't I see her?'

'She's all right . . . she lives in Yorkshire – '

'You told me that!' Ruth shouted, her voice terrifying and
high-pitched, her control dissolving as she grabbed her son's
shoulders tightly. 'Where in Yorkshire? I want to see her –
where is she?'

His face hardened and he turned back to the screen.

SHE DOESN'T WANT TO SEE YOU. SHE
REFUSES TO SEE YOU.

Ruth shook her head and tugged at Graham's arm. 'Why?'

He turned back to the screen;

> YOU GAVE HER AWAY.

'I had to!' she screamed, realising that her son hadn't heard. Quickly, Ruth tugged Graham round to face her. 'I was ill! I didn't know what I was doing,' she said, pleading with him, the whole horror threatening to fall in on her and crush her. 'Oh, please tell her that, Graham, please ... I never meant to let her go.'

There was a look of pity in his eyes as Ruth continued.

'Graham, how did she know where to find you? Why did she come to you after all this time? Why didn't she come to me?'

He turned back to the computer.

> SHE TRACED YOU THROUGH THE
> HOSPITAL AND THEN CAME HERE NEARLY
> A WEEK AGO.

Only a week ago! Ruth thought, snatching at Graham's hand. He shook her off and pointed to the screen.

> SHE LEFT A LETTER

'Where? Where?' Ruth asked frantically, searching through the papers on the table beside them, throwing them on to the floor, desperate, her heart hammering as she looked for the letter from her daughter. 'Where?' she asked again, her eyes wild as she turned to her son. 'Where is the letter?'

He said nothing.

'*Where is the letter?*' she repeated hysterically.

Again he gestured to the screen.

> I BURNT IT. I DIDN'T KNOW THEN IF YOU
> WANTED TO HEAR FROM HER OR NOT. I
> DIDN'T KNOW WHAT TO DO FOR THE BEST
> AND I DIDN'T WANT YOU TO FIND IT
> UNEXPECTEDLY.

Ruth flinched, remembering the letter she had found from

Ken, the letter which he had written to Graham. Slowly she turned and looked at her son, into the dark wells of his eyes, into the unfathomable gaze.

'I want to see her, Graham. I have to!'

He read his mother's lips and looked away. Her hands clenched, Ruth expected him to write something else but he sat motionless in the wheelchair with the computer bleeping in front of him. He's going to punish me, she thought, with a deadening realisation. He's going to make me suffer.

'Graham, I'm sorry I didn't tell you about Laurel,' she began, trying to regain her composure, the words sticking in her throat uncomfortably. 'It was wrong of me,' Ruth trailed off, wondering why Laurel hadn't gone to Kate, or Dino, to anyone other than her son. 'But I need to see her. Can you ask her if she'll see me? Please?'

He nodded and took hold of her hand, gently cradling it in his own. Tenderness and punishment, Ruth thought ruefully.

'Just ask her to see me, will you?'

He nodded, seeing the pain in her eyes.

'Thank you, Graham,' she said finally and then left.

When she returned to the bedroom Ruth closed the door and then began to shake, her whole body trembling, a fine misting of sweat clinging to her limbs. Her breaths uneven, Ruth rested her head against the cold glass of the window and gazed out blindly. She had never believed that she would see or hear from Laurel and winced as she thought back to her birth. With suffocating grief, she remembered Derek, the house on the Coppice and the small patch of garden; thought of every dream she had had about her child, every impression, every moment of guilt and loss. Crying out softly, she closed her eyes and tried to think.

She had longed for her daughter, but how much had Laurel longed for the mother who had given her away? If Ruth had suffered guilt, Laurel had suffered rejection. If Ruth had missed her, how many times did she miss her mother and wonder where she was? And when she found out that she was rich and successful with her own family – how she must have hated her. The bitter truth struck Ruth with all the impact of a blow from a clenched fist. A child could forgive; a woman with a child of her own would never understand the mother who had given her away.

Ruth dressed slowly and then returned to Graham's rooms. He smiled sympathetically and watched as she spoke to him.

'Have you got Laurel's address?'

He nodded.

'Can't you give it to me, Graham? Please?'

He shook his head and, without thinking, Ruth grasped his arm, her face only inches from his. 'What are you doing to me?' she asked, her voice hoarse.

He flinched and glanced down at his arm, where red weals appeared under the grip of his mother's fingers. 'Laurel said she needed help,' he sighed.

'What sort of help?' Ruth asked sharply. 'Money?'

He nodded.

'Well, she can have money, as much as she wants,' Ruth said, trying to smile. 'Tell her that, Graham, will you?'

He signalled with his hands. 'She said she's too hurt and bitter to want to see you, she said she never wants to see you ... but that you owe her something.'

Ruth watched his hands and then recoiled, shocked. 'Oh, God!' she said, her voice dropping to a whisper. 'Tell her ... tell her that I'll help her and her son. Ask her how much money she needs and she can have it.' Ruth looked at Graham, her mind beginning to work more clearly. 'You'll have to write to her and that will take time. I could phone her direct – '

He shook his head vigorously.

'All right, Graham, I won't!' she agreed, in anger and despair. 'But let Kate telephone her – '

In temper he turned to the screen and punched in the words:

SHE SAID SHE WANTED TO CONTACT YOU
THROUGH ME AND NO OTHER WAY.
OTHERWISE SHE WOULDN'T GET IN
TOUCH AGAIN.

Panic welled up in Ruth but she controlled herself, and

with a massive effort, nodded her head. 'All right, Graham. Whatever you say. Whatever she says.'

Ruth's first instinct was to tell Dino everything, but she soon realised that it was not feasible. If she told him he would simply waylay the letters to Laurel, find out where she was and go and see her ... which was exactly what her daughter didn't want. Ruth paced the floor. Maybe Laurel was meeting Graham out of the house, she thought, knowing that if he found out, Dino would have her son watched ... Her stomach lurched. If her children discovered they were being spied on ... she shook her head, the thought of losing Laurel again too horrendous to contemplate. She had no choice, she had to agree to Graham acting as the go-between.

That afternoon Graham asked Ruth for three hundred pounds.

'Three hundred pounds!'

'She needs it,' he signed.

'All right, all right,' Ruth said quickly, getting the money from the safe and giving it to him. 'Just tell her I want to see her, please. Just tell her that.' Her tone pleaded with him, begged him. 'She can have what she wants – just get her to agree to see me, will you?'

He nodded and wheeled himself out of the room.

Having presumed that Graham was going to see Laurel that afternoon, Ruth waited to hear him go out but by six it was apparent that he was not going anywhere. Suffering from a hangover, Dino was in an uncommunicative mood and was slumped in front of the television as Ruth passed the study door. She stopped and looked at him, wanting to tell him everything, for once in her life desperate to confide.

The arrival of Kate interrupted her thoughts. 'What's the matter, Mum?'

'Nothing,' Ruth replied, catching hold of her coat and walking out into the garden. She shivered in the bleak air.

'Tell me what it is,' Kate pleaded. 'It's Christmas Eve, you were full of beans yesterday, the party went well – so it must be something that's happened today.'

'It's Graham – he's heard from Laurel.'

She took in her breath sharply. The winter evening closed in fast, the trees dark shapes against the fading light.

'Did you say that Graham has heard from Laurel? Your daughter, Laurel?' Ruth nodded. 'When?'

'Just lately. She needs help ...' Ruth said, her voice wavering, totally unlike her own, 'and she refuses to see me.'

'She refuses to see you!' Kate said incredulously, her expression hardening as she continued. 'But she's still asking for your help. What kind of help does she need?'

'Financial help.'

Kate sighed. 'Why? Is she in trouble?'

'Graham won't tell me any more.'

'*What!*' Kate said in astonishment.

'He just says that she won't see me and that she needs some money to sort herself out and that she thinks I owe it to her.'

Kate glanced at her mother. She could still distinguish the fine profile in the dying light, the sweep of her hair and the unfamiliar look in her eyes. Suddenly anxious, Kate realised that Laurel's re-emergence had been a body blow for her mother, a blow from which she was reeling badly.

'Some Christmas present!' she said bitterly.

'Maybe she needs the money for Christmas. She has a son – James.'

Kate shook her head slowly. 'How did Graham find out about her?'

'Your father told him when he was drunk,' Ruth said coldly, walking off, her tall figure moving towards the bottom lawn.

Her daughter ran after her. 'But how did Laurel get in touch with Graham – and why him? Why not me?'

'That's what I wondered,' Ruth answered bitterly. 'Graham says that she discovered I was her mother from the hospital records, and then followed the leads until she found out where I was. Apparently she then wrote to Graham.'

'Why write to Graham?' Kate asked softly, her thoughts running on. 'He's handicapped, so why use him as an intermediary?'

'How would Laurel know he was handicapped?' Ruth countered, shivering with cold. 'From her information, Laurel would discover that I was living here with my daughter and my two sons. She had no way of knowing that Graham was handicapped, and she probably chose him because he was the head of the family. She would know that Ken and I were divorced and possibly that he has since died. I'm not married to Dino and so, in her eyes, Graham is the male head of the household and her half-brother. That's why she went to him.'

'So why did Graham keep quiet about it until Christmas Eve?'

The question jolted Ruth and she turned away, walking past the summer house and towards the fish pond. She had asked herself the same question and could not answer it.

'Well, Mum?' Kate persisted.

'I don't know! Perhaps because Laurel hadn't asked him for money until now.'

'It's not ringing true, is it?' Kate said softly. 'I don't understand any of it.'

'I don't care how it sounds!' Ruth cried out, her usual calmness disappearing. 'Laurel is back. For the first time in my life I know where she is. I *have* to trust Graham, he's the only one who can persuade her to come home.'

A bird flew overhead as Kate looked away. She knew what it meant to her mother to hear from Laurel, but she also knew that Ruth was perilously close to collapse, her judgement faulty, panic making her reckless.

'I know how you feel, Mum. But Laurel sounds so hard. I mean, asking for money ... Do you really want to get to know her that much? She might just bring trouble ... and we've had so much of that.'

'She's my daughter!' Ruth said shrilly. 'I should have looked for her before. I could have found her. But I thought ... I thought it would be better to leave her alone. That's what everyone told me.' She smiled bitterly and turned back to Kate. 'How can you ask me to turn my back on her now? Would you want me to turn my back on you if you were in trouble?'

Kate's eyes blazed. 'I wouldn't ask you for money and I wouldn't refuse to see you – '

'You don't know what you'd do! Neither do I. Laurel is bitter and angry and we'll have to wait and see what happens. Graham's doing his best to help – we *have* to be patient, that's all we can do.'

For a long moment both women looked defiantly at each other and then Kate dropped her eyes. 'How is he contacting her?'

'By letter, I think. Or maybe he'll meet her – '

'I could follow him and find out where Laurel is.'

Ruth shook her head violently. 'No! I lost her once. I won't risk that again. Leave the two of them alone – when the time is right Laurel will come home.'

Christmas Day was snowy and cold; the front door jammed as usual and the draughts blew down the corridors making the bedrooms chilled. In an effort to behave as though nothing was wrong, Ruth made lunch and held brittle conversation with her parents, avoiding the look of concern in Dino's eyes. Curiously light-headed, she felt as though she were flying, suspended above them and looking down. They toasted Christmas and later relaxed in front of the fire, Ruth's father laughing with David as they played some computer game together. Graham retired to work and Kate tried to read, her eyes flickering from the book to her mother, her anxiety noticed by Dino, who watched them both. Sitting stiffly in her seat, Ruth waited, expecting the phone to ring or the doorbell to sound and her daughter to stand there, waiting to come in.

But Christmas Day dipped into Christmas night and Graham didn't leave the house and no one called.

Nineteen

'Well, what do you think?' Nina asked her husband over the breakfast table. 'I say she should tell Dino about Laurel. And quickly.'

Tony Milton turned over the bank statement in his thick fingers. 'You've been shopping again. Jesus, Nina, you must cut down.'

She looked at him and said plaintively. 'I can't help it. Spending money is like breathing to me – '

'Then try holding your breath now and then,' he said drily.

'Oh, very funny!' Nina responded, reaching for the toast. 'I was talking about Ruth. I say she should tell Dino about Laurel – '

Tony continued to read, his eyes bulging. 'Nine hundred quid in Harvey Nichols! What did you do, make them an offer for the lease?'

Nina rolled her eyes heavenwards. 'It was the sale. Everybody spends money in the sale,' she said, trying to get his attention from the bank statement. 'Should I have a word with Ruth? Tony! What do you think?'

'I think,' he said, ladling some marmalade on to his bread, 'that you should watch what you spend. Keep a check on it.'

'Preferably a blank one,' Nina responded smartly.

At the same time as Nina was eating breakfast, Ruth was sitting in front of her mirror. Slowly she applied foundation, eye shadow, blusher, her face taking shape and colour as she worked. Sighing, she turned her head from side to side to check her reflection and then clasped on heavy gold earrings before standing up.

'Laurel's back,' she said simply.

Dino stopped dressing and looked at her, seeing the perfect

maquillage and sensing the brittle unease under her movements.

'Your daughter?'

She nodded and walked to the window. A weak winter sun trickled over her, making her fine skin fragile, her eyes almost colourless. 'I wanted to tell you because I need your advice,' she said turning. 'I want your help.'

He moved towards her, but she stiffened, distancing herself.

'Laurel won't see me.'

'She has to see you! She's your daughter. You have a right!' Dino said, incensed.

'I have a right?' Ruth asked, shaking her head. 'No, I don't think so. I gave up all my rights to Laurel when I gave her away. She's angry. I suppose I would be angry too.'

He pulled on his jacket. 'I can find out where she is – '

'No, Dino, I don't want that! Graham is acting as the intermediary, and that's the way she wants it. If I try to find out where she is, she'll disappear ... Laurel needs help and money at the moment,' Ruth said evenly. 'She'll come to me in her own good time.'

'But where's she living?'

Ruth shrugged. 'I've no idea. Graham said that her home was in Yorkshire, but where she is now, God alone knows.'

'She must be living in London otherwise she couldn't be contacting Graham.' He smiled drily. 'This is all a bit ridiculous! Graham is crippled, he shouldn't be doing this.'

'He wants to do it.'

'Maybe, but is he capable?'

Ruth smiled, her eyes distant. He had a peculiar feeling that she was not quite real; almost as though he was talking to her through water.

'One thing I learnt years ago was never to underestimate my son. He might be handicapped but he's very resourceful. This makes Graham feel useful.' She glanced over to Dino. 'When he told me that Laurel had come to him I thought he would resent the fact that I hadn't told him about her, but instead he's helping. Maybe his father's death altered him;

maybe he's less concerned with his own feelings now ... I don't know,' she said, rubbing her forehead with her hands. 'Laurel has a son, James. My grandchild ... I keep thinking about them, wondering what they're like. I keep wondering if she hates me ... I know that if my mother had given me away I would have hated her.'

'No, you wouldn't.'

Ruth shook her head. 'But I would! I can only hope that Laurel isn't like me, because if she is I'll never see her or her son.'

Dino touched her lightly on the shoulder, she seemed frail, ready to break. 'You've never let anything get you down, Ruth, never. Even when terrible things happened, you still kept fighting and you've never given up hope.'

She looked at him calmly. 'I'm not giving up hope, Dino, it's just that now she's within reach she feels further away than ever. Before, Laurel was unreal, now she's here, round the corner, or on a bus. I could see her, pass her in the street ... and I wouldn't know her.' Ruth caught hold of Dino's hand, her nails biting deep into his flesh. 'Graham is my only hope. I have to trust him and hope that he can bring her back to me.'

'Is he the right person to do that?'

She turned, her eyes dull. 'He's all I've got.'

That night Ruth asked Graham if he had given the money to Laurel and he told her he had, refusing to say how, or where. She thought he was carrying the secrecy too far, but did not dare to oppose him, knowing that he could easily change from being helpful to obstructive. He made a difficult intermediary.

Nina followed the train of events with rapt interest, knowing that Ruth was finding the situation hard to cope with, especially as the work at the cinemas increased. Sitting in the sumptuous office at the Belvedere, she looked boldly healthy against the glare of a snowfall outside.

'I bet he's enjoying all this,' she said, lighting a cigarette.

'Who?'

'Graham, who else are we talking about?' she asked, raising

her eyebrows. 'He's been at the mercy of everyone else all his life and suddenly he's in the limelight, playing you all off one against the other.'

'He's trying to help, Nina!'

She tossed her lighter back into her bag. 'I'm not saying he isn't. I'm just saying that he'll be enjoying it, that's all.' She smiled mischievously. 'I can just see him roaring down the High Street on that wheelchair to a secret assignation.'

'That's not funny,' Ruth said coldly.

'Don't be daft! It's terrific, it means he's getting out and about for a change.'

'He could have an accident. Graham is deaf.'

Nina pulled a face. 'He's not blind though, is he? Graham is capable of crossing the road on his own, you know, and if he isn't it's about time he learned.' She inhaled and screwed up her eyes against the smoke. 'Thing is, how long are you prepared to let this go on?'

'As long as it takes.'

'So the ball's in Graham's court?'

'Yes, I suppose so.'

Nina glanced away and walked to the window, tugging off a few dead leaves from a large flower arrangement. 'We go back a long way, Ruth,' she said, without looking round, 'and we've gone through a lot, so we can speak freely to one another, can't we?'

'What is it, Nina?'

'Graham is ... unusual,' she said, tearing one of the leaves carefully. 'I've always loved him, because he was handicapped and because he turned out so good-looking.' She laughed suddenly and dropped the leaf into the waste-basket. 'But he's a very tricky customer. He's resented everything from the day he was born – '

'Nina, just a minute!'

She put up her hands. 'No, hear me out! Graham is resentful. You're his mother and you see him differently. I see him as an awkward little bastard who hated the world for being born crippled, and then hated anyone who took your undivided attention away from him.' She shrugged as Ruth tried to interrupt her. 'OK, you're going to tell me he's changed, and maybe you're right, maybe he does feel so guilty about his father's death that he wants to help, I'm not saying he doesn't, I'm just saying that he can't – '

'Be trusted?'

She smiled ruefully. 'Well, let's put it this way – he needs watching.'

Ruth bristled, but experience told her to listen. Nina was too shrewd to be that far off the mark. So when she went home later, she immediately made her way upstairs to see Graham. He was in the gym, lifting weights, unaware that his mother was watching. Ruth waited by the door, and when he had finished, she moved towards him. He smiled warmly.

'How's things?' she asked, trying to keep her expression cheerful, nonchalant. 'Have you heard any more news from Laurel?'

His eyes flickered with something close to annoyance.

Seeing the danger sign, Ruth sat down beside him and changed the subject. 'Did you finish your computer print-out for your grandfather?'

He nodded.

'And were they pleased?' Ruth asked, looking at her son. His T-shirt was damp under the arms and along his forehead the skin was shiny and smooth as marble.

'They've asked me to do some more ...' he told her in sign language. 'They said it was very good. They said I was very astute.'

'So you are,' Ruth agreed willingly, wondering when it was safe to bring up the subject of Laurel again.

'They said that they could find enough work for me to be full-time employed ...' he continued.

Ruth frowned. 'Do you want that, Graham? It would be tying.'

He smiled bleakly, his white teeth even and clean.

'What else is there to do with my time?' he signed.

Ruth shrugged, embarrassed.

'Laurel needs some more money,' he signed quickly.

The demand shocked Ruth and she glanced away, knowing

she was being manipulated, an unhealthy feeling of unease swamping her.

'Of course Laurel can have as much money as she wants. But what does she need it for? Can't she come to me direct?'

The familiar expression of irritation crossed his face. 'She won't!' he signed emphatically.

'Won't!' Ruth said, her patience snapping. 'For how long, Graham? You ask her, because I want to know! I would rather we met and she told me what she thought of me instead of playing these stupid games any longer!'

'She doesn't want to meet you!' he signed angrily.

Ruth flung up her hands. 'You've made the point, Graham. I understand that my daughter thinks that I owe her something and that I can pay off the debt with money. I don't mind. But she could at least write me a note ... I don't even know what she looks like, or what James is like.'

Graham's face stiffened. 'They're OK.'

'Yes, I know they're OK! But what are they like? Surely you must understand how this is hurting me ...' Her voice broke. 'You've seen them. Tell me about them, please.'

He looked round the gym and then glanced back to his mother, signing slowly. 'Laurel is dark – '

'Dark eyes?' Ruth asked eagerly.

He shrugged. 'Brown.'

She prompted him. 'What else? What colour hair?'

'Brown.'

'Brown! I thought she'd still be blonde like she was when she was a baby. Is she tall?'

His eyes flickered. 'It's difficult to tell from a wheelchair.'

Taking a deep breath, Ruth continued. 'Well, is she slim? Plump? What?'

'Average.'

'And what about James? What does he look like?'

'A child.'

'I know he looks like a child, Graham, he *is* a child! But is he dark like his mother?'

'I don't know,' he signed back.

Her patience finally snapped. 'Perhaps he's bald then? For

God's sake, Graham, you must know!'

He gave her a long look and then signed, 'He was wearing a woolly hat when I saw him.'

Ruth closed her eyes and breathed deeply to steady herself. She had no wish to argue with her son, in fact that was just what she wanted to avoid. Ruth wanted Graham on her side; not against her.

'I'm sorry,' she said, squeezing his hand. 'I get so het up. It's just that this is such a strain – and you've been marvellous.' Ruth watched his face soften, the look of the child again. Aware that his animosity had faded, Ruth relaxed. She had to wait for Laurel ... and she had to wait for Graham to bring her home.

'How much money does she want, Graham?'

The money poured out. Ruth wondered what her daughter needed it for, but gave it to Graham willingly, knowing that even if she asked, his answer would be evasive. Perhaps Laurel had to settle the legal fees for her divorce, Ruth thought, or, God forbid, medical bills, but she never knew for sure, and as the days passed she began to imagine all forms of hardship.

'She could be ill,' she said to Dino repeatedly, 'or James could be ill.'

'Graham would have told you,' he replied, shifting his position in bed. 'Do you want me to have a word with him?'

Ruth flinched in the dark. 'I don't think so, Dino. Graham would look upon it as interference. No, we have to wait.'

He sighed loudly and turned on the light. 'One more week,' he said suddenly.

Ruth turned over to face him. 'What?'

'I said one more week – and that's the limit. If, after another week, Laurel hasn't agreed to see you, then I'll find out where she is myself – '

'But – '

He waved aside her interruption. For nights, Ruth had not been sleeping, her crippling schedule, together with the anxiety about Laurel, exhausting her. Coming in late, she would pour herself a drink and sit in the study, her thoughts wandering.

He had watched her deteriorate and was frightened that before long, she would be ill.

'This has gone far enough, Ruth. I can't see you like this. If Laurel has any compassion she'll listen to reason and meet you. Otherwise, she's not worth bothering about!' He turned his back on her. 'One week – and then I step in.'

When Ruth arrived at the Belvedere the following morning her head was banging and her hands shook. It was obvious that she was running a temperature and when Geoffrey Lynes saw her he asked Bill Pascoe for a coffee and two aspirins.

'Here, take these,' he said, passing them to Ruth. 'You look awful. Why don't you go home?'

'I have some things to do. Besides, I'm better at work.'

He was puzzled; knowing nothing about Laurel he thought she was just being stubborn and challenged her. 'Surely things will wait?'

'No, I have to work!' she said, reaching for the post as it blurred in front of her eyes.

He hovered uncertainly. 'If you're sure.'

Too exhausted to argue, Ruth leant back in her chair. 'Maybe you're right . . . Listen, don't let anyone into the office and tell everyone I'm out.' She sipped the coffee eagerly. 'If I don't feel better soon I'll go home.' He nodded and walked out.

So when the office door jerked open ten minutes later Ruth jumped up quickly, her attitude unwelcoming. It was Nina.

'Oh, it's you . . .'

She looked behind her and then back to Ruth. 'Yeah, it's me. Thanks for the welcome.'

'I didn't want to be disturbed – '

'Well, pardon me! I quite forgot that you'd become such a bloody big shot that I'd have to book an appointment to see you!'

'Nina – '

She shook her head. 'No, bother to explain! So you're too busy, are you? Hell fire, Ruth, you certainly can be a right royal pain in the arse.'

It was Ruth's turn to be angry. 'What is the matter with

you? I just told Geoffrey not to let anyone in because I didn't feel well! He wasn't to bother me unless it was an emergency.'

Nina stood her ground, her hands on her hips. 'Only to be disturbed in case of emergencies, hey? Well, try this on for size – I've just seen your daughter.'

Ruth could feel the colour draining from her face.

'Yes, that's right – I've just seen Laurel and your son.'

Ruth sat down heavily and Nina bent hurriedly over her. 'Oh God, you're not going to faint, are you?'

'I ... don't feel well, that's all,' Ruth said, badly shaken. 'Tell me about Laurel. Tell me where you saw her, Nina.'

She unbuttoned her coat, dropping her voice so low that Ruth had to strain to hear her. 'I was coming up to the house to see Kate; she and I thought we would go shopping this morning as it's her half day at the hospital – '

'I know that, Nina. Go on.'

'Well, I arrived, and Kate was busy on the phone. When she finished she was all apologetic, saying that she had to go into the hospital after all because they needed her ...' She trailed off. 'Are you drinking that coffee?'

Irritated, Ruth glanced at the cup. 'No, I've had enough.'

'You don't mind if I finish it, do you?' Nina asked before continuing. 'Anyway, I told Kate not to worry and then set off for home.' She sipped the coffee. 'Then just as I was going to turn on to the main street, I saw this car parked on the left with a man in a wheelchair beside it.' She paused. 'Of course I thought of Graham, didn't I? And stopped at the junction to get a better look. It was him and he was talking to someone in the car.'

'Who?'

'That's just it – I couldn't see. So, being nosy, I drove round the block and parked almost opposite them for a better look ... and there she was.'

She stopped, drained the cup and leant back.

'So?' Ruth asked, infuriated. 'Go on, Nina! What did my daughter look like?'

'Dark brown hair and eyes, and rather too thin really. Her

face was a bit pinched. Sort of spiky.'

'Was James there? Was her son with her?'

Nina nodded. 'In the back, looking out of the window straight at me. Gave me quite a turn, I can tell you.'

'What's he like?' Ruth asked hoarsely.

'White as a ghost – white face, blond hair, pale eyes and eye lashes. He looks so frail he might break, if you know what I mean.'

'Unhealthy?'

She shrugged. 'How would I know? I'm no authority on kids, but let's put it this way – he looked like a boiled egg would overface him.'

Ruth thought for a moment, fighting dizziness, her mind creating pictures of Graham and Laurel. 'And you said that she and Graham were talking?'

'Non-stop, although it's fair to say that they weren't talking so much as arguing. Graham would say something and then Laurel would react, flapping her arms around like nobody's business.' Ruth could imagine her daughter, could see the thin arms moving, the thin face anxious. 'What sort of car was she driving?'

Nina dug deep into her handbag and passed her a piece of paper. 'Mini, battered old thing.' She pointed to the slip. 'That's the number – I thought it might come in useful.'

Inexpressibly grateful, Ruth looked down at the figures. 'And what about Graham? How did he seem?'

'Like he always seems, but when she was talking he kept stopping her and asking her to repeat things slowly so that he could read her lips. She would do it right for a while and then forget when she got upset.'

'How upset?'

'She cried while I watched them,' Nina said thoughtfully. 'Graham had written something on a pad for her to read and when she looked at it, great tears plopped down her cheeks.'

Ruth's heart shifted. 'She cried?'

'Sure. She looked very upset.'

'And what was James doing all this time?'

'Gazing out of the car window, nothing else.'

Ruth rested her head against the chair and closed her eyes. 'Did Graham give her anything?'

'Like what?'

'A parcel ... or an envelope.'

'Not while I watched them,' Nina said, shrugging, 'but I was there for only ten minutes or so. I can't tell you how long they'd been talking before I came, or how long they continued after I left.'

Ruth opened her eyes and looked steadily at Nina. 'I gave Graham five hundred pounds for Laurel.'

She whistled softly. 'Why?'

'He said she needed it, although he won't tell me what for.' Ruth noticed the shrewd look on Nina's face. 'I had to give it to her.'

'Perhaps she doesn't look upon you so much as a long-lost mother as her own personal National Westminster bank,' she replied with deadly sarcasm.

'Listen, Nina! If my daughter needs the money – '

Undaunted, she interrupted Ruth. 'If she needs the money she could come to you and ask you for it, not send Graham backwards and forwards with the cash.'

'She might need it for rent, or for food.'

Nina shook her head, marvelling at the sheer blindness of the woman in front of her. Astute in business, Ruth was woefully trusting when it came to any matter involving her children. It was a flaw in her character which had led to Graham's over-dependence and her own almost pathological protection of her offspring.

'So Graham is a sort of "meals on wheels" you mean?' she asked archly.

Ruth's face set. 'That wasn't funny.'

'Really? Well, neither is this whole situation!' Nina answered sharply, her own instincts warning her. 'You're being used, Ruth, and you know it. You should have it out with that girl once and for all and not rely on Graham. I've told you before – '

Ruth sighed wearily. 'Yes, I know! You've told me and so has Dino. I understand what you're saying, but I *can't* force the issue. Dino's given me one week to sort it out!' She laughed bitterly. 'One week after twenty-two years.'

The following day Ruth stayed at home. Having spent one more sleepless night she was physically and mentally exhausted when she rose at seven, pulling on her dressing-gown and walking into Graham's room. With eerie calm she told him that Nina had observed his meeting with Laurel, and asked him whether or not she had finally decided to talk to her mother.

He seemed annoyed and answered in sign language, 'She's going back to Yorkshire.'

Ruth looked at his fingers and then back to his face. 'Back to Yorkshire?' she repeated stupidly.

He nodded.

'Why? Did you give her the money?'

He nodded again.

'Then why is she going? What did she say?'

'Nothing much.'

Ruth's throat tightened, the effort of speaking almost physically painful. 'Not even thank you? Not even a message?'

He shook his head, and then touched his mother's arm with a look of pity in his eyes. 'I'm sorry, but she said nothing else.'

'But Graham, she *can't* go back!' Ruth clasped and unclasped her hands desperately. 'Does she need more money? I could pay for her rent in London – anything, just as long as she stays.'

His face softened, the dark eyes unusually kind. 'She says that she wants to go back ... she has her home there.'

'No!' Ruth shouted, letting go of Graham's hands and leaning back in her seat. 'Her home is here now. Tell her I'll pay for James's schooling. I'll buy her a flat! A house! Anything she wants!' Ruth was begging then, her grey eyes almost colourless in the white face. 'Tell her she needn't see me, Graham. Just get her to stay.'

He read Ruth's lips and then signalled, 'She said that she could keep in contact through me. I will deliver her letters to you, or any messages.'

Ruth panicked. 'No! That won't do! Laurel has never once written or rung me. No! If she goes back I'll never see her – I know that!' Her voice was rising, and in an effort to control

395

herself Ruth began pacing up and down Graham's room, her mind racing. Finally, she knelt down beside the wheelchair and looked up into his face. 'Graham, please ask her to stay. She'll listen to you. Please ... for my sake.'

He touched his mother's hair lightly. 'I'll try.'

'Oh, for God's sake try!' she begged. 'Please, please try!'

He nodded. 'But I can't promise.'

Ruth smiled half-heartedly. 'Yes, I understand ... Thank you, oh, thank you, Graham.'

That had been on Tuesday. On Wednesday, Graham told his mother that Laurel had refused to see him. On Thursday she asked for more money; and on Friday Ruth gave Graham £1000.

That afternoon he went out to meet his half-sister. Ruth waited at home. It was precisely one week since Dino had given her his ultimatum. With iron will Ruth controlled herself, waiting by the front door, then by the phone. Minutes dragged into hours and still she waited. Waited for her daughter's footsteps or the sound of her voice. Three o'clock scratched past, as did four and when the phone did ring it was Geoffrey Lynes. Ruth answered him hurriedly, desperate to have the line free again. By four-thirty she was numb with anxiety.

'Hello, Mum,' Kate said, walking in and shaking the rain off her coat. 'Any news?'

'Nothing,' Ruth said, moving towards the kitchen. 'Not a word.'

She followed her mother, taking some bread out of the fridge and beginning to make sandwiches. 'Laurel's a cow.'

Ruth glanced up. 'You shouldn't say that – '

Kate interrupted her mother, her husky voice rising. 'Why not? It's what we're all thinking. Me, Nina, Dino – even Graham, I should imagine, if the truth be known. She's a bitch of the first order, and that's the truth!'

Shocked by the outburst, Ruth rose to Laurel's defence. 'How can you say that! You don't even know her!'

In astonishment she saw her daughter throw down the knife on the kitchen table, her face vivid with anger. 'And I don't bloody want to! I hate her already, I loathe her for what she's done!' She swung round to face Ruth. ' "Laurel this, Laurel that," ' she mimicked. 'Always Miss Perfect Laurel, who's been so badly treated ... poor Laurel, abandoned and left by her mother ... shame on you for leaving such a lovely girl.' She backed away from Ruth as she moved towards her. 'Twenty-two years ago you had her adopted – so what? – if this performance is anything to go by you were lucky to get rid of her.'

Beside herself with rage, Ruth lunged towards the girl, but she ducked and edged her way round the kitchen, still talking. 'I'm sick of her! Sick of her name! Her bloody existence! She's a rotten, conniving, revengeful cow – and you know it!'

Ruth grabbed her arm savagely but Kate still continued. 'You're grovelling because you feel guilty. *You*, of all people! You've given in all the way and she hasn't budged an inch. I'm ashamed of you – you always had such self-respect before.'

Without an instant's hesitation, Ruth slapped her across the face. Kate gasped and shook her arm free. 'You're hitting the wrong daughter,' she said, running out of the kitchen.

Her palm stinging, Ruth sat down heavily at the kitchen table. How dare she, she raged to herself. How dare she say that she had lost her self-respect! Laurel was her daughter, too, why didn't anyone understand that? Incapable of action, Ruth waited in the kitchen. Kate did not reappear and it was much later when the front door opened again and Graham came in. He was wet through, the drizzle having turned into rain, the wheels of his chair leaving marks on the hall floor. Ruth watched him from the doorway, and when he looked up at her, she could see the answer in his face.

'Laurel's going back to Yorkshire, isn't she?'

He nodded slowly, a thin glow of pity in his eyes.

From then on the only contact Ruth had with Laurel was through Graham, and that contact was minimal. She returned to Yorkshire with her child and wrote to Graham once a fortnight, using the Post Office as their collection point. According to Graham, she had resented Ruth's insistence that they should meet and wanted to live her own life as far from her mother as possible. Exhausted and defeated, Ruth did what she had always done when she was in pain – she turned to her work. Becoming rapidly absorbed with the Belvedere, she endeavoured to bury all thought of Laurel, her pride relegating her daughter to a very minor role in her life. And although she appreciated what Graham had done, Ruth never begged him to plead on her behalf again, and he seemed relieved, their usual closeness intensified.

Kate was another matter altogether. After her outburst, she remained hostile towards her mother, avoiding her whenever possible and going out every weekend with friends. Hurt and filled with a sense of deep disappointment, Ruth turned to her work.

'We're booked up for the whole of the year until November,' Geoffrey Lynes told her as he showed Ruth the diary. 'Not bad, is it?'

'It's wonderful,' she said coolly. 'You're a good help.'

He smiled. 'You're a good boss to work for.'

'No bad feelings?' she asked.

'There never were,' he replied carefully. 'Listen, I've been meaning to get something off my chest for a long time. About that fire – '

Ruth glanced up at the man in front of her. Then, slowly, she shook her head. 'No, Geoffrey, don't say anything. Not a word.'

By forcing herself into an even more punishing schedule at work, Ruth had no time to dream of an emotional reconciliation with her daughter; besides, all contact was distant and financial, Laurel continuing to drain her mother as each month a few hundred pounds winged its way from a Maida Vale Post Office to some box number in Yorkshire which only Graham knew. Ruth gave the money willingly, without telling Dino, the cheques the only tangible proof that Laurel and her son were alive.

Nina took a different view.

'Bloody outrage!' she said thoughtfully, watching Ruth and noting the changes in her. She looked older, her face still lovely, but curiously devoid of expression. 'Your daughter is playing you for a sucker. All that money – isn't it about time she reciprocated in some way?'

Ruth shrugged. 'I'm not so sure. Maybe things are better the way they are. She was breaking up the family – '

'How's Dino?' Nina asked deftly.

'He's well. Busy at the bank,' Ruth explained, 'but he gets impatient about Laurel. I can't bring the subject up any longer without an argument.'

'He's had enough.'

'So he tells me,' Ruth replied drily.

'Are you going to keep giving Laurel money?'

'Why not?'

Nina blew out her cheeks. 'Well, let's hope to God she doesn't start developing expensive tastes. Even guilt has its limits.'

But not for Ruth. No amount of money could absolve the past for her. So for months she paid out, on the month, and by summer she had given her daughter £7,500 – all paid via Graham. Not a word of thanks came back; not a letter, not even a photograph – nothing. The only contact Ruth had with her daughter was through Graham, and when she pressed for details, they were always hurtful.

'Laurel doesn't want to see you. She doesn't feel close to you,' Graham explained. 'I'm sorry, but she's not interested.'

Ruth watched her son's fingers as he signed the words and then glanced away. It was always the same – no contact, no warmth, only a few well-chosen words to inflict the most pain.

'But they're both well?' Ruth asked.

'James has had chicken-pox, but he's recovered now.'

'Chicken-pox!' she said, alarmed. 'You're sure he's OK? Has she taken him to a doctor to check him out?' As usual, Ruth reverted to the old ploy. 'If she needs money . . .'

And she did, repeatedly, and her demands became more insistent, escalating from monthly payments to fortnightly, and then weekly. Then, on a steamy afternoon when the air was listless and the sky thick with insects, Graham asked Ruth for £10,000.

'Ten thousand pounds! What for, Graham? What on earth does she want that kind of money for?'

He watched his mother's lips and then signed, 'She says she wants to buy a house and needs the deposit. She said that I should ask you for it. She said you owed it to her.'

Ruth flinched. 'All right, maybe I do owe her something – but the same could be said of her! How dare she make demands like this without even bothering to come and ask me herself!' Ruth looked away. 'And to make you run around doing her dirty work – it's not good enough! I want to see her!'

Graham's face altered from pity to anxiety. 'She won't see you! If you try to find her she said she'll never have anything to do with you again. And she'll never let you near James.'

Her ruthlessness was breathtaking. 'That's blackmail!' Ruth shouted, knowing that she was trapped, and loathing the sensation. 'You can tell Laurel to go to hell!'

Graham read her lips and frowned. 'Are you sure you want me to tell her that?'

Defiantly, Ruth nodded.

'Mother, are you sure? She's your daughter.'

Ruth looked at her son and hesitated, sunlight scorching through the windows and making hot patterns on the carpet. The heat dragged on her and she sat down heavily. 'All right ... I'll write her a cheque.'

'No, she wants it in cash.'

'It's £10,000, Graham! I'll have to go to the bank to draw it out.'

He nodded and signalled back. 'That's all right, she doesn't need the money until the end of the week.'

Afraid to mention the affair to Dino, Ruth withdrew the money and packed it in a small carton, Sellotaping round the sides of the box. Then she passed it to Graham. 'I hope you're not thinking of posting all that money?' Her tone was cold, a winter voice.

He shook his head.

'Is Laurel coming here then?'

A thin film of disquiet clouded his eyes. Knowing how much the charade was taking out of him, and how much he detested having his loyalties divided, Ruth dropped her enquiries. 'You do it your way then.'

Gratefully, her son signed, 'Leave it to me, I'll see that Laurel gets this safely.'

With a feeble attempt at a smile, Ruth left.

For the next eight months Laurel dogged her mother's heels. Every day Ruth waited for news, watching Graham and treasuring each detail about her daughter and grandson. The strain showed easily in Ruth, but although she feared the stress might weaken Graham, his new-found responsibility seemed to steady him, the strange circumstances bringing them closer together. Ruth's relationship with Kate, however, did not improve.

'Where are you going tonight, Kate?'

She stopped by the front door, irritated. 'Out.'

Ruth breathed in deeply. 'I can see that. With whom?'

'Does it matter?' she asked, her expression defiant.

'Of course it does!' Ruth answered vehemently. 'This is ridiculous – we shouldn't be fighting.'

Kate bowed her head, the long fall of hair tumbling over her shoulders. 'I don't want to fight with you either, Mum.' Her voice had lost its bitter edge and she seemed close to tears.

'Kate, I know things have been difficult, but if we can't all pull together we'll tear each other apart – and that's pointless. Laurel isn't a threat to you – she's not interested in becoming another member of this family. She's made that obvious.'

'She's bad news.'

Ruth hesitated before she replied. 'I agree with you ... Laurel's bitter and she's brought us no happiness, only upset.' Gently she smoothed Kate's hair, astonished that she had jeopardised their relationship. 'I don't want you to hate me. But one day you'll have a child of your own and it's difficult to know what's best sometimes.'

'I just worry about you, that's all.' Her eyes met her mother's evenly. 'Ever since Laurel came back there's been a bad feeling. She frightens me.' Some of her foreboding washed over Ruth and she shivered. 'Something's wrong, Mum, and it's hanging over all our heads ... sometimes I think it will crush us.'

Aware of her unease, Ruth rallied for her daughter's sake.

'No one is going to hurt any of us. Would I let anyone harm us?' She smiled, but the attempt was only half-hearted. 'Believe me, Kate, no one is going to hurt my family.'

That evening there was a function at the Belvedere. A leading Tory politician was holding a party, supposedly to ensure some publicity for his latest volume of memoirs. Ruth leant on the rail of the balcony and looked down. The man droned on, while several leading newspaper journalists scribbled idly on to their pads. Uninterested, she glanced away, looking up at the ceiling and along the walls, seeing all her hard work translated into bricks and mortar, her progress monitored in wallpaper and yards of carpet and the layers of gilding.

For once, her work meant little to her and, surprised by her own feelings, Ruth went home. Graham was working in his room and told her that Laurel had received the money and that she would now be able to buy her house. Apparently she had not sent a word of thanks to her mother.

'When is she getting in touch with you again?' Ruth asked.

'I'm not sure.'

She nodded, oddly relieved. 'Thank you, Graham, for everything you've done. I just hope that she's happy in her new house ...' The words sounded forced even to her ears and her voice trailed off.

Graham watched his mother's lips, an expression of intense sympathy in his dark eyes, then he nodded. When Ruth turned to go, he was already back at his computer.

A form of suspended relief took over. It was almost pleasurable not to find Graham waiting for her with another demand for money for Laurel. Ruth even began to indulge herself, believing that Laurel's new home might finally release her from her daughter's clutches. But she knew that when the money ran out, she would be back.

'You're joking!' Robert Floyd exclaimed, immensely amused, his eyes bright with interest. 'What the hell would you want with a place in Paris?'

Ruth uncrossed her legs and stood up. The office was as

sparse as ever; only a large sculpture of a horse's head relieved the austerity. She walked over, appraising it. 'This is nice, Robert, when did you get it?'

'At that exhibition the other week.' He lit a cigar and inhaled deeply. 'Kate made me buy it. Cost a damn fortune.'

Ruth's fingers trailed down the bronze. 'It's splendid. I didn't know my daughter had such a good eye.'

'And an expensive one,' he countered, adding mischievously, 'not that she should ever have to worry about money . . . unless you lose it all again.'

'I'm not certain that I want to buy the premises. I simply want to look and – '

' – expand your empire.'

She turned, shrugging. 'You're against that?'

'Why should I be? You have my intense admiration, especially as your cinemas seem to flourish abnormally. Perhaps you're protected by some Great Film Buff in the sky?'

'It wasn't luck,' Ruth said coldly.

The old man threw up his hands. 'Would I ever suggest such a thing?' He smiled and then added seriously, 'I know you've worked bloody hard. You deserve your success. Just don't overstretch yourself. You should take a holiday sometimes.'

'Your concern for my health is touching,' Ruth said, smiling archly, 'and strangely enough I was thinking of taking a break when I go to France.'

'With Dino?'

Ruth paused for a moment. She hadn't asked him yet, but the holiday was a chance to be alone with him, to spend time with him and cajole him back into good humour – a humour which had been severely tested since Laurel's re-emergence.

'Of course he's coming with me,' Ruth answered coolly. 'Anyway, I must be off now, I just called in to see how you were – '

'You're a bloody awful liar!' Robert Floyd said, laughing. 'You came in to see my reaction to your scheme, that's all. Kate's the only one who comes to see me without an ulterior motive.'

'Have it your own way,' she said, moving towards the door.

'I'll let you know if I intend to buy the cinema when I get back.'

'Yeah, you do that. Only don't ask me for money, I would hate to go out of business at my age.'

The suggestion of a holiday was more than welcome to Dino – until he realised what was behind it. Then his patience snapped.

'You want *another* cinema!'

'I want to have a look, that's all,' Ruth replied calmly.

'Are you crazy?' he asked, sitting down on the bed next to her. 'You've already got far too much work. Drop the idea.'

'Why should I? I'm good at business.'

His temper flared. 'Business! Bullshit! This has nothing to do with business. You collect cinemas – you want them like other women want fur coats.' He leant towards her. 'I don't suppose that it has ever occurred to you that when something goes wrong with one of the children, you buy a cinema! When Graham was ill – you bought a cinema! Now Laurel's disappeared – you're buying a cinema again! It's a way of keeping control. You can hold on to buildings better than you can hold on to your children!'

Ruth bit her lip, stung by the truth in his words. 'That's only your opinion,' she said icily. 'I want to get on – '

'How far?'

'I don't know, Dino!' she shouted. 'As far as I can – as far from Oldham as possible; as far from poverty as I can get!'

He sighed and took hold of her hand. 'You'll have to stop one day, Ruth. One day something or someone will make you stop, and then you'll have to come to terms with yourself. Don't spend so much time looking to the future that you miss what's going on now.'

She softened, suddenly gentle, and put her arms round him. 'Come with me, Dino . . . Please.'

He glanced at her face and then kissed her. 'You do this every time, Ruth,' he said, smiling. 'You can't keep seducing me into a good humour.'

She raised her eyebrows. 'Really? You've never complained before.'

He kissed her throat and then her mouth. 'I'll come to Paris with you ... but buying another cinema is still a bloody stupid idea.'

They left the week after, installing themselves in an exotic hotel in the centre of the capital. The sun was rising and the flowers glowed against the white stonework on the balcony as Ruth stood, looking out. Behind her, birds chattered into the warm air, and in the gardens rows of sprinklers idled round and round drenching the dry grass. She stretched and moved inside, drawing a bath. The tap water was tepid against her body, and when Ruth drew the blind a large butterfly flapped against the window, its wings drumming on the glass like a child's fingers.

Dark, gloomy, riddled with damp, the cinema was impressively grim. Hardly a flicker of the sunlight outside pierced the determined dimness, and the smell of dust and dirt was almost insufferable. Ruth touched the wall of the auditorium and then wiped her hands on a tissue, the grime still clinging to her fingers.

'God, this is appalling,' she said, turning to Dino who was standing with his arms folded, a look of quiet triumph in his eyes.

'It needs decorating,' he said, bursting out laughing just as Ruth did.

She leant against him weakly. 'I have never seen anything so ghastly. Never!'

'Well, it was your idea.'

'Not that it couldn't be renovated,' she said, straightening up and screwing up her eyes to see better. 'It must have been beautiful once.'

'Once is the operative word,' Dino said drily. 'You'd have to spend a fortune on it.'

'They'd be pleased to sell it,' Ruth answered. 'They're not asking much, considering its position.'

Dino remained silent. He had decided it was the best defence; if he argued with her, Ruth would only want the place more.

'Well . . .' she said finally, as they moved out into the blazing street, 'I'll sleep on it.'

They had just returned to the hotel when the phone rang. Apparently the operator had some difficulty connecting the long-distance call, and it was only after Dino lost his temper that the line was connected.

It was Kate. 'Mum?'

Her voice sounded dull over the phone, its usual huskiness pronounced.

'Kate!' Ruth said, surprised. 'What's the matter? Is everyone all right?'

'We're fine,' she said unconvincingly. 'We just wondered when you were getting back.'

A warning bell sounded in Ruth's head. 'On Thursday, as we said. Why? Do you want us back earlier?'

'No . . . that will be OK. Just don't make it any later, will you?'

'Kate, you sound dreadful, what's the problem?' she asked anxiously. 'Tell me, is someone ill? Graham? David?'

'No, honestly, Mum, we're fine. We just miss you, that's all . . . I just wanted to talk to you.'

'Well, we're talking,' Ruth said, signalling to Dino to come and listen to the conversation. 'Are you sure you don't want me to come home?'

Kate seemed suddenly more composed, almost cheerful. 'No . . . I'm sorry if I worried you. Enjoy yourselves and we'll see you Thursday afternoon.'

That night neither Ruth nor Dino could sleep. When she dozed, Dino got up; when he slept for an hour, Ruth was awake. By the time light was creeping up on the city, they were both up and dressed.

'We could be worrying about nothing,' Ruth said repeatedly.

Dino looked at her, his eyebrows raised. 'When did Kate ever ring us on holiday? Since when did she ever sound worried when there wasn't a good reason?'

Ruth shook her head and dragged the suitcases out of the wardrobe. 'Well, shall I pack up or not?'

'You pack, I'll ring the airport.'

They were due to catch the afternoon flight, but a storm blew up and grounded all the planes. With mounting irritation, the passengers were ushered back into the airport lounge, Ruth nervously fiddling with her hand-luggage. It took three hours for the storm to blow itself out, and after an uneventful flight, they finally came down in misty London at two a.m. Shivering, Ruth waited as Dino hailed a taxi, her eyes itching with tiredness.

The miles slipped languidly under the wheels as they tracked from Heathrow to Hampstead. Road after sleepy road passed by, a few lonely people drifting in the barren streets. When the car finally turned into their road Ruth glanced over to the house, expecting to see it in darkness. Instead, from almost every window, lights blazed, and as she hurried down the drive the front door opened and a figure stood silhouetted there.

Twenty

Nina heard the frantic knocking and ran down the stairs two at a time to pull open the door. 'God, Mrs Corley – what the hell is happening?'

The woman rushed past her, her uniform dishevelled, her normally tidy hair undone. 'I had to come, Mrs Milton! I couldn't think where else to go. Mrs Floyd's away, you see, and I . . .' She broke off, incoherent.

Nina grabbed hold of the woman and shook her so hard that her glasses slipped down her nose. 'Tell me what's happened!'

But Mrs Corley was too much in shock to be coherent and just kept clenching and unclenching her hands.

'Where is Kate?' Nina asked. 'Where's Graham?' The woman stiffened in her arms. 'Mrs Corley! What's going on?'

Her eyes flicked to Nina and then flicked away. Then as though some kind of reasoning came back to her, Mrs Corley suddenly caught hold of Nina's arms and said blindly, 'David! I left David –'

Without hesitating, Nina grabbed her coat and flung open the front door, running down the street towards Ruth's house, her high heels clicking on the stone pavement.

Ruth ran towards her house quickly, although Dino had already raced up the steps, and as he did so the figure turned and moved back into the hall. Ruth followed him, arriving to find Kate standing in the doorway of the lounge. Around her there was chaos. Cushions were thrown about, chairs pushed aside, and a glass had been thrown against the far wall and smashed. On the low table in front of the fire was a child's picture book, and on the settee was a shabby scarf, well worn and losing some of its colour.

'What on earth is happening here?' Dino said, turning round

and looking at the mess. Kate stood facing him, her hands down by her sides, her face expressionless. 'Kate! Answer me!'

She flinched when he shouted, but made no attempt to explain. Thinking she was in shock, Ruth signalled Dino to be quiet, then walked over to her daughter and took hold of her hand. It was cool, the palm dry.

'Kate, I'm home now. Tell me what's happened.'

Her head moved as she looked at Ruth and then, as though she finally realised where she was, she withdrew her hand. 'You're back early,' she said woodenly, bending forward and picking up a cushion. Her body seemed stiff and uncoordinated, her voice monotonous.

'We caught an early flight home – we thought you sounded worried on the phone.'

Illogically cheerful, she turned to Dino. 'You shouldn't have worried, I told you not to. Everything's fine, all under control.'

It was like talking to an automaton, he thought. 'Kate! This is the last time I'll ask you – what happened?'

Upstairs, a door banged. Remembering her son, Ruth ran up to David's room. He was fast asleep, totally oblivious to the chaos around him. With enormous relief, Ruth left the room, headed for the stairs which led up to the second floor and knocked at Mrs Corley's door. When there was no reply, she walked in. The main room was empty, as were the others. Fighting real panic, Ruth went downstairs to Graham's room. Again, it was empty.

Fear made Ruth run downstairs into the lounge, her feet drumming down the stairs, her breath coming in gasps. Kate had moved from her place by the window and was sitting in front of the fire, the lamps only half-illuminating her and making shadows under her eyes and beneath the firm line of her chin. Dino was standing beside her and shrugged when he saw Ruth.

'Where's Mrs Corley, Kate?'

She did not answer her mother.

'Where's Graham?'

Again she did not answer, only looked away from the fire towards the window again. Dear God, Ruth thought, what is the matter with her? 'Answer me!' she shouted, too frightened to keep calm any longer. 'Tell me what's going on!'

Kate had no chance to reply before the front door banged back on its hinges with the full force of someone slamming it against the wall behind. Ruth spun round, startled, and saw Graham move across the hall. He stopped when he saw his mother, the handsome face altered, the hair falling across the dark eyes. Stunned by the look on his face, Ruth hesitated, unable to move towards him or speak.

Instead, it was Kate who broke the silence. Getting to her feet she said. 'Ask your son what's the matter. Ask your beloved, indulged son what he's done ... ask him!'

Ruth flinched, turning from her daughter to Graham. She knew that he hadn't heard what his sister said, but he knew enough to move, wheeling himself across the polished hall floor towards the lift. Dino was there before he was and stood in front of the doors, blocking Graham's way. 'I want an explanation – now!'

Jerking up his head, Graham looked at Dino with an expression dangerously close to fury. His face was white and his eyes were fixed and black in his head. 'Tell me!' Dino shouted hoarsely. 'Or by Christ I'll beat it out of you.'

'I ...' Graham trailed off, his voice incoherent.

'Tell me in sign language!' Dino shouted.

Behind her, Ruth could hear Kate sobbing and turned, her throat dry. Her family seemed to be breaking up before her eyes. Everything she treasured, everything she had worked for over the years. 'You tell me, please ... please, Kate. I can't stand this, please tell me.'

Her daughter hesitated, glancing across to Graham. Knowing her so well, Ruth could see in her face the same expression she had used so often as a child, the expression of loving which told her mother she was going to lie for him, to cover up.

'Kate, please ... '

Without taking her eyes off her brother, she began. 'I was supposed to be working at the hospital late today but instead I swapped shifts and came home early ... ' She paused, a look of disbelief on her face. 'When I got to the end of the road I met Mrs Corley who was on her way to collect David from school. Mrs Harvey was shopping and the house was quiet when I got here. I thought Graham would be upstairs working, but when I got in I could hear a voice in the lounge – someone shouting – and I walked in.'

She stopped, and then continued more slowly. 'There was a young woman in the room, shabbily dressed, with a little boy. She was pleading with Graham and begging him for something. The child was silent and when he saw me he hid behind his mother. Graham hadn't heard me come in, of course, and so I had the advantage ... I knew she was Laurel and that the child was her son – I also knew from what she said that she was frightened ... '

'Laurel here?' Ruth asked. Laurel, her daughter, the child born so long ago, the child who hated her.

Kate nodded, but never once took her eyes off Graham. He watched her coldly from his wheelchair.

'She was saying something like, "I don't want anything except to see her", and then "She's my mother".'

Ruth's heart shifted, her mind running over the words, trying not to believe them. She turned to look at Graham. There wasn't a flicker of fear in his eyes.

'She said that she couldn't stay in London any longer and that he had to beg you ... '

'Beg me to do what?' Ruth prompted her, her voice ice-cold.

'ASK HIM!' she shouted, pointing to her brother. 'Ask him what he's done. Ask your son!'

Clasping both arms Ruth swung her daughter round to look at her. 'No! You tell me. I trust you to tell me the truth and I want to know, now! What has Graham done?'

Kate tensed in her mother's grasp and turned back to him, her husky voice steady. 'Your son,' she spat out the word, 'told Laurel that you hated her! That you had always hated her and never wanted to see her or have any contact with her. He told her that you wanted to forget her and that you never wanted to see her because she reminded you of the past ... '

Ruth struggled to breathe, her whole body trembling.

'Your son said that you wanted to buy her off and he gave her three hundred pounds to prove it. He said that there was no room in this family for anyone else and that you didn't want her or her son ...'

Kate's eyes were still fixed on Graham's. 'He said that he was sorry she was divorced and in trouble but he'd asked you and you'd refused to help – '

'No!' Ruth said, her voice low, betrayed. 'I don't believe it! Laurel refused to see *me*. She refused to see *me*!'

'No, Mum, she didn't,' Kate said, touching her mother's arm and seeing the hopeless look on her face. 'When Laurel saw me she panicked, grabbed the little boy and ran out of the house. Graham tried to stop me, but I followed them and caught up with them in the High Street. She was so upset, Mum ... I took her for a coffee and after a while she began to talk. She was so sorry to have been a bother to us.' She spat the words out bitterly. Ruth was still dumb, uncomprehending. 'I asked Laurel what she wanted and she just said that Graham had got in touch with her before Christmas – extending the olive branch.'

Ruth glanced over to her son. He must have guessed what was going on but his face betrayed nothing. I loved you, she thought, how could you do this? You were everything to me, I would have died for you.

'Graham traced Laurel through the hospital. Then he wrote to her, saying that he wanted to get in touch with his long-lost sister and make up for what you'd done.'

Ruth remained motionless, unable to look at her son.

'She came down like a lamb and met him, and over the weeks she asked to see you.' Kate's voice cracked. 'That was all she wanted – to see her mother – and all the time he was telling her that you refused to see her. He lied to you!'

She swung round and passed Ruth, reaching Graham's wheelchair and striking him across the face just as Dino moved forward between them. Her blow caught her brother across the mouth and a thin trickle of blood ran down his chin and the white front of his jumper.

Startled, Dino caught hold of her and held her tightly to

him while she continued to talk. 'He played you one against the other ... one against the other,' she repeated hoarsely, turning her head away from Dino and watching her brother as he looked up at her, a bleak smile on his lips. 'And he was enjoying himself – LOOK AT HIM – he's enjoying himself!'

'Why?' Ruth asked dully. 'I don't understand. Why?'

'For revenge! Because he wanted you to love *him* and no one else. Not me, not David, not even his father – just him. He thought you'd betrayed him, just like father betrayed him when he died! Don't you see? You let him down ... ' She was almost hysterical, 'so he decided to punish both of you. You, because you had betrayed him, and Laurel because she was your daughter and another drain on your affection.'

'But it wouldn't have made any difference!' Ruth said wildly, without understanding her son. Graham loved her, needed her. She had nursed him since he was a child ... theirs had been a special love. 'It's not true, Kate ... I would still have loved him if I'd loved her.'

'THAT'S NOT ENOUGH!' she shouted blindly. 'Nothing is enough for Graham. No amount of loving, no amount of devotion, nothing is sufficient. He's sick!' she said, shaking off Dino's arms and standing by the door. 'He's sick and he's dangerous.'

Ruth leant against the hall table, her legs weak, feeling a thin stream of ice water in her stomach and a dull buzz in her head. Graham made no further attempt to move and Kate stood where she was, her eyes fixed on her brother.

'I gave him almost £20,000 for Laurel ... ' Ruth said dully, ignoring the look of surprise on Dino's face. 'He must have ... he *did* give it to her, didn't he?'

For a minute Kate looked as though she might lie to cover up for him, and then she turned to face her mother, her chin raised.

'When I asked Laurel about the money, she said that Graham had given her three hundred pounds, supposedly from you, to buy her off. No more.'

'But there was all that money for her!' Ruth said stupidly.

413

'Money for Christmas and for her rent, and then the deposit for the house ... '

Out of the corner of her eye, Ruth could see Dino's expression tighten. He looked from Ruth to her son, and then back to Kate.

'Why is there all this mess in the lounge?'

She swallowed and then continued. 'Laurel kept begging to see Mum. She kept saying that she wouldn't get in the way and that she didn't want anything. Her husband had left her and she'd got a divorce, but when Graham first wrote to her he'd suggested that maybe, after you'd both met, you would like her to live nearby ... so she'd sold up her home in Yorkshire and come down. She was living in some hotel in Paddington.'

Ruth closed her eyes; she knew what such places were like; knew what they felt like; smelt like; and how people became trapped in some of them for life. Her confusion turned to anger suddenly. 'And then what?'

'When she was here, Graham told her that you didn't want her near you and that she'd have to go back home. That's what the three hundred pounds was for. Nothing about a deposit on a house. God, Mum, she's got nothing! Neither has the boy.'

Ruth turned and looked at her son; he looked back with her father's eyes and for a minute she couldn't believe any of it.

'I told her that I wanted her to return to the house and wait for you to come home,' Kate continued, 'but she wouldn't. She was too frightened of Graham and she thought you'd be angry. Nothing I said could convince her. She just kept repeating that she'd been a nuisance and didn't belong with us ... I talked to her for a while and asked her for the name of her hotel, which she gave to me.'

'And then you came back here?' Dino asked her quietly. She nodded. 'And Graham was still here?'

Again she nodded. 'He must have known what she'd tell me, but he was as cool as ice, and when I told him I knew he just sneered at me and told me to grow up.' She glanced at him quickly and then glanced away, incredulous. 'I asked him why he'd done it and he told me you had it coming.' She turned to Ruth. 'He said he'd been waiting to get even with you.'

'Get even!' Ruth repeated numbly. No, not her son, this was someone else. She hadn't loved Graham for so long without knowing him. She was his ears, she listened for him; when he had asthma she breathed for him; she gave him her strength. 'I loved him,' she said pitifully. 'Why would he punish me?'

Kate glanced away, hardly able to bear the look on her mother's face.'When I came back David was home and Mrs Corley was making dinner for him. I went upstairs, but Graham wouldn't answer me and pretended he couldn't hear. I followed him into the gym and watched him practise on the bars, my temper boiling. He seemed unconcerned, not slightly bothered about what he'd put you through for more than a year!' She dug her hands into the pockets of her jacket. 'I kept asking him for an explanation ... I'd known for days that something was going to happen ... and he just kept pulling himself up on the bars and lifting those bloody weights. I could have killed him!'

Graham was motionless in his chair; the blood had dried on his lip and looked dark, almost black.

'Finally he went downstairs for something to eat. I followed, like a lap dog. David was about to go up to bed – it must have been nearly nine-thirty by then – and Mrs Corley was chatting to him. We went into the kitchen and Graham got something out of the fridge. I kept on and on at him to explain and finally he flew into a rage and threw the bread knife at me. Luckily David had gone into the lounge for something, and Mrs Corley kept him out of the way. I picked up the knife and chucked it in the sink as Graham went into the lounge ... God, if you'd seen him, he looked so different ... I stood in front of him and told him what I thought about him ... ' She spun round to Dino. 'I thought I was safe! He was in a wheelchair, after all. But he suddenly lunged forward and caught hold of my skirt. I slipped and he kept striking me around the head and shoulders. The lamps fell over and everything got messed up as I tried to get away from him, but I couldn't, and it was only when I got to the bar and grabbed hold of the glass and hit him that he stopped ... I thought he was going to kill me.' She paused, shaking. 'Then I threw the glass at him, but it missed, and when I looked up again he'd gone ... '

415

She stopped talking. Ruth stood immobile, hearing the clock behind her and the fire crackling in the lounge. Under the bright hall light Graham's wheelchair threw a black shadow along the floor and half way up the far wall. He looked bigger and older than she remembered him. Nothing like the child he had been, she thought, nothing like the child she gave birth to.

Time suspended itself. Only Dino moved, walking into the study and picking up the phone. After a while they could hear him talking. '... yes, all right. As soon as you can. Thank you.'

He came out under the light. 'They're coming for Graham, from the clinic.'

Ruth nodded once. The effort jolted her, rocked her, and when she turned back to her daughter she was white, ice-cold, pale as snow. 'Where is Laurel now?'

'I tried to ring the hotel earlier,' Kate answered, not wanting to strike the final blow, '... they told me she'd checked out ... I'm so sorry, Mum.'

They came for Graham within the half-hour, during which time Ruth took Kate upstairs and drew a bath for her while she undressed. Along her upper back and shoulders there were innumerable bruises, and down one-third of her right arm was a dull purple patch, rapidly darkening. Dino stayed with Graham downstairs in the hall, under the white light. He leant against the lift and folded his arms, watching the young man in front of him. Neither spoke; Graham indifferent, his eyes remote, his expression cynical. Feeling a sense of outrage, Dino stood guard, listening to the sounds above him, remembering the peculiar lack of reaction in Ruth.

Laurel's disappearance was the *coup de grâce*. Until then, Dino knew that Ruth had hoped to dredge something up from the nightmare, thinking that whatever happened to Graham, she would be reunited with her daughter. But when Kate told her Laurel had gone, slipping back into that hopeless limbo where she had hovered for so long, it had been impossible for Ruth to accept, and he had seen, with hopeless pity, her reaction – the shock, followed by withdrawal.

Ruth had rocked, almost as though the words had been a

blow to her. Then as he watched her, she straightened up, her tall figure walking stiffly towards the stairs, her face immobile and cold. No warmth, nothing, only the expression of incalculable grief.

Nina arrived just as they were waiting for Graham to be collected. She rushed in, breathless, Tony following close behind in the car. He was still wearing pyjamas under his navy overcoat, his face dull with tiredness.

'What the hell happened?' Nina asked Dino, glancing round. 'It looks like a battlefield in here.'

'It's Graham – he attacked Kate.'

Her expression hardened. She glanced at Graham disbelievingly, her small face pinched with shock. He regarded her with complete disinterest.

'Is she all right?'

'Shocked and bruised,' Dino answered. 'I rang the clinic and they're coming for him.'

'Why did he do it?' Nina asked, baffled, her hands raking her hair back from her face.

'They were arguing about Laurel.' Dino shrugged. 'Graham had been lying to his mother all along. He'd contacted Laurel and invited her down to London, then he told her that Ruth didn't want to see her.' In complete frustration, he threw his hands up, 'All the time that Ruth was begging Graham to bring Laurel home, she was pleading to see her mother. She only wanted to see Ruth.'

'Bastard,' Nina said briskly, her back turned towards Graham, her fury palpable in the cool hall. 'How's Ruth. How's she taken it?'

Dino hesitated. Nina noticed his reluctance, and prompted him. 'Is she OK?'

'She's too shocked to make sense out of anything,' he said finally. 'Ruth's done what she always does, she's rallied, put on a brave face.'

Nina patted his arm absent-mindedly and then walked upstairs. There was no one in the bedroom so she instinctively made her way to Graham's room. Ruth was packing for her

417

son, folding his clothes tidily, her hands smoothing the articles, rearranging them repeatedly. Her expression was bland, her eyes unfocused. Nina ran over and hugged her, although Ruth was totally unresponsive.

'I'm so sorry ...'

'I can't believe it, I can't believe he would do it,' Ruth said, pulling some T-shirts out of a drawer. 'Kate found them, you know, and ran after Laurel. She told her what Graham had done.' She stopped suddenly, slapping her hands against her thighs. 'What has he done?'

'Ssshhh!' Nina said quickly, worried about the imminent hysteria in Ruth's voice and the jerky movements. 'Kate's all right and Laurel's OK –'

'She's gone,' Ruth said flatly. 'She checked out of the hotel and left London – she thought it was all her fault. She's gone.'

She said it with finality as though it was over, done with. Finished.

'We can find her!' Nina insisted. 'It can't be that difficult. Tony and Dino can find her.'

Throwing everything out of the case Ruth began to fold and unfold Graham's clothes again. Her expression was fixed, the pain clawing at her. 'I don't believe it!' she said finally, her voice firm. 'Graham couldn't do such a thing ... I know my son.' Haven't we been friends for years, she thought. We loved each other. 'I know my son. He wouldn't do this to me.'

Speechless, Nina said nothing in response.

With an air of grim calm, Ruth turned back to the case and continued packing. Every time she thought about Graham she saw him as a child in his pram, those dark eyes watching her; remembering how he'd tried to walk and how much he'd struggled. All the times he'd fallen, all the times she had worried about his asthma, his deafness, his exercises – all the days and nights spent listening in the darkness for the sounds of his breathing.

'He has to go to the clinic ... to stay,' Nina said bluntly.

Ruth tensed. 'For a while maybe.'

'No – for good! He's too old and too dangerous to live here.'

Ruth turned, her arms full of Graham's clothes, her face coldly angry. 'He's my son.'

'So's David. And Kate is your daughter, and so is Laurel!' Nina snapped back. 'You can't pander to one child, you have to think about the others.' She stood up to face Ruth, her voice rising. 'What about the next time, hey? What about the time he hits David, or you? What then? He's too strong for you to cope with and too bloody clever – I told you, before all of this happened, that you had to watch him.' She breathed in deeply, her voice softer. 'He's not safe. I'm sorry ... but he's not normal.'

Her words hit out and made Ruth gasp. 'He'll change –'

'No he won't! He's nineteen years old, he's a man, not a child. You have to face it.'

Scornfully, Ruth walked out of the bedroom and headed for the stairs. Kate was standing in the corridor, dressed in a towelling robe, her hair hanging loose on her shoulders. She watched her mother descend, her eyes fixed on her son in the hall beneath. Ruth regarded him closely for a long time, seconds passing as she studied each feature of that well-loved face. Despite everything Graham had done, when she looked into his eyes her heart turned with pity. With infinite tenderness, he put out his arms and circled his mother's waist, his head resting heavily against her stomach. Silently, Ruth held him. She was still holding on to her son when the attendants arrived to take him to the clinic.

He went without a murmur and did not look round. Dino closed the door and turned, astonished to find that Ruth had already gone back upstairs. Kate hovered in the hall, her arms wrapped around her body, hugging herself. Confused by Ruth's attitude, Dino pulled the girl to him and they comforted each other.

'Can I get you anything, Kate?'

She smiled slightly. 'No ... thanks. I'll just go to bed.' She seemed about to move and then paused. 'Graham will be all right at the clinic, won't he?'

'He'll be better there than he was here, Kate.'

'But he won't have to stay there permanently, will he?'

She knew the answer; they both did.

'We'll see,' he said quietly, watching her mount the stairs and make her way back to her room. With a heavy heart, Dino turned off the lounge, landing, and hall lights. The darkness leapt out at him from the corners and made shadows up the stairs.

A voice broke into the silence suddenly. 'Someone turn the bloody light on! I can't see a damn thing and all I need is a broken leg to really finish the night off.'

He had forgotten Nina was in the house. Hurriedly flicking the lights back on Dino watched as she came down the stairs two at a time, rushing towards the lounge and pausing in the doorway, her face a study of total disbelief.

'Well, I'll be damned!' she said, turning to Dino and pointing to the vision in front of her. Tony was asleep in one of the easy chairs, snoring softly in the middle of all the chaos. 'Would you Adam and Eve it!' she said, jerking her head towards her husband. 'Nothing affects him! Not a damn thing – he could sleep anywhere.' She walked over and poked him in the stomach.

He woke quickly. 'What the –'

'Tony, we should go home now.'

'Home?' he repeated.

'Yeah, home. You know, the square building with the chimneys.'

He smiled sheepishly and got to his feet, obviously still half asleep. When they reached the door Nina turned to Dino, a look of concern on her face. 'If you need anything, just ring.'

He nodded and glanced towards Tony. There was a heavy stubble on his chin and his soft white flesh looked grey from lack of sleep. Automatically, he extended his hand. 'Thanks for . . .' he started, trailing off in embarrassment.

Nina raised her eyes to Dino as she steered her husband out of the door. 'Well, it's been fun,' she said drily. 'We must do it again some time.'

Dino smiled affectionately and shook his head. 'Go home,' he said softly. She shifted the car into gear and then wound down the window. The engine purred in the night.

'Don't worry about Ruth, or Graham ... you did the right thing. Stay with her, Dino, she needs you.'

Ruth woke in the morning and remembered, the pain wracking her. She covered her eyes with her hands and thought of everything which had been said, remembering that Graham had gone away and that Laurel was missing. Gasping, she turned, thinking she would go mad with anguish, the terrible sense of loss tearing at her. Flinging out her hand she felt the bed empty next to her and sat up, her mind clearing. So Dino had already left for work, she thought, getting up and walking to the bathroom. It wasn't true what they all said about Graham – he wasn't that kind of boy, he was her child, after all, and a mother knows her own child ... Hesitating, Ruth pulled some clothes out of the wardrobe. She would ring the clinic and have a word with Dr Throop, she thought. There had to be some explanation.

'He needs controlling,' Dr Throop said firmly.

Her heart lurched. 'Controlling? What does that mean? I don't want him on drugs, Dr Throop.'

'Mrs Floyd, your son was in a terrible state last night; we had to settle him down and sedating him was the only way possible. He can be very violent.'

Ruth clung on to the receiver grimly. What was everyone talking about, she thought blindly. Graham wasn't ill, it was all just a misunderstanding.

'I think it would be inadvisable to visit your son for a while, Mrs Floyd. He should settle down again first.'

Ruth winced. This was a conspiracy, they were all trying to keep her from her son! First Laurel, now Graham, she thought wildly. They were taking her children away from her one by one ...

'But ... how long will it take?'

'One never knows with Graham,' he said calmly.

No one ever knew with Graham. Not even his mother or his

sister; not even the people who had loved him and lived with him, and lied for him. Not even them. Ruth put down the phone and went up to see her daughter, watching Kate sleep, a dark bruise just apparent on her bare shoulder where her nightdress fell back.

The house shook itself into life around her. Mrs Harvey made breakfast and David came in shortly afterwards with Mrs Corley. She seemed embarrassed by her actions of the previous night and kept trying to excuse herself.

'You see, Mrs Floyd, I didn't know quite what to do. I didn't want to go to the police. And I knew that Mrs Milton was a good friend of yours and would be discreet.'

Ruth smiled woodenly. 'It's all right. I'm so sorry if anything frightened you.'

Mrs Corley glanced up, surprised by the choice of words. 'It was just that Graham was out of control, Mrs Floyd, and I was worried about David and wanted to keep him out of the way. It never occurred to me that Graham would hurt Kate.'

Ruth turned away, suddenly unable to continue the conversation. Of her four children, two were separated from her and another was suffering. Only David was totally impervious to the situation and came down soon afterwards, wearing his headphones. He seemed cheerful, eerily so.

'Take those things off,' Ruth said.

'WHAT!'

Quickly, she snatched the headphones off her son's head and put them on the table. 'You'll deafen yourself.'

He frowned. 'No, I won't. I like music.'

'I don't care!' Ruth said sharply, too sharply. 'You can have them when you come home, but not until then.'

David hesitated, about to argue, and then thought better of it. 'Where's Graham?' he asked innocently.

Mrs Corley glanced over to Ruth, waiting breathlessly for her answer. 'He's been ill . . .' his mother explained calmly. 'He had to go back to the clinic.'

For an instant, there seemed to be a flicker of relief in David's eyes.

*

By ten-fifteen in the morning, Ruth was at work, sitting in front of the valuable antique desk and reading and rereading letters which all meant nothing. Names and addresses all pooled into one; phone calls and queries meaningless; her mind occupied with the constant replaying of the scene from the previous night. 'Laurel only wanted to see you ...' Kate had said; '... only wanted to see her mother.' Ruth slammed the drawer of her desk, her mind alternating between total acceptance of the truth and complete denial. She knew she should hate Graham; should feel despair at losing Laurel again; but she was too traumatised to react properly.

Even when she had come across the child's book and the head scarf which Laurel had left behind, she had not lost control. Snatching them up, she had pressed them against her mouth, her eyes closed against her tears. The scarf smelt of wool, like a school uniform, and the label was worn so much that the wording was indecipherable. For a while Ruth had sat on the settee and held the objects in her hands – for the first time since her birth, possessing something of her daughter.

And, relying on the fact that work had always been her way of coping with pain, Ruth had gone to the cinema. Usually anything could be forgotten when she was at work ... but not that morning. Unable to concentrate, Ruth reluctantly drove home. Illogically, she rang the hotel and asked for Laurel, putting down the phone when they told her she had left ... She's gone, Ruth thought dully, Laurel is gone. The child I gave away has now abandoned me. What had it all been for, she asked herself. What had all the struggles, the fights, the marriages, births – what had they all been for? She had lived her life for her children, hauled herself away from Oldham, left the bleak heights of Oldham Edge and the grimy streets for London and the future she had so assiduously made for herself. And for her children – Ruth's children.

What did any of it matter now, she asked herself desperately. The house, the possessions, the business, the money ... Ruth sat up suddenly, her eyes wide open, alerted. She thought of everything that had been said the night before and remembered the money ... If she believed what they said, and *if* Graham hadn't given it to Laurel – where was it? Quickly Ruth made her way to Graham's rooms. The bedroom was tidy, the computer turned off, the screen blank.

One by one Ruth took down his files, and then felt along the shelf. There was nothing. Her heart banging, she looked under his bed and then in his cupboards, feeling amongst the clothes for a box or a large envelope. Again, nothing. It never occurred to Ruth that he might have put the money in the bank, or spent it. There was nothing on which Graham could have spent it. Numbly, she searched. And found nothing.

In the gym she even toppled his equipment, frantic to find the money; hoping that Kate had been mistaken and that he had given it to Laurel after all. He couldn't have kept it, Ruth thought to herself, he's given it to my daughter, just as he said he would . . . Sweat poured down her back as she searched and her hands slipped on the weights, some crashing to the floor as she moved them. The daylight swept into the room and along the bare floorboards, making dashes under the bars and along the white walls. Everything Ruth touched felt of her son; smelt of him; ached with him. Her son, her child – Graham. As a last resort, she went into the bathroom. His toiletries were arranged within easy reach for him; the straps swinging slightly with the breeze from the open window.

Pulling over the laundry basket, she rummaged through the washing, tipped out the contents of his wash-bag, and emptied the pockets of his bathrobe. And still Ruth found nothing. Exhausted, she sat down on the edge of the bath, even permitting herself a slight smile. They were wrong, she thought, Graham *had* given the money to Laurel, he hadn't lied to her. But some instinct filtered through to Ruth, some deep intelligence which told her to keep looking; told her that Graham *had* taken the money. She looked round frantically, her eyes taking in every detail of the bathroom. Think, she said to herself, think – if the money is here it must be found. The solution came to her suddenly; if Ruth wanted to find it she had to think like Graham; she had to think like a person in a wheelchair who would only be able to find a few hiding places within easy reach. Ruth shifted her position on the side of the bath and crossed her legs, one foot banging against the side of the bath. The noise echoed.

Alerted, she tapped it again. It echoed. With a deep sense of dread, Ruth slipped to her knees and tapped the panel. There was a space behind. Looking round she could see nothing with which to prise it open and rushed into the other room to find a large, heavy paper knife. Carefully, she slid the knife into the slot between the wall and the bath panel and eased it apart. It took several moments before the side suddenly fell forward and revealed the space behind. Ruth's hand trembled as she felt into the darkness ... and found the box.

It was an old shoe-box which had once held some trainers, and when she slipped off the elastic band and lifted the lid the money looked up at her, row after perfect row. Apart from the three hundred pounds he had given to Laurel which was supposed to buy her off, all the money remained.

The room shifted in front of Ruth's eyes. Dizzy, she leant against the bath and laid her head on her knees, her breathing laboured. Images of Graham flashed into her mind; the baby, the child, the man; handsome, cunning, intelligent – treacherous. She sighed and then shivered, past ghosts walking over her, dancing on her dreams. She could have deluded herself; she would have done before ... but not now. Graham had committed the one sin Ruth could not forgive, he had deprived his own blood, his own half-sister, allowing her to suffer while he had everything. He could have punished his mother over and over again, but he had punished her child instead. The difference sentenced him.

When Ruth finally found the strength to move, she struggled to her feet, the box clenched firmly in her hands. Decided on her course of action, she swore that her daughter would have that money, pound by pound, and that wherever Laurel was, she would find her.

The heavy storm pelted on the windows; rain lashing the trees and making fast puddles in the driveway. Ruth heard the car pull in and the sound of the front door opening, watching as

Dino walked in, his clothes drenched, his hair wet and plastered to his head.

'You should change,' she said coolly. 'Have a bath, or something.'

He nodded and moved towards the stairs. 'Do you want anything?' he asked, aware of her strangeness.

'No, I'm fine.'

'Listen, Ruth –'

She cut him off. 'I don't want to talk now.'

'Well, I do!' he responded, his voice as cold as hers. 'I want to talk, and I want to help you. I don't want to be cut out – I can't help what happened. I can't help the fact that Laurel and Graham have gone, all I can do is help.'

Ruth turned away, 'I don't want to talk about it.'

'Why not? What are you trying to prove, Ruth? That you can cope with anything? That you don't need to grieve?' He pushed back his wet hair. 'Even when such terrible things happen you don't turn to me,' he said disbelievingly. 'We should share things, Ruth. Good and bad, we should share.'

He stopped, surprised by the look on Ruth's face. The coldness had vanished, in its place was confusion, an unexpected vulnerability which saddened him.

'You stupid woman, don't you know how much I love you?'

Ruth faltered. Over the years they had always argued and fought bitterly; at times, Dino would return to his flat to cool off, at other times Ruth would leave for the cinema. But now she realised with a jolt that she needed him too much to risk losing him.

'I love you,' she said softly, her confidence failing her, her composure breaking, peeling from her, leaving her fragile. Her gentleness touched him.

'God, you drive me mad!' he said, catching hold of her, his face against hers, the rain damp on his skin. 'I'm sorry about the children, but we'll find Laurel again, I promise you.'

She hugged him tightly.

'I'm too old for all this trauma,' he continued, teasing her. 'All this passion is bad for my heart.'

She punched him lightly in the stomach. 'You thrive on it, you moron.'

With a look of deep tenderness, he asked, 'Ruth, would you do something for me?'

'Anything.'

'Then marry me.'

Laurel disappeared without trace, although they spent weeks trying to find her, Nina ringing Ruth constantly to ask for news.

'Tony says no one can just go missing. She must be claiming child benefit or social security – you could find her through that.'

Ruth sighed. 'We're working on it, but with no success so far.' She pushed away the papers on her desk and swivelled her chair round to the window. 'I'm frightened that Laurel might not believe Kate. Maybe she still thinks I don't want her.'

'No way!' Nina said emphatically. 'She's just confused, that's all. You wait and see, she'll turn up again.' There was a pause on the line. 'Have you seen Graham?'

'No. Dr Throop keeps insisting that I don't visit ... besides, I can't face him at the moment.'

'I'd face him ...' Nina said crisply, 'with a mallet.'

'So how long is he in the clinic this time?' Robert Floyd asked Kate, as he leant back in his chair. The office was thick with the inevitable cigar smoke, a copy of that day's paper on his desk.

'We don't know.'

'Vicious boy. I always said so. I told your mother too, not that she paid a blind bit of notice ... Too much of his father in him.'

'I wonder if it was my fault,' Kate said softly.

The old man glanced over to her. If Graham was like Ken, he thought, Kate was her mother's child.

'I feel guilty, as though I should have done something ...' she continued, '... to cover up for him, or prevent all of this happening.'

427

'Your mother spent years castigating herself too,' Robert Floyd said bluntly, trying to shock Kate into reason, 'but at least it served to motivate her. It got her a fine business and a lot of money, because she used it to spur herself on. But that's rare, guilt seldom brings any rewards. To most people it's pure shit.'

Kate nodded, the point taken. 'Do you think Laurel will ever get in touch?'

'Listen, I'm a tired old man who's seen a lot. I admire your mother, Kate, and I'll never forget what she did for my son ...' He paused, his eyes brilliant with cunning. 'And I *always* pay my debts.'

Kate looked up, scrutinising his face and trying to read the unfathomable expression there. 'What are you up to, Grandfather?'

'Wait and see,' the old man said, getting to his feet.

'But –'

'No buts. I'm hungry. Let's eat.'

April slipped through their fingers and there was still no word of Laurel. Ruth worked on, making a bid for the cinema in Paris, and looking forward to the day when the pain would begin to fade. But the nights still haunted her, her dreams curling into the dark. Laurel appeared, running through a maze and looking for her. Once, she met Ken and he told her that he'd been calling repeatedly but Ruth never came. Then Laurel turned away, lifting her son and throwing him over the wall of the maze to where Graham sat on the other side, his wheelchair making a huge shadow on the cool grass.

'What is it?' Dino said, turning to Ruth in the dark and holding her. 'It was a dream ... only a dream.'

Clinging on to him, she fell back to sleep.

Kate came into Ruth's dream then, dressed from head to foot in red, her face turned away. When she looked towards her mother it was with Graham's eyes, and at the far end of the maze David was calling for Ruth, waving his arms to get her attention, while behind him she could see the shadow of Graham's wheelchair.

Panicking, Ruth woke and got out of bed. The early morning was cold and the radiator in the bathroom was faulty again. Being a Sunday, no one else was up, the house silent with sleep. Fumbling with her dressing-gown, Ruth went downstairs. The kitchen welcomed her and Barnie yawned as she came in, his thin legs poking out of his basket, the fur round his mouth grey with age.

'Hi, old fella,' she said, stroking his head. 'Just you and me awake, hey?'

Outside noises filtered in; the milkman delivering his round and the sound of next door's poodle barking uselessly. Ruth made herself some tea and sipped it slowly, as Barnie jumped on to her lap and fell back to sleep, his rib-cage rising and falling as he breathed. Many unrelated things flicked in and out of her mind: Joanie's hard face the night she had brought Ken home; the way he died; and the time Graham first went to the clinic. She closed her eyes, remembering Dino's mother, and the smell of mimosa on the villa walls.

It was effortless to slip back and remember Derek and Oldham; Nina as she had been; and her mother's hat shop. Easy to be a gangly, over-tall girl in a small town, eager to please, a girl with such a long journey to make. Ruth shifted her position, thinking of the park in Oldham and George Armani and Laurel ... She had to be out there, Ruth thought to herself, Laurel had to be there, somewhere. Maybe asleep, maybe looking out of a window. But alive ...

And as she thought of Laurel Ruth thought of Graham and shook her head, trying to rid herself of the memory, thankful only that Kate had managed to tell Laurel that her mother loved her ... She must realise that whenever she needed or wanted her, Ruth would come. But as she thought of her daughters, Ruth thought again of her elder son, and decided on her course of action. Graham was treacherous and deceitful, but he was her child ... she would talk to Dr Throop again. She would talk to his doctor and they would find a solution, Ruth thought grimly. Graham could be helped ... he *had* to be helped.

The morning yawned in and she was just going back upstairs

when she heard a noise. Surprised, Ruth stopped to listen. The noise was repeated, a slow knocking on the front door, followed by a timorous jab on the bell. Ruth glanced at the clock – it was twenty past eight, the Hour of the Angel. With cautious steps, she walked over to the door.

Against the cool May morning a woman stood motionless, a child beside her, the light pooling over her dark hair and illuminating the pale skin like an alabaster figure in a dawn garden. Ruth stood motionless, and looked at her; looked into the dark eyes and the small, sparse face, noticing how the cold made patches on her cheeks and how her hand clasped the child's.

'Laurel?' Ruth said hoarsely.

The woman frowned momentarily, but made no movement.

'What's your name?' Ruth asked, her voice wavering.

'Mary . . . They called me Mary.'

Ruth stared blindly at the girl. You were always Laurel to me, she thought, unable to believe that her daughter was real; that the child she had given birth to, the child she had lost twice, was now within reach.

Laurel was the first to break the silence. With one careful movement she placed her hand against her son's back and gently pushed him towards Ruth, saying, 'James, this is your grandmother.'

Ruth looked down at the child and then knelt beside him, holding him and cradling the fragile blond head against her own, the tears pouring down her cheeks.

Laurel walked in, closing the door behind her. Tenderly she touched her mother's face.

'It's all right . . . everything's all right. I've come home.'